THREE NOVELS

TRANSLATED FROM
THE CZECH BY
M. AND R. WEATHERALL

INTRODUCTION BY
WILLIAM HARKINS

A Garrigue Book
Catbird Press

THREE NOVELS

HORDUBAL, METEOR, AN ORDINARY LIFE

BY KAREL ČAPEK

This is a reprint of a trilogy of novels originally published separately in Czech as *Hordubal, Povětroň,* and *Obyčejný život* in 1933-1934, published separately in Great Britain in 1934-1936 by George Allen & Unwin Ltd., and published in a single volume in 1948 by George Allen & Unwin Ltd. in Great Britain and by A. A. Wyn in the United States. This is a reprint of the second impression of the one-volume version published by A. A. Wyn in 1949. The introduction has been added, and the translation of the afterword by Karel Čapek has been revised by Robert Wechsler.

CATBIRD PRESS, 44 North Sixth Avenue, Highland Park, NJ 08904, 201-572-0816. Our books are distributed to the trade by Independent Publishers Group and can be ordered and charged by calling 800-888-4741.

Library of Congress Cataloging-in-Publication Data

Čapek, Karel, 1890-1938
Hordubal, Meteor, An ordinary life; Three Novels by Karel Čapek, translated by Maria and Robert Weatherall; introduction by William Harkins.
ISBN 0-945774-08-7 (pbk.)
I. Title. II. Title: Hordubal. III. Title: Meteor. IV. Title: Ordinary life.
PG5038.C3A28 1990
891.8'635--dc20 89-23957 CIP

Contents

Introduction

Karel Čapek has remained, over the decades since his death in 1938, the great national writer of his Czech people. At the same time, he has also enjoyed special favor in the English-speaking world, to the extent that all of his major and many of his minor works are available in English translations.

If we inquire concerning the secret of such popularity, an answer is not easy to give. Čapek turns out to have written many types of literature and to have meant many things to many people. One thinks first of his utopian or, to use today's terminology, dystopian works (a dystopia is a utopia gone amok): the play *R.U.R. (Rossum's Universal Robots)* (1920), the novel *The Absolute at Large* (1922), or the somewhat later novel *War with the Newts* (1936). These works, for all their penetrating insight into how human progress can be our own worst enemy, are also admirable for other qualities: the dramatic expressionism of *R.U.R.*, with its robots marching in step to epitomize the dangers of mechanization; the trenchant satire and parody of the two novels, the first burlesquing a world of technological overproduction, the second describing man's subjugation by a species of giant, intelligent newts which mankind had previously subjugated for its own industrial and military purposes. In a Swiftian vein, these novels mock the seeming achievement of our modern, civilized and technological world.

Standing next to this theme of the disasters facing our modern civilization is the theme of war. It first appears in the satirical revue *From the Life of the Insects* (1921), which Karel Čapek wrote with his brother Josef. In the third act of the play, one tribe of ants conquers and exterminates another. The war theme figures by implication in the scientific fantasy *Krakatit* (1924), in which Čapek foresaw how the power of atomic energy might be used for military purposes. Finally, his two late, anti-Nazi plays, *The White Plague* (1937) and *The Mother* (1938), finally accept war (Čapek had been a pacifist), but only on the ground of justifiable self-defense or, more precisely, the defense of others more defenseless. One does not normally think of Čapek as an anti-war author, but perhaps this theme did as much to establish his reputation, particularly in the modern theater, as did the theme of scientific dystopia.

Although his best-known works tend to be about social problems, Čapek was essentially a humanist. His concerns were not specifically political—about *man*—but rather stemmed from his interest in and love for *men* and for how they were affected by and could respond to the modern world. It is Čapek the humanist who is most keenly reflected in the work I consider to be his masterpiece, and it is with perhaps the most agonizing theme of our time—the search for identity—that he has made his mark.

This masterpiece is the trilogy of novels contained in the present volume. The literary theoretician and critic René Wellek has described this trilogy as 'one of the most successful attempts at a philosophical novel in any language.'

Czech literary critics came to refer to this trilogy as Čapek's 'noetic' [i.e., epistemological] work. Epistemology is that branch of philosophy which deals with the possibility and truth status of knowledge, and the terms as used here refers to the theme of a search for individual identity in the chaotic modern world. At first glance we can agree with this definition, but as we read and reread the three novels, the term appears increasingly inadequate: not only self-knowledge is involved here, but also the very nature of society and of human feeling. The deepest significance of the trilogy is its embodiment of the spirit of democratic humanism.

The three novels of the trilogy mark Čapek's transition from his earlier, somewhat superficial philosophy of relativism—expressed particularly sharply, if somewhat facilely, in the novel *The Absolute at Large*—to a new philosophic absolutism. This transition was to serve the writer well in his duel with Nazism (if relativism made everyone somehow right, then Hitler would have to be right as well). This transition is orchestrated for the reader of the trilogy in the form of a Hegelian logical triad (or dialectic) of thesis, antithesis and synthesis.

Hegel's triad was an attempt to get away from the static Aristotelian rules of logic and to find a more dynamic logic that could explain change, progress and organic growth. For Hegel, each thesis implied a contradictory thesis, or antithesis, and this conflict ended in another thesis, or synthesis, which implied a contradictory thesis, and so on.

The first novel of the trilogy, *Hordubal* (1933), maintains the relativist attitude toward truth characteristic of Čapek's earlier period: the truth of Hordubal's life and thoughts can never be discovered. But this epistemological concept is voiced as a point of departure in Čapek's search for man's truth. Like a domino, it completes an old pattern and begins a new one.

Hordubal also connected with Čapek's earlier fiction in a more specific respect: based on a story drawn from real life, it deals with problems of police investigation and judicial trial. In these qualities, it may be viewed as a continuation of Čapek's detective stories with a philosophical twist, *Tales from Two Pockets* (1929).

In *Hordubal* Čapek's relativism takes the form of a series of attempts by different observers to reconstruct the logic of Hordubal's motives and actions, which we see from Hordubal's perspective in the first part of the novel. All fail, necessarily, because Hordubal's secrets and his personality are essentially unique and incommunicable. Thus the thesis of our logical triad: all humans are distinct and unknowable.

In its authorial technique, *Hordubal* is more traditional—less original, perhaps—than the following two volumes of the trilogy. Its strongest qualities relate to its use of vivid symbolic imagery: e.g., the phallic, masculine horse associated with the hired man Manya, contrasted with the peaceful, brooding cow Hordubal reveres. Čapek manipulates these and other symbols with intense pathos. Indeed, although the novel as thesis concludes that we cannot know the secrets of another's heart, Čapek has, through the miracle of a work of art, communicated these secrets to us.

The second novel, *Meteor* (1934), attempts the reconstruction of the life story of an unknown man, dying from a plane crash. Three versions are given: a nun's dream, a clairvoyant's fantasies and, finally and most completely, a writer's artistic reconstruction. All three attempts are limited by both the personalities of their narrators and their means of perception.

The ultimate implication of relativism is that there can be no truth whatsoever: if there is no one truth, then there can be no truth, only a forest of different and conflicting 'truths' through which we wander aimlessly. However, the philosophers José Ortega y Gasset and Karl Mannheim had, in the 1930s, pointed out an escape from this paradox, to which Mannheim gave the name 'perspectivism.' Different truths are the products of different perspectives, but observations made according to these different perspectives add up to a coherent and consistent truth, not to contradictions. And, in fact, the three stories told in *Meteor* about 'Case X' are not totally contradictory, but overlap and could be gathered together into a more or less consistent and harmonious whole.

This 'perspectivist' structure of perception may remind one of the distortions involved in a cubist painting, which are intended to simulate a three-dimensional view of an object. 'Literary cubism' is best known in modern French poetry. In Czech literature, the concept is associated with Karel Čapek and his brother Josef, who was also a cubist painter. In Karel's novel *Meteor,* we find the cubist concept fully realized. *Meteor* thus constitutes the antithesis of the trilogy: perspectives about a human life are indeed many, but people are not therefore unknowable; rather, the perspectives may be accumulated to construct a coherent truth.

Throughout the trilogy, Čapek was preoccupied with the theme of individual identity: in *Hordubal* the issue, while present, is still tangential; in *Meteor* it comes to the center of the stage; and in *An Ordinary Life* (1934), the final volume of the trilogy, it becomes more focal still, since not only are we concerned with the question of what the principal character is like, but it is he himself who undertakes the search for his identity. A retired railway official attempts to write the story of his life, but what he originally conceives as a simple, unencumbered, 'ordinary' story suddenly becomes a thicket of tangles and contradictions. These can be resolved only by the postulation of variety, of a whole host of personalities within him, some buried and silent, others potential, still others alive in rebellion. And here we have the synthesis of the triad: the plurality of perspectives without corresponds to a plurality of personalities within the individual.

But if this is true, then we have a metaphysical basis on which to establish the unity of society: the individual repeats within himself the variety of persons around him; therefore, he can empathize with others and they with him. And this society will be democratic insofar as nothing separates the plurality within from the one without. Hence Čapek has given a literary and philosophical solution to the troubling problem of democracy and a pluralist society.

He has also contributed a kind of psychoanalysis largely independent of Freud's. This effort is especially apparent in *An Ordinary Life,* where introspection leads to the breakdown of the ordinary man's jejeune self-evaluation and to the discovery of the deeper, more complex truth of a variety of persons within. Like Freud, Čapek emphasized childhood development and childhood sexual expression, but without any predisposition to an Oedipal Complex or a unilateral source of life energy such as Freud's libido.

Although the three volumes of the trilogy are strikingly different in style and approach, and none of the characters or plot elements figures in more than one of the volumes, yet there is much to hold the trilogy together. The Hegelian triad is one such link. Another is the symbol of the human heart: in *Hordubal* the heart, sent off for medical examination, is lost (implying that Hordubal's grief, his noblest aspect, is no more). In *Meteor* the heart is the organ implicated in the death of 'Case X;' while in *An Ordinary Life* the retired railway official dies from heart failure.

This central symbol of the heart is perhaps evidence that the trilogy is not purely or even primarily 'noetic.' No, it has to do with humanity, with human action and perception. And, in spite of Čapek's self-proclaimed 'optimism,' it is tragic and pessimistic. Hordubal's pitiful, self-sacrificial love leads him only to death. *Meteor*'s 'Case X' flies home to recapture his own identity, only to crash in the culmination of a violent, reckless, heedless life. The 'ordinary man' only pursues his analytic self-discoveries when he is about to die.

'Is it all worth reading?' old Mr. Popel asks of the doctor who has handed him the reminiscences of the 'ordinary man.' As a scientist, the doctor, of course, has no opinion. Reading the trilogy brings only sadness to those touched by it, just as it brought sadness to the 'ordinary man.' Obsession and tragedy are the two pillars of Čapek's art in this great work.

Still, if the characters and events in the trilogy are tragic, the vision of a democratic society based on man's perception of his own plurality is not. The contradiction may seem a paradox; but perhaps Čapek is hinting, as he and his brother Josef had so many years before in *From the Life of the Insects,* that while individual life is necessarily tragic, social life can sometimes transcend tragedy and become heroic and an occasion for optimism.

William Harkins
Columbia University

HORDUBAL

BOOK I

CHAPTER I

THAT man sitting second from the window, the one with his clothes all creased; who'd think that he's an American? Don't tell me! Surely Americans don't travel in slow trains; they go with the express, and even then it's not fast enough for them, the trains are quicker in America they say, with much bigger carriages, and a white-coated waiter brings you iced water and ice-creams, don't you know? Hello, boy, he shouts, fetch me some beer, bring a glass for everyone in the carriage, even if it costs five dollars, damn it! Good Lord! That's life in America, you know: it's no use trying to tell you.

The second one from the window dozed with his mouth open, all sweaty and tired, and his head hung down as if he were lifeless. Oh, God, oh, God, it's already eleven, thirteen, fourteen, fifteen days; for fifteen days and nights sitting on my box, sleeping on the floor, or on a bench, sticky with sweat, stupefied, and deafened with the rattle of the machines; this is the fifteenth day; if only I could stretch my legs, put a bundle of hay under my head and sleep, sleep, sleep . . .

The fat Jewess by the window squeezed herself gingerly into the corner. That's it, at the end he'll go off, and fall on me like a sack; who knows what's wrong with him—looks as if he's rolled on the ground in his clothes, or something; you seem a bit queer to me, I should say, I should like to move right away; oh, God, if only the train would stop! And the man, second from the window, nodded, bent forward, and woke with a jerk.

"It's so hot," said the little old man, looking like a hawker, cautiously beginning a conversation. "Where are you going to?"

"To Kriva," the man got out with an effort.

"To Kriva," repeated the hawker professionally and graciously. "And have you come far, a long way?"

The man second from the window made no reply, he only wiped his moist forehead with his grimy fist, and felt faint with weakness and giddiness. The hawker gave an offended snort and turned back towards the window. The other hadn't the heart to look through the window, he fixed his eyes on the filth on the floor, and sat waiting for them to ask him again. And then he would tell them. A long way. All the way from America, sir. What do you say, all the way from America? And so you are coming all this distance for a visit? No, I'm going home. To Kriva, I have a wife there, and a little girl; she's called Hafia. She was three years old when I went away. So that's it, from America! And how long were you there? Eight years. It's eight years now. And all the time I had a job in one place: as a miner. In Johnstown. I had a mate there; Michal Bobok was his name. Michal Bobok from Talamas. It killed him; that was five years ago. Since then I've had no one to talk to—I ask you, how was I to make myself understood? Oh, Bobok, he learned the lingo; but you know, when a chap has a wife, he thinks how he'll tell her one thing after another, and you can't do that in a strange tongue. She's called Polana.

And how could you do your job there when you couldn't make yourself understood? Well, like this: they just said, Hello, Hordubal, and they showed me my job. I earned as much as seven dollars a day, sir, seven. But living's dear in America, sir. You can't live even on two dollars a day—five dollars a week for bed. And then the gentleman opposite says: But then, Mr. Hordubal, you must have saved a nice tidy bit! Oh, yes, you could save. But I sent it home to my wife—did I tell you that she's called Polana? Every month, sir, fifty, sixty, and sometimes ninety dollars. I could do that while Bobok was alive, because he knew how to write. A clever man, that Bobok was, but he got killed five years ago; some wooden beams fell on him. Then I couldn't send any more money home, and I put it in a bank. Over three thousand dollars, I tell you, sir, and they stole it from me. But that's impossible, Mr. Hordubal! What did you say?

Yes, sir, over three thousand dollars. And you didn't prosecute them? Now I ask you, how could I prosecute them? Our foreman took me to some kind of a lawyer; he patted my shoulder. O.K., O.K., but you must pay in advance; and the foreman told him he was a swine, and pushed me down the stairs again. It's like that in America, no use talking. Jesus Christ, Mr. Hordubal, three thousand dollars! That's a big sum of money, it's a whole fortune, God in Heaven, what bad luck! Three thousand dollars, how much is that in our money?

Juraj Hordubal felt a deep satisfaction: You'd all turn and look at me, all you people here, if I began to tell you; people would rush from all over the train to look at a man who had three thousand dollars stolen in America. Yessir, that's me. Juraj Hordubal raised his eyes, and looked round at the people; the fat Jewess pressed herself into the corner, the hawker seemed to be offended, and looked out of the window, working his jaws, and an old woman, with a basket on her lap, eyed Hordubal as if she disagreed with something.

Juraj Hordubal closed up again. All right then, it's all the same, I needn't worry about you; for five years I've not spoken to a soul, and I managed that. And so, Mr. Hordubal, you're coming back from America without a cent? Oh, no, I had a good job, but I didn't put my money in the bank again, you bet! In a box, sir, and the key under my shirt, that's how it was. Seven hundred dollars I'm taking home. Well, sir, I would have stayed there, but I lost my job. After eight years, sir. Locked out, sir. Too much coal, or something. From our pit six hundred were given leave, sir. And everywhere and everywhere there was nothing but people being sent away. No job for a man anywhere. That's why I'm coming back. Going home, you know. To Kriva. I have a wife there and some land. And Hafia, she was three then. I have seven hundred dollars under my shirt, and once more I shall begin to farm, or I shall work in a factory. Or fell trees.

And then, Mr. Hordubal, weren't you lonely without your wife and child? Lonely? My God! But I ask you, I sent them money, and I kept thinking, this will buy a cow, this an acre of land, this something for Polana, but she'll know herself what to buy. Every dollar was for something, And the money in the bank, that was enough for a herd of cows. Yess'r, and they pinched it from me. And did she ever write to you, your wife? She didn't. She can't write. And did you write to her? No, sir, can't write, sir. Ever since that Michal Bobok died I haven't sent her anything. I only put the money by. But at least you telegraphed to her that you were coming? What for, why, why waste money on that? It would give her a turn if she got a telegram, but she won't get it from he. Ha, ha, what do you think! Perhaps she thinks your dead, Mr. Hordubal; don't you think if she hasn't heard a word from you for so many years——? Dead? A chap like me, dead! Juraj Hordubal blanced at his knotted fists. A fellow like that, what an idea! Polana is sensible, she knows that I'm coming back. After all, we're all mortal; what if Polana is no longer alive? Shut up, sir; she was twenty-three when I went and strong, sir, as strong as a horse—you don't know Polana; with that money, with those dollars I kept sending her, with those she wouldn't be alive? No, thank you.

The hawker by the window scowled and mopped her brow with a blue handkerchief. Perhaps he'll say again: It's so hot. Hot, sir! You call this hot? You ought to be on the lower deck sir; or below in the shaft for anthracite. They put niggers down there, but I stood it, yess'r. For seven dollars. Hello, Hordubal! Hello, you niggahs! Yes, sir, a man can stand a lot. Not horses. They couldn't send any more horses down below to haul the trucks. Too hot, sir. Or the lower deck on the boat. . . . A fellow can stand a lot if only he can make himself understood. They want something from you, you don't know what; and they shout, get into a temper, shrug their shoulders. Now I ask you, how could I find out in Hamburg how to get to Kriva? They can shout, but I can't. To go to America's nothing; someone puts you on the boat, someone waits for you there—but back, sir nobody will help you. No, sir. It's a hard job to get home, sir.

And Juraj Hordubal nodded his head, then it nodded by itself, heavily and listlessly, and Juraj fell asleep. The fat Jewess by the window turned up her nose; the old woman with the basket on her lap and the offended hawker glanced at each other knowingly: Oh, oh, that's what people are like now: like cattle——

CHAPTER II

WHO's that there, who's that on the other side of the valley? Look at him; a gentleman, wearing shoes, perhaps he's an engineer, or something like that, he's carrying a black box, and trudges up the hill—if he weren't so far away, I'd put my hands to my mouth and halloo to him: Praised be to Jesus Christ, sir, what's the time? Two minutes past twelve, my friend: if you weren't so far away I'd shout and ask whose cows you're minding, and then perhaps you'd point and say: That with the white patch on her face, that red and white, that one with the star, that roan, and this heifer belong to Polana Hordubal. Well, well, my lad, they're nice cows, a pleasure to look at; only don't let them get down to Black Brook, the grass is sour there, and the water's foul. Just think of that, to Polana Hordubal; and before she'd only got two cows; and what about it, boy, hasn't she got some oxen as well? Good Lord, and what sort of oxen, from Podoli, with horns spreading out like arms; two oxen, sir. And any sheep? Both rams and ewes, sir, but they are grazing up on Durna Polonina. Polana is rich and clever. And has she got a husband? Why do you wave your arms about like that? Polana has no husband? Oh, what a stupid fool; he doesn't recognize me, the man; he shades his eyes with his hand, and stands staring, staring as if he were a gate-post.

Juraj Hordubal felt his heart thumping right up in his throat; he had to stop, and catch his breath, ahah! ahah! It's too much, it's so sudden, it makes him shake like a man who has fallen into water: all of a sudden he's at home, he only stepped over that stony gully, and it overwhelmed him on all sides: yes, that gully was always there, that blackthorn bush was there, too, and even then it was scorched by the herdsman's fire; and again mullein flowers in the ravine, the road vanishes in the dry grass, and in the dry thyme, here is that boulder grown over with bilberries, gentian, junipers, and the border of the wood, dry cow droppings, and the forsaken hay-hut; there is no America any more, eight years have vanished; everything is as it was, a shiny beetle on the head of a thistle, smooth grass, and far away the sound of cow-bells, the pass behind Kriva, the brown clumps of sedges, and the way home, a road trodden by the soft steps of mountain men, who wear home-made shoes and have never been to America, a road smelling of cows and of the forest, warm like an oven, leading into the valley, a stony road, trampled down by farm animals, swampy near the springs, bumpy with stones; oh, Lord, what a fine footpath, as swift as a brook, soft with grass, crumbling with stone chips, squelching in the hollows, curving under the trees in the wood: no, sir, no clinker sidewalk that squeaks under your boot, like they have in Johnstown, no railings, no hosts of men tramping to the mine, not a soul anywhere, not a soul, only a road leading down, the stream, and the sound of the cow-bells, the way home, dropping downwards, the little bells of the calves, and beside the stream the blue wolf's bane——

Juraj Hordubal descended with long strides: What difference does a box make, what difference do eight years; this is the way home, it just takes you along, like the herd returning at dusk, with full udders, ting-tang from the cows, and the little bells of the calves: why not sit down here and wait till dusk, come into the village when the cow-bells are ringing, when the old grannies come out on to their doorsteps, and men lean on the fence: look, look, who's coming here? Why me—like a herd from the pasture—right into the open gate. Good evening, Polana, even I am not returning empty.

Or no, wait till dark, until God's cattle have gone, until everything has fallen asleep; then knock on the window, Polana! Polana! God in Heaven, who's there? It's me, Polana, so that you are the first to see me; glory to God! And where's Hafia? Hafia's asleep; am I to wake her? No, let her sleep. God be praised.

And Hordubal quickened his pace still more. Oh, Lord, a man does move when his thoughts run ahead of him! You can't keep pace with them, never mind how much you stretch your legs; your mind runs away in front, and has already reached the rowan-trees at the edge of the village, sssh, geese, sssh, and you're already at home. You ought to make a sound like a trumpet: where are you all, see who's coming, the American, tram-tara, you do gape, boys, hello! And now silence, here we are at home, Polana is in the yard beating out the flax, to steal up to her, and cover her eyes—Juraj! How did you recognize me, Polana? Glory to God, to think that I couldn't remember your hands!

Hordubal ran along the gully, unconscious of the box in his hand, there where all his America was packed up, the blue shirt, the Manchester dress, and the teddy-bear for Hafia. And this here, Polana, is for you, material for a frock, like they wear in America, a cake of scented soap, a handbag with a chain, and this, Hafia, is a flash-light, you press this button here, and it lights, and here I've got pictures for you which I cut out of the newspapers—ach, lassie, I had lots and lots of them, for eight years I kept saving them up for you, any I came across; I had to leave them behind, I couldn't get any more into the suit-case. But wait, there are lots of other things in the box!

And here already, thank God, the road crosses the brook; no iron bridge, only stepping stones, you have to jump from one to the other, and balance with your arms; ah, there by the roots of the alders we used to catch crayfish, with our trousers rolled up, wet right up to the shoulders; and is the crucifix still there at the bend of the road? Praise be to Jesus Christ, it is, leaning over the cart-track, soft with the warm dust, and smelling of cattle, straw, and corn; and Michalcuk's orchard fence must be here; yes, here it is, grown over with elder and hazel as it was then, and tumble-down as it used to be; glory to the Lord, now we are in the village, safe and sound, Juraj Hordubal. And Juraj Hordubal stopped: Why the deuce has the box suddenly become so heavy, just to wipe the sweat off, and Jesus Maria, why didn't I wash myself at the brook, why didn't I take my razor out of the box, and the little mirror, and shave at the brook! I must look like a gipsy, like a tramp, like a robber; what if I go back and wash myself before I let Polana see me? But you can't do that now, Hordubal, they're looking at you from behind Michalcuk's fence, behind the ditch with burdocks a child is standing still and gaping. Shan't you call to him, Hordubal? Shan't you shout, hello you, are you one of Michalcuk's? And with a patter of bare feet the child took to flight.

Why not go right round the village, thought Hordubal, and come home by the back way? What an idea! They would rush at me: You there, what are you up to? Get off down the road or you'll be beaten! What's one to do, I must go right through the middle of the village; oh, God, if only that box didn't weigh so much! The face of a woman at the window behind the geraniumst sunflowers gaping at you, an old woman pours out something in the yard, as if she had eyes in her back, the children stop and stare, look here, look here, there's a strange man coming, old Kyryl works his jaws, and doesn't even raise his eyes; once more stab to the heart, God be with us, and with bowed head we pass through the homestead gate.

Oh, you booby, how could you make such a mistake! Don't you see that this isn't Hordubal's wooden hut, stable, and barn made of logs? it's a real farm, a brick building, with slates on the roof, and in the yard an iron pump, an iron plough, and a set of irron harrows, why a proper farm; quick, Hordubal, disappear quickly with that black box of yours, before the farmer comes and says: Now what are you looking for here? Good afternoon, didn't Polana Hordubal once live here? I'm sorry, sir, I don't know what I've done with my eyes.

Through the doorway Polana emerged, and stopped dead, as if turned to stone, with her eyes staring, and she pressed her hands firmly to her breast, as she breathed quickly and in gasps.

CHAPTER III

AND then Juraj Hordubal didn't know what to say: he had thought out so many opening phrases, why was it that none of them would do? He won't put his hands over Polana's eyes, he won't tap on the window at night, he won't return with the cow-bells tinkling, and with words of blessing; but dirty and unkempt he rushed in. Well, what wonder if a woman gets frightened? Even my voice would be strange and stifled—Lord tell me what I can say with such an inappropriate voice!

Polana drew back from the entrance; she stepped back—too far; oh, Polana, I could have slipped past—and murmured with a voice which was hardly a voice, and hardly hers: "Come in, I—I'll call Hafia." Yes, Hafia, but before she comes I should like to put my hands on your shoulders, and say, Well, Polana, I didn't mean to frighten you; thank God, I'm home at last. And see, see how she's furnished the house: the bed's new, and deep with feathers, the table's new, and heavy, sacred pictures on the wall; well, my lad, even in America they don't have it better: the floor's made of boards, and geraniums in the windows: you are a good manager, Polana! Very quietly Juraj Hordubal sat down on the box. Polana is clever, and she knows her way about; from what you can see you would think that she owns twelve cows, twelve or even more—Praise be to God, I didn't toil in vain; but the heat in the mine, my God, if you knew what a hell! Polana did not return; Juraj Hordubal felt uneasy somehow, like someone quite alone in a strange room. I will wait in the yard, perhaps I might wash in the meantime. Ah, pull my shirt off, and pump cold water over my shoulders, over my head, and hair, and splash about with the water, and neigh with pleasure, ha! but that would hardly be the thing to do, no, not yet, not yet; just a drop of water from the iron pump (there used to be a wooden coping here, a bucket on a pole, and that deep darkness below, and how damp and cool it felt when you leaned over the coping) (and this is like America, where the farmers have pumps like this) (with the full bucket into the cowshed, and water the cows till their muzzles shine with dampness, and they snort loudly), with a drop of water he moistened his grimy handkerchief, and wiped his forehead, hands, and neck. Ach, ah, that's nice and cool. He wrung the handkerchief out, and looked round for somewhere to hang it. No, not yet, we're not at home yet; and he pushed it, still wet, into his pocket.

"Here's your father, Hafia," Hordubal heard someone say, and Polana pushed towards him a girl of eleven, with shy, pale blue eyes. "So you're Hafia," murmured Hordubal in embarrassment. (Ah, God, a teddy-bear for a big child like that!) and he wanted to stroke her hair, just with his fingers, Hafia; but the girl drew back, she squeezed herself against her mother, and kept her eyes fixed on the strange man. "What do you say, Hafia?" said Polana harshly, giving the girl a push from behind. Oh, Polana, leave her alone—what if a child does get frightened! "Good evening," whispered Hafia, and turned away. Juraj suddenly began to feel queer and his eyes filled with tears; the child's face danced before him and grew dim, but, what's that—eh, oh, nothing, but I haven't heard 'good evening' for so many years. "Come and see, Hafia," he said hurriedly, "what I've brought for you."

"Go, you silly," said Polana, giving her a push.

Hordubal knelt down before the box, Mother of God, everything has got messed up during the journey! He searched for the electric lamp. Hafia will be astonished! "So you see, Hafia, you press this button here, and it lights." But what's wrong, it doesn't want to light; Hordubal pressed the button, turned the little thing round and round, and became filled with sadness. "What's wrong with it? Ah, perhaps it's dried up inside there where the electricity is—you know, it was so hot on the lower deck. Well, it did shine brightly, Hafia, like a little sun. But wait, I've got some pictures for you. Now you'll see something!" Hordubal fished from the box cuttings from the papers and magazines which he had placed between a few articles of clothing. "Come here, Hafia, this will show you what America looks like."

The girl writhed with embarrassment, and looked inquiringly towards her mother. Dryly and severely Polana motioned with her head: go! Timidly and unwillingly the child shuffled towards the tall, strange man. Oh, if only you could dash out of the door and run, run to Marica Zofka, to the girls who there behind the barn are rolling a pleasant little puppy into a pillow——

"Look, Hafia, look at these ladies—and see here, see how these people are fighting with each other, ha, ha, what? That's football, you know, a game they play in America. And see here, look at these big houses——"

Hafia's shoulder was now touching his, and timidly she whispered: "And what's this?"

A wave of pleasure and emotion ran through Juraj Hordubal: See how the child is getting used to me already! "This . . . you know, this is Felix the cat."

"But it's a pussy," objected Hafia.

"Ha, ha, of course, it's a pussy! You are clever, Hafia! Yes, it's . . . a sort of American tom-cat, all right."

"And what's he doing?"

"There . . . he's licking a tin out, do you understand? a kind of milk tin. It's an advertisement for tinned milk, you know."

"And what does it say?"

"That . . . that's something in American, Hafia, you won't understand that; but look at these ships," said Hordubal, quickly turning the conversation. "I sailed in one like that."

"And what's this?"

"They're chimneys, you know? These ships have a steam engine inside them, and at the back there's a kind of . . . er . . . propeller . . ."

"And what does it say?"

"You can read that some other time, you know how to read, don't you?" said Hordubal, turning away. "And this here, you see, two cars ran into each other . . ."

Polana stood on the doorstep with her hands folded on her breast, and with dry, unblinking eyes she looked round the yard. There in the room behind two heads were bent together, a man's slow voice tried to explain this and that. "That's how they do it in America, Hafia, and here, see, I once saw this myself," and then the voice halted, faltered, and murmured: "Run, Hafia, run and see what mammy's doing."

Hafia dashed towards the entrance as if released.

"Wait," said Polana, stopping her, "ask him if he wants anything to eat or drink."

"Never mind, my sweet, never mind," cried Hordubal, moving towards the entrance. "It's kind of you to think of it, thank you very much, but there's no hurry. Perhaps you have some other work to do——"

"There's always something to do," Polana suggested vaguely.

"So you see, Polana, so you see, I won't disturb you; just get on with your job, and in the meantime I . . . I'll——"

Polana raised her eyes to him, as if she wished to say something, as if she wanted suddenly to say something very much, until her lips quivered; but she suppressed it, and went out to do her work; for there's always something to do.

Hordubal stood by the door, and looked after Polana. What if I went after her into the shed—no, not yet, not yet; the shed's dark, well, somehow it's not the thing to do. Eight years, my lad, are eight years. Polana is a sensible woman, she's not going to jump round my neck like a youngster; you'd like to ask her this and that, what are the crops like, the cattle, but God be with her, she has some work to do. She always was like that. Quick at work, active, sensible.

Hordubal looked thoughtfully into the yard. A clean yard, with cinquefoil and chamomile blossoming here and there, no trickle of liquid manure running away. What about having a look round the buildings—no, not yet, not yet; for Polana herself will say: Come and look, Juraj, see what I've done, everything is made of brick and iron, everything new, it cost so much and so much. And I shall say: Good, Polana, I am also bringing you something for the farm.

Polana works well: and she's straight, as straight as a youngster. Lord, what a straight back! She always carried her head well, even when she was a girl—Hordubal sighed, and scratched his head. Well, then, Polana, you give the lead, for eight years you've been your own mistress, it can't just end with a snap, you yourself will say that it's good to have a man in the house.

Hordubal looked thoughtfully round the yard. Everything is different, and new; Polana has done very well; but that manure, my lad, somehow I don't like that manure. It's not from the cows, it's stable manure. Two sets of harness hang on the wall, there are horse-droppings in the yard—Polana didn't say that she has horses; but listen, horses, that's not a woman's job. It takes a man to look after a stable, that's it. Hordubal wrinkled his forehead and felt worried. Yes, that's the tap of a hoof against the wooden boards; the horse scrapes with its foot, perhaps it wants a drink, I'll fetch him some water in the canvas bucket, but no: not till Polana says: Come, Juraj, have a look round the farm. In Johnstown they had horses down below in the mine; I used to go and rub their noses—you know, Polana, there were no cows there; just catch hold of a cow by the horn, and waggle her head. Na-na-na, you old beggar, heta! heta! But a horse—well, thank God you'll have a man here.

But then came a whiff of something familiar, an old smell of something from childhood. Hordubal sniffed slowly with satisfaction: wood, the resinous smell of wood, the scent of spruce logs in the sunshine. Juraj felt himself being drawn towards the heap of logs. Rough bark is good for a rough hand, there's a stump as well with a hatchet stuck in it, a wooden trestle and saw, his old saw, with its handle worn smooth with his horny hands. Juraj Hordubal sighed, glad to be home, safe and sound, he took off his coat, and wedged the log into the firm arms of the trestle.

Pespiring and happy Juraj began to saw wood for the winter.

CHAPTER IV

JURAJ straightened himself, and wiped the sweat away. Well, sure, this is a different job, and a different smell from that down there in the pit; Polana has a nice, sweet-smelling wood, no stumps, no dead branches. The ducks quacked, the geese made an uproar, and a wagon rattled and moved with glorious speed up the narrow road. Polana darted out from the shed, and ran, ran (Ach, Polana, you run like a girl), she opened the gate wide. Who is it, who's coming here? The whip cracked, hi, warm golden dust rose in a cloud, a team clattered into the yard, the wagon rattled, and on it was a fellow standing up bravely, Magyar fashion, holding the reins high, and cried whoa, in a high voice. He jumped from the wagon, and with the flat of his hand he patted the horse's neck.

Polana came up from the house, pale and resolute. "This is Stepan, Juraj, Stepan Manya."

The man who was bending over the traces straightened himself briskly, and turned his face towards Juraj.

You're a bit dark, thought Hordubal to himself. Lord, what a raven!

"He came here as a farm worker," Polana explained, drily and deliberately.

The man muttered something and bent to the traces, he took out the pin and led the horses away, holding them both by one hand, the other he gave suddenly to Hordubal. "Got here safe, mister!"

Hordubal quickly wiped his hand on his trousers, and gave it to Stepan. He felt embarrassed, and yet somehow greatly flattered. He became flustered and mumbled something, and once more he shook Stepan's hand in the American fashion. Stepan was short but wiry; he only reached up to Juraj's shoulders, but he gave him an insolent and piercing glance.

"Nice horses," murmured Hordubal, and he tried to rub their noses; but they shied and began to prance.

"Look out, mister," shouted Manya, with a spiteful sparkle in his eyes. "They're Hungarian."

Ah, you darkie, you think I don't know much about horses? Well, as a matter of fact, I don't, but they'll get used to their master.

The horses jerked their heads, ready to dash away. Keep your hands in your pockets, Hordubal, and don't get out of the way in case the black one thinks you're afraid.

"This one is a three-year-old," said Manya, "from an army stallion. Whoa," he jerked the horse's mouth. "Stand still, you devil! Whoa." The horse pulled, but Stepan only laughed; and Polana came up to the horse and gave him a piece of bread. Stepan's teeth and eyes sparkled after her as he held the horse by the rein. "Hi, you! S-s-s!" It seemed as if he were forcing the horse into the earth, in the effort he hissed through his teeth; the horse stood with its neck beautifully arched, as it felt for Polana's palm with its lips. "Hi," shouted Manya, and, holding on to their heads, he took them into the stable at a trot.

Polana looked after them. "I've been bid four thousand for him, but I shan't take it," she said brightly; "Stepan says he's worth eight. We shall cover that little mare in the autumn——" Well, the deuce knows why she halted as if she had bitten her tongue. "I must get the fodder ready for her," she said, hesitating, and not knowing how to get away.

"So, so, fodder," Juraj agreed. "A nice horse, Polana; and what can he pull?"

"It's a pity to put him in a wagon," said Polana, testily. "He's not a cart-horse."

"Well, I just wondered," Hordubal managed to say. "Of course it's a pity for a nice colt like him. You've got some fine horses, it's a pleasure to look at them."

At that Manya emerged from the stable, carrying the canvas buckets for water. "You'll get eight thousand for him, mister," he asserted confidently. "And that little mare ought to be covered in the autumn. I've the offer of a little stallion for her, what a demon, eh!"

"Brutus or Hegüs?" asked Polana, turning half-way.

"Hegüs, Brutus is too heavy," said Manya, revealing his teeth beneath his black moustache. "I don't know what's your opinion, mister, but I don't care much for heavy horses. They're strong, but they've no blood, sir, no blood."

"Well, yes," agreed Hordubal uncertainly, "it is like that with horses. And what about heifers, Stepan?"

"Heifers?" exclaimed Stepan. "Ah, you mean cows. Ah—yes, mistress has two cows, for milk she says. You haven't been in the stall yet, sir?"

"No, I—you know I've only just come," said Hordubal, becoming embarrassed: Well, that heap of cut wood can't be denied—at the same time, he felt glad that he had begun so easily to talk to Stepan, like a master to a workman.

"Yes," he said, "I was just going there."

Stepan obsequiously led the way, carrying two buckets of water.

"We've go here—mistress has a young foal only three weeks old, and a mare in foal, she was covered two months ago. This way, sir. This gelding here is already nearly sold, two thousand five hundred sir. He's a good horse, but I have to work the three-year-old to give him some exercise. He won't stand quiet." Manya again showed his teeth. "The gelding will go to the army. All our horses have gone to the army."

"Well, well," said Juraj. "Yes, it's nice and tidy here. And have you been in the army, Stepan?"

"In the cavalry, sir." Manya showed his teeth, and gave the three-year-old a drink. "Look, mister, what a lean head, and what a back. Come up! Now then! Look out, sir! My, what a rascal!" he said, patting the horse on the neck. "Now, sir, that's a horse for you."

Hordubal didn't feel at ease in the strong odour of the stable. A cowshed had a different smell of milk, manure, and grass, and home. "Where's the foal?" he inquired.

The foal was young and curly, and just sucking; it was all legs.

The mare turned her head, and with knowing eyes looked at Hordubal: Well, who are you? Juraj melted and patted the mare on the flank; her skin was warm and as smooth as velvet.

"A good mare," said Stepan, "but heavy. Mistress wants to sell her—you know, master, a farmer won't pay a full price for a horse, and in the army they only want light horses. Heavy horses are no use. A stable all alike is better," Stepan opined. "I don't know what you think, sir——"

"Well, Polana understands," murmured Hordubal, half-heartedly. "And what about oxen, hasn't Polana got any oxen?"

"What does she want oxen for?" grinned Manya. "A mare and a gelding are enough for the land—beef doesn't pay, mister. Perhaps pig-breeding. Have you seen what a boar mistress has got? Six gilts, sir, and forty young ones. Weaners fetch a good price, dealers come a long way to get them. Sows as big as elephants, with a black snout, and black hooves——"

Hordubal shook his head dubiously: "And what about milk—where do you get milk for them?"

"From the farmers, if you please," laughed Manya. Eh, you, want our boar for your dirty sow? There isn't a boar as good as he is in the whole country. How many buckets of milk, and how many sacks of potatoes will you give for him? Well, sir, you sweat for nothing here. Too far from the town, it's difficult to sell anything. The people are stupid, sir. They grow things only for their guts. Let them give stuff away if they don't know how to sell."

Hordubal nodded vaguely. That's true, we used to sell very little, only a few hens and geese. Well, this is something different. Polana knows how to manage things, that's true.

"Sell a long way away," said Stepan thoughtfully, "and only then, if it's worth while. Who'd go to the market with one pat of butter? They can see from your face that you've got nothing; well, then, either put the price down, or go to the devil!"

"And where are you from?" asked Juraj.

"From down there, from Rybary, do you know the place, sir?"

Hordubal didn't, but he nodded: so, from Rybary; what master wouldn't know?

"That's a different country, sir, rich and as flat as you like. Take the swamp at Rybary—why, all the country here would go into it like a pea in a pocket; and grass, sir, grass, up to your waist." Manya waved his hand. "Ah, it's a lousy country here, you begin to plough, and you only turn up stones. With us if you dig a well, there's black soil right down to the bottom."

Hordubal's face clouded. What do you know, you Tartar—I, I've ploughed here and turned up stones; but, Lord, the woods, and meadows! In a bad humour Juraj went out of the stable. A lousy country, you say, well what made you push your nose in here, you devil? Isn't it good enough for the cattle? But, glory to God, this is the time for the cattle, already they tinkle in the valley and ring round the village; bells, with a cracked sound, deep and slow, slow like the step of a cow; only the little high-pitched bells of the calves dash about. Well, well, even you will grow up, and go heavily and seriously like cows, as we do. The sound of the herds drew nearer, and Juraj felt like taking off his hat as if it were the angelus. Our Father, which art in Heaven; like a river, the sound came nearer—it broke up into heavy drops, it spread over the whole village; one cow after the other left the herd, and bim bam, bim bam, made for her shed, the scent of dust and milk, bim bam in the gate, and, nodding their heads, two cows ambled into Hordubal's yard, wise and gentle creatures and made for the cowshed door. Hordubal heaven a deep sigh. Well, I've also come home, thanks to the Lord, this is the home-coming. The sound of the herds dispersed over the village, and died down, a bat began its zig-zag flight after flies in the wake of the herd. Good evening, master! From the stable, with a long moo, the cow made herself heard. Well, well, I'm coming. In the dark Juraj entered the shed, felt the horns, the hard and hairy forehead, the damp muzzle, the softly folded skin on the neck; he felt for the tin pail, and the stool, and sat down to the full udder; he milked one teat after the other, the milk rang as it struck the empty pail; and thinly, under his breath, Juraj began to sing.

A figure with a dark silhouette stood in the doorway. Hordubal stopped singing. "It's me, Polana," he murmured apologetically. "So that the cows get used to me."

"Won't you come to supper?" Polana inquired.

"Not till I've finished milking," replied Hordubal from the darkness. "Stepan can have his with us."

CHAPTER V

Juraj Hordubal sat down at the head of the table, folded his hands, and said grace. That's as it should be now that you are master. Polana sat with closed lips, her hands clasped together, Hafia stared and didn't know what to do, Stepan frowned stubbornly at the floor—What, you, you don't say grace, Polana? Well, Stepan may be of another creed, but grace is the proper thing at table. Look at them, they grow peevish, they eat fast, and silently. Hafia toys with the food on her plate—"Eat, Hafia," said Polana, admonishing her drily, but she herself hardly put anything into her mouth; only Stepan, leaning over his plate, made a loud noise as he took food from his spoon.

After the meal Manya wondered what to do with himself. "Wait a bit, Stepan," Hordubal urged him. "What did I want to say—Yes, and what was the harvest like this year?"

"The hay was good," said Manya evasively.

"And rye?"

Polana looked sharply at Stepan. "Rye," Manya said slowly: "Why, as a matter of fact, mistress sold those top fields. It wasn't worth the trouble, sir. All stones."

Inside Hordubal something snapped. "All stones," he mumbled, "yes, all stones; but, Polana, a field is the foundation——"

Stepan showed his teeth with self-assurance. "It wasn't worth the trouble, mister. The fields near the river are better. We've had maize as tall as a man."

"Near the river," said Hordubal taken aback. "So you've bought, Plana, some land in the plain?"

Polana was about to say something, but she swallowed it. "Manor fields, mister," explained Manya. "The soil's like a threshing floor, deep, good for sugar beet. But sugar beet's a poor business. It's a bad time, sir, better put your money in horses: a horse turns out well, and you get more for a horse than for a year of forced labour. If we only had another piece of land in the plain, and built stables down there——" Stepan's eyes sparkled. "Horses aren't goats, sir, they want flat land."

"The owner is willing to sell those fields," Polana remarked, almost to herself, and began to figure out what they would cost; but Hordubal wasn't listening; he was thinking of the rye and potato fields that Polana had sold. They were all stone certainly, but hadn't they been stone for ever? That, my lad, was part of the job. Two years before I went away I turned a piece of waste land into a field—eh, what do you know of hard work in the fields!

Hafia came stealthily to Stepan and leaned with her elbow against his shoulder. "Uncle Stepan," she whispered.

"What is it? smiled Manya.

The little one wriggled shyly. "I only——"

Stepan held her between his knees and rocked her: "Well, Hafia, what did you want to say?"

Hafia whispered into his ear: "Uncle Stepan, I've seen such a beautiful little puppy to-day!"

"Have you really?" inquired Manya importantly. "And I've seen a hare with three little ones."

"Oh, I say," exclaimed Hafia in amazement, "and where?"

"In the clover."

"And shall you shoot them in the autumn?"

Stepan looked sideways at Hordubal. "Well, I don't know."

A good fellow, thought Juraj to himself with relief, the child loves him; she wouldn't come to me. Children get used to things; but that she didn't mention those pictures I brought her from America! I ought to give something to Stepan—an idea struck him, and he looked round for his wooden box.

"I've put your things out on the dresser," said Polana. She always was so careful, mused Juraj gravely, going up to the pile of things from America. "This is for you, Hafia, these pictures, and this teddy-bear here——"

"What is it, uncle?" murmured Hafia.

"It's a bear," Manya explained. "Have you ever seen a live bear? They live away there in the mountains."

"And have you seen them?" urged Hafia.

"Yes, I have. They growl."

"This, Polana, is for you," mumbled Hordubal shyly. "They're silly things, well, but I didn't know what . . ." Juraj turned away, rummaging in his possessions for something he could give to Manya. "And this, Stepan," he said shyly, "perhaps might suit you: an American knife, and an American pipe——"

"Ach you," Polana burst out, almost choking, her eyes filling with tears as she rushed out of the room. Well, Polana, what is it?

"Thank you very much mister." Manya bowed, showing all his teeth, and gave his hand to Juraj. Eh, you, what strong hands you've got! It would be worth while to take you on. Well, praise be to God, sighed Hordubal with relief, that's over.

"Show me the knife, uncle," begged Hafia.

"Look," said Stepan boasting, "this knife has come all the way from America. I will carve an American doll for you with it. Would you like it?"

"Yes, uncle," cried Hafia, "but you will, won't you?"

Juraj smiled broadly and happily.

CHAPTER VI

BUT it wasn't all over yet. Juraj knew what was expected of him. When a man returns from America he must show himself in the pub, meet the neighbours, and stand them drinks. Let them all see that he's not come back empty handed, and in disgrace. Hi, landlord! drinks all round, and look sharp; what, you've forgotten Hordubal, and aren't I the miner from America? Let them know all over the village that Hordubal's come back. Eh, let's go and have a look at Hordubal, hi, missus, my coat, and my hat——

"I shall be back soon, Polana, go to bed, and don't sit up for me," urged Juraj, and he tramped ostentatiously through the dark village towards the public house. What different smells a village has: wood, cows, straw, hay, here's the smell of geese, and there it stinks of mayweed and nettles. In the pub old Salo Berkovic was no longer there, a red-haired Jew got up from the table and inquired suspiciously: "And what would you like, sir?"

Someone was sitting in the corner: who could it be? It might be Pjosa, yes, it was—Andrej Pjosa, called Husar, stared at Juraj as if he wanted to shout: Is that you, Juraj? Oh, yes, it's me, Andrej Husar, you see it's me.—Well, Pjosa didn't shout, he sat and gazed; and Hordubal, to show that he belonged to the place, said: "Is old Berkovic still alive?"

The freckled Jew placed a glass of brandy on the table. "It's six years ago since he was buried." Six years? eh, Pjosa, that's a long time; what's left of a man after six years—and what after eight? Eight years, I haven't drunk brandy for eight years: my God, I should have liked to drink it sometimes—to drown my sorrow, to spit at the strangeness, you know; but they wouldn't let them make brandy in America. At any rate, I sent more dollars to Polana; and, see, she bought horses and sold some land. All stones, they say. And you, Husar, you haven't sold any land? Well it's clear that you haven't been in America.

The Jew stood at the bar, and stared at Juraj. Shall I begin a conversation with him? the Jew wondered. He's not talkative it seems, he looks so, so, better not interfere; what fellow from the district can it be? Matey Pagurko has got a son somewhere, maybe it's Matey's son; or it might be Hordubal, Polana Hordubal's husband, who was in America——

Juraj blinked his eyes. The Jew turned away and busied himself arranging the glasses on the counter; and what about you, Pjosa, why do you keep your eyes down? Am I to speak to you by name? That's it, Andrej Pjosa: you get out of the habit of talking, your mouth turns wooden, but—well, even a horse, even a cow wants to hear a human voice. It's true Polana was always quiet, and eight years don't make you talk, loneliness doesn't teach you to talk: I don't know where to begin myself: she doesn't ask—I don't speak, she doesn't talk—I don't want to ask. Eh, what, Stepan is a good workman, he even does the talking for her. She sold the fields and bought a pusta in the plain, and there you are.

Hordubal sipped his brandy and nodded his head. This stuff burns, but you get used to it. Stepan—seems to be a good chap, apparently; he understands horses, and he likes Hafia; and as for Polana—a woman gets used to things, and what is to come will come by itself. Eh, Pjosa, and what about your wife—is she strange sometimes? Well, you beat her, but Polana is—like a lady, Andrej. That's it. She's sensible, hard-working, and clean—praise be to God. She is strange, certainly; and she carries herself like no other woman in the village. I don't know how to manage her, Husar. I ought to have rushed into the house like the wind, and danced her round until she was out of breath. That's how its done, Andrej. But I—you see, I couldn't do that. She was scared, as if I were a ghost. Even Hafia is frightened somehow. And you, Pjosa. Well, here I am, what am I to do? If the twig doesn't break it will bend. Good health, Andrej! Andrej Pojsa called Husar got up, and went towards the door as if he hadn't noticed anything. At the door he turned, glanced back, and burst out: "Back safe, Juraj!" You are a queer bird, Husar; as if you couldn't sit down with me—don't think that I've come back like a beggar: I've a nice couple of hundred dollars, even Polana doesn't know of it yet. Well, you see, Pjosa did recognize me; well, look here, that came by itself, the other will come by itself, too. Hordubal felt happier. "Hi, Landlord, bring me another one!"

The door flew open, and a fellow elbowed his way through it, he filled the room at once.—Why, it's Vasil Geric Vasilov, my best pal; with only a glance he was already at the table, Vasil! Juraj! The embrace of a fellow like that is rough, and smells of tobacco, but it's good, eh, you Vasil! "Welcome, Juraj!" he cried, looking worried, "and what brings you here?" "And why not, you camel, did you want me to die there?" laughed Hordubal. "Well," said Geric evasively, "it's not a good time for farmers now. You're all right, aren't you? Praise to God at least for that." You are queer, Vasil, you only sit on the edge of the chair, and you empty your glass at one gulp. "What's the news?" "Well, the old Kekercuk's dead, a week after Christmas, may he rest in peace; and on Sunday young Horolenko married Michalcuk's girl; last year the devil brought us foot-and-mouth disease—Ach, Juraj, they've made me mayor here, I'm an official, you know, it's only a nuisance——" The conversation fell to pieces, Vasil Vasilov somehow didn't know what to say, he rose and gave his hand to Juraj: "Good luck, Juraj; I must go."

Juraj smiled, and turned his glass round with heavy fingers. Vasil is no more what he used to be, ah, God in Heaven, how he knew how to drink until the windows rattled; but he came to me, and embraced—pal. Good luck, Juraj; why did you behave like that, is it written on my face that my homecoming wasn't a success? Ah, it wasn't, but that will come yet; slowly, slowly, I shall come back; every day, bit by bit, and look, soon I shall be at home. I've got money, Vasil; I could even buy land if I wanted, or cows, twelve cows if I like; I shall take them out to graze on the meadows myself, perhaps as far as Volov Chrbat; in the evening I shall return, with twelve bells ringing, and Polana will run swiftly to open the gate, like a young girl——

Silence reigned in the public house, the Jew drowsed behind the bar; yes, loneliness is good for a man; his head keeps on turning, turning, but in that way, my friend, he gets his ideas straightened out. To return step by step, and slowly like the cows; but what if I dash in like a team, charge into the yard, and make the sparks fly—stand up, hold the reins high, and jump down—here I am, Polana, and now I shall not let you go; I shall carry you in my arms into the house, and I shall hold you to me and squeeze the breath out of you. You are soft, Polana. Eight years, for eight years I've been thinking of you; and only now shall I go to you. Hordubal bit his teeth together until the muscles bulged out in his cheeks. Hi, wild horses, hi! Let Polana see—her knees will tremble with fright and pleasure, let her see: her man is coming back.

CHAPTER VII

In the moonlight Hordubal returned, drunk because he was unused to brandy, and unused to such thoughts, for he was going to a woman. Why do you make me feel so cold, moon—aren't I going so silently and lightly that I don't even shake the dew from off the grass? Hi, you dogs, all over the village, it's Juraj Hordubal going home, after eight years the chap's come back, feeling his arms curve to hold a woman. Yes, now I have you in my arms, and even that's not enough, I should like to press you to my mouth, and feel you with my fingers, Polana, Polana! And why do you make me feel so cold, you? Yes, I am drunk, because I need courage, because I want to dash headlong home; close my eyes, wave my arms, and jump head first—— Here you have me, Polana, here, and here, and here, everywhere, where are your hands, your legs, your mouth; eh, how big you are, how much there is of you, from head to toe, when shall I hold you all.

Hordubal went on through the moonlight night, quivering in every part of his body. You wouldn't shout, you wouldn't say a word in the moonlight night, you wouldn't break into its smooth surface: silence, silence, that light shadow is you, don't call to me by name, it's me; I hold you as silently as a tree grows, and I shan't break into this smooth surface, I shan't say a word, I shan't breathe; ah, Polana, you could hear a star fall.

But no, the moon doesn't shine on us, to us it doesn't seem so chill, it shines over the dark wood, and with us it's dark, a darkness that seems alive; you must feel with your hands in the dark, and you find your wife, she sleeps—no, she's not asleep, you can't see her, but there she is, she laughs quietly at you, and makes room for you; what a space for such long limbs, there's no room for you, you must squeeze yourself into her arms; and she whispers into your ear, you don't know what it is—the words are cold, but the whisper is warm, and dark, in a moment the darkness has become thicker, so dense and heavy, that you can feel it, and it is the woman, her hair, her shoulders; and she breathes, she draws in her breath between her teeth, she breathes darkly into your face—eh, Polana, Hordubal burst out, ah, you!

Silently Juraj unlatched the little gate leading into the yard, and trembled. Polana was sitting on the doorstep in the moonlight, waiting. "You, Polana," he murmured, and his spirit fell. "Why aren't you asleep?"

Polana shivered with cold. "I'm waiting for you. I wanted to ask you. Last year we sold a pair of horses for seven thousand; so what you—what do you think?"

"Y-Yes," said Hordubal, hesitating. "That's good, well, we'll talk about it to-morrow——"

"I want to do it now," said Polana harshly. "That's why I've waited for you. I don't want to look after cows any longer . . . drudge in the fields . . . well, I don't want to!"

"You won't," said Hordubal, glancing at her hands, shining white in the moonlight, "now I'm here to do the work."

"And what about Stepan?"

Juraj was silent, he sighed. Why talk about it now? "Well," he murmured, "there'll not be work enough for two."

"And what about the horses?" interposed Polana quickly. "Somebody must look after the horses, and you don't understand them——"

"That's true," he said evasively, "but we'll manage somehow."

"I want to know!" urged Polana, clenching her fists. Eh, how quick you are! "Just as you like, Polana, just as you like," Juraj heard himself say. "Stepan can stay, my sweet; . . . I must tell you, I've brought some money with me. . . . I will do everything for you."

"Stepan understands horses, you won't find another like him. He's worked for me for five years." Polana rose, strange and pale in the moonlight. "Good night; don't make a noise; Hafia is asleep."

"What—what you—where are you going?" exclaimed Hordubal, taken aback.

"Up in the loft. You sleep in the room, you are master here." In Polana's face there was something hard, something evil. "Stepan sleeps in the stable."

Hordubal sat motionless on the doorstep, and looked at the moonlight night. So, so. I don't want to think, my head has become wooden: and what is it that sticks in my throat so that I can't swallow it? You sleep in the room, you are master here. That's it.

Somewhere in the distance a dog barked, a cow rattled her chain in the stall. You sleep in the room. Eh, stupid head! You turn it, and nothing, nothing—it only throbs. Master, she said. All this is yours, master, these white walls, yard, everything. What a master you are. You have the whole room for yourself. You alone will roll on the bed—well master? And what if I can't get up. My head is so heavy—perhaps it's the brandy, the wood spirit the red-haired Jew gave me, but didn't I come from the pub as if I were dancing. Yes, that's it, in the room, Polana wants to honour her master, he shall sleep like a guest. A great weariness came over Hordubal. Well, yes, she wants me to rest, to be comfortable after the journey; yes, I can't even get up, it's silly to have legs like jelly. And the moon has already hidden herself behind the roof.

"Eleven o'clock has struck, every creature praise the L-O-R-D." That's the night watchman calling—they don't call like that in America—it's strange in America. He mustn't see me here, that would be a shame. Hordubal grew frightened, and silently, like a thief, he stole into the room. He took off his coat, and heard a faint breathing. God be praised, Polana was only joking, she's asleep here. Ah, what a stupid! And I like a log in the yard! Juraj stole silently, silently, up to the bed and groped with his hands: here some hair, there a small thin arm—Hafia. The child whimpered, and buried her face in the pillow. Yes, it's Hafia. Juraj sat down silently on the side of the bed. I'll cover her tiny legs. Oh, God, how can I get into bed? I shall only wake the child. Perhaps Polana wanted her to get accustomed to her father. That's it, father and child in the room, and she in the loft.

An idea struck Juraj—and, well, it wouldn't let him rest. She said: I'm going to sleep in the loft. Perhaps she said it on purpose: you silly, you can come after me, you know where I am: I'm going to sleep in the loft. There's no Hafia in the loft. Hordubal stood up in the darkness, like a pillar, and his heart beat fast. Polana is proud, she wouldn't say: here you have me: you must go after her as if she were a girl, you must feel about in the darkness, and she will laugh quietly; ah, Juraj, you silly, for eight years I've been thinking of you.

Silently, silently, Juraj crawled up into the loft. Ah, how dark it is, Polana, where are you, I can heart your hear beating. "Polana, Polana," whispered Hordubal, groping in the darkness. "Go, go away," came a dithering groan from the darkness. "I don't want you! Please, please, please." "I . . . nothing, Polana," murmured Hordubal, deeply confused, "I only . . . to ask you if you are comfortable here——" "Please, go away, go," came a terrified groan from the darkness.

"I only wanted to tell you," stammered Hordubal . . . "My dear, everything shall be just as you want . . . you can even buy land in the plain . . ."

"Go, go away," cried Polana, at her wits' end—and Juraj never knew how he got down, somehow, as if he were falling headlong into an abyss. But no, he didn't fall, he sat on the bottom step, and felt as if he were falling into an abyss. So far, Jesus Christ, to fall so far! And who's wheezing here? It's me, it's me. I'm not grunting, I'm only trying to get my breath, and it's not my fault if I groan, again and again! Well, grunt; you are at home now, you are master here.

Hordubal halted, he sat on the step, and peered into the darkness. You sleep in the room, she said, you are master here. So that's what's wrong with you, Polana: You've been your own mistress for eight years, and now you're angry because you'll have a master over you. Eh, my sweet! look what a master! He sits on the step, and whimpers. You'd like to wipe his nose with your apron. Hordubal felt his face move. He touched it. My God, it's a smile! Hordubal smiled into the darkness: What a master, farm worker! Mistress, a farm worker has come to look after your cows, and you, Polana, shall be like a lady. Well, you see, everything can be set right; horses and cows, Stepan and Juraj. I shall breed cattle for you, Polana, a pleasure to look at—and sheep; you shall have everything, you shall be mistress over everything.

So now, it was already easier to breathe, and he didn't groan any more, be began to breathe deeply, like a pair of bellows. What do you think, ma'rm, a farm worker doesn't sleep in the room; he should go and sleep with the cows, that's his place. At any rate, it's not so lonely, you can hear something breathing; perhaps he says something aloud, and then gets frightened, but you can talk to a cow: she turns her head, and listens. You sleep well in a cowshed.

Silently, quietly, Juraj stole into the cowshed; the warm smell of cattle greeted his nostrils, a chain jingled against the stanchion. Heta, you cows, heta, it's me; thank God, there's straw enough for a man.

"Midnight has struck, every creature praise the L-O-R-D, and Jesus Christ His Son." No, it's not like this in America. "Take care that light and fire do no harm to anyone——"

Tu-tu-tu went the night watchman's horn, as if a cow had lowed.

CHAPTER VIII

STEPAN was hitching the horses to the wagon. "Good morning, mister," he called, "don't you want to have a look round the meadows?"

Juraj frowned slightly: Am I a bailiff to drive about in a carriage and look round the fields? Eh, well, there's nothing to do, there's nowhere to take a scythe to the corn, why shouldn't I have a look at Polana's farming?

Stepan wore wide linen trousers and a blue apron—it was clear that he was from the plain, and he was as dark as a gipsy. "C-c," he clicked to the horses, and with a rattle and clatter off they flew. Juraj had to hold fast to the wagon, but Stepan stood erect, his tiny hat perched at the back of his head, the reins held high, and he played with the whip over the horses' backs. Well, well, slowly, there's no hurry.

"But, my lad," said Juraj, somewhat discontented, "why are you pulling at the horses' mouths? You see how they chafe, it hurts them."

Stepan turned and showed his teeth. "It has to be like that," he said, "so that they carry their heads high."

"And what for?" objected Hordubal. "Let them carry their heads as they grew."

"It pays very well, mister," Stepan explained. "Every buyer looks whether a horse carries his head high. Look, look now they're going very well: on their hind legs, with their front ones they only just scratch the ground. C-c."

"And don't make them go so fast," cried Hordubal.

"They learn to trot," said Manya, indifferently. "Let them learn. What can you do with a slow horse?"

Does Stepan drive Polana about like this? wondered Hordubal. The whole village turns to look: That's Hordubal's wife on the wagon, fine, like a lady: she folds her arms, and sits erect. And why shouldn't she feel proud? thought Juraj. Praise be to God, she's different from the other women, firm and erect, like a pillar; she's made the farm like a castle; she got seven thousand for a pair of horses, well, then, she can carry her head high. It pays very well, my lad.

"Now there's that flat land," said Stepan, pointing with his whip. "Right up to those acacias it belongs to the mistress."

Hordubal climbed down from the wagon as if broken. You've shaken me about, you devil. So this is that flat land; grass up to the waist, but dry and hard—don't tell me, this isn't soil for sugar beet, it's a steppe.

Manya scratched his head. "If you bought this land as far as there, mister, you could keep thirty horses here."

"We-ll," objected Hordubal, "it's not very rich, my good fellow."

"What do you want with rich land?" grinned Manya. "A horse must be dry, mister. Or do you want to feed horses for the butcher?"

Hordubal made no reply, and, going up to the horses, he rubbed their noses. "Well-well-well, little chap, don't get frightened, you're a nice one. What are you pricking your ears for? And you, ah, you're a knowing one! Why are you pawing the ground? What do you want?" Stepan unharnessed the horses, he straightened himself, and said, somewhat sharply: "Don't talk to the horses, mister. It makes them soft."

Hordubal looked up with a start: so that's how you talk to your master! And, well, perhaps so that the horses don't get used to me. I won't meddle with your horses, you camel; well, well, you needn't frown.

Stepan let the horses loose to graze, and took up the scythe, ready to cut some grass. What a blockhead not to have taken another scythe with him! Juraj sighed, and looked out over the plain to the hills behind Kriva. There at any rate were real fields —all stone, perhaps, but they were fields: potatoes, oats, rye— somewhere there rye was still growing, somewhere there they were already cutting the corn. "And who bought those fields of ours up there, Stepan?"

"Someone called Pjosa," said Manya.

Ah, Pjosa, Andrej Pjosa Husa; that's the reason why he didn't speak to me in the pub; he was ashamed because he had deprived a woman of her field. Juraj looked up over the hills. Strange, as if Hordubal's fields had run down the hills, and settled in the plain.

"And Rybary is down there?" inquired Juraj.

"Down there," said Stepan. "Over there, about three hours away."

Three hours away, see, it's a long way yet to Rybary. Out of boredom Hordubal picked a halm of grass and began to chew it; it was rather harsh and sour. The grass up there, on the slopes, tastes quite different, spicy, of thyme. Juraj walked slowly over the meadow, further and further. What a flat land, nothing to see but the sky, and even the sky isn't the same as up there; it looks dusty. And here's a field of maize as tall as a man, all green stuff; ach, Lord, it looks so untidy—just let the sows in, there would be a grunting! While a field of rye is like a velvet coat. Acacias—Juraj didn't like the acacias; up there there are blackthorns, spindle-trees, and mountain-ash, and none of those good-for-nothing acacias. I can't even see Manya now, in that apron of his, and high boots. And what about not talking to the horses! A horse is a wise animal, like a cow; it learns quietness through talking.

A flat plain spread out before Juraj, he was overcome with loneliness, it was almost like the sea; what could he do there! He turned towards the hills; ah, you, even you are eaten away by the flat land, it makes you look small and stupid. But to tramp up them, my friend, then at least you learn what the earth is like. And Juraj could not stand it any longer, he hastened back to the village, leaving Stepan behind with his team. I'll look at the crops, he thought to himself, but he kept going for an hour, and still the hills were far away in front, and it was so hot, not a breath of air was stirring. So here's your flat land. Who would have thought that Stepan had taken me so far? Only c-c, and we were already at the other end of the earth. Polana has keen horses: what's the good of a slow horse, mister?

Hordubal had already been going for two hours, and there at last was the beginning of the village; gipsies, the scoundrels, rolling about among hemlocks and thorn-apples, and there already was the smithy. Hordubal halted, something came into his head, ah, Polana, I'll show you! He barged his way into the blacksmith's shop. Hello, my man, make me a latch, well, what kind of a latch, for a door. I'll wait till you've made it. The smith didn't recognize Hordubal, it was dark inside the shop, and he could not see for the blaze. Well, if you want a latch, I'll make it for you; and he began hammering hard on a big one. Well, my man, what are Polana's horses like? Why, like demons, but for the gentry; no good for work, uncle. When you shoe them, aha! it needs two fellows to hold devils like them.

Hordubal looked at the glowing piece of iron. I shall bring you something, Polana, something for the house. And what's a horse like that worth? The smith spat. God's my witness; they say they want eight thousand for it. All that money for a horse! If the wild terror falls lame what have you got? A little Hutsul horse is better, or a heavy gelding, with a back like an altar, and a breast like an organ—ei, they were horses, they used to have on the estate! But now—a tractor! The squire is selling his meadows: what's the use of hay, he says, what good are horses, now they've got machines——?

Hordubal nodded. Yes, machines like they have in America. I must see that Polana doesn't go wrong. Machines will come, and what shall you do with horses then! Aha, so you see; no, no, Polana, I shan't let you have my dollars to buy meadows. Fields and cows; they're something different—a man can't fill his belly with machines. And it doesn't pay, they say. Well, perhaps not, but you've got milk and corn anyhow.

Hordubal went back home, carrying the piece of iron still

warm. Polana—perhaps she's cooking the dinner. Juraj stole up the steps to the loft, and fixed the latch on the inner side of the little door. So, and now the staple—Polana climbed up the steps, and knitted her brows, to see what Juraj was tinkering at up there. What will she ask? No, she won't, she only looks on with a fixed gaze. "It's already finished," murmured Hordubal. "I've only fixed up a latch for you, so that you can lock yourself in."

CHAPTER IX

AND already it's so dull for you, Jura, Juraj; you walk round the farmyard, gaze about, and you don't know what to do. Grow savoys? That's no job for a man. Feed the hens? Feed the pigs? Oh, that's an old woman's job. The wood's already sawn, and chopped up, you've mended the fence, you've patched up this and that; you slouch like old Kyryl, who mumbles to himself over there in Michal Herpak's farmyard. And the neighbours' women peep. That's a fine farmer, hands in his pockets, and yawning. May you jaw fall off!

Down there in the meadows—is Manya: what am I to do there? Don't talk to the horses, and so—stay there alone, what's there for me in the plain? Look at him, a farm worker from somewhere, and says, if you do this and that, mister. And look, I shall; it's not for you to order me about, but if it's of wood I shall make it. In the old days forests were cut; and they don't sell the wood any more, they say, it rots on the ground, the saw-mills stand——

God, to mind the cows once again! Not two young heifers, people would laugh, but twelve cows; and drive them perhaps as far as Volov Chrbat, with a heavy stick in my hand ready for a bear. And nobody would say: don't talk to the cows. You have to shout at cattle.

But Polana wouldn't even listen—the butcher gives you eight hundred for a cow, she says, and yet he lets you have it as a favour. Well, never mind the butcher—for myself I'd rear cattle: but if you don't want, all right. I shan't stick the money in the plain for you.

Or harness cows to the wagons and go to the fields to bring the harvest home. The man walks, walks, with one hand on the yoke, get on! O—ou! No hurry, only as much as the cows can manage. Even in America I didn't get used to any other pace; only the cows' pace. And going down with a load of sheaves, to catch the wheel by the spokes, and hold all the loaded wagon in your hand—God be praised, at any rate you realize that you've got hands. That's a man's job, Polana. Ah, God have mercy, what vanity—but one's hands get soft; and what able hands they are, hard, American ones.

Yes, Polana, you can run about, you've always got something to do, here the hens, there the pigs, there something in the dairy, but it's a shame for a fellow to lean on the fence. If only you said, You, Juraj, you could do this and that; but you're like an arrow, no one can talk with you. I could tell you things—perhaps this: in America, Polana, a fellow can sweep, wash the dishes, and wipe the floor, and he's not ashamed; they have a good time, those women in America. But you—you scowl as soon as I touch anything: it's not right, you say, people will laugh at you. Ah, what's it matter! let them laugh, the silly fools. I do something in the stable, I give the horses food or drink—and again Stepan scowls. Don't talk to the horses, he says, and so on. Right-ho, you! And he's always scowling. Well, well, don't eat me with your eyes. He doesn't even talk to the mistress, he hardly opens his mug, and only with those eyes of his. He's bitter, he's all yellow with bitterness, it gnaws his entrails. And Polana is frightened of him, too, she says: Go, Hafia, and tell Stepan to do so and so, ask him about this and that—Hafia isn't frightened of him. She calls him uncle, and he takes her on his knee: This is how the colt jumps, Hafia, this is how the mare goes—and he sings, but as soon as he sees anyone it's as if someone cut him short, and he crawls away into the stable.

Hordubal scratched his head. And the deuce knows why Hafia is so frightened of me. She plays and plays, but as soon as I come she stops, and she doesn't take her eyes from me, only off and away. Well, run. Eh, Hafia, I should like to make wooden toys for you, if only you would lean against my shoulder and look—ooh, what's it going to be? And what couldn't I tell you about America, child! there are negroes there, and such machines—eh, God be with you, Hafia, run along to your Stepan. Don't beat her, Polana, you can't tame anyone with force; but if you sat down sometimes, if we only talked to one another, Hafia would come, and she would listen, she would put her elbow against my knee—I could tell her many odd things, the child would listen with her mouth wide open. Well, in winter perhaps, in winter, by the fire——

Below from the village came the noise of geese, and the rattling of a cart—that's Manya coming back. Juraj waved his hand, and retired behind the barn. What, am I to stand here, just staring at you! You bring a load of hay, and you make as much noise as if you'd brought God knows what. And here is silence, here you are at the back of the world. They let the orchard go to ruin, we used to have pears and plums here, and now nothing. Those old trees ought to be cleared away, and young ones planted in the autumn, but no; there's nothing old left, nothing that was here before, except those barren trees: stay here with God. There used to be a shady little orchard, but now pigs root there; and nettles; oh God!

Don't you realize, I saw many things in America; I had a look, and see, this or that could be done here, too. They have nice things there, handy ones—just take their different machines! Or this—grow vegetables. Or rabbits. But it's best with rabbits when you've plenty of leaves from the vegetables. And then, many things might be done. I would do everything, if only, Polana, if only you took a glance to see what Juraj is doing. And what is it going to be, Juraj? Cages for the rabbits, Hafia will be pleased, you'll even be able to make her a little fur coat. Or a pigeon-house, for instance. And then, wouldn't you like some bees! I could make a bee-hive, not out of a log, but a bee-hive with a little piece of glass at the back, so that you can see inside. In Johnstown there was a miner, a Pole, a great bee-keeper; just think, he even had a wire mask for his face. You learn a lot. If only you wanted, Polana, if only you looked—there would be lots of things. Or ask: how do they do so and so in America? Well, you never ask, it's difficult to tell you anything. A man is too shy to do something only for his own interest, for himself—as if he were only playing: but for someone else—he spits in his hands, and even whistles. It's like that, Polana.

Glory to God, I can hear the cow-bells ringing, it's evening already; they must be tied up, given water, patted, Hafia will shout: Stepan, daddy, supper; Stepan eats noisily, Polana is silent. Hafia whispers to uncle Stepan, well, what is there to do; good night everybody. Hafia in the room, Polana in the loft, Stepan in the stable—walk round the yard once more, and crawl into the cowshed to sleep. And there, with my hands under my head, I can even explain aloud what we could have, and how things might be done.

And the cows—as if they understand; they turn their heads and look.

CHAPTER X

"TELL them, Hafia, that I'm not coming back till the evening."

A slice of bread and bacon, all is ready, and now for the hills. Hordubal felt free and almost homesick, like a child that has escaped from its mammy. And he looked over the village as if something had changed there. What was it? This used to be Hordubal's field? It was, without a doubt—all stones, they said, and yet Pjosa had a crop of barley here, he's got potatoes here, and a little patch of flax; see how Pjosa's field and Hordubal's have been joined together. But there, higher up, by the mountain-ash—from there you can see the whole village. There you can marvel at God's wisdom: Kriva, the village is called, and really it is crooked, bent into an arch, like a cow lying down. One roof next to the other, all the same, like a flock of sheep: but that white building is Polana's. As if it didn't fit in here, thought Juraj; the roof is red, new—one might ask who has come here? Someone from the plain, where people have no wood, and must use brick——

The plain. From here even the plain is visible. Blue, level—like the sea, well, a weary waste. That's why they go so fast: the road is dismal, a man walks—walks, and it's as if he trod on one spot. You don't go to the plain just to see things; while here—like a feast day, you only need follow your nose, and there's always something to lead you farther: there past the bend in the road, over the stream, there to that spruce, up over the clearing, and then, when you've got there, into the wood: the wood faces the midday sun, all beech-trees, the trunks light and grey, as if mist were lying there; and here, there, everywhere cyclamen in flower, like tiny glowing flames. And here, look what a pale brown mushroom, it lifts the dead leaves, ah, what a sturdy white stem; and do you know what! I shall let you stay, mushroom, and I shan't pick you either, cuckoo-flowers and campanulas, but a bunch of strawberries for Hafia, down below at the edge of the wood, where they are sweetest. Hordubal stopped and held his breath: deer; there on the other slope a doe was standing, blonde and sleek, like last autumn's leaves, she stood in the bracken, alert and inquisitive. What are you, a man or a stump? A stump, a butt, a black branch, but don't run away; what, even you are afraid of me, wild creature? No, she's not afraid; she nibbles a tiny leaf, she looks, chews her cud like a goat. Beh, beh, she says, she stamps her little hooves, and trots away. And Juraj was suddenly overwhelmed with joy, he went upward with a light step, thinking of nothing. He just went, and went, feeling at peace with the world. I have seen some deer, he will say to Hafia in the evening—ooh, where? Well, up there—there are no deer, Hafia, in the plain.

And here it is already—nobody knows what it is really: some kind of a log hut, now in pieces, logs strewn about, but logs. Good Lord, a belfry might be built of them, grown over with Night-shade, and Herb-Paris, with wild lilies, Verasrum, Crane's-bill, and ferns, truly, a strange spot, as if haunted—here the wood faces north; a dark wood, grown over with moss, the soil is black, and squelchy, yes, it's haunted here, they say, and some mushrooms, whitish, translucent, like jelly, wood sorrel, and darkness, always so dark here, not even a squirrel to be heard or a little fly; it's such a dark wood, young children are frightened to come here, and even a big chap crosses himself. But here already is the edge of the wood, you wade through bilberries up to your knees, and lift the branches, and see how much lichen hangs here, brambles catch you by the legs, eh, man, it's not so easy to get through the wood to the upland clearing, you must tear your way through the thicket like a boar; and bang! as if you had been shot out of the wood, as if the wood itself shot you out, you stand in the clearing, praise be to Jesus Christ, here we are!

The clearing is wide: spruce-trees here and there, big and mighty like the church, you could take your hat off, and greet them aloud; and the grass, velvety, smooth, very short, you walk on it as if on a carpet; the long and wide clearing between the woods, it stretches far and wide, it has the sky above, it has gathered the woods round its waist: like a man who bares his chest, and lies, lies, and looks up into God's windows—ah, ahah, that's breath for him! And Juraj Hordubal felt suddenly as small as a little ant, and he ran over the wide clearing, where to, little ant? Well, there, up to the top; do you see there, those little red ants grazing? That's where I'm making for. The clearing is big.

Big, sir: you would say a herd of oxen? Those red dots? God has it very nice: he looks down, and says to himself: that black dot there is someone called Hordubal, that bright dot there is Polana; I must look and see, will those two dots meet? or shall I push them together with my finger? And here from the hill something black dashes directly at me; it runs, it rolls down the slope, what are you? Oh, you are a black cur, you'll bark yourself hoarse, get off, do I look like a robber? Come here, you're a brave little dog; I'm going to the herdsman up there. Already you can hear the cow-bells. Hajza, the herdsman kept shouting: the oxen with big, quiet eyes gazed at Juraj, they swished their tails, and went on grazing; the herdsman stood motionless, like a juniper-tree, and looked round for the newcomer.

"Hi," cried Juraj, "is that you, Misa? Well thanks be to God!"

Misa said nothing, he only stared.

"You don't know me? I'm Hordubal."

"Ah, Hordubal," said Misa, without surprise; why should he be surprised.

"I've come back from America."

"What?"

"From America."

"Oh, from America."

"Whose cattle are you looking after, Misa?"

"What?"

"Whose cattle are they?"

"Oh, whose cattle. From Kriva."

"So, so, from Kriva. Nice beasts. And what about you, Misa, are you all right? I've come to have a look at you."

"What?"

"Well, to have a look at you."

Misa said nothing, he only blinked his eyes. One's not used to talking up here. Hordubal lay down on the grass, propping himself up on his elbow, and he began to chew a piece of grass. It's a different world here, you needn't talk, it's not necessary. From April till September, Misa watches the herds here, he doesn't see a soul for a week at a time——

"And what, Misa, have you ever been down there on the plain?"

"What?"

"Have you been on the plain, Misa?"

"Oh, on the plain. No, never."

"And up there, on the Durnoj, have you been there?"

"Yes, I have."

"And there behind that hill, you haven't been there?"

"No, I haven't."

So you see, and I—I've been as far as America; and what have I got for it? I can't even understand my wife——

"There—there are other pastures there," said Misa.

"And tell me," inquired Juraj, as he used to when he was a boy. "What was that log hut in the wood?"

"What?"

"That log hut, there in the wood."

"Oh, that log hut." Misa thoughtfully pulled at his clay pipe. "Who knows? The robbers wanted to build a fortress there, they say. But who knows?"

"And is it really haunted there?"

"Oh, that," said Misa vaguely.

Hordubal turned over on his back. It's fine here, he thought to himself; what's going on down there below?—already you yourself don't know. People swarm there in the farmyard, they get in each other's way, it's a wonder they don't go for one another like cocks; till your tongue aches because it itches so much to shout out——

"Have you got a wife, Misa?"

"What?"

"—whether you have got a wife?"

"No, I haven't."

In the plain there aren't clouds like these; the sky's empty there, but here—like the cows on the clearing; you lie on your back and mind them. And it's as if they were sailing, and you were sailing with them, sailing away somehow, strange that you are so light and can soar with them. Where are they going, these clouds, where are they off to in the evening? As if they melted away, but can anything vanish like that?

Hordubal leaned on his elbow. "I wanted to ask you, Misa—do you know a herb for love? So that perhaps a girl might fall in love with you?"

"Oh," murmured Misa, "I don't need that."

"Not you, but someone else might."

"And what for?" inquired Misa, indignantly. "There's no need."

"But do you know such plants?"

"I don't." Misa spat out. "I'm no gipsy."

"But you know how to cure people, Misa, don't you?"

Misa said nothing, he only blinked his eyes. "You don't know what you'll die of," he said suddenly.

Hordubal sat erect with a throbbing heart. "Do you think, Misa, that . . . soon?"

Misa blinked thoughtfully. "Oh, God knows. Does a man live long?"

"And how old are you, Misa?"

"What?"

"How old are you?"

"Oh, that I don't know. What's the good of knowing?"

Ba, what's the good of knowing? Juraj murmured; what's the good of knowing?—say, what's Polana thinking about? Down there a man torments himself with it; but here—well, think what you like, my dear, if you were happy you wouldn't think. It's strange, how far away everything is from here, so far, that you feel homesick. A man feels—as if he were looking on himself as well from a great height, as he runs—about the yard, gets angry, and worried, and all the while he's just a little ant, irritated, not knowing how to get out.

A great peace fell on Juraj, so great that it was like a pain. Look at him, such a rough and strong fellow, and he sighs, sighs under the burden of relief. Ah, I shouldn't like to get up yet, and take it down into the valley, and how about not liking: I couldn't. To lie silently, silently, so that it gets straightened out; to lie like this for days, perhaps for weeks, and wait till it falls into place; let the sky turn round, let the ox put his head down and sniff, let the marmot peep, is it a stone? it's a stone, and hop on it to sit up and sniff. With his hands spread out Hordubal lay on his back. There is no Hordubal, or even a Polana—only the sky, the earth, and the sound of the cow-bells. The clouds melt away, and nothing is left behind, not even as much as when you breathe on the glass. The ox thinks what a struggle he has, and it is only cow-bells from afar. What's the use of knowing? Gaze. God gazes, too. What a big eye, peaceful like the eye of a beast. The wind, as if time itself were flowing and roaring; where can it all come from? And what's the use of knowing?

Evening came on, and Juraj began to descend, he went over the clearing, and slipped into the wood, with long and light steps he walked; the burden of peace had already settled into place in him, and he need not even think of it. All right, Polana, all right, I shan't run about under your nose any longer, the yard is too small for two of us. I shall find a job somewhere, and if not, I shall sit up here, and wait, wait till the evening. Why not—does a man live long? Why, I ask you, should two little ants get in one another's way? there is so much space that you don't even understand where it all comes from; and I—even from a distance I can look. Praise be to God, there are hills enough from which you can see your home. You can crawl as far as the Creator's collar, and look down at yourself. Like the clouds, rise—and dissolve, like breath.

Already the cow-bells could be heard, but still Hordubal sat on the thyme-covered baulk with a bunch of strawberries in his hand, and looked down on the new red roof. The farmyard, too, could be seen like the palm of a hand. To take Hafia there, and show her. See here, Hafia, isn't it like a toy? In the yard a small bright little figure emerges, and stands, stands. And there, see, from the stable a dark little figure comes out, goes up to her, and also stands still. And they don't move—like toys. Ants would wave their feelers, and run about, but men—are more mysterious: they stand next to one another, and nothing happens. What's the good of knowing? thought Hordubal, but it's strange that they stand so long, so motionless; one's uneasy—it's dreadful that they stand so motionless. And was it peace, Juraj, that you brought with you from up there? The heaviness that knocks you down? You have had too much of something up there, and it's sadness; you spread your hands out, and now you carry a cross. And those two there below stand, stand—ah, Jesus, if only they would move at last! And then the bright little figure tore itself away, and went in; the dark one stands, doesn't move, and, glory to God, already it's gone.

Hordubal returned with a bunch of strawberries—he had nothing but that little bunch, and yet he forgot it in the yard. Four people at the evening table; he was almost on the point of beginning—I saw some deer, Hafia—but he didn't say anything, words stuck in his mouth like pieces of food, Polana ate nothing, as pale as if she were carved out of bone, Stepan scowled over his plate, screwed his face about, crushed bread with his fingers, suddenly threw his knife down, and ran out as if he were choking.

"What's the matter with uncle Stepan?" murmured Hafia.

Polana said nothing, she gathered the plates from the table, so deadly pale that her teeth chattered.

And Hordubal took himself away to the cows, the bald-headed

one turned her head towards him, until her chain rattled. What is it, master? Why do you sigh so loudly? Eh, bald one, what's the use of knowing, what's the use of knowing?—but it's heavier, heavier than a chain. Up there we could make our bells ring, you and I—what space there is, there's space for God there, too, but among men it's close, two, three people, bald head, and so close together! can't you hear their chains rattling?

CHAPTER XI

THAT night Manya got drunk, like a beast; not in Kriva, but away at Tolcemes, at the Jew's; he fought with the other fellows, and he used his knife and got stabbed, they say, who knows; towards morning he returned, swollen and sore, and now he sleeps it out in the stable. The horses ought to be watered, thought Juraj, but I shan't meddle with your affairs. If I'm not to talk to them, all right; look after them yourself. And Polana—like a shadow, better not see her. Well, things are in a state. Hordubal frowned. What is one to do?

It was hot, hot as if it were going to thunder: nasty flies, oh, what a vile day! Juraj slouched into the orchard behind the barn; but even there somehow—What is there to do here? Only the nettles smell, and why are there so many broken pots here? such gipsy rubbish—Polana's like a shadow: she stays somewhere inside the house, and nothing—God be with you; but you know it's hard for a man here. Hordubal uneasily rubbed his moist neck. Well, the storm will come, Stepan ought to cart the hay home——

He climbed over the fence, and made his way round behind the village, to look at the sky, what it was like. The village from the back—as if you looked at a table from underneath, all wood and framework, as if nobody saw you, as if you were playing hide and seek with the whole world; just fences, and burdocks, savoys eaten with caterpillars, here a refuse dump, hemlocks, thorn-apples, and gipsies, gipsy huts behind the village—Juraj halted, and hesitated: oh, God, where am I! Polana is alone, Stepan unconscious in the stable . . . Hordubal's heart began to thump. Devil take the gipsy! She just sat on the ground, old crone, dreadful, combing a child for lice.

"And what would you like, sir," the gipsy woman croaked.

"Gipsy, gipsy," shuddered Juraj, "can you make a love potion."

"Ei, I can," the gipsy woman grinned, "and what will you give me?"

"A dollar, an American dollar," Hordubal burst out, "two dollars——"

"Wah, you carrion," the gipsy woman cried, "for two dollars, look here, you can't couple a dog for two dollars, you can't even charm a cow——"

"Ten dollars," whispered Hordubal in excitement, "ten, gipsy!"

The gipsy woman grew calm at once. "Give them to me," she commanded, stretching out a dirty paw.

Juraj's fingers trembled as he rummaged feverishly for the money. "But make a good charm, gipsy, not for a night, not for a month, not for a year——So that the heart grows soft, the tongue loose, so that she will be glad to see me——"

"Hi," the gipsy murmured, "Ilka, make a fire!" She rummaged in her bag, her hands were hooked and wrinkled like a bird's claws. Ah, what a shame! The sky is growing wilder, there will be a storm. Make it, gipsy, make it well—Eh, Polana, look where you've taken me!

The gipsy prattled, throwing pinches from her bag into the little cauldron; it smelt vile; she mumbled something, shaking her head, and making charms with her claws. It was terrible for Juraj. Let me fall down on the spot! This for you, Polana, for you, only you—What a crime!

Juraj ran home, carrying the charm, he ran, the storm was coming. The cows were trotting with their load of sheaves, children scampering home, the dust rose in columns. Perspiring freely Hordubal opened the little gate leading to his home, he had to stop and lean, his heart throbbed, that for you, Polana. And suddenly from the stable the three-year-old ran out, stopped, neighed, and galloped to the gate.

"O-o-o!" shouted Juraj, waving his arms to stop him. Polana ran out from the house. The horse was up on its hind legs, it spun round, dashed round the yard, with its head high, and its back pressed down, and it dug its hooves into the ground.

And where has Hafia got to? She ran across the yard to her mammy, squealing with terror, and fell . . . Polana shrieked, and Hordubal gave a roar. Oh, wooden legs! Why don't I dash forwards——? And then from the stable Manya flew, his white sleeves fluttered, the horse reared itself up, and to its mane a man was hanging, he tore at the horse, eh, you don't shake him off, like a wild cat on its neck. The horse sprang away, shook its head, threw its back up; bang, Manya was on the ground, but he clung to the mane, kneeling, and tore at the horse. And only then did Hordubal's legs untie themselves, and he ran for Hafia. The horse dragged Manya over the yard, but Stepan now dug his heels in, and pulled, pulled at the mane. Hordubal pressed the child to his breast, he would have liked to carry it away, but he forgot—such a sight it was; the man and the beast. Polana's hands were on her heart. Then Manya gave a high-pitched laugh, neighed like a horse, and galloping and jumping he led the snorting stallion into the stable.

"Now, take the child," said Hordubal, but Polana heard nothing. "Polana, do you hear, Polana?"

For the first time Juraj put his hand on her shoulder. "Polana, Hafia!" She lifted her eyes. Ah, have you ever had such eyes before, have you ever breathed like this, with your mouth half open? How beautiful you were—and now it's vanished.

"Nothing happened to her," she mumbled as she carried the sobbing child into the house.

Manya emerged from the stable, he wiped the blood from his nose with his sleeve, he spat blood from his mouth. "It's all right now," he said.

"Come," muttered Hordubal, "come, Stepan, let me bathe your head."

Stepan snorted with delight under the stream of water, and splashed cheerfully and copiously. "But that was a job, wasn't it?" he prattled in a lively tone. "The little stallion got rattled, mister, that's why he was so wild." Manya showed his teeth, he was wet and dishevelled. "Ei, he will be a stallion!"

Juraj wanted to say to Stepan: Well, you are a champion, you did do it well; but among men—there's no need. "There will be a storm," he murmured, and strolled away behind the barn. In the south the sky was heavy; storms which come from below are never good. The little stallion got rattled, and one can't even move one's legs to save the child. Maybe I'm already old, Polana, or what. Strange, my legs were like wood, as if charmed.

Lord, how dark! It began to thunder. The gipsy woman made a charm, and see, the little stallion got rattled; and I didn't catch hold of the horse's mane, nothing, only shuddered, and gaped. I, no, but Stepan did. Why shouldn't he, he's young? Ah, Polana, Polana, why did you look so, why were you so beautiful!

And already it was there, there; the storm—like a frightened horse it ran, sparks from under its hooves, neighing. You don't catch hold of the horse's mane any more, your legs won't let you, they falter. You don't spring, don't yell; Stepan does. Damn, it's a miserable charm from that gipsy: the little stallion got rattled, and so. And you think: That's all for Polana. So why didn't you spring at the horse? Polana would have looked with her hands on her breast, and her eyes—as never.

Juraj blinked his eyes, he didn't even feel the warm drops on his face. The sky was rent, crashed, and rattled; Hordubal crossed himself hurriedly, and felt an urge to run for shelter. No, not yet, first throw the gipsy woman's charm into the nettles. And then with a jump under the shed and watch the storm.

CHAPTER XII

WHERE else would he be? He had crawled behind the barn, to think. For instance, he thought: Well, let's admit that I'm old; but I ask you, how does it happen? You live, you feel nothing, you are the same as yesterday, and suddenly—old. As if somebody had bewitched you. You don't catch hold of a frightened horse by the mane any more, you don't fight in the pub any more; you pick up the child instead of catching the horse. And to show you, once upon a time even I fought in the pub, gloriously, with Geric, in fact, ask Vasil, Polana. And suddenly—old; Polana's not old.

Well, then, perhaps I'm old. To pick up a child is also good. Eh, Polana, I could show you—for instance, what a farmer I am. You could live like a lady, maids to do the work, and you only shout: Hi, Maryka, feed the hens; now then, Axena, water the cows. It's true they stole three thousand dollars of mine, but I still have seven hundred, we might start on many things. Ah, my dear, I wasn't in America for nothing; young, not young, at least I've learned how and what in the world. And that it doesn't pay to keep cows, they say, and such-like things. What about it, you must know how to sell. In America, say—there a farmer doesn't wait till the butcher comes; he goes himself to the town, and makes a contract; so much and so many times a year, so many and so many churns of milk a day, all right. That's how it's done. I ask you, why shouldn't it do here as well? Buy a pony and a cart—sell your horses, Polana, I want a pony that you can talk to—and drive to town. Well, the American knows his way about, he didn't go abroad for nothing; he takes home a belt full of money. And then the neighbours would come—Could you, Juraj, sell for us a couple of geese in the town? Why couldn't I, but not like this, with only one goose under my arm; but fifty, a hundred geese a week—I should make coops, off with a load of geese to town.

That, my friends, is how business is done. Or wood for burning, fifty loads of wood. Potatoes—in wagons. Look at Hordubal, what ideas he's brought back with him from America! And even you, Polana, would say, Juraj is clever, no youngster could be more active; Hi, Maryka, Axena, take master's boots off, he's back from the market. And what have you been doing all the day, my dear? I looked after the farm for you, scolded the servants, and then, well, I've been waiting, Juraj, for you.

Hordubal sat on a stump, and blinked his eyes. Try it, why not? A fellow is young as long as he begins something new. And if not that, well, in a different way. For instance, buy the rock below Mencul—stone like marble, and cart the blocks to town; Good Lord, have they any stone in the plain? Only mud and dust, the sky is dusty, too. And perhaps break the stone oneself—didn't I break a bit of stone in America? And dynamite, my friend, I can manage. You make a hole, put the cartridge in—all clear, bang—and crash! Well, Polana, that's a man's job, what? What's catching a little stallion compared with it? And with a red flag in your hand—look out, they're firing the charge. I should make glorious bangs, and you other one—you catch horses in the field. Oh, there are still things here to be found out. What have you got in the plain? Nothing, the plain. But here—near Kysla Voda there's iron, the water is all brown with rust. Under Tataruka some kind of glistening stone like pitch. Old women say that there are treasures in the mountains. Walk about the hills as far as beyond Durny there, beyond Cernyvrch, beyond Tatinska, beyond Tupa—who knows what might be found. Oh, my friend, in these days they search even below the ground. At home nothing, not a word. To-morrow, Polana, I'm going to Prague, to talk with some gentlemen about something—and stop. And then experts will come, and straight to Hordubal's: Good day, is Mr. Hordubal at home? And Mr. Hordubal here, Mr. Hordubal there; you have found a treasure, a mineral that we've been looking for

for fifty years.—Well, why not? All stone, they say—ah, do you know what that stone is made of? You don't, so don't talk.

Hordubal felt rather ashamed. Perhaps these are silly ideas; but the stone below Mencul—isn't silly. For that I must have oxen, a pair, two pairs of oxen—say those from Podoli, grey ones, with horns like arms, ah, what animals! And with a load of stone into the plain—to walk in front of the oxen, and only hi up, hazza! And you with your horses—make way for the oxen, to the other side of the ditch! And whose oxen are they? Hordubal's, nobody in the country has such animals.

Hordubal took the little bag from under his shirt and counted his money over. Seven hundred dollars, that's over twenty thousand; very nice, Polana! With that we can begin a new life. But you will see yourself what a champion Juraj is. And that wisdom is strength. A horse like that which carries its head high is worth a lot, but look at an ox: he nods his head, he carries the yoke on his back, but he does more work.

Juraj nodded, and strolled into the yard. In the yard Polana was shelling green peas; she just raised her eyebrows, swept the empty pods from her lap, and turned into the house.

CHAPTER XIII

HORDUBAL sat in the pub, and felt happy. Praise be to God, to-day it's noisy here: Michalcuk's here, and Varvarin, Mechajl's Poderejcuk, Herpak called Kobyla, Fedeles Michal, and Fedeles Gejza, Feduk, Hryc, Alexa, Hryhorij, and Dodja the ranger, all neighbours, and to shoot wild boars, they say, they do a lot of damage in the fields. Hryhorij owns the rock below Mencul, it would be a good thing to talk with him, to begin at the thin end, and cautiously: for instance, that the road into the fields ought to be mended with stone. Eh, thought Juraj in annoyance, but I haven't any fields now. Pjosa has them, he sits there and frowns. I've got no fields, what do I care about the wild brutes? Let them chase them away themselves; what I—I don't belong here. Hordubal felt gloomy; let them look after their own troubles, I've got mine.

In the meantime the men discussed what and how, when to begin, and from which side. Juraj slowly sipped his beer, and thought of his own worries. She just raised her eyebrows, and into the house. Well, Polana; sometime perhaps you would like to begin, and then, Juraj, what about this and what about that; and I shall just raise my eyebrows, and go to the pub. So that you may also know how it feels. What, have I a mangy snout, what, do my eyes run, or have I a dreadful mug like the tramp Laslo? Yes, I'm old, and everywhere coal has eaten into me; I'm all gristle, nothing else is left of me; all back because I crawled on all fours in the mine; all paws, and all knees—if you only knew in what tight places I had to hack the coal! Even now, when I cough, I spit black, Polana. Well, there's not much of me that you can like; but I can work, my dear, and you will see——

"Hi, American," grinned Fedeles Gejza, "you haven't shown yourself yet. Well, have you come to treat your countrymen?"

Hordubal nodded: "I have, I have, but to treat them in the

American fashion. Jew, bring Gejza a glass of water! And if it's not enough for you, Gejza, a whole pail, at least you can wash your mug in it."

"And is my mug any concern of yours," laughed Gejza, "if my wife likes it?"

Juraj's face darkened. What does your wife matter to me? Look at him, to treat him! And what, I would; ah, God, neighbours, I would gladly drink with you, hold shoulders with you, and sing, sing till my eyes closed. But I've got my dollars for other things; I've got an idea, a good one, an American one. But wait till I begin to blow the stone up. Good Lord, Hordubal, has he gone mad? Aren't there enough stones here? And after a while—see, the American, he can skim cream even from a rock.

Fedeles Michal began to sing, the others joined in. Ah, it's good to be among the lads. How long is it since I heard—how long ago now—— Juraj half closed his eyes, and in a subdued voice he joined in—taida—taida—taida, and suddenly—the deuce knows what made him begin to crow—he sang, sang, sang at the top of his voice, until his whole body swayed with the tune.

"Hi, you," shouted Fedeles Gejza. "A fellow who won't drink with us ought not to sing with us. Sing at home, Hordubal!"

"Or bring Stepan here," said Jura Feduk, joining in. "They say he knows how to sing better than you."

Hordubal got up, there was no end to him, he almost reached to the ceiling. "You sing, Gejza," he said mildly. "I was ready to go home in any case."

"And what should you do at home?" grinned Fedeles Michal. "You've got a workman there."

"He's a big farmer," Gejza hinted. "He pays a man to work for his wife."

Hordubal turned sharply. "Gejza," he muttered between his teeth, "who do you mean?"

Gejza rocked spitefully on his feet. "Who? There's only one farmer like that."

The men began to get up. "Let him be, Gejza," Varvarin begged; somebody took Juraj gently by the shoulders, and led him away. Hordubal tore himself free, and went up to Fedeles, it was a wonder that he didn't touch him with his nose.

"Who?" he said hoarsely.

"There's only one so daft," said Fedeles Gejza, very distinctly, and then suddenly, as if he lashed out: "But whores like Polana are common enough."

"Come out," cried Hordubal hoarsely, making his way out of the pub, between the shoulders of the other fellows. Gejza followed him behind, he opened the clasp-knife in his pocket. Mind, Hordubal, mind your back! But Hordubal paid no heed, he forced his way out, with Gejza behind him, the clasp-knife in his hand held so tightly that his palm sweated.

They all crowded out of the pub. Juraj turned to Fedeles: "You," he muttered. "Well, come!"

Gejza had his hand with the clasp-knife behind his back, he grunted deeply, ready to spring; but Hordubal, with arms like a windlass for a well, caught him by the hips, hands or no hands, he lifted him, spun round, and threw him to the ground. Gejza fell on his feet, hissing with rage. Again Hordubal lifted him high, and threw him to the ground, up high, and to the ground, as if he wanted to beat the floor with him; suddenly Gejza's knees gave way beneath him, and he dropped to the ground, with his arms spread out, and crash! his head banged against a bucket, and he lay as if he were only a heap of clothes.

Hordubal breathed heavily, looking round at the men with bloodshot eyes. "I didn't know," he murmured apologetically, "that there was a bucket there."

At that moment he received a whack on his head, and another, and another. Two, three, four men silently struck Hordubal on the head till it rattled. "Get off," he roared, waving his arms in the darkness; he struck somebody's nose, sank to the ground, and tried to get up. "They're fighting," yelled someone; Hordubal tried to get up, he couldn't, he tried to get up under the blows, and groaned, Oh—oh, and still he tried to get up——

"What, you here!" cried a quick and breathless voice, and crashed with a horse-whip into the gasping heap. And on their heads! Somebody howled with rage, look out for the knives! Vasil Geric Vasilov breathed heavily, and brought the horse-whip in jerks across Hordubal's body. Juraj tried to get up. "Clear off, you," the mayor thundered, lashing with his whip. Ah, if you weren't an official, and what an official! But Vasil Geric Vasilov is a famous fighter. And then even the women came cautiously into the road, with their hands folded, looking in the direction of the pub.

Juraj Hordubal tried to get up, his head was on Vasil's knee, and someone was washing his face, it was Pjosa. "That wasn't a fair fight, Vasil," the American groaned. "They struck me from behind, and two to one——"

Ach, Juraj, there were six of them, the bastards, and they all had sticks from the fence. Your head must be made of oak, or it would have cracked. "And what about Gejza?" the battered one inquired anxiously.

"Gejza has had enough, they've taken him away," the mayor explained.

Juraj sighed with satisfaction. "He'll keep his mouth shut now, the swine," he murmured, trying to get up; praise be to God, he felt better already, he stood and held his head. "Why did they go for me like that?" he wondered. "Come and have a drink, Vasil. They wouldn't let me sing, the dirty devils."

"Go home, Juraj," the mayor advised him. "I'll go with you, they may be waiting for you somewhere."

"As if I were afraid of them," said Hordubal gaining courage, and he staggered home. No, I'm not drunk, Polana, but they beat me at the pub. Why did they do it? Only for fun, my dear, for a lark, I tried my strength with Fedeles Gejza.

"And do you know, Vasil," explained Juraj, somehow exhilarated, "I had a fight in America, lad, a miner went for me with a hammer, a German or something, but the others—they took the hammer away from him, and made a ring, and then we fought; but only with our bare fists. Eh, Vasil, I got a whack on my mouth, but the German went to the ground. And nobody interfered."

"You, Juraj," advised Geric seriously. "Don't go into the pub again, or there'll be another fight."

"And why?" exclaimed Hordubal in astonishment. "I didn't do anything to them, did I?"

"Well," said the mayor evasively, "they've got to fight with somebody. Go to sleep, Juraj; and to-morrow—send that workman away."

Hordubal darkened. "What do you say, Geric? Are you going to meddle with my affairs too?"

"Why have a stranger in your home?" said Vasil evasively. "Go, go to bed. Eh, Juraj, Polana isn't worth fighting for."

Hordubal stood still like a pillar, and blinked. "So, even you are as mean—as the others," he at last was able to say. "You don't know, Polana, you—— Only I know her, and you—don't you dare——"

Vasil put his hand on his shoulder. "Juraj, for eight years we've had her under our eyes——"

Hordubal quickly tore himself away: "Go, go, or—Geric, as long as I live, as God is above me, I don't know you, and you were my best pal."

Hordubal didn't turn round again, and he staggered home. Geric only gave a snort, and long and silently he swore in the darkness.

CHAPTER XIV

In the morning Stepan harnessed the horses to the wagon, he was going down into the plain. Hordubal came out from the cowshed, he looked queer, swollen, and with bloodshot eyes. "I'm coming with you, Stepan," he said shortly.

C-c, the wagon flew through the village, but Juraj didn't look at the people or the horses. And a bit behind the village, "Stop," he ordered, "and get down from the wagon, I want to tell you something."

With insolent and flashing eyes Stepan scrutinized the battered face of his master. "Well, what?"

"Listen, Manya," began Hordubal in a faltering voice. "There are vile rumours about Polana—and you. I know they're lies—but we must stop them. Do you understand?"

Stepan shrugged his shoulders. "No, I don't."

"You must leave us, Stepan. It's—because of Polana. To shut people's mouths. It has to be, do you understand?"

Stepan fixed insolent eyes on the evasive ones of his master. "I do."

Juraj waved his hand. "And now, be off with you."

Manya stood still, clenched his fists, and looked as if he wanted to fight.

"You've got your work to do, Stepan," murmured Hordubal.

"Very well," hissed Stepan; he swung himself up into the wagon, turned round with the whip, and crash! he struck the horses over the head.

The horses backed, reared, and broke into a wild gallop; the wagon flew and rattled as if it would break into a thousand pieces.

Hordubal stood on the road, enveloped in dust; then he slowly made his way back to the village, walking home with lowered head. Eh, Juraj, that's how the old people go.

CHAPTER XV

In a week Hordubal grew thin, like a skeleton. And why not, I ask you? Is it a small thing to get things straight in the morning, feed the pigs, curry-comb the horses, take the cows to the pasture, clean the cowshed, and get the child off to school; then go with the horses down to the plain, the maize is ready for harvest; home at midday, cook something for the child's dinner, water the horses, feed the hens; and again go to the plain for a bit of work, then in the evening come home quickly, get supper ready, look after the cattle, with clumsy fingers even mend Hafia's little skirt; well, a child must play, how soon she tears her frock. It's difficult to be in so many places at once, it's hard not to forget one for the other. In the evening he sank into the straw like a log of wood, and still he could not fall asleep because of worries, whether he had forgotten something. Ah, God, he had, he hadn't watered the geraniums in the window; and Hordubal got up wearily to water the geraniums.

And Polana—as if she didn't exist; she locked herself in the room and sulked. What to do, thought Hordubal, greatly embarrassed; the wife is angry, because I didn't ask her advice. What do you think, Polana, I want to send the workman away. Eh, woman, have sense after all: could I have told you, Polana, such and such rumours as there are about you? And what am I to tell you; well, I sent the workman away, be angry; I shan't drive you to work with a stick. Oh, Lord, Polana's hands are wanted here; only a week, and it's as if everything had got into a mess; who would have thought how much work a woman like that does—a man doesn't even do half as much. But she will see it herself, her temper will go, and she will laugh. What a camel is Juraj, he doesn't know how to put things straight, or cook—well, what do you expect from a man!

Once—he caught sight of her; he came back for something,

and she was standing at the door. Like a shadow. Rings round her eyes, and a perpendicular furrow on her forehead. Hordubal turned away—I nothing, my dear, I haven't seen you. And she vanished—like a shadow. At night when Hordubal crawled into the straw, he heard a door open silently somewhere. That's Polana. She goes out into the yard, and stands, stands—— And Juraj, with his hands under his head, blinked in the darkness, and shuddered.

Cows, horses, Hafia, hens, pigs, field, flowers—Lord, that's bad enough, but the worst job is to keep up appearances. So that wagging tongues won't be able to say that at Hordubal's so and so. I have a married sister, she could help, she could cook, but no, thank you nicely, we don't need her. The neighbour looks over the fence: Hordubal, send Hafia over to me for the day, I'll look after her. Thank you very much, neighbour, much obliged, but please don't bother yourself; Polana's not very well, she has to lie down a bit, I like to do her work. What, let you push your nose——! I meet Geric, he looks at me, a word of greeting is in his mouth. You go your own way, I don't know you. And Hafia is frightened; she looks at me, with open eyes—well, she misses Stepan. What was I to do, child? there were such rumours, put it to the peoples' account.

Cows, horses, maize, pigs—yes, clean out the pig-sty, and water the cows. And here, see, I must clean the ditch out so that the slush can get away. Hordubal set to work, he snorted with eagerness. For a time the only thing in the world was the pig-sty; you wait, Polana, you'll be astonished when you come here—a pig-sty like a parlour. Now some clean water. And Hordubal went with the bucket to the well.

In the yard, on the shaft of the wagon, Manya was sitting; he played with Hafia on his knee, and talked to her about something.

Juraj set the bucket down on the ground, and with his hands in his pockets he went straight up to Stepan.

With one hand Manya moved Hafia away, and the other he put in his pocket; he sat still, with eyes as narrow as caraway seed, and something was sticking out of his hand and pointing at Hordubal's belly.

Hordubal grinned. Old boy, I know from America how to use a revolver. Here you are, he took from his pocket a clasp-knife and threw it on the ground. Manya put his hand in his pocket and kept his eyes fixed on his master.

Hordubal leant forwards with the hand on the wagon and looked down at Manya. What am I to do with you here, he thought. Lord, how am I to begin with him?

And Hafia didn't know either how it would end, and with gaping mouth she looked from her father to Stepan, and from Stepan to her father.

"Well, Hafia," murmured Hordubal. "Are you glad that Stepan has come back to you?"

The little girl said nothing, she only turned her eyes towards Manya.

Hordubal rubbed his neck doubtfully. "And why are you sitting here?" he said slowly. "Go and water the horses."

CHAPTER XVI

AND then he went straight to the room, and knocked at the door. "Let me in, Polana!"

The door opened, and Polana stood there like a shadow.

Hordubal sat down on the box, with his hands on his knees, and looked at the floor. "Manya has come back," he said.

Polana said nothing, she only breathed heavily.

"There were some—rumours," murmured Juraj. "About you . . . and about him. That's why I sent him away." He snorted with annoyance. "And he's come back, the rogue. Things can't go on like this, Polana."

"Why?" burst out Polana sharply. "Because of those stupid rumours?"

Hordubal nodded gravely. "Because of those stupid rumours, Polana. We're not the only ones here. Stepan—is a man, let him defend his own self against human tongues; but, you—eh, Polana, after all, I'm your husband—at least in public. So there."

Polana leaned against the door, her legs felt weak, and she didn't speak.

"It seems," murmured Hordubal, "it seems that Hafia is used to Stepan—he's good with the child. And horses—they miss Manya. He worked them hard, but even that they liked." Juraj lifted his eyes. "What should you say, Polana, if we betrothed Hafia to Stepan?"

Polana's heart sank. "But that is impossible," she cried in terror.

"Yes, that's true, Hafia is young," said Hordubal thoughtfully. "But to betroth isn't to give away. In the old times, Polana, they betrothed even children in the cradle."

"But Stepan—Hafia is fifteen years younger than he is," objected Polana.

Juraj nodded. "Like you, my dear. It's sometimes like that. But Manya can't stay here like a stranger. As Hafia's bridegroom

—that's different: he belongs to the family, he's working for his little wife——"

It began to dawn on Polana. "And could he stay here then?" she asked, tense and breathless.

"Yes, why shouldn't he? As if he were with his own parents. Who's the stranger? He's our son-in-law. And people's mouths would be shut. At least they'd see that . . . that it was only spiteful gossip. That's because of you, Polana. And otherwise—well, it seems as if he likes Hafia—and he understands horses. He's not keen on work, it's true—but does a hard worker ever get rich?"

Polana was so perplexed that she began to frown. "And do you think that Stepan would be willing?"

"He will, my dear. I've got some money—well, he can have it. I ask you, what am I to do with the money? And Stepan—is greedy; he would like to have fields, horses, the plain as far as you can see—his eyes will just shine. He'll fall on his feet—will he think it over!"

And Polana's face again became impenetrable. "Well, do as you like, Juraj. But I shan't tell him about it."

Juraj rose. "I shall tell him myself. Don't worry. I shall even get advice on this and that from a lawyer. There will have to be some kind of an agreement, I think. Well, I'll even arrange for that."

Hordubal stood waiting, perhaps he thought that Polana would say something. But she was suddenly seized with activity: "I must get the supper ready."

And Juraj strolled behind the barn as he used to do before.

CHAPTER XVII

MANYA took his master to Rybary, to talk with his parents. C-c. The horses, with their heads up, were a pleasure to look at.

"And so you, Stepan," said Hordubal pensively, "you have an elder brother, a younger one, and a married sister. . . . Hm, there are enough of you. And tell me, isn't it flat in your district?"

"Flat," said Stepan quickly, and his teeth shone. "We breed buffaloes mainly—and horses. Buffaloes do well in the swamp, mister."

A swamp, thought Juraj. "And wouldn't it be possible to drain it? I've seen that kind of thing in America."

"Why drain it?" laughed Stepan. "There's land enough, mister. It would be a pity for the swamp, reeds grow there; we make baskets in the winter. We have wicker instead of planks. Wagons of wicker work; fences, stables—all made of wicker, look at that lambing pen there."

Juraj didn't like the plain, it was endless, but what could he do? "And your father's alive, you say."

"Alive. He'll be astonished to see who I'm bringing him," said Manya rather proudly, boyishly. "But there, that's Rybary already." And with his little hat stuck at the back of his head, cracking his whip, he drove Juraj, like a baron, into the village and up to the Manyas' home.

A small, stocky boy came out of the hut. "Look here, Dula," shouted Stepan. "Put these horses under cover, and give them a drink and a feed of oats. This way, mister."

Hordubal just ran his eye over the farm; the tumble-down barn, the pigs rooting in the yard, hen turkeys preening their feathers; in the framework of the door a big bodkin was sticking——

"That's a bodkin, sir, for making the baskets," Stepan explained. "And we shall build a new barn in the spring."

On the doorstep old Manya was standing with a long moustache under his nose. "I've brought you, dad, the farmer from Kriva," announced Stepan, puffing himself up. "He wants to talk with you."

Old Manya led his guest into the room, and waited suspiciously for what was to come. Hordubal sat down with dignity, but only on the end of the chair, to make it clear that the business was not over yet. "Well, Stepan, tell him what we've come for."

Stepan showed his teeth, and poured out all the great news: that his master there would let him have his only daughter, Hafia, when she grew up; and so he wanted to talk with his father, to come to an agreement.

Hordubal nodded his head: yes, that's it.

Old Manya began to be interested. "Hi, Dula, bring some brandy! You are welcome, Hordubal; and was the journey pleasant?"

"Good."

"Thank God. And have you had a good harvest?"

"Very fair."

"And your family well?"

"Very well, thank you kindly."

Having said everything that was right and proper, old Manya began: "And so you have only one daughter, Hordubal?"

"Well, only one has come up."

The old man sniggered, but kept his wits about him. "Don't say that, Hordubal, you may have a son yet. A fallow field is fertile."

Juraj only jerked his hand to signify dissent.

"Perhaps a little boy will be born, an heir," the old man grinned, keeping his eyes open all the time. "And you look well, Hordubal; you will farm for fifty years yet."

Hordubal slowly rubbed his neck. "Well, as God wills. But Hafia need not wait so long. Thank God, I have a dowry for her."

Old Manya's little eyes gleamed. "Why not, that's understood. In America, they say, you've only to pick up money lying on the ground, isn't that so?"

"It's not as easy as that," said Hordubal cautiously. "And you know, Manya, money. You keep it at home—they steal it; you put it in a bank—they steal it as well. A farm would be better."

"Holy truth," agreed old Manya.

"I've been looking round here," Hordubal went on considerately. "Your soil can't support many people. All swamp and common. It seems to me that a farmer would have to have lots of acres of pusta if he's going to live on it."

"Well, that's true," growled the old man suspiciously. "It's not easy to divide a farm here. Our oldest, that's Michal, should inherit the farm, and the other two—only shares."

"How much?" Juraj shot out.

Old Manya blinked with surprise. Eh, you, why don't you give me time? "Three thousand," he murmured, squinting at Stepan.

Hordubal quickly figured it out. "Three times three—then nine, your farm's worth ten thousand, you say?"

"What's that you say, three times three?" The old man was vexed. "The daughter ought to get a share as well."

"That's true," admitted Hordubal. "So let's say—thirteen."

"Oh, no, not that," the old man shook his head. "And you, Hordubal, you're only joking?"

"No joking," insisted Hordubal. "I should like to know, Manya, how much a farm like this would cost in the plain?"

Old Manya was puzzled, Stepan's eyes bulged: will the rich man Hordubal buy Manyas' farm?

"A farm like this you wouldn't get for twenty thousand," the old man faltered.

"With the whole lot?"

The old man jeered. "That's good, Hordubal! We run four, five, horses in the yard."

"I'm counting without the horses."

Old Manya became serious. "And after all, what do you want, Hordubal—have you come to buy the farm, or to betroth your daughter?"

Hordubal grew hot. "Buy the farm—me, buy a farm in the plain? Would I buy mud? No. Rods for whistles, eh? No, thank you, Manya, but wait a moment; if we two come to an agreement, if your Stepan is betrothed to Hafia, you would leave your farm to Stepan. After the wedding—your Michal would have his share paid out by me. And Dula as well."

"And Marja?" murmured Stepan.

"And Marja—you haven't got anyone else, have you? Let Stepan farm here in Rybary."

"And what about Michal?" the old man inquired, not being able to follow.

"Well, he will get his share, let him go with God. A young man—he would rather have money than land.

Old Manya shook his head. "No, no," he murmured. "That won't do."

"And why shouldn't it?" Stepan burst out eagerly.

"You get out of here, hurry up," the old man cried. "What has our talk got to do with you?"

Growling and offended Stepan slouched into the yard. Dula, of course, was with the horses.

"Well, what about it, Dula?" said Stepan, putting his hand on his shoulder.

"A nice horse," said the boy like an expert. "Can I have a ride on him?"

"Too good for your backside," murmured Stepan, nodding his head in the direction of the room. "Our old man——"

"What?"

"Oh, nothing. He's doing what he can to spoil my happiness."

"What happiness?"

"Oh, nothing. What do you know!"

Silence reigned in the yard, only the sow grunted to herself;

the corncrakes could be heard in the swamp, and the frogs had begun.

"And shall you stay in Kriva, Stepan?"

"Perhaps—I've not decided yet," boasted Stepan.

"And how about the mistress?"

"That's none of your business," said Stepan darkly. Look at the mosquitoes! And the swallows, it's a wonder they don't scrape the ground with their bellies. Stepan yawned nearly wide enough to dislocate his jaw. What are the old beggars up to inside there? Let them bite their noses off!

Stepan was ruffled, and out of boredom he pulled the bodkin from the door frame, and stuck it in again with all his might. "Now you pull it out," he said to Dula.

Dula pulled it out. "Now who can stick it in furthest?" For a short time they amused themselves by sticking the bodkin into the door until splinters began to fly. "And what now?" said Dula. "I'm going after the girls. With you there's no fun any longer."

Dusk slowly fell, over the plain the horizon became flushed with a purple mist. Should I go in? thought Stepan. Not on purpose—hurry up, the old man said, what has our talk got to do with you? Is the American Hordubal giving his daughter to him, or to me? I ought to be able to look after myself, and instead —hurry up! And why do you order me about, raged Stepan, I already belong to another family!

At last Hordubal swayed out of the door, he was tipsy with brandy—they must have come to some agreement, the old people —old Manya came with him, and patted him on the back. Stepan stood at the horses' heads, holding the bits by the reins, just like a groom; even Hordubal noticed it, and he nodded approvingly to Stepan.

"So on Sunday in the town," cried old Manya, and C-c, the wagon started.

"A pleasant journey!"

Stepan glanced out of the corner of his eye at his master, he didn't want to ask; perhaps he would begin himself——

"There—our river," he said, pointing with his whip.

"M . . . m."

"And there, that wagon with the reeds, that may be our Michal. We use reeds for bedding instead of straw."

"So."

And still nothing. Stepan drove the horses as nicely as he could, but his master only nodded his head. At last Manya couldn't stand it any longer. "Well, mister, how much have you given them?"

Hordubal raised his eyebrows. "What?"

"How much have you promised them, mister?"

Hordubal said nothing. Only after a little while: "Five thousand each."

Stepan thought it over, and then spat between his teeth: "Then they've robbed you, mister. Three thousand would have been enough."

"M . . . m," murmured Hordubal. "Your father—as hard as oak."

Ah, so, thought Stepan. He gives to others, and me—as if he wanted to rob me.

"And you—five thousand as well," added Hordubal. "To put into the farm, he says."

Good, thought Stepan. But now, when I'm nearly his son—how will it be with my wages? He can't pay me like a farm-hand. Perhaps he might give me that colt? Sell it, Stepan, aren't you one of us already?

"And drive properly!" commanded Hordubal.

"Yes, mister."

CHAPTER XVIII

THEY drove back from the town; it was sealed. They had come to a proper agreement at the Jewish lawyer's, but it had cost two hundred crowns—and put that there, if you please, and write this here. Well, a farmer is cautious with property, my lad, he doesn't want to let himself be caught, and yet he mustn't forget to make over to Hafia one-half of the farm in Rybary. Good, said the lawyer, we'll put in a clausula. Aha, my lad, there's even that in it. And then they all signed it: Juraj Hordubal three crosses, in the name of the Father, the Son, and the Holy Ghost. Old Manya—three crosses. And Michal Manya, a nosegay stuck in his hat, blew himself up and signed importantly with his full name. Marja, the spouse of Janos, with a silk scarf on her head, and Stepan all festive—and still someone has to sign? Oh, no, Dula must be with the horses, and he's not yet of age. So, finished, gentlemen, and I wish you much happiness. It cost two hundred; well, a thorough job, there's even a clausula in it.

And then all to the pub, to drink on it. Willy nilly Juraj Hordubal talked familiarly with old Manya, they even quarrelled as if they were relatives. "And let's go, Stepan." Stepan would have liked to talk with Hordubal as if he were his father, but was any talk possible with him? He sat on the wagon, holding on with both hands, deep in thought, and he hardly spoke. This is a strange betrothal, eh, thought Stepan, you never feel at ease with the master. C-c.

And so they drove into Kriva at a nice trot, the horse-shoes clattered. Juraj Hordubal peered out from beneath his brows, and suddenly, with his hand above his head, he snapped his fingers, and sang, whooped, and yelled as if he were at a carnival. He must be drunk—the people turned. Why is Hordubal the American in such high spirits? On the village green there were girls and boys, they had to drive at a walking pace, Juraj stood up, placed one hand on Stepan's shoulder, and shouted to the people: "What do you say to the son-in-law I'm bringing? Eh, hurrah!"

Stepan tried to shake himself free, and hissed: "Keep quiet, mister."

Hordubal gripped his shoulder, so that Manya nearly cried out with pain. "Look here," he cried, "I've got a son-in-law for Hafia, we're celebrating the betrothal——"

Crack went the whip into the horses! Stepan frowned, and bit his lips until it was a wonder they didn't bleed. "Hold yourself together, mister, you're drunk!"

The wagon rumbled into Hordubal's yard. Juraj let Stepan go, and suddenly became silent and serious.

"Walk the horses round," he commanded, "they're covered with sweat."

CHAPTER XIX

AND Polana didn't know what to think of Juraj. He wanted to drag Stepan to the inn. What, he said, you're not a workman any longer, you're like our son. And instead of crawling behind the barn he walked about the village, stopped, and began to chat with the old women: "I've betrothed Hafia," he said. Well, she's only a child yet; but she got to like Stepan when she hadn't her father at home; and Stepan, neighbour, Hafia is as dear to him as a holy picture—eh, it's a pleasure to have such children. And he praised Stepan to heaven; what a good worker he was. He'll make a good farmer, he said. He'll inherit the farm in Rybary from his father. Round the village he had plenty to say, but at home—as if he were tongue-tied, do this and that, Stepan, and nothing else.

Juraj went round the village looking for those he had not spoken to yet, he waved his hand to Fedeles Gejza, but he avoided Geric. Geric even held his hand out, but Juraj turned away. As long as I live I don't know you: we're not on speaking terms, I don't want to know what you're thinking about.

The women laughed: queer betrothal. The bridegroom scowled like thunder, and avoided conversation; he was consumed with rage. The bride—at the stream she played with the children, her skirt tucked up to her waist; she hadn't yet learned to feel ashamed. And Hordubal waved his arms about on the village green, he was proud of his future son-in-law. Only Polana—a strange woman, it's true, but she looked dark, she saw that there was something for the people to laugh at, she didn't even put her nose outside the gate. That's how it was, people, and don't think that everything was in order.

Didn't Hordubal notice that Stepan was displeased? Perhaps he did, but he avoided him. He merely gave him orders over his shoulders, what he had to do, and at once made for somewhere else. And Stepan looked after him as if he wanted to bite his head off.

But Manya wouldn't give in any more; he waited for his master, with his teeth clenched so tightly that the muscles twitched beneath his skin. His master was walking across the yard. "You ought to drive down, Stepan," and already he tried to escape, but Manya stood in his way. "I want to talk with you about something."

"Well, what is it this time?" said Hordubal evasively. "You'd better look after your own business!"

Stepan was almost ashy with rage—strange, he always used to be so yellow. "What are you saying about me, and about Hafia?" he burst out vehemently.

Hordubal raised his eyebrows. "What am I saying? That I have betrothed my daughter to the farm-worker."

Manya blew himself up with rage. "And why—why you—people laugh at me now, wherever I go. 'When will the christening be, Stepan?' they say, and 'run, Stepan, there's a gander chasing your bride——' "

Hordubal began to rub his neck. "Let them laugh. They'll get tired of it."

"I've got tired, mister," said Manya, grinding his teeth. "I—don't want to be a laughing-stock."

Hordubal breathed deeply. "And I don't want to be a laughing-stock either. That's why I betrothed you. So what do you want?"

"I won't," said Manya, grinding his teeth, "I—I shan't stay here as the bridegroom of a sniffling baby."

Hordubal, with his hand still behind his neck, sized him up with his eyes. "Stop, what did you say? That you won't?"

Manya nearly cried out with rage. "I shan't! I don't want to! Do what you like, but I——"

"You won't?"

"I won't."

Hordubal snorted. "You wait here."

Manya swallowed hard, it was a shame for him to be jeered at by the whole village, better run away, or something——

Hordubal came out from the hut, rapidly tearing some paper in his hands into smaller and smaller pieces. He looked at Manya, and threw the bits in his face. "Well, you're not betrothed any longer. You can tell your old man that I've torn the agreement up." His arms flew up, he pointed: "And there's the door, get out!"

Manya took a deep breath, his eyes were as narrow as caraway seeds. "I shan't go from here, mister!"

"You will. And if ever you come again—I've got a gun!"

Stepan grew red. "And what—if I don't go?"

With Hordubal's chest pushing against his Manya retreated. "You look out!" he hissed.

"You won't go?"

"Not till the mistress says so—no!"

Hordubal gave a kind of growl, and suddenly—his knee dug into Manya's belly.

Manya bent double with pain, and then one hefty hand seized him by the collar and the other by the trousers, they raised him, and over the fence into the nettles.

"Well," panted Hordubal, "if you couldn't go by the gate, so over the fence." He strolled back, rubbed his neck; there was such an unusual warmth in his neck——

Somewhere behind a fence a neighbour jeered.

CHAPTER XX

Polana, of course, locked herself in the room, and was as silent as if she were dead.

In the early morning Hordubal harnessed the three-year-old into the wagon, and the heavy gelding, a badly balanced team: the gelding kept his head down, and the stallion carried his high —a strange pair.

"Tell your mother, Hafia, that I'm going to the town; I shan't be back till evening, if God allows."

Let the cows moo with hunger, let the horses tap with their hooves, let the sows grunt, and the young pigs squeal; but Polana will stop sulking, they won't let her, she's a farmer's wife after all, she'll go and look after the animals, can anyone be angry with God's creatures?

The gelding kept his head down, and the stallion carried his high. Stepan also carries his high—he used to work the three-year-old with the little mare—they go well together, he said. Na, na, why do you bite the gelding, you scoundrel? But Polana will come out when I'm away, she'll feed the animals, and cheer up. And see, even at this pace we're getting to the town.

First to the lawyer, and, if you please, sir, I should like to make my last will and testament: I have a wife, she's called Polana; it's right and proper that the wife should inherit what the man leaves.

"And what have you to leave her, Mr. Hordubal: a farm, money, securities?"

Hordubal looked at him suspiciously: Why do you want to know? "Just write: everything that I possess."

"Well, let's write: all my chattels and effects, movable and immovable——"

Hordubal nodded: now, if you please, it says quite clearly, all the chattels and effects, movable and immovable, for her fidelity, and conjugal love.

Now sign here, in the name of the Father, and Son, and the Holy Ghost. Hordubal still hung back. "And then, if you please, would it be possible for me to go to America again?"

"Oh, not at all, Mr. Hordubal; in America they've got too many workers now, they don't want to let any more in——"

"Hm, so. Perhaps there's a mill here in the town?"

"Oh, a factory. There are factories here, but they are closed, they don't work. Bad times, Mr. Hordubal," the solicitor sighed, as if he himself carried the burden of bad times.

Hordubal nodded. What can a man do, men are no longer required. Nobody wants a man like Hordubal; it's a shame for such able hands. But perhaps they want horses, horses who can carry their heads high.

Juraj Hordubal inquired for the commandant of the cavalry. There, they said, in the barracks. And what do you want, uncle, are you looking for your son? No, not my son, but I should like to sell this three-year-old, sir. We don't buy horses here, said the soldier, but he let his hands run over the horse; he touched its legs and withers. A horse like a deer, uncle.

And then an officer came, and shook his head. To sell a horse? A nice animal, and it's been ridden already? He's not had a saddle on yet, you say, only been ridden bare back—by the horseman. And soon about five officers had collected. And well, uncle, can we try the horse? Why not? said Hordubal. But he's very wild, sir. Eh, what, wild; let me have him, boys, a bridle, and a rug, it would be a marvel if it threw Tony.

Before you could count five, mister officer was sitting on the horse's back. The stallion bucked a bit; reared, and mister officer was on the ground. He fell nimbly on his backside, he only laughed, and now, boys, catch the horse on the barrack square. The fat mister commandant laughed till he had to hold his sides. "Well, my man, an excellent horse; but keep it at home for a bit, we shall have to write for a permit before we can buy it——"

Hordubal frowned, and he harnessed the horse into the wagon.

"What am I to do, sir? I shall have to sell it either to a gipsy or to the butcher."

The commandant scratched his head. "Listen to me, it's a pity for the stallion. Do you want to get rid of him in any case?"

"Yes, get rid of him," murmured Hordubal. "He doesn't suit me."

"Eh, then leave him here," mister commandant decided, "and we shall give you a receipt to show that the horse is with us. And then later we shall write and say what we'll give for it. Will that suit you?"

"Yes, why not?" said Juraj. "He's a nice horse, sir, he carries his head high. Eight thousand, they say."

"In that case, take him away," said the commandant quickly.

"Well, say five," said Hordubal hesitating. There was another fat military gentleman, he nodded his head a little. "That would do," the commandant said. "We shall write to you. If you're not satisfied—you can take the horse away. Will that do? And now we'll give you that receipt."

Hordubal drove home, in his pocket he had the receipt with a seal, and the bag with his dollars. The gelding trotted on, hanging its head. The stallion was not there any longer. As if Stepan had gone a second time, now that the three-year-old was gone. It would be better to sell the filly as well and the mare with the foal. —Eh, little gelding, I only tickle your back with the reins and off you trot. And why not talk to the horse? When a man talks, the horse turns his head, and swishes his tail; it's clear that he understands. Also he nods his head because he's thinking. A long way yet, my boy, but you go well uphill. Na—and don't begin to shy, it's only a little stream over the road. Never mind the fly, I'll drive it away myself. Hi! And in a low voice, and slowly, Juraj began to sing:—

Oh, Polana, Polana,
Unlucky Polana,
Let God be with you,
Polana, Polana.

CHAPTER XXI

HORDUBAL was strange and restless: early in the morning he disappeared, let God look after the farm, and the devil knows what he was up to. The other day as far as Tibava; And you, Geletej, do you want a man for your cows, or in the fields? What, a workman, Hordubal, I've got two sons, who is it you're trying to find a job for, cousin? And in the Tatin range, the ranger Stoj lives there; Are there any trees to fell, he inquired. Trees, no my boy, thousands of trees lie rotting in the wood. Is that so, then good-bye. And isn't there a railway being built somewhere, or a road, a quarry being worked? What are you thinking about, uncle, everybody has forgotten us here; who is there to build for?

Well, what am I to do? Sit down somewhere and wait till dusk. Far away the cow-bells are ringing, the herdsman cracks his whip as if he were shooting, somewhere the herdsman's cur is barking. In the fields—someone is singing. What am I to do? Sit and listen. How the flies buzz, one close to my face, you can listen, for hours, and it's never silent, life is always going on; perhaps a beetle chirps, or the squirrel is disturbed, and everywhere the peaceful sound of God's cattle mounts to the heavens.

And in the evening to slouch home. Hafia brings the food—eh, what food, even a dog wouldn't eat it; but I'm not hungry, anyhow. Of course, Polana has no time to get my supper ready. It's night already, the people have gone to bed; and Hordubal walked round with a lantern, doing what jobs he could: cleaning out the cowshed, putting manure on the heap, fetching water. He worked quietly, so as not to wake anybody, and he pottered about doing what it's a man's job to do. The eleventh hour is striking—every creature praise the L-O-R-D, and Juraj quietly crawled into the cowshed. Well, cows, well, there won't be quite so much for Polana to do in the morning.

And again as far as Volovo Polje, looking for work. Hi,

Harcar, don't you want someone to help you? What you, have you gone mad, or have they let you out of clink? Looking for work now, after the harvest? And what have you got to talk about? thought Hordubal, I've got enough money in my bag to buy half of your farm; you needn't puff yourself up so much. Slowly Hordubal tramped home, and what to do at home? Oh, only to cross those hills, there's nothing to do in this strange country.

Juraj sat by the edge of the wood above Varvarin's field. There too he could hear the cow-bells, they may have been from the Lehoty district. What's that Misa doing up there on the clearing? Below was a brook, and by the brook—a young woman was standing. Juraj screwed his eyes up to see her better. Doesn't she look like Polana? Ah, no, not that, how could Polana be here? From this distance any woman would look like Polana. And from the wood a dark fellow came running. That's not Manya, thought Juraj, how could Stepan come from this side? The dark man reached the young woman and stopped, he stood, and talked. How can they have so much to say? wondered Hordubal. Some girl maybe, and her sweetheart—a stranger from Lehoty, or from Volovo Polje; they meet on the sly, so that the boys at home don't give him a hiding. And those two below stand and talk; well, talk, I'm not looking. The sun is over Mencul, won't it be night soon? And those two stand there below, and talk. And what can I try yet?—perhaps in the salt mines they might have work for a miner. It's true, the mines are a long way away; but who will mind how far I have to go. Those two stand below and talk. It will be useless to ask in the mines——

No, they're not talking, but there's only one there now, who seems to be rocking about. But no, there are two of them, and they rock about, as if they were fighting. And it's because they're holding each other so tightly that they look as if there were only one staggering there. Hordubal's heart missed a beat. I'll run down there. No, I'll run home, and see if Polana's there. Surely she's at home, where else could she be? Lord, these legs—like lead. Hordubal got up and hastened along the wood, he ran along the footpath, he dashed to the village. Ough, I've got a pricking feeling in my side, as if someone had stuck one of those bodkins into me. Already he was out of breath, and he ran! ran with all his might. Glory be to God, here already is the village! Juraj went at a quick pace. Why does it prick so in my side? God, if I only get there, only a but further now, there's the gate, I must press with all my might on my ribs so that it doesn't prick so much, and run up to the gate——

Hot and sweating Hordubal leaned against the gate-post, he felt dizzy, he gasped for breath as if he were sobbing. The yard —empty; perhaps Polana is in the room, or somewhere. Suddenly Juraj became deadly indifferent as to where she was, he couldn't get as far as the room, he couldn't get his voice to speak, he breathed in gasps, and he had a job to hold himself up or his legs would have given way beneath him.

The little gate opened, and Polana slipped into the yard, breathless and flushed; she was taken aback when she caught sight of Juraj; she stopped, and said, rather too hastily: "I've only been to see a neighbour, Juraj; at—Herpakova, to look at her baby."

Juraj pulled himself up to his full height, and raised his eyebrows. "I didn't ask, Polana."

CHAPTER XXII

AND he would have liked to go behind the barn as usual, but he couldn't, the pain stabbed him to the heart. He tried to pretend that he had taken a fancy to the spot: to sit there, on the kerb-stone at the gate, and look at the yard. Polana—all of a sudden she was bustling with work; she fed the hens, she swept the doorstep, everywhere something—"Herpakova has got a little girl," she communicated glibly. Eh, Polana, what makes you so keen on talking now?

"Mm," murmured Juraj casually.

Dusk fell; Polana opened the gate so that the cows could come from the pasture. "You, Juraj," she began tentatively, "you said that you would buy some more cows——"

"There's no need," mumbled Hordubal.

Nodding their heads the cows went into the shed, bim bam, bim bam. Juraj rose, God be praised, I can manage already. "Good night, Polana," he said.

"What—you won't have any supper?"

"No."

Polana stood in his way. "Juraj, I shall make you a bed in the parlour. What will people say if you, the farmer, sleep with the cows!"

"Never mind," said Juraj, "They'll say many things yet."

Polana watched him darkly as he went into the shed. What an old back Juraj has!

Juraj lay down in the straw. He could not feel the pricking in his side any longer, but his heart felt heavy, oppressive. The farm was falling into silence somehow. Hafia prattled uneasily in a subdued voice, as if someone had shouted to her, be quiet, don't shout so loud! As if someone were very ill.

And silence, the farm was asleep. Sighing deeply Hordubal groped his way out of the straw, he lit the lantern, and went to have a look round, to see if there was any job to do. And again it pricked, blast it. The stable ought to be cleaned out, and the horses given fresh bedding, but Juraj only meditated, I should like to, I should; why is it that somehow I don't care to-day? He looked at the hens in the loft, the pig-sty, the barn, he climbed the ladder to the hay loft. What if the hay gets hot? Ah, my side hurts. He walked round the yard, and he even went into the orchard. What there? Eh, well, only perhaps there might be somebody. Who could it be there? Well, no one, but you never know. And what about the loft—Polana doesn't sleep there any more, there's maize there: Polana has moved into the room. Hordubal held his breath to keep from groaning, and he climbed up to the loft; he tried to open the door, but he couldn't, he only heard some trickling noise when he shook it. Oh, that's the heap of maize which has slipped down and blocked the door. There's nobody there either. And who could be there? What a silly!

Hordubal stood in the yard like a black pillar, and uneasily scratched his neck. And after all, what am I doing, he wondered, what am I chasing round here for? Manya has lived here for so many years; well, I didn't watch, I didn't run round the yard with a lantern; why do it now? Somehow he felt dull and indifferent. If I were lying in the shed, and heard some steps—should I get up? No, I shouldn't. Should I shout: Who's there? I shouldn't. I should only hold my breath. Ah, Lord, have I to watch grown-up people? Well, I did once, it's true, and I made as if I had some job to do in the dark. After all, can you watch and keep somebody's heart? Stupid, you are stupid! Well, what—let Manya come back—what does it matter? It's all the same, everything is all the same. Nothing hurts now. When the house is burnt down the roof doesn't leak. At Herpaks' the child began to cry. So you see, perhaps it is true that Polana went to have a look at the baby. Why not? women—like mad with children. That must be Herpakova feeding her child. Do you remember, Polana, how you fed Hafia? Only just moved your shoulder, and your breast slipped into your bodice—it's eleven years ago now. And you—to America—you silly, silly——

Hordubal blinked at the stars. Lord, how many they are—how many more have come through since then! In those days there weren't so many that you almost felt frightened of them. It's all the same. As if everything was slipping away from you, one thing after another. America was, coming home was. Geric was, Fedeles, Manya—how much it was; and now there's nothing left. All the same. Well, praise be to God, it makes it easier for a man.

Tu-tu-tu the night watchman chanted in the distance—and so many stars that you shivered.

Good night, good night, Polana, good night!

CHAPTER XXIII

EARLY in the morning before anyone was awake Juraj had left the village behind him, and made for the hills. To Misa. And what was he going to do there? Oh, only talk with him. It's still misty, you can't see the hills. Juraj shivered a bit; but that pricking feeling was no longer in his side; he only found it a bit difficult to get his breath, perhaps it was the mist. He climbed up to the field that used to be Hordubal's, and he had to stop to catch his breath; Pjosa has got it ploughed already—all stone, they say, and see, even to Pjosa the field is worth the trouble. Hordubal sighed deeply, and tramped upwards into the hills. The mist lifted and rolled away over the forest. Only a bit longer, and it will be autumn. Hordubal climbed, keeping his hand pressed to his side: Well, it pricks a bit, but it's all the same now, up or down. And this isn't mist, it's a bank of clouds; you can tell by the smell how it's soaking with water. Mind your head or you'll knock into it. And now it's rolled away over the hill, and now again you're in it, and you can't see three yards in front of you, you just keep on going, forcing your way through a thick fog, and you don't know where you are. And Hordubal gasped as he climbed slowly and laboriously into the clouds.

A cold drizzle began to fall. Above on the clearing Misa threw a sack over his head, and cracking his whip, hazzo ho, he was driving the cattle to the hut. You couldn't make out if it was an animal, bush, or boulder; but Cuvaj was a clever cur, he ran round the herd, and kept the cattle moving, but only the sound of the bells could be heard in the mist.

Misa sat at the entrance to the hut and gazed into the mist; the clouds opened for a moment, and you could see the cattle bunched together; and then again everything was enveloped in mist, and only the rain pattered. What time can it be? surely nearly midday. And then Cuvaj sprang up, he sniffed in the mist, and growled faintly.

Out of the mist the shadow of a man appeared. "Are you there, Misa?" cried a hoarse voice.

"I am."

"Thank God!"

It was Hordubal, drenched to the skin, and with his teeth chattering: from his hat water ran in a stream as if from a gutter.

"What brings you here in the rain?" inquired Misa, rather vexed.

"In the morning . . . it wasn't raining . . ." gasped Juraj. "It was such a clear night . . . and it's good that it rains, we need it."

Misa blinked his eyes thoughtfully. "Wait a bit, I'll make a fire."

Hordubal sat on the hay, and gazed into the little fire; the wood crackled and smoked, Misa put a sack on his back, and a feeling of warmth spread over Juraj's body. Ugh, why it's hot, as hot as it was down there in the mine. Juraj's teeth chattered, and he patted Cuvaj's wet coat, who stank at his side. Oh, well, I smell myself like a drenched dog. "Misa," chattered Juraj, "and what's that hut for in the wood?"

Misa boiled water in the little kettle, and threw some herbs into it. "I know, you don't feel well," he growled. "And what are you doing running about in the rain, you doodle?"

"There was a shaft in the mine . . ." said Juraj hurriedly, "where water was always dripping, always. Tic-tic-tic, like a clock ticks. And—do you know, Herpakova has had a baby, Polana went to have a look—and there's no job anywhere, Misa, men aren't wanted any longer, they say."

"And yet new ones are born," murmured Misa.

"Must be born!" prattled Juraj. "That's because women are—You aren't married, you don't know anything, you don't know anything—What have you to talk about, if you haven't got a wife? Eh, my lad, there are lots of things to think about. For instance, that they put down: for her fidelity and conjugal love. Otherwise God knows what people would say. And it is a pity that they robbed me of three thousand dollars; she could have been like a lady, eh? What do you say, Misa?"

"Well, that's true," mumbled Misa, blowing into the fire.

"So you see, and then they say I'm a fool. They envy me because I've got a wife who carries her head high like a thoroughbred. People are like that: they want to do you down. And instead, she only went to a neighbour's to look at the baby. All vile gossip, Misa. Tell them that I saw her myself coming from the neighbour's house."

Misa nodded his head thoughtfully. "I'll tell them, I'll tell them everything."

Juraj sighed. "That's why I came to see you, you know. You haven't got a wife, you've got nothing to be spiteful about. They —they wouldn't believe me; but you'll tell them, Misa. It's clear, she had to have a workman while the master was away; but she locked herself in the loft, a latch as big as a thunderbolt; I've seen it myself. And that Geric has got something to say! Eight years, he says, and so. Tell me, who knows her better—Geric or I? She only just moved her shoulder, and her breast slipped into her bodice. And that fellow down there, the one at the stream, he was a chap from Lehota, I saw him, he came from Lehota. And people—gossip at once."

Misa shook his head. "Now, drink this, it's good for you."

Juraj sipped the steaming beverage, and gazed into the fire. "You've got a nice job here, Misa. And tell them, they've got faith in you, you're a knowing one, they say—that she was a good and faithful wife——" The smoke made his eyes smart, and tears stood in his eyes; his nose seemed to stick out sharply. "It's only me, only me, who knows what she's like. Eh, Misa. I'd go to America like a shot, and earn more money for her——"

"Drink the whole lot at once," urged Misa. "It will warm you up."

A heavy sweat broke out on Hordubal's forehead, he felt weak, and happy. "I could tell you things about America, Misa," he said. "I've forgotten a lot already, but wait a bit, I shall remember——"

Misa quietly made up the fire; Hordubal breathed deeply, and his teeth chattered in his sleep. Outside the rain had stopped, from the spruce-trees behind heavy drops were still falling; and the mist kept on rolling. At times a cow gave a moo, and Cuvaj went to look if the herd was all right.

Misa felt something at his back, it was Hordubal's eyes; for a while Juraj had not been asleep, and he was looking round with sunken eyes.

"Misa," he said hoarsely, "can a man take his own life?"

"What?"

"I asked if a man could take his own life?"

"Why do you want to know?"

"To get away from his thoughts. They're thoughts, Misa, which have nothing to do with you. You think . . . let's suppose . . . that she lied, that she wasn't with the neighbour . . ." Juraj screwed his mouth up. "Misa," he groaned, "how can I get rid of them?"

Misa blinked his eyes. "Eh, it's very difficult. Think it out to the end."

"And what if at the end there's . . . only the end? Can a man put an end to himself?"

"There's no need," said Misa slowly. "Why? Even then you'll die."

"And—soon?"

"If you want to know—soon."

Misa rose and went out of the hut. "And sleep now," he said, halting at the door, and then he vanished—as if into the clouds.

Hordubal tried to get up. Praise to God, I'm a bit better already, but my head is somehow dizzy, and my body so queer, limp, as if it were made of rags.

He staggered out, into the mist, he could not see; only hear the ringing of the cow-bells, a thousand cattle grazing in the clouds, and bim bam with the bells. Juraj walked and walked, he really didn't know where. But I must go home, he thought, and so he had to go forwards. But he didn't know whether he was going uphill or down; perhaps down, because—he felt as if he were falling; perhaps always—upwards, because he went with difficulty, and breathed heavily. Eh, it's all the same, only home. And Juraj Hordubal plunged into the clouds.

CHAPTER XXIV

It was Hafia who found him in the cowshed. The cows were uneasy, and Polana sent her: "Go, have a look." He was lying on the straw and there was a rattling in his throat.

And he didn't mind any longer when Polana led him into the parlour, he only tried to raise his eyebrows. She took his clothes off, and put him to bed.

"Do you want anything?"

"No," he chattered, and went to sleep again; he dreamed of something, and they disturbed him—what was it? But Geric was not in America, they mixed everything up, now start again right at the very beginning. If only something didn't weigh so heavily on my chest, it must be that dog, Cuvaj, right on my chest he lies, and sleeps. Juraj passed his feverish hand over his hairy chest. Just sleep, you hairy one, and how your little heart beats! Ah, you beggar, but you are heavy!

He slept for a time, and when he opened his eyes Polana was standing in the door, and looking inquiringly. "How are you?"

"Better, my dear." He was afraid to talk, for things might go lost and change again into his hovel in Johnstown. But this is—like home: the painted cupboard, the oak table, oak chairs—Hordubal's heart throbbed: but I've come home at last! Lord, what a long journey, a fortnight on the lower deck and in the train—you feel quite broken down. But I mustn't move, or it will disappear again; better close my eyes, and just realize that it's here——

And then it all got mixed up again: the miners in Johnstown—Harcar—they fight Hordubal; Juraj flies through the mine, dodges about, catches hold of the ladder, and struggles upwards; a cage crashes down from above, it will smash his head, it certainly will—and Hordubal woke to his own groaning. Better not sleep, it's better here, and with staring eyes Juraj clutched the peaceful furniture. It's better here. Hordubal made signs with his finger in the air, and told Misa about America. Old boy, the hardest job for me—only, hello, Hordubal, and off I went. Once a shaft fell in, even the breakdown gang wouldn't go there. Twenty dollars I got then, the foreman himself shook my hand—like this, Misa, like this. And Hordubal descended in the cage, always down; a fat Jewess sat there, and an old man, and they looked severely at Hordubal. A hundred and eighty-one, eighty-two, eighty-three, Juraj counted and shouted: stop, that's enough, it doesn't go any lower, it's the bottom of the pit. But the cage kept going down, all the time, it got warmer, he couldn't get his breath, these devils take you down to hell. It seemed to Juraj as if he would suffocate, and he woke.

Dawn came; Polana stood at the door looking intently.

"It's better already," murmured Hordubal, and his eyes glowed. "Don't be angry, Polana, I shall get up soon."

"Just keep lying," said Polana, drawing nearer. "Have you got any pain?"

"No, I haven't. In America I had it as well—flu, the doctor said. And in two days—like a horse. I shall get up to-morrow, my dear. I make a mess here, don't I?"

"Do you want anything?"

Hordubal shook his head. "I'm quite well. Only—only water in a bucket, but I could do it myself——"

"I'll bring it straight away." And she went.

Hordubal heaped the pillows behind his back, and put his shirt straight over his chest. So that Polana doesn't see me so undressed, he thought. And if I could wash and shave! But Polana will come, she'll be here directly. Perhaps she'll sit down on the bed while I drink. Juraj moved to make room, so that she could sit down, and he waited. Perhaps she's forgotten, he thought, she's got plenty to do, poor girl—if only Stepan would come back! I'll tell her when she comes: "And what, Polana, if Manya came back?"

Hafia came through the door, carrying a glass of water; she carried it so carefully that her tongue was sticking out.

"You are good, Hafia, "sighed Hordubal. "And say, is uncle Stepan here?"

"No."

"And what is mammy doing?"

"She's standing in the yard."

Hordubal no longer knew what to say, he even forgot to drink: "Well go," he muttered, and with a jump Hafia was out of the door.

Juraj lay silently listening. In the stable the horses' hooves clattered. Will Polana give them water? No, she's feeding the sows, I can hear their contented grunting. How many steps a woman like that must make, he wondered. Stepan ought to come back; I shall drive to Rybary, and I shall say to him: What, you sluggard, get a move on with the horses, Polana can't manage all the work. I shall go perhaps in the afternoon, thought Juraj, and then a veil spread before his eyes, and everything vanished.

Hafia peeped through the door, she changed from one foot to the other, and stole away again. "He's asleep," she whispered to her mother in the yard. Polana said nothing, her thoughts were on something else.

Towards midday, Hafia again stole on tiptoes into the parlour. Hordubal was lying with his arms behind his head, and looking up to the ceiling.

"Mammy wants to know if you want anything?" she recited.

"I think, Polana," said Juraj, "that Stepan ought to come back."

The girl did not understand and opened her mouth: "And how are you?" she says.

"All right, thank you."

Hafia ran out. "He's all right, he says," she announced to Polana.

"Quite all right?"

"Hm," murmured the girl.

And then the afternoon silence fell. Hafia did not know what to do. You must stay at home, Polana said, in case your father wants something. Hafia played in front of the house with her doll, which Stepan had cut out for her. "You mustn't go away," she said to the doll. "Master is lying down, you must watch the yard. And don't cry, or I shall spank you."

Hafia went on tiptoes to peep into the parlour. Her father was sitting on the bed, nodding his head.

"What is mammy doing, Hafia?"

"She's gone somewhere."

Hordubal nodded. "Tell her that Stepan must come back. And Stepan can get that stallion back. Would you like to have some little rabbits?"

"I should."

"I shall make you a rabbit hutch, one like the miner Jensen had. Eh, Polana, in America there are things—I shall do everything." He nodded his head. "Wait, I shall take you up on the clearing, there's a strange hut—even Misa doesn't know what it is. Go, go tell mammy that Stepan will come back."

Hordubal felt satisfied, he lay down, and closed his eyes. It's as dark here as it is in the mine. Bang, bang, with the hammer at the rock. And Stepan grins, all stone, he says. Yes, but you don't know, you greenhorn, what work is. A fellow is known by what he does. And what's the wood like, my sweet, you've got in the yard. All straight logs. And I—I used to chop up old stumps. That's a job for a man, to chop up stumps, or dig out stones from the ground. Hordubal felt satisfied. I've done a lot, Polana, ah, God, a lot. It's all right, it is as it ought to be. And Juraj, with his hands crossed, fell asleep.

He woke in the dusk, because the darkness felt oppressive. "Hafia," he shouted, "Hafia, where's Polana?" There was no answer, only from the distance came the sound of the cow-bells, the herds coming from pasture. Hordubal sprang up from the bed, and pulled on his trousers; I must open the gate for the cows. I feel all dizzy, that's from lying down. He groped his way out, into the yard, and opened the gate wide. He felt queer, he gasped for breath. But praise be to God, I'm already up and out. The sound of the cow-bells draw nearer, it flowed like a river: everything ringing, as if with cow-bells, and the tinkling of the calves.

Juraj felt like kneeling down; never before had he heard such great and glorious ringing. Nodding their heads, looking tremendous, two cows came into the yard, with full and gleaming udders. Juraj leaned against the gate, and he felt as well, as peaceful, as if he were praying.

Polana ran through the gate, hasty, breathless. "You've got up already?" she burst out. "And where's Hafia?"

"Well, up," murmured Juraj apologetically. "I'm all right now."

"Go, go and lie down again," commanded Polana. "In the morning—you'll be quite all right."

"As you like, my sweet, as you like," said Juraj obediently and kindly. "I should be too much in the way here." He closed the gate, latched it, and slowly went into the parlour.

When they took him his supper, he was asleep.

BOOK II

CHAPTER I

"JURAJ HORDUBAL has been murdered!"

Geric, the mayor, hastily pulled on his coat. "Run, boy, for the police," he commanded quickly. "Tell them to go to Hordubal's."

In Hordubal's yard Polana was running about, wringing her hands. "Oh, Lord, Lord," she cried, "Who's done it! They've killed him, they've killed him!"

Hafia looked on from a corner, the neighbours stared over the fence, a body of men forced its way through the small gate. The mayor went straight up to Polana, and put his hand on her shoulder. "Stop that. And what's happened to him? Where's the wound?"

Polana trembled: "No—no—I don't know, I haven't been there, I couldn't——"

The mayor gave her a shrewd glance. She was pale and rigid, she only forced herself to run about and lament. "And who saw him?"

Polana pressed her lips tightly together. But then the police came and shut the small gate in front of the people's noses. It was the fat Gelnaj with his coat unbuttoned, and without a rifle, and with him was the new man, Biegl, who sparkled with freshness and zeal.

"Where is he?" inquired Gelnaj in a subdued voice. Polana pointed to the parlour and began to wail.

The American Hordubal was lying on the bed as if he were asleep. Gelnaj took his helmet off to the dead, but not to make it appear so, he wiped away the sweat. Geric hung about gloomily by the door. But Biegl went up to the dead man, and leaned over the bed. "Look here on his chest," he said. "A drop of blood. It looks as if they'd stabbed him with something."

"A family affair," murmured the mayor.

Gelnaj turned slowly. "What do you mean by that, Geric?"

The mayor shook his head. "Nothing." Poor Juraj, he thought to himself.

Gelnaj scratched behind his ear. "Look, Charley, a broken window." But Charley Biegl pulled away the shirt on the dead man's chest, and looked beneath. "I wonder," he said slowly. "It wasn't a knife, and hardly any blood——"

"That window, Biegl," repeated Gelnaj. "That's something for you."

Biegl turned towards the window. It was shut, only one pane was broken. "Ah, look here," he said with interest. "Well, this way—but nobody could crawl through this hole, Gelnaj. And, here on the glass are scratches made by a diamond, but on the inside! That's queer!"

Geric tiptoed up to the bed. Eh, poor devil, how your nose sticks out! And your eyes are closed as if you were asleep——

Biegl cautiously opened the window and looked out. "That's as one would expect," he announced with satisfaction. "The bits are outside, Gelnaj."

Gelnaj snorted. "So you think, mayor," he said with deliberation, "it's a family affair, what? And I haven't seen Stepan Manya here."

"He may be at home, in Rybary," the mayor suggested uncertainly.

Biegl nosed round everywhere. "Nothing's been disturbed, nothing broken——"

"I don't like it, Charley," said Gelnaj.

Biegl showed his teeth. "Very stupid, isn't it?" But wait, it will all work out nicely. I like straightforward cases, Gelnaj."

Gelnaj rolled out into the yard, fat and respectable. "Come here, Hordubalova. Who was in the house last night?"

"Only me—and Hafia here, my daughter."

"Where did you sleep?"

"In the room, with Hafia."

"This door leading into the yard was locked, wasn't it?"

"Yes, it was locked."

"And in the morning it was still locked? Who opened it?"

"I did—when it got light."

"And who found the corpse first?"

Polana kept her lips closed tightly, and gave no answer.

"Where is your workman?" inquired Biegl suddenly.

"At home, in Rybary."

"How do you know that?"

"Well—I only think——"

"I'm not asking you what you think. How do you know that he's in Rybary?"

"—I don't."

"When was he here last?"

"Ten days ago. He got the sack."

"When did you see him last?"

"Ten days ago."

"You're lying," said Biegl, making a random shot. "You were with him yesterday. We know that."

"It's not true," cried Polana in terror.

"Confess, Hordubalova," Gelnaj advised her.

"No—yes. He saw me yesterday——"

"Where?" demanded Biegl.

"Out there."

"Where, out there?"

Polana glanced quickly here and there. "Behind the village."

"What were you doing there? What? Answer me quick!"

Polana said nothing.

"You had an appointment with him, hadn't you?" Gelnaj began again.

"No, God is my witness! We met by accident——"

"Where?" demanded Biegl again.

Polana turned her hunted eyes to Gelnaj. "We met by accident. He only asked me when he could come for his things. He has some clothes still here, there in the stable."

"Aha, your husband sacked him on the spot, didn't he? Will you please tell me why?"

"They had a quarrel."

"And when was he to have come for his things?"

' To-day—this morning."

' And did he?"

"No, he didn't."

"Because he came last night," interrupted Biegl.

"No, he hasn't been here! He was at home!"

"How do you know that?"

Polana bit her lip. "I don't."

"Come, Hordubalova," said Biegl sharply. "When you see the victim you'll tell us some more."

Polana staggered.

"Let her be," growled Geric Vasil Vasilov. "She's going to have a baby."

CHAPTER II

Gelnaj sat in the yard, and let Biegl pry round all the farm buildings. He sniffed and sniffed, and his eyes shone with zeal. He poked about in the stables and cowshed, he went round everything and then he began to search about in the loft; he grew livelier, he enjoyed it so much. What a job! thought Gelnaj to himself; gipsies are enough for me, and to keep order—— Well, let Charley enjoy himself.

From the parlour the doctor emerged, and went to wash his hands at the pump. Biegl was already on the spot, and inquired impatiently: "Well, what, what was it?"

"That will come out at the post-mortem," replied the doctor. "But I should say that it was probably a nail, or something. Only two, three drops of blood—queer."

Polana brought him a towel.

"Thank you, marm. And tell me, was your husband ill in any way?"

"He was in bed yesterday, he had some kind of fever."

"Aha. And you're going to have a baby, aren't you?"

Polana blushed. "Not till spring, sir."

"It won't be in the spring, mother. Some time early in the new year."

As Polana went away Biegl winked with pleasure. "So then we have a motive, Gelnaj. Hordubal only came back from America in July."

Gelnaj snorted. "Hordubalova thinks that it was somebody from outside. Some time ago her husband had a fight in the pub, she says, and badly mauled Fedeles Gejza. He knocked him on the head. Gejza is a ruffian. It may be vengeance, she says. There's another nice motive for you there, Charley."

The doctor also glanced after Polana, and said, absent-mindedly: "It's a pity that you will lock her up, and I like maternity cases. I get nothing to do with births here, women have children like cats. With this woman it's likely to be a more difficult delivery."

"Why?"

"Old and thin. About forty, isn't she?"

"Oh, no," said Gelnaj. "Hardly thirty. And so Hordubal was ill? How can you tell then when a man's dead?"

"A medical secret, Gelnaj, but I'll tell you. Under the bed there was a full pot."

"I hadn't noticed that," said Biegl enviously.

"So good-bye, gentlemen," said the doctor, swaying as he marched away on his stumpy legs. "And you'll let me know about the inquest, won't you?"

"I shall have another look round the house yet," mumbled Biegl, "and then we could go to Rybary."

"And what do you keep on looking for, Charley? Another motive?"

"Clues," said Biegl drily. "And the instrument."

"Aha. I wish you well."

Gelnaj strolled to the fence, and began a conversation with a neighbour; he teased her until she gave him a slap with her dish-cloth and a bunch of flowers. In a corner near the shed Hafia was crouching, terrified. Gelnaj made faces at her, and grinned so fiercely that she was frightened at first, and then began to mimic him. When after a long time Biegl came out of the barn, Hafia was sitting on Gelnaj's knee, telling him that she was going to have a rabbit-hutch.

"I've not found anything more," said Biegl irritably. "But I shall come back here again. It would be strange if I—— Did you tell Geric to get a cart for us to go to Rybary?"

"It's waiting already," said Gelnaj, dismissing Hafia with a pat on her seat.

"Well, what, Gelnaj, what do you think of it?"

"I'll tell you what, Biegl," growled Gelnaj thoughtfully. "I shan't think anything about it at all. After twenty-five years I've had enough of it. I don't like it."

"Well, a murder isn't a trivial thing," said Biegl expertly.

"Oh, not that so much, Charley," said Gelnaj, shaking his head. "Only, you know, a murder in a village musn't be taken like that. You're a townee, you don't see the point. If it were robbery with violence, I should damned well nose about like you. But a murder in the family—And I'll tell you, I'm not surprised that they killed Hordubal."

"Why?"

"—He was unlucky by nature. He had it written on his face, my boy."

Biegl grinned. "The devil had it written on his face. A young farm hand slept in the house, that's the whole case. Gelnaj, man, it's such a simple case——"

"Oh, no, cases in a family are never simple," growled Gelnaj. "But you'll see, Charley. To murder for money, that's simple, it can be done in two ticks; but think, for days and weeks to have it inside you, for days and nights to brood on it—in that case, Biegl, it's as if you poked your nose into hell. It's clear to you because you're new to the place; but I knew them all, Charley, all three. But what's the good of talking? let's go to Rybary."

CHAPTER III

"Is Stepan at home?"

"No, he's gone to the town."

Biegl pushed Michal Manya out of his way, and rushed into the house. Gelnaj in the meantime began to talk to old Manya and Michal about the weather, hares, and that the sewage was running out on to the road.

Biegl returned, followed by Stepan, pale and rebellious, with bits of hay sticking to his clothes.

"So why did you say that he wasn't at home?" demanded Biegl of Michal.

"In the morning he said that he was going to the town," mumbled Michal. "Is it my job to watch him?"

"And all the time he was hiding in the hay! What were you hiding there for, you?"

"I wasn't," scowled Stepan. "Why should I? I was asleep."

"Perhaps that's because you didn't sleep enough last night, eh?"

"Yes, I did. Why shouldn't I?"

"Well, why were you asleep when we came?"

"Because I've got nothing to do here. I had enough to do when I was at work."

"He worked yesterday, if you please; he was ploughing all day," put in old Manya quickly.

"I didn't ask you," snapped Biegl. "Get off into the house, and Michal as well."

"Oh ah," sighed Gelnaj. "And what have you got to say, Stepan, to what's happened to Hordubal?"

"I haven't done anything to him," burst out Stepan.

"So you already knew that someone had killed him?" began Biegl victoriously. "And who told you about it?"

"—Nobody. But when you see policemen—you can guess that something's wrong with Hordubal."

"And why with Hordubal?"

"Because—because we had a quarrel," said Stepan, clenching his teeth and fists. "He threw me out, the dog!"

Biegl was rather disconcerted. "Take care, Manya. So you admit that you parted with Hordubal in anger?"

Stepan was vexed and showed his teeth. "Everybody knows that, don't they?"

"And did you want to revenge yourself on him?"

Stepan snorted. "If I had met him—I don't know what I should have done."

Biegl stood thinking for a short time: Stepan wasn't going to give in easily.

"Where were you last night?" he asked pointedly.

"I was at home, here, I was asleep."

"That remains to be seen. Is there anyone who can prove it?"

"Yes. Michal—Dula—our old man. Ask them."

"It's not your business to give me advice," rapped out Biegl. "You talked with Hordubalova yesterday afternoon. What about?"

"I didn't talk with her," replied Stepan harshly and deliberately. "I didn't see her at all."

"You're lying! She told me herself that she had an appointment with you—that you asked her when you ought to come for your things——"

"I haven't seen her for ten days," insisted Stepan. "Since I stopped work, I haven't been in Kriva, and I haven't seen her."

"Be careful," stormed Biegl. "I'll teach you to talk sense! Get a move on, and show me where you slept last night."

Stepan shrugged his shoulders, and led Biegl into the house. Gelnaj knocked at the window: "Hi, you old fellow, come here!"

Old Manya shuffled out, and blinked his eyes suspiciously. "Beg your pardon, what's happened?"

Gelnaj waved his hand. "Someone had a go at Hordubal

last night, he got a whack on the head. Listen, my friend, didn't Stepan do it?"

The old man shook his head. "Oh, not that, I tell you, Stepan couldn't have done that. He was at home, he was asleep. Hi, Michal, come here! Tell us where Stepan was last night."

Michal thought for a bit, and then said, slowly: "Well, where could he be? He was asleep upstairs with Dula and me."

"I see," nodded Gelnaj, "I knew it straight away. And Hordubal isn't popular in the village. You know, a rich American, and he doesn't even entertain his neighbours."

Old Manya lifted his arms. "I say, rich! Under his shirt he carries a bag with nothing but dollars——"

"Have you seen them?"

"Yes, I have, for he came here to buy our farm, and he showed me the money. More than seven hundred dollars, I tell you. Unpopular in the village, that may be; a proud man has no friends."

Gelnaj nodded thoughtfully. "And what have you got here, Manya, this splintered door?"

"That's done by sticking the basket needle into it. It's there the whole year round."

"Show me what it looks like," asked Gelnaj, becoming interested. "I didn't know that baskets were made with a needle."

"Oh, the stems are plaited with the needle—like this," said Manya, showing him with his finger. "It was still here yesterday," he grumbled. "Don't you know where it's gone, Michal?"

"Don't worry," murmured Gelnaj indifferently. "When I'm going past some time, I'll look in. But you oughtn't to let that sewage, Manya, run out on to the road. It's not your road."

"When we begin to manure the field, the heap will be carted away——"

"You ought to have a proper cistern, one made of concrete. You need some money in the farm, eh?"

"Oh, that, yes, we do," simpered the old man. "To build a

new barn—but Michal here is a ne'er-do-well. Stepan has more sense for farming. Stepan, he would make a farmer."

Dula returned from the fields, bringing on the wagon a small cock of hay, but he drove along in great style.

"Come here, boy," shouted Gelnaj in a fatherly manner, "I only want to get things straightened out. Where was Stepan last night?"

Dula opened his mouth, and looked questioningly at his father and at Michal; no one made the slightest sign. "He was here," mumbled Dula. "With me and Michal, he slept in the loft."

"Well, you've said it," said Gelnaj approvingly. "And what, shall you join the cavalry?"

The youngster's teeth glistened. "Of course I shall."

From the house Biegl emerged, silent and irritated. "Come here, Gelnaj. I've given Stepan several on the jaw; and now I've locked him in the parlour."

"You oughtn't to have done that," said Gelnaj. "Infringement of personal freedom, and so on."

Biegl grinned disrespectfully. "What do I care? The worst is that I haven't found anything. And what about you?"

"Alibi as plain as a pikestaff, Charley. The whole night long he slept in the hay like a good boy."

"They're telling lies," burst out Biegl impatiently.

"Of course. It's in their blood, my friend."

"But at the court they'll change their tune," promised Biegl.

"And that's because you don't know them. They'll either refuse to give evidence or they'll all perjure themselves wholesale. In a village, Charley, it's like a national custom."

"Well, what am I to do?" frowned Biegl. "What do you think, Gelnaj, ought we to arrest Stepan now? You can bet your life that he did it."

Gelnaj nodded. "I know. Only—look out, Biegl," he began to say, but did not finish; for just then there was a slight clatter, and Biegl roared: "Stop him!" and off he dashed round the corner of the building. Gelnaj slowly followed. There were two men on the ground, but Biegl was on top. "I'll hold him for you, Charley," offered Gelnaj.

Biegl got up, and by twisting Stepan's arm he made him get up too.

"Up you get," he puffed breathlessly. "I'll give you something for trying to run away."

Stepan hissed through his teeth, and his face was screwed up with pain. "Let go," he growled. "I—I only wanted to go to Kriva—to get my things——"

Dula forced his way between the two policemen. "Let him go," he shouted, "let him go, or——"

Gelnaj put his hand on his shoulder. "Slowly, boy. And you, Michal, don't you try to interfere. Stepan Manya, I arrest you in the name of Law. And now come quietly, you camel!"

They drove Stepan Manya to the town. He didn't ride behind the little stallion with his head up, and yet people stopped and looked back. On each side sat a policeman with a rifle between his knees; Stepan was between them; his little hat was not stuck at the back of his head, and he didn't look round at the plain. There—the river, and here horses grazing, a swamp glistened between the rushes; but Stepan only gazed at the tawny back of some horseman——

Gelnaj unbuttoned his uniform, and began to talk. He talked familiarly with Stepan, but said not a word about Hordubal; only about farming, about his home at Rybary, about horses—Stepan at first would hardly open his mouth, but later his tongue became loose. Yes, that little stallion; the master got a bad price for him, who knows who he sold him to, and for how much; he could have had eight thousand for him, he ought to go to a stud farm, but first put that black filly to him—eh, sir, I should like to see what would come of it! Manya's eyes lit up. And he sold a horse like that! It's a sin. He ought to have sold the gelding, or the mare with the foal—but that little stallion—— Stepan became so moved that he began to foam at the corners of his mouth; and Biegl was upset and thought that one ought not to talk with the culprit, except in an official capacity.

"Eh, sir," said Stepan, almost to himself, "if that stallion were in the shafts, I'd take the reins myself—it would be a ride!"

CHAPTER IV

"Look here, Gelnaj," explained Biegl in the evening. "Someone in the house did it; he broke the window from inside to make it look like a burglary. He couldn't get in by the door because it was bolted. So he was either in the house already in the evening——"

"He wasn't," said Gelnaj. "Hafia told me that Uncle Stepan hadn't been with them in the evening."

"Very well. Or someone in the family let him in at night; but then it couldn't have been a stranger. Stepan was there for five years as a worker. The whole village knows that for those five years he had relations with Hordubalova——"

"No, only for four years. The first time they were together in the straw, afterwards the mistress went to him every night in the stable. Hafia told me that, Charley."

"That Hafia of yours seems to know a lot," scoffed Biegl.

"Well," said Gelnaj, "you know, a country child——!"

"Well, go on: Hordubalova is expecting a child—it is common sense that it's with Stepan, because Hordubal, the American, only came back in July. Hordubalova knew that it would come back on her; Hordubal wanted her for himself——"

Gelnaj shook his head. "It might not be like that, Biegl. He used to sleep in the cowshed, and she in the loft, or in the room. I know that from the neighbours."

"—But she kept on with the workman."

"That's just what I don't know," said Gelnaj thoughtfully. "Hafia thinks not. But during the last few days Polana used to go away, behind the village. The neighbour saw her go off."

"Man," exclaimed Biegl in astonishment, "you know as much as an old woman. But I want myself to get a logical picture."

"Aha. And can't you work it out on your own, Charley?"

"No, I must get it straight in my head by talking about it. That fool Hordubal trusted Stepan so much that he betrothed his little daughter, Hafia, to him. But, tell me, isn't it absolutely mediaeval—to betroth a child!"

Gelnaj shrugged his shoulders.

"But then it somehow dawned on him that his wife was leading him a pretty dance, and he threw Stepan out of the house."

Gelnaj snorted with disapproval. "And what are you trying to tell me, Biegl? First Stepan went away from the Hordubals, and only afterwards did he betroth Hafia to him. Ask the wives in the village."

"That doesn't agree with my idea," said Biegl, growing confused. "Well, man, how does it really hang together?"

"I don't know, Charley, I have no—what do you call it? logical picture. It's a family affair, and not one of those clear-cut cases. Not at all, it can't be clear. You've got no family, Biegl, that's it."

"But, Gelnaj, after all, it's as easy as A B C: Polana wanted to get rid of her husband: Stepan—would like to marry and take the farm. Those two came to an understanding, everything ready. Yesterday Polana ran for Stepan——"

Gelnaj shook his head. "Wrong again. Hafia told me that Hordubal sent her himself yesterday to fetch Stepan back. And it's not my affair! Biegl, but hadn't the victim a bag under his shirt with money in it?"

Biegl was taken aback. "What, a bag? He hadn't got anything."

"So you see," said Gelnaj. "And they say that he had more than seven hundred dollars. Have a look for those dollars, Charley."

"You think—murder and robbery?"

"I don't think anything, but the money's gone. Old Manya saw it once with Hordubal. Manya wanted to build a new barn——"

Biegl whistled quietly. "Ah, so! Then the real motive would be money!"

"Might be," nodded Gelnaj. "It usually is. Or say vengeance. Biegl—there you have another motive which might do. Hordubal threw Stepan over the fence into the nettles. For that, Charley, in a village, the usual thing is a clasp-knife. You can choose which motive you like."

"Why do you tell me that?" frowned Biegl.

"Well, so that you can make a logical picture for yourself," said Gelnaj innocently. "And perhaps Manya killed him because of that stallion."

"That's nonsense!"

"Just so. In a family they murder for nonsense, my dear Biegl."

Biegl shut up sulkily.

"Don't get angry, Charley," growled Gelnaj. "Instead I'll tell you how Hordubal was murdered. With a bodkin for making baskets."

"How do you know that?"

"It was lost yesterday at Manya's farm. You can look for it, Biegl."

"What does it look like?"

"I don't know. I think it looks like some kind of a needle, but that's all I know," said Gelnaj, carefully cleaning his pipe. "Except that at Manya's they're going to cart the manure heap away."

CHAPTER V

GELNAJ and Biegl were drinking wine and waiting for the doctor to return from the post-mortem.

"And where did you find that glass-cutter?"

"At Hordubals', in the room. What have you got to say to that?"

"These peasants are like that," said Gelnaj, very upset. "They hate to throw anything away even if it incriminates them. They think it may come in handy sometime——" he spat expertly. "A stingy lot——"

"Hordubalova said that the glass-cutter had been there for ages, even before her husband went to America. But Farkas, the glazier, says that he can remember Stepan buying it there about a month ago."

Gelnaj whistled. "A month ago! Look here, Biegl, that's strange: that they'd thought of it a month ago. To kill somebody quickly, I could do that myself, but to think over it day by day—And you haven't found those dollars yet?"

"No. In that room I unearthed a flash-lamp. I'm trying to find out where Stepan bought it. That's another proof, isn't it? There's enough evidence for the woman to be arrested as well. But they say that we ought to find some definite proofs."

Gelnaj fidgeted on his chair. "Charley, since it's you—I know something too. They say that Stepan's brother-in-law, someone called Janos, had let it out that about a week ago Stepan came to him in the field, and said: 'You, Janos, you could have what you like, a pair of oxen, perhaps, and you could choose them yourself at the market—for a small job,' he said, 'just to put Juraj Hordubal out of the way.' "

"That's good," acknowledged Biegl. "And what did Janos do?"

" 'Get on with you,' he said to him, 'and have you money for it, Stepan?' 'I haven't,' said Stepan, 'but the mistress has:

we've promised each other to get married when Hordubal's gone.' "

"Then we've got them," said Biegl with relief, "and they're both in it."

Gelnaj nodded. But at that moment the doctor appeared, coming from the post-mortem, hurrying on his stumpy legs, and looking round with short-sighted eyes.

"Doctor," shouted Gelnaj, "won't you stop for a minute?"

"Ah," said the doctor bluntly. "Well, perhaps. Bring me some brandy. He's already begun to smell, poor chap. Not a pleasant job. Aha," he sighed, putting down his empty glass. "And do you know, gentlemen, that they killed a dead man?"

Biegl's eyes opened wide. "Why, how's that?"

"Very likely he was breathing his last, a comatose state. Nearly dead. Pneumonia in a very advanced stage, the right lung already septic, as yellow as gall. He wouldn't have lived till morning."

"So it wasn't necessary then," said Gelnaj slowly.

"That's true. A dilatation of the aorta—as big as your fist. Even if he hadn't had pneumonia, the slightest excitement would have finished him off, poor chap."

The policemen maintained an uneasy silence. At last Biegl cleared his throat, and inquired: "And what was the cause of death, doctor?"

"Well, murder. He was stabbed in the left chamber of his heart. But because he was at the last gasp there was little loss of blood."

"And what do you think it was done with?"

"I don't know. A nail—or, to put it briefly, with a thin, pointed metal object, about ten centimetres long, round in section—are you satisfied?"

Gelnaj played with his glass with his fat fingers to hide his confusion. "And, doctor—couldn't it be said that he died of pneumonia? See here, when he would have died in any case—why make such a fuss——?"

"That won't do, Gelnaj," burst out Biegl. "It's murder!"

The doctor's glasses glistened. "It would be a pity, sir. An interesting case. You rarely come across a murder with a needle or something similar. I shall put the heart in spirit, and send it"—he began to grin—"to a specialist. So that you can have it as clear as a pikestaff, gentlemen. It's no use, it's murder within the meaning of the law. Oh, God, but how unnecessary!"

"Well, that's that," grumbled Gelnaj. "And this jackass calls it a simple case!"

CHAPTER VI

BUT the bottle with Hordubal's heart was broken in the post, and the spirit ran out; so that the heart of Juraj Hordubal reached the learned gentleman's study in a very bad state.

"What are they sending me this for?" inquired the angry white-haired gentleman. "And what have they written? That they diagnosed a wound with a sharp instrument. These country doctors!" The professional expert sighed, and looked at Juraj Hordubal's heart from a safe distance. "Write: a stabbing wound is ruled out, the hole is too small—it's a shot through the muscle of the heart from a weapon of small calibre—most probably a Flobert. Take it away!"

. . . . .

"Well, now we've got it," said Gelnaj to Biegl, as he returned from Rybary. "And it says, Charley, that Hordubal wasn't stabbed, but was shot from a Flobert. So there!"

Biegl's hands fell. "And what does the doctor say to that?"

"What can he say? He's furious. You know him, don't you? And he sticks to his own opinion, he says. Well, then, a Flobert; the bullet hasn't been found, it's true; but what can one do? You must look for someone who has a Flobert."

Biegl threw his helmet into the corner. "I shan't leave it like that, Gelnaj," he threatened. "I shan't let anyone butt in here. Good Lord! I'd nearly finished, it all fits in, and now this! Tell me, can we go to the court—with this? Where shall we find a Flobert, man?"

Gelnaj shrugged his shoulders. "So you see, this is because you wouldn't let poor Hordubal pass to heaven with pneumonia. You deserve it, and so does the doctor."

In a rage Biegl sat down on his chair. "This, Gelnaj, has spoiled all my pleasure. The greatest pleasure I ever had."

"Well, what is it?"

"I've found the dollars. Something over seven hundred, and the bag as well. They were behind the beam in the loft in Rybary."

Gelnaj was surprised, and he took his pipe out of his mouth. "Well, that's something, Charley," he said with appreciation.

"But it took some finding," said Biegl, with satisfaction. "I've added it up: do you know how long I was searching round in Rybary? No less than forty-six hours. I didn't leave one little straw untouched. Stepan can stuff himself with his alibi. What do you think, Gelnaj: will it satisfy the jury? The money has been found, the glass-cutter that Stepan bought isn't bad either, then you've discovered contradictions in their statements, and a motive like a traction engine."

"Four motives," suggested Gelnaj.

Biegl shook his head. "Not at all! It was just an ordinary, mean, ugly murder for money. I'll tell you how it happened. Hordubal knew that Manya had relations with his wife, and he was scared of him. That's why he carried his money under his shirt, that's why he betrothed him to Hafia, that's why he threw him out in the end, that's why he locked himself in the cow-shed. Quite a clear case, Gelnaj."

Gelnaj blinked thoughtfully. "And I've always got those horses in my mind. Stepan liked horses. He didn't talk of anything else but them, to buy more land, and breed nothing but horses. There was a piece of land for sale behind Hordubal's meadows. Perhaps Manya wanted Hordubal to buy it, and he wouldn't, and carried his money under his shirt—I shouldn't wonder, Charley, if it wasn't for that."

"Anyway, it comes to the same thing: for money. It certainly wasn't because of love for Polana."

"Who knows."

"No. Gelnaj, you're an old policeman, and you know the people in the village; but I'm young, and I damned well know something about women. I've had a look at Polana. She's a plain, bony woman—and old, Gelnaj; it's true she's had relations with the farm-hand—I think it must have cost her a heap of money. But for her, Gelnaj, Hordubal wouldn't let himself be killed, for her Stepan wouldn't commit murder. But for money—it's quite clear. Hordubal was a village miser, Polana was after the money so that she could keep her lover, Stepan would do anything for brass—and there you've got it, Gelnaj. In all this there wasn't as much love as that," Biegl snapped his fingers. "A dirty case, man, but quite simple."

"Well, have you got it all together, Biegl?" said old Gelnaj. "Like the public prosecutor. According to you it's so simple——"

Biegl grinned with self-esteem.

"—but according to me, Charley, it would be simpler still if the Lord had taken Juraj Hordubal. Pneumonia, amen. And after a time the widow would marry the farm-hand—a baby would be born—But you don't like that Biegl, it's such a simple story."

"No. I like to find out the truth, Gelnaj. That's a job for a man."

Gelnaj blinked thoughtfully. "And you have a feeling, Charley, that you've found it? The real truth?"

"—I'd like to find that needle yet."

BOOK III

THE State *v*. Stepan Manya, twenty-six, farm-worker, single, Reformed Church confession,

And Polana Hordubalova, *née* Durkotova, widow, thirty-one, Greek Orthodox confession,

For the murder of Juraj Hordubal, farmer, of Kriva, and for being an accomplice in the murder of the said Juraj Hordubal respectively.

Accused, stand up. You have heard the charge. Are you guilty or not guilty?

The accused pleaded not guilty. He said that he had not killed Juraj Hordubal; he slept that night at home in Rybary. The money behind the beam—he got from the farmer, as a dowry, he said, if he married Hafia. He had not bought the glass-cutter. He had not had any relations with the other accused. He had nothing further to say.

The accused pleaded not guilty. She did not know anything of the murder until the morning. Questioned as to how she discovered that Juraj Hordubal was dead, she said that she only noticed the broken window. She had not had any relations with the other accused. The farmer himself bought the glass-cutter years ago. The murderer must have gained entry through the window, because the door into the yard was bolted, all through the night.

Having said that she sat down, deathly pale, not at all attractive, in an advanced stage of pregnancy; because of her pregnancy, the proceedings had to be expedited.

And the process rolled on with the inexorable routine of the judicial machine. Protocols were read and opinions given, notes rustled, the jury put on a pious air and pretended to follow with understanding every word in the official bill. The accused sat as still as a doll, only her eyes wandered restlessly. Stepan Manya from time to time wiped his forehead, and tried to follow what was being read: who knows if there's a hitch in it, who knows what the learned gentlemen will spin out of it: with his head respectfully bowed Manya listened, moving his lips as if he were repeating every word.

The court came to the cross-examination of the witnesses.

Vasil Geric Vasilov, mayor of Kriva, was called; a tall, broad-shouldered farmer; slowly and seriously he repeated the words of the oath. He was one of the first to see the corpse. It's true that he said that it was a family affair. Why? It's only common sense, your honour. And, are you aware, Geric, that Polana Hordubalova had relations with Stepan Manya? He was aware. He spoke to her himself about it before Juraj came back—— And was Hordubal in the habit of treating his wife badly?—He should have beaten her, your honour, declared Vasil Geric Vasilov, to chase the devil out of her. She would not even prepare meals for Juraj.—Perhaps Hordubal complained of his wife?—He did not, he only avoided people; he perished with grief, like a candle.

Polana sat erect, and gazed into the void.

The police sergeant, Gelnaj, gave testimony which agreed with the indictment. He went over the tangible evidence: Yes, this is the window from Hordubal's parlour, here on the inner side it is cut with a diamond. That day it was rainy, there was a puddle outside the window: but inside the parlour there was no trace of mud, and on the window-sill the dust was undisturbed. Could a man crawl through this hole? No; in any case he would have had to get his head through, and that's impossible.

The assistant policeman, Biegl, gave evidence; he stood at attention, and sparkled with zeal. His answers agreed closely with the indictment. He found the glass-cutter in the cupboard, which was locked; Hordubalova did not want to let him have the key, she said she had lost it. He broke the cupboard open, and found the key at last at the bottom of a bucket of oats. He also found Hordubal's dollars at Rybary. And there's something else, your honour, which I thought I ought to bring, reported Biegl, in a louder voice, and he produced something from his handkerchief.

He had found it only yesterday, when the Manyas were carting the manure heap away. It had been thrown into the midden.

Biegl laid on the table before his honour a thin, pointed object, about fifteen centimetres long, with a circular section. What is it?—It's a bodkin for making baskets, which belonged to Manya and was lost on the day of the murder.—Biegl didn't move an eyelash, but he enjoyed his triumph, and basked in the general interest. For five weeks he had been looking for this miserable needle, and here it is.

Accused, do you recognize this needle?

No, I don't. And Manya sat down, gloomy and sulky.

The doctor gave evidence. He wished to make it clear that the murder was committed with a thin, pointed object, round in section. If Hordubal had been shot the projectile would have remained in the body, and it was not there; at great length the doctor explained the difference between a wound from a shot and from a stab; and besides, a rifle of such small calibre must have been fired at such a short range that the shirt would have been burned, and perhaps the skin on the chest as well.

Could the wound have been inflicted with this object?

It could. One can't say with certainty that it was, but this object is sufficiently sharp, and thin, to produce a similar wound. It would do very well, thought the doctor. Yes, and death ensued almost immediately. And the rash doctor hurried away.

The prison doctor gave evidence. Polana Hordubalova, according to the usual signs, was in the eighth month of pregnancy.—Accused, said the judge, you need not get up. Who is father of the child which you are expecting?

Juraj, whispered Polana with her eyes on the ground.

Hordubal returned five months ago. With whom then have you the child.

Polana remained silent.

Old Manya declined to give evidence; Stepan buried his face in his hands; the old man dried his tears in his red handkerchief. By the way, Manya, do you recognize this object?

Old Manya nodded. Oh, it's our needle, it's for making baskets. He was pleased, and would have liked to put it in his pocket. No, no, my good man, it must stay here.

Michal and Dula also declined to give evidence. Marja Janos was called. Do you wish to give evidence? Yes. Is it true that your brother Stepan asked your husband to murder Juraj Hordubal? It is true, your honour, but my husband—not even for a hundred oxen, he said. Did Stepan have relations with the accused? Eh, he had, he himself boasted of it at home. Stepan is a bad man, your honour. It was not good to betroth him to a child; God be praised that nothing came of it.—And was your brother very angry when Hordubal threw him out? Marja crossed herself: Ah, Lord, like a devil: he wouldn't eat, or drink, or even smoke.—The witness stood down, and at the door she cried: What a shame, your honour.—May I leave this money to help Stepan?—No, no, woman, there's no need of money, go with God.

Janos was called. Do you wish to give evidence? As you wish, your honour. Is it true that Stepan asked you to murder Hordubal? The witness was embarrassed and blinked his eyes. It is true that he said something about it. You are poor, he said, you would earn some money.—And what were you to do for the money?—How do I know, your honour, such silly talk.—Did he tell you to kill Hordubal?—No, I should not say so, your honour. It's a long time ago. It was only a talk about money. Why should I carry such stupid things in my head? And I'm a fool, he said. A fool, well perhaps a fool, but it won't bring me to the gallows, my lad.—Aren't you drunk, my man?—I am, your honour; I had a glass to give me courage; it's not easy to talk to you gentlemen.

The trial was then adjourned until the next day. Stepan's eyes sought Polana's, but Hordubal's widow looked as if carved out of ivory, as if she did not know of him: bony, unattractive, wooden. No one looked at Stepan, only at her. Him, a dark-looking lout! Is it seldom that one fellow kills another? But this

—his own wife, I ask you, what a life if you can't even trust your own wife! Even at home in bed you can't feel safe, they'll stick you like a pig. Hordubal's widow passed through a corridor of hate which closed behind her like water. Eh, with a stake he ought to have beaten her to death, like a wolf when it's caught in a trap. She ought to hang, said the women. There's no justice in the world if she's not hanged. Oh, get on with you, you old hens, growled the men, women, you know, are not hanged; lock her up for life.—If women judged they'd hang the bitch for certain. I'd put the rope round her neck myself.—Don't you talk, Marika, it's not a woman's job. But they'll certainly string Stepan up.

Yes, yes, Stepka; and he didn't kill one of his own family. If they don't hang Polana, won't women soon be killing their husbands? Any woman might get it into her head—in a family, my friends, in the married state, there's no lack of reasons. No, no, she ought to be hanged. And how can they hang her when she's expecting a baby? That, that will be no baby, it will be the devil himself.

Simon Fazekas called Leca was called to give evidence. He saw Polana standing with Stepan on the day when the murder took place, behind the brook. Stepan Manya, do you still decline to admit that on that day you were in Kriva, and talked with Polana Hordubalova?—I was not there.—Accused, did Manya talk with you behind the brook?—He did not.—But you told the policemen that he did.—The policemen forced me.

Juliana Varvarinova, Hordubal's neighbour, made her statement. Yes, she used to see Hordubal, he walked about like a body without a soul. Polana would not cook for him, after he had sacked Stepan, but she used to cook chickens and young pigs for the farm worker. She slept with Manya every night, may God not punish her, the neighbour spat out,—but when Hordubal returned who knows where she met the farm worker; she never set foot in the stable again. In the last few days Hordubal even used to go round at night and shine a light everywhere, as if he were keeping watch.

And listen, witness, you saw Hordubal throw Stepan over the fence. Had Stepan his coat on then? He had not, he was only in his trousers and shirt. And did he go away without the coat? Yes, your honour. So this coat which he is wearing now must have been left behind with his things at Hordubal's? Stepan Manya, when did you go back to Kriva for this coat?

Stepan stood up, and blinked uncertainly.

You took it away the night that Juraj Hordubal was murdered. You can sit down. And the public prosecutor made a note with an air of having won a victory.

Take both the accused away, commanded the president of the court, as Hafia Hordubalova was called to give evidence.

A blue-eyed, pretty little girl was brought in; there was a breathless silence.

You needn't be afraid, little one, come here, said the president of the court, paternally. If you don't want to you needn't give evidence. Do you wish to make any statement?

The girl stared and looked questioningly at the learned gentlemen in gowns.

Do you wish to give evidence? Hafia nodded obediently. Ye-es.

Was your mother in the habit of going into the stable when Stepan was there? Ye-es, every night. Did you see them together sometimes? I did, once Uncle Stepan held her in his arms, and threw her down in the straw. And what about the farmer, your daddy, was he sometimes with your mother? No, not daddy, only Uncle Stepan. And when your father returned from America did your mother go to your uncle? Hafia shook her head. And how do you know? Because my father was at home, said the child quietly with experience. But Uncle Stepan used to say that he would not stay here, that everything was different.

Was your father good? Hafia shrugged her shoulders in embarrassment. And Stepan? Oh, Stepan was good. Was your mother good to your father? No. And to you? did she like you? She only liked Uncle Stepan. Did she cook for him well? She did, but he used to give me some of it. And who did you like best? The girl wriggled shyly. Uncle Stepan.

And what happened, Hafia, that evening when your daddy died? Where did you sleep? With mammy, in the room. Did anything wake you? It did. Somebody knocked at the window, and mammy sat up on the bed. What happened next? Next, nothing, mammy said that I ought to sleep, or did I want to get a spanking. And did you sleep? Yes, I did. And didn't you hear anything more? Nothing. Only somebody was walking in the yard, and mammy was gone. And who was walking—do you know? The girl opened her mouth with astonishment. Why, Stepan. Who else would mammy be with?

A silence fell on the court so painful that it was difficult to get one's breath. There will be an interval, commanded the president hurriedly, and he himself led out Hafia by the hand. You are a good little girl, he mumbled, good and sensible; but you should be glad that you don't understand what it's about. The jury searched in their pockets for something to give Hafia; they pressed round her, patted her, and stroked her hair.

And where's Stepan? inquired Hafia in a silvery voice. And here was the fat Gelnaj, he puffed and made his way to Hafia: Come, little one, come, I'm going to take you home. But the corridors were full of people, who gave Hafia, this one an apple, that one an egg, or a piece of cake, they sniffed into their handkerchiefs, and shed copious tears. Hafia kept tight hold of Gelnaj's fat finger, and she was near to crying herself; but Gelnaj said, Don't cry, I'll buy you some toffee, and she jumped with pleasure.

The trial proceeded; sometimes as if it had run into a knot, which several hands had to unravel. Pjosa called Husar gave evidence, Alexa Vorobec Demetrov, and his wife, Anna, and the wife of Kobyla Herpak, gave evidence about the woman, Polana Hordubalova. Ah, God, what things people know of others, it's a shame; the Lord need not pass judgment, people judge. And a man called Misa, a shepherd, asked permission to make a statement. Come here, witness, you need not take the oath.

What?

You need not take the oath. How old are you?

What?

How old are you, Misa?

Oh, I don't know, What does it matter? In the name of the Father, Son, and Holy Ghost. Juraj Hordubal asked me to give a message that his wife was good and faithful.

Wait, Misa, what message did he send? When did he tell you that?

Oh, when—well, I don't know. It rained then. He told me to tell them. You, Misa, they'll believe you.

God be with you, my man, and you came all the way from Kriva for this?

What?

You can go, Misa, we don't want you any more.

Oh, thank you, God bless you.

Farkas the glazier gave evidence. Stepan Manya bought the glass-cutter from me. And do you know him? Why not, it's that one there, the yellow one. Stand up, Manya; do you admit that you bought this glass-cutter from Farkas the glazier? I do not. You may sit down, Manya, but you won't help yourself like this.

Barah's wife gave evidence, Hryca's wife, and Fedor Bobal's wife. What a shame, Polana, eh! They point their fingers at you, they tell of your unchastity, women stone the woman caught in adultery. No one looks at Stepan Manya now, in vain you cover your pregnant womb with your crossed hands, you can't cover your sin; Stepan killed, but you sinned. Look at her, the huzzy, she doesn't even bow her head, she doesn't cry, she doesn't prostrate herself and touch the ground with her head, she looks as if she wanted to say: go on, talk, talk, what does it matter to me?

Accused, have you anything to say against the statement of Marta Bobalova?

I have not. And she did not bow her head, she did not blush with shame, she did not fall down with dishonour: like a statue.

Are there any more witnesses? Very well, the trial is adjourned until to-morrow. But that little Hafia gave her evidence very nicely, didn't she? Such a baby, my friend, and what an experience she's had already! Dreadful, dreadful. And yet her evidence —like a clear stream flowing. So matter-of-fact in everything— as if there was nothing amiss in what she were saying. But the whole village is against Polana. It's a bad case for Polana; for Stepan, of course, as well, but why worry about Stepan—a subordinate figure? Yes, yes, the village has come to understand that a question of morals is at stake, my friend. You might say, the people of Kriva are avenging an order which has been violated. Strange, usually, when this and that happens in a family, people don't take it so seriously, do they? It seems as if Polana did not only commit adultery but something worse as well. What do you say? Well, an offence against the community; so she incurred the hostility of the village.

Be cursed, Polana! Haven't you all seen, how she carried her head? That she felt no shame! She even smiled when Fedor Bobal's wife said that the women wanted to smash her windows for her adultery. Yes, her head still higher, and she smiled as if she had something to be proud of. Oh, go on, uncle, I should like to see her myself, then; and is she nice-looking? I hope God doesn't punish me, nice-looking! She must have cast a spell over Stepan, I say, she must have blinded his eyes; thin, I tell you, and her eyes—only to stab with; she must be evil, I think. But the child, like a picture; we all cried—when one thinks of her, an orphan! And you see, even before the child that woman wasn't ashamed, she committed adultery before her own daughter. Well, a devil, I say. Oh, you ought to go and see her, uncle!

Let us in, let us in, we want to see her, the huzzy! Oh, well, we'll keep together, and stand as if we were in church, but do let us in! Don't push so much, you people, your fur coats will make the noble court stink! Get away from that door!

Look at that one sitting so up straight and gaunt, that's her. Really, who'd ever say it was her? She looks just like any ordinary woman. And where's Stepan? Oh, you can only see his shoulders. And the one who's just getting up, the tall one in the gown, he's the public prosecutor himself. Silence, silence, now you will hear something.

Gentlemen of the jury, I have gone through the facts of the situation as they were ascertained by the exemplary work of the police (in the body of the court Biegl prodded Gelnaj), and as they emerged in the statements of the witnesses. I should like to take this opportinuty of thanking them all. Gentlemen, in my long career I have never attended a trial in which the statements of the witnesses were imbued with such a deep, such a passionate devotion to the cause of justice as in this case. The whole village, the whole population of Kriva, men, women, and children, came before you, not only to give evidence, but to complain to God, and to man, of an adulterous woman. It is not I in the name of the law, but the people themselves who are the prosecutors, and plaintiffs. According to the letter of the law you are going to judge a crime. According to the conscience of these, God's people, you are going to judge a sin.

The public prosecutor was certain of his case, but at that moment he hesitated. (Why do I talk about sin? Do we try the souls of men, or only their deeds? Only deeds, that's true—but do not deeds spring from the soul? Eh, mind the blind alleys! After all, the case is so simple——) Gentlemen of the jury, the case which you have to decide is clear, terribly clear in its simplicity. You have here only three persons. The first is the farmer Juraj Hordubal, a simple man, a good fellow, perhaps with a rather weak mind. He worked hard in America, he earned five to six dollars a day, four of which he sent to his family, to his wife, so that she could have an easier life. The voice of the public prosecutor acquired a strange throaty sharpness. And this money, earned with blood and sweat, the woman gave to—a young farm worker, who had no scruples in being kept as the paramour of an ageing mistress. Would Stepan stop at anything for money! He broke up the home of the emigrant, he estranged the mother from her child, and prompted by his mistress, he killed the sleeping husband for a bag of money. What a crime—what a sin of avarice! (The public prosecutor paused. Crime, not sin. This isn't God's judgment.)

And then here is—this woman. As you see her, cold, calculating, hard. Between her and the young farmer there could be no affection, not even sinful love; only lust, only sin, only sin.—She sustained the instrument of her lust, she pampered him, not even for her own daughter did she care. God touched her with his finger; in her sin she became pregnant. And then the husband returned from America, God himself sent him to punish the adultery in his house. But Juraj was weak; no one of us, no other man would, I hope, have borne in silence what this man suffered, this weak-minded husband who perhaps only wanted to have peace in this home. But with his coming the flood of dollars stopped, the mistress had no longer the means with which to retain the favour of a young ne'er-do-well. Stepan Manya left the service of sin; and then the incomprehensible weakling, Hordubal, undoubtedly under the instigation of his wife, himself offered him the hand of his little daughter, he offered him money and his farm if he would return. . . .

The public prosecutor felt himself choking with disgust. And even that was not enough. It seems that Stepan sponged on him and threatened him. Then at last, even the poor victim could bear no more, and he threw the good-for-nothing out of his house, but from that moment he was afraid for his life, and he looked for work anywhere on the other side of the hills, at night he went round with a lantern and kept watch. The vile plan, however, was ready; the old peasant was too much in the way of the base woman and the greedy workman; adultery and avarice combined against him. The victim fell ill, he could not keep guard, and could not defend himself; the following morning he was found stabbed through the heart. He was killed while he was asleep.

And is this the end? The public prosecutor seemed surprised

himself; he had a splendid and eloquent peroration ready, but somehow it stuck in his throat, and suddenly snap, the end; he sat down, and he himself did not know how it had come about. He glanced inquiringly at the president of the court, he seemed to nod and acquiesce: the jury swallowed something in their throats, they sniffed, and wiped their noses, and two began to cry openly. The public prosecutor sighed with relief.

Manya's counsel stood up, a big man, and a barrister with a great reputation. The public prosecutor, at the end of his able speech, appealed to the heart of Juraj Hordubal. Allow me, gentlemen of the jury, to begin the defence of my client with this same heart. And as night follows day it's clear that the prosecution itself admits that there are discrepancies in the expert evidence. Was the heart of Hordubal stabbed through or shot? Was the instrument of murder that inconspicuous needle belonging to Manya, or a gun carried by some person unknown? For myself I incline to the view of the learned scientific expert who with absolute certainty speaks of a gun of the smallest calibre. Well, gentlemen, if Juraj Hordubal was shot, the perpetrator of the deed was not Stepan Manya. And so on: step by step the famous barrister tore the body of evidence to shreds, and emphasized each point with his fat hand. There is not one single piece of evidence incriminating my client, it is all circumstantial. I do not appeal to the feelings of the noble jury, I am sure that on the evidence brought before them by the prosecution, and what has emerged during the trial, they cannot find Stepan Manya guilty. And the famous barrister sat down victoriously and with deliberation.

As if one had pressed a button, a new black figure sprang up, Polana Hordubalova's counsel, a young and handsome man. There was not one single bit of direct evidence against his client which suggested that she had been an accomplice in the murder of Juraj Hordubal; it had all been deduced from suggestions, from circumstances, and from hypothetical interrelations. Gentlemen of the jury, those interrelations are founded on the suppositions

tion that Polana Hordubalova had a motive for desiring the death of her husband, that is to say that she was unfaithful to him. Gentlemen, I pray you: if conjugal infidelity were a sufficient motive for murder—how many men, how many women, here in the town, in the village, in Kriva itself, would now be alive? Rather let that go; but I ask you, how do we know that Polana Hordubalova committed adultery? All the people of the village, it's true, have made their way here, and given evidence against the accused. But, gentlemen, pause and think: which of us is safe against one's next, and one's neighbours? Do each of you realize what the others say of you? Perhaps even worse things than of this unhappy woman; no integrity can protect you against lying and dishonourable gossip. The prosecution did not deny itself one witness who was jealous and brave enough to disgrace a defenceless woman——

On behalf of the witnesses I wish to protest against this insinuation, interrupted the public prosecutor.

It is not in order, said the president of the court. I trust that it will not be repeated.

The nice-looking little fellow made a polite and sprightly bow. As you please. We have heard the witnesses who have had something to say against Polana Hordubalova. But the court forgot to call one witness for this woman, I should like to call him the crown witness; that is the murdered man, Juraj Hordubal.

The nice-looking little fellow waved a sheet of paper in the air. Gentlemen of the jury, ten days before his death, Juraj Hordubal, the farmer from Kriva, made his last will and testament. And in it, as if he had a premonition that his voice would be needed, he ordered this to be written (in a high-pitched voice charged with emotion the young counsel read) All my property movable and immovable I bequeath to my wife, Polana, *née* Durkotova, for her fidelity and conjugal love. Note, gentlemen, if you please—For her fidelity and conjugal love! This is the testament of Juraj Hordubal, this is his testimony. You have heard Misa the herdsman say that Hordubal himself wished to let you know that Polana was a good and faithful wife. I was—I admit—surprised at Misa's statement; it sounded to me like a voice from the other side of the grave. Here you have a written testimony, the testimony of the only man who really knew Polana. The farm worker, Manya, boasted to his sister that, he said, he had had relations with his mistress. So it appears from the farm worker's statement, and so (here he struck the paper with his hand) it appears from the statement which her husband made before God. Gentlemen, it is for you to decide which of these two you are to believe.

The young counsel thoughtfully lowered his head. If by this the charge of adultery against my client falls to the ground, no motive remains for which she should be rid of her husband. You may object that she is in the eighth month of pregnancy; but gentlemen, I can refer you to several medical authorities to show how fallacious the determination of the stage of pregnancy may be. And the bright little fellow rattled off a number of authorities and scientific views. Manya's experienced counsel shook his head. That ruins his case, the jury don't like scientific arguments; but that with the will was pretty clever. Just imagine, gentlemen of the jury, that you find Polana Hordubalova guilty, and that the child of Juraj Hordubal, a living testimony of fidelity and conjugal love, is born in prison, branded as the child of an adulterous mother. By everything that is holy I warn you, gentlemen of the jury: do not commit an error of justice against an unborn child.

The nice-looking fellow sat down and mopped his brow with a perfumed handkerchief. Congratulations, muttered the old warrior of the court into his ear, it wasn't at all bad. But now the public prosecutor rose for his final speech. His face was flushed, and his hands trembled. If a child, then a child, he ejaculated hoarsely. Counsel for the defence, the child of Juraj Hordubal, Hafia, has given evidence. Her statement you will hardly call—(with his fist on the table)—gossip. At least I hope not (The nice-looking fellow bowed and shrugged his shoulders.) After all, I am grateful to you for producing the last will and testament of Juraj Hordubal. That alone was necessary (the public prosecutor straightened himself up as if he were growing) for us to form a complete picture of the character of this woman, almost diabolic, who—who already had the plan prepared to do to death her dull, good-natured weakling of a husband—and still she thought out the last subtle point of her plot: to compel the poor fellow to leave to her alone, to her alone, everything he possessed—and still give her what amounts to a moral alibi—for her fidelity and conjugal love! And the good man obediently went—so that not one penny should come to little Hafia, but to her, Jezebel, so that she could pay her lover and wallow in sin.—The public prosecutor choked with passionate indignation.—This is no longer a trial, in very truth it is God's judgment over the sins of the world.—The tense and laboured breathing of the devout people in front of him was clearly audible.—And now a bright light has fallen on the case of Juraj Hordubal. The cold, calculating, cynical will which was able to induce the hand of the illiterate Juraj to make three crosses under this ghastly and incriminating document—the same dreadful will, gentlemen, inspired the hand of Stepan Manya—the murderer. This little village paramour was not only an instrument of adultery—he also became an instrument of murder. This woman is guilty, cried the public prosecutor, making a violent gesture and pointing at her. That testament convicts her—only the devil himself could have thought out that hellish sneer—for her fidelity and conjugal love! Jezebel Hordubalova, do you admit at last that you murdered Juraj Hordubal?

Polana raised herself, livid, ungainly with pregnancy, and moved her silent lips.

Don't tell them anything, someone said harshly and hastily. I'll tell them myself. Stepan Manya stood up, his face awry with the mental strain. Hon . . . Honourable judge, he stammered, and suddenly he was seized with a violent fit of sobbing.

Rather taken aback the public prosecutor bowed in his direction. Please calm yourself, Stepan. The court will gladly hear what you have to say.

It—it was—sobbed Stepan—me.—I only wanted revenge—for—for—because he threw me over the fence—and the people laughed at me! I couldn't even sleep—I had to do something to him—I had—to have my revenge—That's why I went——

Did the mistress open the door for you? inquired the president.

No—she didn't—she didn't know anything. . . . I, in the evening—nobody saw me—Hordubal slept in the parlour—and I went to the loft —and hid there——

In the body of the court Biegl excitedly prodded Gelnaj. But that's not true, he blustered—he couldn't get into the loft, the door was held down with maize! I was there the first thing in the morning, Gelnaj! I'm going to tell them——

Sit still, growled Gelnaj, holding Biegl down. You ass, don't you dare!

And at night, stammered Stepan, wiping his nose and eyes, at night I crawled down—into the parlour—Hordubal was asleep —and I killed him with the needle—it didn't—it didn't want to go into him—and he didn't—didn't move—Stepan staggered, and the attendant handed him a glass of water from the president's table. Stepan drank gratefully and copiously, and wiped the sweat from his forehead. And then I cut the hole in the window —and took the money—to make it look as if burglars—and—back to the loft—and out by the window. Stepan gasped. And then I knocked at the window—for the mistress—to tell her that I had come for my coat.

Polana Hordubalova, is that true?

Polana rose, her lips were pressed together. No, it's not, he didn't knock——

The mistress doesn't know anything about it, broke in Stepan. And it's not true that she had relations with me. Once—ye-es, once I wanted to throw her down on the straw, but she defended herself—and Hafia came. And then nothing, nothing more——

That's good, Stepan, said the public prosecutor, bending forward. But I have one question more to ask. Up till now it was not necessary. Polana Hordubalova, is it true that before this Stepan here you had another lover, the farm worker Pavel Drevota?

Polana faltered and gasped, raised her hand to her forehead, and the attendant half led her, half carried her out.

The trial is adjourned, announced the president; on account of the new points revealed by the confession of Stepan Manya, the court will meet to-morrow at the place where the deed was committed.

. . . . .

Biegl waited in Hordubals' yard for the noble court to arrive. And then the distinguished gentlemen drove up. Biegl saluted, solemn and erect, the people stood watching in the road behind the fence, gazing into the Hordubals' yard, as if God knows what might appear—a great day for the policeman.

Biegl led the noble court to the loft. The loft is just as it was, nobody has set foot in it since the day of the murder. Even then the door was held down with maize; if anybody had tried to push it up the maize would have fallen down here on the steps. And Biegl pushed against the door, the heap gave way, and down fell a stream of maize. If the gentlemen will kindly go up, said Biegl politely. In the loft was all God's blessing from the plain, heaps of reddish maize, one felt like wading and jumping in it. And this is the little window; so Manya went out this way, he said——

But this window is latched on the inside, a member of the jury discovered, and looked round importantly. If nobody has been here since the day of the murder Manya could not have got out this way.

That's true, he couldn't; on the window-sill here there are bottles and tins covered with years of dust, these farmers never throw anything away! If Manya had crawled out this way he would have moved this rubbish away first, wouldn't he?

Yes, of course he would have to. And what's outside, under this window.

The parlour where Hordubal was killed, and the little garden in front of the house. Will the gentlemen kindly go and look there as well? The noble court betook itself with dignity to the little garden. One of the lower windows had been taken out: This is where the opening was made in the glass. Just above us is that little window in the loft through which Manya jumped out, so he says. I searched here immediately after the murder, said Biegl modestly, and below the window there was not a single footprint; there was a flower bed, freshly dug, and it had rained just before——

The president of the court appreciated the point and nodded. It's obvious that Stepan is lying. But perhaps you ought to have gone and looked in the loft immediately after the murder.

Biegl brought his heels together. Your honour, I did not want to disturb the maize. But to make certain I nailed down the door so that nobody could get in. I only took them out this morning. I tied a piece of thread on the door——

Good, good, mumbled the president, now satisfied. You thought of everything, mister, mister——

Biegl puffed out his chest. The assistant policeman Biegl.

Another gracious nod. Among us, gentlemen, there is no doubt that Stepan Manya lied. But now we are here perhaps it would interest you to look into the parlour.

From the table a big, broad-shouldered, heavy farmer stood up; they were just having dinner. This, if you please, is Mechajl Hordubal, the late farmer's brother; he is managing the farm at present.

Mechajl Hordubal bowed deeply to the gentlemen. Oxena, Hafia, quick and bring chairs for the gentlemen.

There's no need, my man, no need. And why haven't you had a new window put in here? It lets the cold in.

And why buy a new window, I ask you? The window is at the court, it would be a pity to buy a new one.

So, hm. And I see you are taking care of Hafia here. She's a clever girl, look after her well, the orphan. And this—your wife, isn't she?

Yes, your honour, Demetr Varivodjuk Ivanov's daughter, from Magurica.

And you are expecting a baby, I see.

Well, if God gives, His name be praised.

And—do you like it here in Kriva?

Well, yes, said Mechajl and waved his hand. If you'll excuse me, do you think I could get to America to find work, your honour?

Like Juraj?

Yes, like Juraj, God grant him eternal peace. And farmer Mechajl accompanied the departing gentry to the gate.

. . . . .

The noble court returned to town. Gee up, little horses, gee up, you bring an important load. And the village looked like Bethlehem, just like Bethlehem.

The president leaned towards the public prosecutor. It's not late yet, we could get it through by evening, perhaps there won't be so many speeches as there were yesterday——

The public prosecutor blushed faintly. I don't know myself what came over me yesterday. I spoke as if I were in a trance, as if I were not an official but an avenger—I just wanted to preach and thunder.

It was as if were we in church, said the president thoughtfully. You know those people in the court didn't even breathe. A strange people. I felt it myself: that we were passing sentence on something graver than crime, that we were judging sin—Praise be to God, to-day the court will be empty; no sensation, it will go smoothly.

. . . . .

It went smoothly. To the question if Stepan Manya was guilty of the crime of murder committed against Juraj Hordubal, eight of the jury answered yes, and four answered no.

And to the question if Polana Hordubalova was guilty of being a party to the said murder, all twelve answered yes.

In accordance with the verdict of the jury the court condemns Stepan Manya to penal servitude for life,

And Polana Hordubalova, *née* Durkotova, to penal servitude for the period of twelve years.

Polana stood lifeless, holding her head high; Stepan Manya sobbed violently.

Take them away!

. . . . .

The heart of Juraj Hordubal was lost somewhere, and was never buried.

METEOR

CHAPTER I

THE trees in the hospital garden sway with the gusts of a strong wind. And at each gust they become more and more worked up, the wind makes them desperate, and they jostle like a crowd in a panic; now they stop, and tremble. It did make us run; hush, can you hear anything? Yes! run, here it comes again.

A young man in a white coat saunters round the garden, puffing a cigarette. Apparently a young doctor; the wind ruffles his young hair, and his white coat crackles like a flag flapping in the wind. Tear and toss wild wind; don't the girls like to run their fingers through such a bristly and conceited mane? What a head, ruffled and erect! What a youth! What impudent conceit! Along the path a young nurse runs, the wind moulds her apron round her shapely thighs, with both hands she tidies her hair, looks up to the tall and fluttering figure, and hurriedly tells him something. Well, well, sister, why such glances, and why that hair——

The young doctor throws away his cigarette in a fine curve, and with long strides makes straight across the lawn to the ward. Ah, someone is dying, you must go with a professional step that indicates haste, but not excitement. The right thing for a doctor is to go to a call quickly, but quietly and deliberately; so look out, young man, that on the spur of the moment you don't overhurry yourself going to the bed of a dying man. But you, little sister; you run with the light steps of haste in which charitable and official eagerness finds expression, if we take no notice of the fact that with regard to your personal appearance it is very becoming for you. A girl like a peach, they say; too good for a hospital.

So, is that so, a man is dying; in the racket of the wind, during the flight of the terrified trees, someone is dying; they're used to it here, but all the same—— Over the white cover a feverish hand wanders. Poor, restless hand, what do you want to clutch? What would you like to throw away? Is there no one to hold you, well I'm here, don't be frightened, don't grope about, there's no dreadful solitude to frighten you. The young doctor bends down, the tufts of his hair fall over his forehead, he takes that groping hand by the wrist and mumbles: Pulse like a thread, *in extremis*; fetch the screen, sister.

But no, we won't set this long-haired, frivolous fellow by the bed of a dying man, while the organ of the tempest booms, *vox celestis, vox angelica*, amid the wailing of the human voice. No, no, sister, this isn't the end, only a fit—let's say, it's something wrong with his heart. This deadly sweat, and feverishness, is only anxiety, he thinks he's suffocating; we'll inject some morphia, and he'll go to sleep.

The poet turned back from the window. "Doctor," he inquired, "what ward is that one opposite?"

"The Medical ward," murmured the surgeon, busy watching the flame of the spirit lamp. "Why?"

"Well, only——" said the poet, again turning to view the crowns of the trees tossing in the wind. So, after all, that nurse is from the Medical ward, and you needn't imagine her lips trembling over the gory butchery of the operating table. Here, take it, sister, and cotton-wool! Cotton-wool!—No, it's not like that; she stands like a log, for she doesn't know much yet; and she only sees the ruffled mane of that fellow in the white coat. It's like this really, it's like this: she's head over heels in love with him, and she has meetings with him in his room. What a guy! How touzled and sure of himself, the braggart! Don't be shy, little girl, nothing will happen; I'm a doctor, and I know all about it.

The poet grew peevish. Oh, we know that; every fellow has it in him, that frenzy, that agony, when in some desirable woman he recognizes another man's mistress. Let's say sexual envy; let's say jealousy. It may well be that sexual morality is based on this displeasure felt when other people enjoy something together. The wind shows the nice shape of her thighs: that's all. And I—fancy all this twaddle at once. I'm too personal.

Irritable and peevish, the poet looked at the garden tossed by the wind. My God, what empty violence, how depressing the wind is!

"What?" said the surgeon.

"How depressing the wind is."

"It's gets on one's nerves," said the surgeon. "Come and have a drink of coffee."

CHAPTER II

THERE was an aroma of iodoform, coffee, tobacco, and maleness. A good, strong smell, something like a field dressing station. Or perhaps not, wait a bit: a quarantine station. Tobacco from Cuba, coffee from Porto Rico, and wind in Jamaica; stuffy, the wind, and the flurry of the tossing palm trees. Seventeen new cases, doctor, they're dying like flies. Out with the carbolic, quick with the chloride of lime; get a move on, men, and keep a watch on all the roads; nobody must move from here, the plague is on us. Yes, not a single person, till we've all gone under. The poet began to grin. But in that case, doctor, I should have to take the position of responsibility—I, the author. I lead in that battle, an old colonial surgeon, a veteran of plague epidemics, who knows the ropes; and you are my scientific assistant. Or perhaps not, not you, but that hairy fellow from the Medical ward. How are your cultures getting on? The fellow's eyes stick out in terror, the tufts of his hair fall over his forehead. Doctor, doctor, I think I've caught the infection. Well, that will make the eighteenth case; get him to bed. I shall sit up with him to-night, sister. See, see how that girl looks, how she looks at his hair all clammy with fever! I know she loves him; silly girl, she'd kiss him if I went away —she'll be getting the infection next. How those battered Creodoxas rustle and sigh! Feverish hand, what would you like to clutch? Don't reach after us, we don't know, we can't. Give me your hand, I will take you so that you need not be afraid. Pulse like a thread, *in extremis*; fetch the screen, sister.

"Sugar?" said the surgeon.

The poet tore himself from his brooding. "What?"

In silence the surgeon placed the bowl of sugar in front of him. "I've had lots to do to-day," he said vaguely. "I'm looking forward to the holidays."

"Where shall you go?"

"Shooting."

The poet looked attentively at the taciturn man. "One day you ought to go a long way—for tigers or jaguars. While there are still some left."

"I should like to."

"Listen, doesn't it strike you? Can't you imagine—shall we say, the dawn in the jungle, the warbling of some strange bird, something like a xylophone soaked in oil and rum."

The surgeon shook his head. "I don't imagine anything. I . . . I have to take damned good care to keep my eyes open. To see, don't you know? And when you're shooting," he added, squinting with his eyes, "you must keep your eyes open too if you want to see properly."

The poet sighed. "Well, you're lucky, my friend. Always when I look I imagine something at the same time. Or rather it's like this: it begins to take shape in my mind by itself, it goes on, and begins to exist as something apart—Of course, I interfere; I advise, improve, and so on, do you understand?"

"And then you write it down," murmured the surgeon.

"No, not at all! Not usually. Such trash. In the short time you were making coffee, two perfectly silly stories took shape like that about your long-haired colleague from the Medical ward. I beg your pardon," he inquired suddenly, "what kind of a man is he?"

The surgeon hesitated. "Well," he said at last, "a bit of a braggart. . . . A big dose of self-conceit—as is usual with young doctors. Otherwise," with a shrug of the shoulders, "I don't know what you would find interesting in him."

The poet could not restrain himself. "Is there anything between him and that little nurse?"

"I don't know," snorted the surgeon. "Is it any business of yours?"

"No," said the poet contritely. "After all, is it any business of mine how things are in reality? My task is to invent, isn't it, to play, pretend——" The poet leaned forward with his heavy shoulders. "That's just the trouble, sir: reality means such a frightful lot to me. That's why I invent it, that's why I always have to invent something to catch hold of it. What I see with my eyes is not enough, I want to see more—and so I invent stories. Please tell me, is there any sense in it? Has it anything to do with life at all? Supposing that just now I'm working on something——

Let's suppose that I'm writing something," repeated the poet after a pause. "I know that it's . . . only a fiction. And I know, my friend, what fiction is, I know how it's done: one part experience, three parts phantasy, two parts logical construction, and the rest artful guile: that it is fresh, that it is topical, that something is being solved or proved in it, and chiefly that it's effective. But one thing is peculiar," the poet burst out, "that all these tricks, all that miserable literary hack-work leaves the man who performs it with an accursed and passionate illusion that it has something to do with reality. Imagine a conjurer who can produce rabbits from out of a hat, and who really believes at the same time that he does truly and honestly conjure them out of the honest hat. What madness!"

"Something of yours didn't come off, isn't that it?" inquired the surgeon dryly.

"No, it didn't. I was walking along the street one evening, and I heard a woman's voice behind me which said: 'But you won't do that to me, surely.' Nothing else, only those words—perhaps no one even spoke, and it only seemed so to me. You won't do that to me, surely."

"Well, and what next?" asked the surgeon, after a pause.

"What would come next," frowned the poet. "From that . . . a story has grown. That woman was in the right, you understand: a frayed, evil, unhappy woman—And the misery, my friend, in which those people live! But she was in the right; she is the family, the household, she is in a word, order; while he——" He made a gesture with his hand. "A dirty dog, such a blind and physical revolt, a lout, and a brutal fellow——"

"And how did it turn out?"

"What?"

"What was the end of it?" asked the surgeon patiently.

". . . I don't know. She ought to have been in the right. In the name of everything in the world, in the name of every law she ought to have been in the right. Do you understand, it all depended on the fact that she was right." The poet began to break up a lump of sugar. "But that fellow took it in his head that he was also in the right. And the more awful and damnable he was, the more he felt that he was right. For it was evident," mumbled the poet, "that he was suffering too, do you understand? There was nothing that could be done; once he began to live in reality, he was not to be ordered about, and he just went his own way, doomed, and inevitable——" The poet shrugged his shoulders. "So you see in the end it was I myself who was that lout, that depraved and desperate wretch; the more he endured, the more it was I—and you call it fiction."

The poet turned towards the window, for there are some things that are more easily spoken into the void. "It won't do, I must get rid of it. I should like to . . . I ought just to play with something . . . with something unreal. That has nothing, nothing, nothing to do with reality . . . or with myself. To be free for once from that terrifying personal experience. Tell me, must I suffer every human agony? Just for once I should like to invent something very remote, and fantastic—as if I were blowing rainbow bubbles."

The telephone rang. "Well, why don't you do it?" asked the surgeon, lifting the receiver, but he had no time to wait for the answer. "Hello!" he said into the telephone. "Yes, speaking—What?—Oh!—So let them take him to the operating theatre—Of course—I'm coming straight away."

"They've brought someone in," said the surgeon, hanging up the receiver. "He fell from the sky—I mean an aeroplane crashed and caught fire. What the devil, in such a storm! The pilot is burnt to cinders, they say; and the other—well, a poor wretch." The doctor paused. "I shall have to leave you here. But wait, I'll send you a patient—an interesting case, medically trivial, I only took an abscess from his neck; but the man is a clairvoyant. Strong second sight, and that sort of thing. But don't you believe him too much." And the surgeon bolted out of the door like a shot, without waiting for the poet's protest.

CHAPTER III

WELL, so this is the clairvoyant, this pitiable figure in striped pyjamas, with a bandaged neck, and his head on one side, poor devil! It hangs on him as if on a peg, he shuffles to the table, and with cold and trembling fingers lights a cigarette. If at least his eyes were not so close together, and sunken, if only they were not so distracted, if only he would look at things! Good God, nice company the doctor presented me with! What can you talk about with such a spectre? Certainly not about terrestrial things; as everyone knows, it's rather tactless to begin to talk about the latest news with someone from beyond the grave.

"It is a wind out there," said the clairvoyant, and the poet breathed a sigh of relief. May the weather be blessed, for it's a familiar subject with people who have nothing to say to each other. It is a wind out there, he said, and yet it wasn't worth his while to look out through the window at the tragic flight of the trees. Well, a clairvoyant! Why should he look? He fixes his eyes on the tip of his nose, and see, already he knows that the wind is raging outside. Strange things! You can say what you like, but this is second sight, isn't that right——

What a sight, those two; the poet leaned forward with his heavy shoulders, stuck his chin out, and with tactless curiosity, yes, with a certain amount of hostility, he sized up the bowed head, the thin chest, and the thin, protruding beak of the little man opposite. Was he going to bite him? No, not that, for somehow he felt repelled by him, partly for this and that in his physical appearance, and partly because he was a clairvoyant; as if he were something impure and loathsome. But the other—perhaps he didn't even see; he gazed, without looking, his head to one side, like a bird. And the state between them was cold, tense, and repellent.

"A strong character," murmured the clairvoyant, as if to himself.

"Who?"

"The man they've brought in." The clairvoyant blew out a thick cloud of smoke. "In him there's . . . a frightful intensity, what shall I call it: a flame, fire, heat. . . . Now, of course, it's only a conflagration burning down."

The poet grinned; he could not stand such misplaced bathos.

"So you've already heard of it, too?" he observed. "Aeroplane on fire, and so on. . . ."

"An aeroplane?" replied the clairvoyant absent-mindedly. "So that's it, just think of it, he was flying in a wind like this! Like a flaming meteor, about to burst into pieces. Why was he in such a tremendous hurry?" The clairvoyant shook his head. "I don't know, I don't know anything; he's unconscious, and he doesn't know what's happened to him. But even from the sooty fireplace you can judge how far the flame burned up. How deeply it burned! And how the embers still glow!"

The poet snorted with disgust. No, absolutely, I can't stick this morbid dummy. Yes, it was a devil of an ember, if we realize that the pilot got fried to death; and this striped scarecrow here doesn't even say poor fellow. It's true, of course: why had that bolt from the blue to fly in such a wind?

"Strange," murmured the clairvoyant under his breath. "And from such a distance! His way lay across the ocean. Queer how the place where a man was last still sticks to him. The sea has stuck to him."

"By what signs?"

The clairvoyant shrugged his shoulders. "Just the sea and the distance—There must have been many ways in his life. Do you know where he came from?"

"You ought to be able to tell that yourself?" said the poet, as pointedly as he could.

"How can you tell?—He's unconscious, and doesn't know

anything. Can you read a closed book? It can be done, but it's difficult, very difficult."

"Reading closed books," murmured the poet. "I'm inclined to think, to say the least, is a waste of time."

"Perhaps it is for you," thought the clairvoyant, squinting in the direction of the corner. "Yes, for you it is futile. You are a poet, aren't you? Be thankful that you haven't to think precisely, be thankful that you needn't try to read closed books. Your task is easier."

"Meaning what?" challenged the poet defiantly.

"This and nothing else," said the clairvoyant. "To invent and to perceive are two separate things."

"And of us two, you are the one who perceives, aren't you?"

"A pretty good guess this time," said the clairvoyant, nodding his head as if to punctuate the conversation with his nose.

The poet began to grin. "I should say that we two don't intend to understand each other, don't you think so? Well, it's true, I only invent things, I imagine what I like, don't I? Just a casual whim——"

"I know," exclaimed the clairvoyant, interrupting him. 'You ALSO thought of that man who fell out of the blue. You ALSO imagined the sea behind him. I know. But you hit on the idea only by a kind of conclusion that most of the air lines link up with the ports. A perfectly superficial reason, sir. From the fact that he MIGHT have come from the sea it doesn't follow that he really did come from there. A typical *non sequitur*, sir. It's not permissible to draw conclusions from possibilities. And so that you may know," he burst out testily, "that man really has got the sea behind him. I know."

"How?"

"Quite certainly. By the analysis of the impression."

"You saw him?"

"No. I needn't see a violinist to recognize what he's playing, need I?"

The poet thoughtfully stroked the back of his neck. "The

impression of the sea—Perhaps that's because I like the sea. But I'm not thinking of any sea that I've ever seen. I'm imagining a sea warm and thick like oil, and it glistens as if it were greasy. It is all seaweed, like a meadow. And from time to time something flashes up, and sparkles heavy like quicksilver."

"They are the flying fish," observed the clairvoyant, apropos of something he was thinking of himself.

"Damned man," mumbled the poet, "you're right, they're flying fish."

CHAPTER IV

It was a long time before the surgeon returned. At last he came, and murmured absent-mindedly: "Oh, you're still here!"

The clairvoyant with his melancholy nose gazed at some place in the void. "Severe concussion of the brain," he said. "Evidently an internal injury. Fracture of the lower jaw, and of the base of the skull. Superficial and severe burns on the face and hands. Fractura claviculae."

"Correct," said the surgeon thoughtfully. "He's in a bad way. And how do you know all this, may I ask?"

"You have just been thinking of it," said the clairvoyant, as if by way of apology.

The poet frowned. Go to Jericho, magician, do you think that you impress me? And if you repeat word for word what one is thinking about, don't imagine that I shall believe you.

"And who is he really?" he asked, to change the subject.

"Who knows," muttered the doctor. "All papers on him were burnt. They've found some French, English, and American coins in his pocket, and a Dutch dubbeltje. Perhaps he flew by way of Rotterdam, but the aeroplane wasn't one of the regular liners."

"Didn't he tell you anything?"

The surgeon shook his head. "Nothing at all. Completely unconscious. I should be astonished if he says anything at all."

The silence became oppressive. The clairvoyant got up, and slouched towards the door. "A closed book, eh?"

The poet frowned after him until he had disappeared down the corridor. "Were you really thinking what he said, doctor?"

"Why, of course. That was the statement that I had just dictated. I don't like this thought-reading. From a medical standpoint," he said thoughtfully. "It's an indiscretion." With this, apparently, he let the matter drop.

"But that's humbug!" the poet burst out indignantly. "It's impossible for one man to know what another thinks! To some extent you can deduce it logically—When you came back I knew at once that you were thinking . . . of that man who fell from the blue. I saw that you were worried, that you were in doubt about something, that it was extremely serious. And I said to myself, wait, perhaps that means an internal injury."

"Why?"

"From reasoning—logical deductions. I know you, doctor, you don't let your mind wander; but when you came back you made motions as if to unbutton your operating coat, although you had already taken it off. From this it was obvious that in your thoughts you were still with your patient. Aha, I said to myself, something is preying on his mind. Perhaps something that he can neither see nor touch—most probably an internal injury."

The surgeon nodded moodily.

"But I looked at you," the poet went on. "That's the whole trick: to observe and deduce—that, at least, is straightforward work. But that magician of yours," he muttered spitefully, "just looks at the tip of his nose, and tells you what you're thinking about. I watched him carefully, he didn't even squint at you. It was . . . disgusting."

And again the only sound was the booming of the wind. "Even now, doctor, you're thinking about that case. There's something peculiar about him, isn't there?"

"He's got no face," said the surgeon in a low voice. "He's been burned so badly. . . . No face, or name, or consciousness. If only I knew something about him!"

"Or this: why did he fly in such a wind? Where was he so dreadfully keen on going to? What was he afraid of losing? What senseless and impatient motive shot him forth? At any rate, he wasn't afraid of death. I'll pay you pilot, ten times over if you'll take me where I want to go. If it's a gale from the west, all the better, at least we shall fly faster—And nothing has been found on him . . . ?"

The surgeon shook his head. "Well, come, have a look at him, if you can't let the matter drop," he said suddenly, getting up.

The sister of mercy sitting beside the bed rose with difficulty; she had fat, swollen legs, and a flat and colourless face, a weary vessel of charity. The old man on the next bed turned his face away; he was too interested in his own suffering to attempt to bridge the gap that lies between the sick and the healthy.

"He hasn't regained consciousness yet," reported the sister of mercy, folding her hands on her bosom; apparently it should be like that when a nun stands to attention, an old amazon reporting; only her eyes blinked anxiously, with human feeling. The poet remembered the expressive eyes of the monkeys, and felt ashamed. Yes, but these eyes are so unexpectedly and strangely human!

And so this is him, this is the case! With a quivering heart he had prepared himself for a sight from which he would fly in terror, with his hands on his mouth and sobbing with fright; and instead everything was very clean, almost pleasant, nothing but a huge ball of white bandages skilfully applied. Upon my word, a clean job, cleverly done; and it has hands made of cotton-wool, gauze, and calico—big white paws lying on the cover. What a dummy they can make out of nothing but cotton-wool and bandage; you wouldn't even say——

The poet knitted his brows, and gasped. But it breathes; just slightly, those folded white paws rise and fall a tiny bit as if it were alive. And that dark gap here between the bandages is perhaps its mouth; and those dark hollows in the tender little crown of cotton-wool—ah, Lord, no, thank God, they're not blind eyes, they're not human eyes, no, they're only closed eyelids; it would be dreadful if he saw! The poet leaned over the clean bandaging; and suddenly the closed lids flickered. The poet started back, he felt faint and sick. "Doctor," he gasped, "doctor, won't he come round?"

"No, he won't," said the surgeon thoughtfully, while the sister of mercy blinked her eyes as regularly as water drips. The panic of compassion relaxed; these two were so calm. Be quiet, be quiet, everything is in order; as regularly as water drips the white sheet over the unconscious man rises and falls. Everything is in order, there is no confusion, or terror, no longer is there any disaster, nobody runs and wrings his hands; even pain is stilled when it becomes a part of order. On the next bed the patient groaned regularly and indifferently.

"Poor fellow," muttered the surgeon, "he's maimed like the Saviour." The sister of mercy crossed herself. The poet would have liked to make the sign of the cross over that bandaged head, but somehow he felt too shy even to do that; he glanced in embarrassment towards the doctor. The surgeon beckoned. "Let's go." And out on tiptoes. There's nothing to talk about now; let the sheet of order and silence close over it, let not that unbroken stillness be disturbed; be quiet, be quiet, as if departing from something strangely and intensely venerable.

Not until they were at the gate of the hospital, where the confusion and noise of life began, did the surgeon remark thoughtfully: "It's strange that so little is known about him. We must register him as Case X." He waved his hand. "You'd better not think about him any longer."

CHAPTER V

He has already been unconscious for two days, his temperature is rising, and his pulse grows feebler. Without a doubt life is escaping somewhere; ah, God, what a nuisance! how are we to mend the tear of which we have no knowledge? Well, then, we can do nothing but look at that dumb body with no face, or name, not even palms on which it would be possible to read traces of its past life. If he only had a name, if only, at least, he had some sort of a name, he would not be so—well, what? —disturbing perhaps, or something. Yes, you call it a mystery.

The sister of mercy, it seems, has chosen this hopeless case for the object of her special personal attention; tired and weary she sits on the hard chair at the foot of the bed, which bears above it no written name of a man, but only the Latin names of his wounds, and she never lets her eyes wander from this white, feeble, and faintly breathing chrysalis; apparently she is praying. "Well," mutters the surgeon, without a smile, "a quiet patient, eh? You seem to have taken to him."

The sister of mercy blinked rapidly as if she wanted to defend herself. "But he's so lonely! He hasn't even got a name——" As if a name were some support to a man. "I dream about him at night," she said, passing her palm over her eyes. "If he should happen to come round, and wanted to say something—I know that he wants to say something."

The surgeon was about to say: Sister, this man won't even say good night to us, but he kept it to himself. Instead, he just lightly patted her shoulder. Here in the hospital one doesn't squander words of appreciation. The aged nun fished out a big, stiff handkerchief, and blew her nose with emotion. "So that at least he has somebody," she explained slightly confused—she seemed to fill out with all her care, sitting broader and more patiently than before. Yes, so that at least he's not so lonely.

That he is not so lonely, yes; but has such a fuss like this with a patient ever been made before? Twenty times a day the surgeon wanders aimlessly down the corridor to have a glance, as if only by the way—Nothing new, sister? No, nothing. Everybody sticks his head into number six; doctors, nurses—Isn't so-and-so here?—but that's only an excuse so that for a moment they can stand over that bed without a name, over that man without a face. Poor fellow, they say with their eyes, and go away on tiptoes; and the sister of mercy rocks slightly, almost imperceptibly at her important and silent post.

And now already it's the third day; all the time deeply unconscious, but the patient's temperature rises above a hundred and four; he is restless, his hands fidget above the cover, and he mutters incoherently. How his body fights for existence; consciousness and will are no longer present to defend themselves, only the heart beats like a weaver's shuttle in a tangled warp; already it runs light, carrying no thread through the texture of life. The machine has ceased to weave, but it still runs on.

The sister of mercy never takes her eyes from that bed of coma; the surgeon would like to say to her, Well, sister, it's no use, and God knows that it's hopeless for you to sit here, better go and rest. Her eyes blink with apprehension, she certainly has something on the tip of her tongue, but discipline and fatigue close her lips; besides people say little, and talk in a low voice over this bed. "Come to see me afterwards, sister," says the surgeon as he goes on his daily round.

Heavily, like a piece of wood, the sister sits down in the surgeon's room, not knowing how to begin, she keeps her face averted, and emotion brings up red spots on her face. "What is it, sister?" inquires the surgeon to make it easier for the old woman, as if she were a little girl, and then she bursts out: "I dreamt of him again to-day for the second time."

So now it's out, and the doctor didn't burst into laughter, or say anything that would have confused the sister; on the contrary, he looked at her with eyes full of interest, and waited for her to go on.

"Not that I believe in dreams," she declared self-consciously, "but if on two nights you have a dream which keeps going on, there's something behind it. It's true that sometimes I try to interpret my dreams, but that's only because I'm lonely; I'm not expecting a sign. None of my dreams ever came true, so it's not because I'm superstitious that I'm interested in them. I know that dreams return and repeat themselves; but to keep going on, as reality does, is something different. If there is something in my dream which I ought not to divulge, Mother of God forgive me! I am more accustomed to doctors than to priests, and I will tell you everything as if it were a confession."

The surgeon nodded with understanding.

"I shall tell you everything," the sister continued, "because it concerns your patient; but it will be the main points which I have sorted out and arranged in my mind. When I dreamt it it was mostly in pictures which were continually changing; some were quite clear, but others were involved, discontinuous, sometimes crowding one on top of the other, sometimes as if several came all at once. At moments it was as if that man was really telling me something, and then again as if I myself were looking at something taking place; it was so confused and puzzling that even in my dream I wished that I could wake, but I couldn't. That dream was so vivid and strong that it went on even in the daytime; but then I could get it into better shape and sequence without those pictures. That wasn't a dream any longer. All things would become mere dreams if there were not some order in them; order is something that only occurs in reality. That is why that dream moved me so much, because I found more order in it than dreams usually have; and I can only tell you what its meaning seems to me now."

THE SISTER OF MERCY'S STORY

"TWO nights ago he appeared to me for the first time. He was wearing a white suit with brass buttons, leather leggings, and a white helmet on his head; but the helmet was not like an army one, and I have never seen such a dress. His face was as yellow as a gipsy's, and his eyes feverish, something like the eyes of a man with typhoid fever; he might have had a fever, for he rambled in his talk.

When you dream of someone, you don't hear him speak, nor do you see him move his lips; you just KNOW what he is saying to you, and I never have been able to discover why it is like that. I only know that he spoke to me, that he talked very fast in some foreign language, which I could not understand; I remember that several times he addressed me as 'Sor,' but I don't know what that means. He was agitated, and almost desperate, because I couldn't understand him, and he talked for a long time. But afterwards, as if he had become conscious of where he was, he began to talk—I was going to say, in our language, but that was only because I could suddenly understand it.

'Sister,' he said, 'on my knees, I beg you please, do something for me if you can; for you know what a state I'm in. God. What a misfortune, what a misfortune! I don't even know how it happened; it was as if the earth suddenly flew up against us. If only I could write on the cover with my finger, I'd make it all clear; but you see what I look like.' He showed me his hands, they were not bandaged; but I don't know now why they seemed so dreadful. 'I can't, I can't,' he moaned, 'look at these hands! I'll tell you everything; but for God's sake help me just to get this one thing done. I flew like mad to get everything settled; but suddenly the earth tilted violently, and began to fall on us. I know that something happened; a flame sprang out towards us, such as I have never seen before, and I saw many things; I saw a ship burning, people burning, I saw a whole mountain burning, but I shall not tell you about that; nothing matters any more but just one thing.'

'Just one thing,' he repeated; 'but now I see that it is the whole of life. Ah, sister, didn't they tell you what happened to me? Haven't I been injured in my head? For I've forgotten everything. I only remember my life. I've forgotten everything that I ever did; I can't remember anywhere where I've been, or people's names, and I don't know what my own name is; all that is accidental and of secondary importance. I certainly must have had concussion of the brain if I can't remember anything but what really took place. If they told you my name, you can be certain that it's not my real one; and if I begin to babble something about islands and adventures put it down to my derangement; I do not know to what these ruins belong, and it's no longer possible to make out of them the story of the man. The whole of man is in what is left for him to accomplish; all the rest is made of bits and fragments which can't be compassed with a glance. Yes, yes, yes, sometimes you dig up something that is past, and think; this is what I am. Only my case is more difficult, sister; something happened that shattered my memory; nothing intact was left in me but what I still wanted to do.' "

CHAPTER VI

THE sister of mercy swayed slightly as she told her story, with her eyes fixed on the floor, as if she were reciting something that she had learned by heart. "It is strange how such a dream is clear and hazy at the same time, I don't know where we were; he was sitting on some wooden steps, which led up to some kind of a straw hut——" She hesitated for a moment. "Yes, that hut was supported on posts, like the legs of a table; and he was sitting with his legs apart on the lowest step, and he knocked out his pipe on the palm of his hand. His face was lowered, you could only see his white helmet; it looked as if he had his head bandaged.

'You know, sister,' he said, 'I can't remember my mother. Strange, although I never knew her, in my mind something has remained like an empty and blind spot where something ought to be. So you see, my memory was never complete, for there was no mother in it.' He nodded his head as he spoke. 'It was always like an empty spot on the map of my life; I never knew myself completely because I never knew my mother.'

'As for my father,' he went on, 'I must say that our mutual relations were never very good, or intimate. As a matter of fact there even was between us a silent and unreconcilable hostility. That is, my father was an exceedingly righteous man; he held an important position in his business, and he considered his life fulfilled because in every respect he did his duty. The duty of a man then is to be devoted to his work, to get rich, and on top of that to be respected by his fellow citizens; these are all such big undertakings that they can only be ended by death. He died pompous and tranquil, as if content that that task he had accomplished too. With me he never talked except to admonish, giving himself as an example; most probably he thought of human life as something already complete, like a house that one inherits, or a firm taken over by a successor. He had a very high opinion of himself, his principles, and his virtues, and to him his life seemed to be something worth handing on like a legacy. Perhaps he cared for me in his way, and thought about my future; but he could not imagine a future except as a repetition of his own experiences. For that I hated him so that with all my might I tried to thwart, mischievously and secretly, everything he might have expected from a good and sensible child; I was lazy, obstinate, and wicked, and even as a boy I slept with the servants—I still remember the roughness of their hands; in secret I filled his house with unruly elements, and I think that I often shook the confidence of the old man; for in me life itself must have appeared as something prodigal and wild over which he had no power.'

'I am not going to describe to you, sister, the life of a young adolescent. Ah, yes, it was all as one would expect; except for this and that I have nothing to feel ashamed of. It's true that I was a naughty and depraved child, but as a youth I was not much different from the rest; just like them I was chiefly full of myself: my loves, my experiences, my views, anything that was mine. Only later a man realizes that these were all not so much his, and his alone, but that they are common experiences through which he had to pass, while all the time he feels that he was the first to discover them. From childhood more stays in one than from adolescence; childhood, yes, that is complete and fresh reality, while youth—God knows where it gets so much of its conceit and unreality; that is why usually it is forgotten and lost. No, thank goodness, it isn't everyone who finds out how he was cheated, and how stupidly he was taken in by life. I have nothing to remember; and when something comes back to me, I feel that it is no longer myself, and that it doesn't concern me.'

'By then I was no longer living with my father; he was something alien and remote, like no one else, and when I stood by his coffin it was awful and impossible for me to have sprung from this alien body already changed by putrefaction; in no way, in no way could I any longer communicate with the departed, and the tears which rose to my eyes only came from the realization that I was alone.'

'I have perhaps already told you that from my father I inherited quite a large fortune; but even that seemed strange and alien to me, as if it still carried some of the respectability and sense of duty of my father. He built up his estate as something in which he would still live; his money was to have been a continuation of his life and status. I did not like it, and I took my revenge by making use of it only for my laziness and self-indulgence. I did nothing because I was not driven to do anything through necessity; but, please tell me, what reality is it that is not hard and stubborn like stone? I could indulge in all my whims; it is a dreadful bore, sister, and to think out how to kill time is harder work than breaking stones. I was good for nothing, and believe me, a capricious man gets less from life than a beggar.'

He paused a moment, and then said: 'As you see, I certainly have no reason to lament my early life. If I refer to it now, it is not to drink from the well of youth. I am ashamed that I was young, for through it I wasted my life. It was the silliest and most senseless period of my life; and yet just towards its end I met with an event, of which the import escaped me then. I call it an event, although it was nothing like an adventure; I got to know a girl, and I made up my mind that I would make use of her; it's true that I was in love with her, but even that in youth is nothing extraordinary. God knows she was not my first love, not even the strongest of my passions, the names of which I have already forgotten.' "

CHAPTER VII

THE sister of mercy shook her head anxiously. "He said all that as if he had something to confess, and it was clear that he did not want to keep anything back from me. He is certainly preparing for death; but for me nothing is left but to pray that God by a miracle, or by grace, will accept this confession made in the dream, and to an unworthy person, as valid; perhaps he will also bear in mind that a man who is unconscious cannot bring himself to the due repentance necessary for perfect penance.

'I must describe to you,' he said later, 'what she was like. Strange: I can't picture her face any longer; she had grey eyes, and a voice rather harsh, like a boy. She also had lost her mother when she was a child; she lived with her father whom she adored because he was a fine old gentleman, and a very noble engineer. To please him, and at her own wish, she studied engineering, and went into a factory; sister, dear sister, I wish that you could imagine her in that workshop of machinery among the steam-hammers, lathes, and half-naked men who pounded at the glowing metal. At that time she was a little girl, an elf, a brave little creature, and the mechanics adored her; she moved in a world of a strange gentility because she lived among men. Once, yes, once she took me into the workshop, and then I fell in love with her; she was so fragile, so bravely sweet among those strong male backs glistening with sweat, with that small, rather harsh little voice of hers, and with her technical authority over fire, iron, and labour. You might say that this was not a place for a girl; God pardon me for my sins, but it was in that very place that I first felt a desire for her in a tormented and absurd way, in a moment when she was examining her work, scrutinizing it with her long knotted brows. Or again, as she stood with her big father, and he laid his hand on her shoulder as if she were a son of whom he was proud, and upon whom he bestows his work. The workmen called her Mister, and I fixed my eyes on her girlish shoulders tormented by a desire which almost disconcerted me as if there were something unnatural in it.'

'She was immensely happy: happy with the pride of her old father, and of herself, happy because people liked her, and that she was earning her own living, happy with quiet and serene content. Her eyes radiated peace, her boyish voice was low and said little; I loved the blue-print stains on her hands and fingers. As for me, I was young, and therefore vain, I was a dandy, so of course I gave myself an air of self-assurance; but that girl puzzled me. I thought that she intended to become a sexless being, and out of some kind of spite I made up my mind to humble her as a woman; I thought that if I seduced her I should somehow score over her. Perhaps I felt ashamed before her for myself, for the tedium and triviality of my life, and so, just for that, I wanted to gloat over the glory of a male conquest. You understand that this is how it seems to me now; but then it was only love, desire, a dreadful desire to bend over her, and press from her the sob that she loved me.'

He became serious, and thought for a moment. 'And now, sister, I am coming to things about which it is not easy for me to talk; but I want to tell you everything. It was not a first love, in which no matter how you think, it follows inevitably and almost unaware; I wanted to have her, and I searched for means which would deliver her to me. I am ashamed to remember how stupid and gross, how futile, all those worldly tricks of mine appeared beside the strange and almost rough sincerity and integrity of that virgin girl. I realized that she was above it, and above me, that she was of finer stuff than I, but it was no longer possible for me to turn back. Men are strange, sister. I was so engrossed with tormenting and vile thoughts of how in some mean way, through a lie, or hypnosis, drugs, or by any other means, I could seduce and dishonour her, like a temple is dishonoured—listen, sister, I am not keeping anything secret from you: I seemed like a devil to myself.

And all the time while I was degrading her in my mind, she loved me. Sister, she loved me, and one day she revealed her love to me as simply as a blossom falls from a tree. It was so different—O Lord, it was so different from what I in my passion could imagine. First that alone, that I was as clumsy as a boy who falls in love for the first time.'

He covered his face with his hands as he said that, and became still and silent. 'Yes, I was a pig,' he said afterwards, 'and I deserve everything that came to me afterwards. I was bending over her, lying with closed eyes, and I tried to enjoy to the full my apparent triumph. I should have liked to see the tears well up from under her eyelids, to see her cover her face with shame and despair; but her face was calm and serene, and she breathed like someone asleep. I felt depressed, I wrapped her up, and turned to the window to work up the devil of my pride. When I turned back she looked at me with full and clear eyes, and she smiled as she said: "Well, now I belong to you!"

'I was horrified—yes, I was horrified with astonishment and humiliation. There was in her so much light, clarity, transparency, I don't know what to call it. Just simply—Now I belong to you, and everything is all right; here we've got it, here we are, and nothing can be done about it. What a relief, how clear it was, what a simple and tremendous solution. Yes, it was solved, and with the most definite certainty, and the most complete fullness; this sensible little maid spoke with assurance and without hesitation. Well, now I belong to you. Think how proud she was, how satisfied with herself because she had found this holy, this bright, and certain living truth; her eyes were still wide open with that astonishing and tremendous discovery, and she became filled with the great peace of something decided for ever. The same small features which for a few seconds were broken with confusion and pain now took on a new and final expression—the expression I should say of a man who has found himself. Yes, now I know what I am. I belong to you, and what has occurred was in order, and the order of things has been accomplished. As when water closes over the ripples, becomes smooth again, and you can see the bottom.'

'Sister, I'm not keeping anything back from you. If she had dug her hands into my eyes, if she had been shaken with sobs, if anything of her had cried out with reproof, What have you done to me, you vile person? I should have felt nothing but delight in victory. A delight both bad and good, pride, magnanimity, and repentance, what do I know; I should perhaps have fallen on my knees, vowing an oath, and kissing her hands, stained with red lead and pencils. But this victory was not for me; for me was only the confusion, and shame, into which I began to fall. I tried to stammer something about love; she raised her brows as if in astonishment. Why talk about that, need we yet? I belong to you, and this means everything, love, acquiescence, reality, yes it means everything. It would be vulgar and immodest to prattle of sentiment and gratitude. What's the good of talking? It has happened, I am yours; and if you have still to talk, it would be as if there were something here that needed explaining away. Ah, sister, sister, don't you understand how wise and mature that was, how dignified and pure! Isn't it as if I had intended to sin, and she had made a sacrament of it? What shame, I did not know what to say; she looked at my rooms with interest, as if she were seeing them for the first time, and she hummed a little tune to herself, she who never sang. She did not actually say so, but she just felt at home, that she belonged there.'

'She smiled, and sat down beside me, and with her small and rather harsh voice she spoke—not of the present, or the future, but of herself, of her childhood, of the affections of a girl; she was giving me her past, as if it all ought to belong to me. I could not get rid of a strange feeling of humiliation and inferiority; I wanted to embrace her again, but she just raised her hand—that alone was sufficient for her defence. No, she said without embarrassment, let us wait. Everything was so simple and matter-of-fact. If I belong to you, it is no folly, but a real thing, lasting, and valid. She kissed me on the mouth, as if to say, don't frown, little one, as if she were my mother, as if she were older and stronger than I, and more mature—It was almost unbearably sweet, and at the same time, God forgive me, as humiliating as a blow.'

'Then she left me—you know that, sister, the heaviest step is going away. In the way in which a man walks away he reflects his embarrassment, incertitude, rashness, self-assurance, frivolity, or vanity. Mind your back, for we are not protected when we go away. I don't know how she went away. She stood in the door with her head slightly lowered, and then she vanished. So lightly and silently. This is important because that is how I saw her for the last time.'

'For that same night I ran away like a scamp.' "

CHAPTER VIII

THE sister of mercy blew loudly and indignantly into her stiff handkerchief, and continued: "That is what he told me. His act was abominable, and it seems as if he is sorry for it; but I must say that he ought not to exculpate so completely the girl, who, as he says, had given herself of her own will. Even if, according to his description, she was gentle and sweet, she deserved the punishment that fell upon her, and we might say that to some extent that man was God's instrument; but that does not mitigate his guilt.

'When I think now,' he said afterward, 'of the strange motives which led to my flight, I see them in a different light to what I did then. At that time I was young, and I had a number of more or less adventurous and hazy plans; besides that I still had in me, from my childhood, a feeling of revolt against any kind of duty. There was in me a violent, anxious aversion to anything which would bind me, and this cowardice I felt to be the expression of my liberty. The depth and fixity of her love terrified me; although she stood above me, I was frightened that I should be bound for ever. I felt that I must decide between myself and her, and I decided for myself.'

'Now I know more, and I see things in a different light. Now I know that she was more complete than I, that everything was decided in her, and nothing in me, that she was mature, while I was still a confused, adolescent, irresponsible boy. What I felt in myself to be a revolt against entanglements was the fear of her superiority, the fear of that great certainty. The virtue of belonging to someone was not given to me, I could not say: I belong to you too, just as you see me here, unchangeable, complete, and final. There was not in me the fullness of a man that I could give to her. I can go through it with you without emotion as if it were a bill, but I can talk like this because it is the ledger of my life. Debit, credit. She gave me herself; she said: Well, now I belong to you. And I—everything I had was love, was passion, a doubtful promise, something like an unsigned cheque.' He laughed quietly. 'For I am a man of business, sister, and I should like to get my accounts in order. My flight, you know, was the flight of an insolvent debtor. I owed her myself.'

It seemed to me (said the sister of mercy) that he was grinning as if he was jeering at me; I tried to speak, but then he grinned still more, and began to disappear. With an effort I tore myself from my sleep, disturbed with such a vivid dream. I prayed for him and for the girl, and I tell you the whole day long it stuck in my head. The following night I lay awake for a long time, but as soon as sleep came over me he was already there as if he had been waiting for it. Again he was sitting on the steps with a lowered head; he seemed sad and uneasy. Behind the cottage a field was waving in the wind, grown over with something that looked like maize, or reeds in a swamp.

'It's not maize,' he said suddenly, 'it's sugar-cane. It seems that I have been buying cane on the islands for many years, and getting rum out of it, aquardiente, as they call it there, but that is not the point. In reality I was nothing more than an immature boy who had run away into the world. I feel annoyed for having described it to you in a not very suitable manner, and it is worth while for me to correct your unfavourable impression. Yes, for instance, I know that to a certain extent you condemn that girl; in what I told you about her behaviour you are inclined to see weakness towards temptation and sinful satisfaction of the flesh. If that were so, then what I took to be her tremendous honesty, and patience of perfect love, was only the illusion of a young enamoured man; but then, sister, that perfect love must have been in me, without my knowing it, and my flight would have been sheer madness. It would have been unintelligible, and unintelligible my whole life would have remained. I know, this is what is called an indirect proof. You can object that life is meaningless, and inexplicable, but I see that you do not think that it is.

'I have another direct proof that what I have described to you is correct. It is the life which I led myself after that strange flight. By this flight I must have committed something extremely cowardly; I must have violated some mystic order, for ever since then a curse had been lying on me. By that I do not mean the troubles that I had to face, but that from that time on I had neither stability nor fixity in anything. I tell you, sister, that after that I lived a bad life: the life of a man who is unforgiven. I use your words to express it, for I am too much a man of the world, and I should say that I lived like a piggish prodigal, a lost hound, a deceitful rogue, and God knows what else, miserable and inconstant, you can imagine: and all because at a certain point I failed dismally. I was too empty, flimsy, and green to be able to face when I met it all of a sudden the fullness of life, yes, how shall I describe it; I have in my mind something that means order and persistence, achievement, value, the peace of something complete for ever. If genuine reality is something which is, and which therefore endures, then I ran away from reality; it was an accursed flight for I never found it again. You can't realize, sister, how frail and ephemeral is all evil; it must perpetually renew itself, but in vain; in baseness a man does not fulfil himself, and the blasphemer, murderer, the jealous, and the rake live lives that are strangely fragmentary and unsettled. Ah, I can't piece together all my life; it is all chips, rubble, and scraps, which won't fit together to form any picture. In vain, in vain I struggle with my petty and sinful acts; they are incoherent and confused, nothing but broken threads and chaos, without head or tail. That's how it is, that's how it is, amen, and you call it a bad conscience.

'I can show you my pockets; they used to be crammed with gold. I can bare my shoulders; they bear the marks of the lash of a whip and of the teeth of mulattos. Feel here; my liver is hard and swollen with heavy drinking. Once red fever got me, and another time they hunted me with guns like a deserter. I could tell you of fifty lives, and they are all false; only their scars are left now. This is the hut where I lay, on the point of death, and abandoned like a sick cat; I went over my different lives, and I could not get them all straight; I think I must have invented them during my fever, they were only vile and awful dreams. Twenty years or so, and only muddled, senseless, fleeting dreams. Then they took me to the hospital, and nurses in white aprons cooled me with ice. God, how good it was, how cool it was, poultices and white aprons, and all that—you know, somehow as if I mattered; but death had already entered me.'

CHAPTER IX

"I SHOULD say, God's finger," remarked the sister of mercy. "Illness is a warning, and the Church does wisely in sending its servants to the beds of the sick, to point the way at that cross-road. But in these days people are too much afraid of illness and death, and because of that they cannot recognize that warning, and they cannot read *mene tekel* when it is written with the fiery hand of pain.

'Death entered me then,' he said. 'They got me past the worst, but I lay stretched out, as weak as a fly. I can't say that I was afraid of death; I was amazed that I was able, that I could die at all, that is, go through so serious and far-reaching an experience; I faced it like a task I wasn't fitted for. I felt as if I were being asked to do something too great, important, and decisive for me, and as if it were hopeless to try to object that I was not ready for it; and I felt a kind of tremendous uncertainty or anxiety. Strange, before that I had faced death so many times, and God knows my life was active, and often dangerous enough; but until then Davy Jones had only been for me a matter of risk or chance, I could laugh at him, or defy him, but now he seemed to be something inexorable, and, like some solution, inexplicable, but supremely valid, and final. Sometimes weakness and indifference gained the upper hand, and then I said to him, Well, all right, I shall close my eyes, and you get it done, but quick; I don't want to know anything. But at other times I was angry at my childish cowardice. But it's nothing, I said to myself, it's nothing very hard, it's only the end. Every adventure has its end, and this will only be one more. But strange enough, however much I thought about it I could not think of death as an end, snip, like cutting a thread. I looked at it then from close enough, and it seemed to me to be something vast and enduring; I can't say what, but a tremendous space in time, for death is lasting. I will tell you, it was this very permanence that frightened me so terribly; I despaired of being equal to it, for I had never undertaken anything permanent, and I never signed a contract that would bind me for any length of time. I had had plenty of opportunities to settle down and live respectably without any great effort, but every time I was filled with violent and overwhelming loathing; I took it to be part of my character that needed change, moods, and adventure. And now, now I had to meet this contract for eternity; I was soaking with cold sweat, and I gasped with terror. But it's impossible, it's not for me, it's not for me, God in Heaven, help me, for I'm not ready yet to decide for ever. Ah, yes, if, say, you could make an experiment with death for three months, for half a year—well, here's my hand; but don't ask me to say to you: Well, now I belong to you.'

'And this, sister, was like lightning, or revelation. Again I saw that girl as she lay full of certainty and joy, as she said quietly: Well, now I belong to you. And again I stood puny and humiliated before that courage to live while I fluttered ridiculously before the decision to die. And I began to understand that life like death has the elements of permanence, that in its way, and with its own small means, it has the will and the courage to last for ever. And these are the two parts which mutually complete and fit into each other. Yes, it's like that: only a fragmentary and casual life is swallowed up by death, while that which is complete and real attains its fulfilment. Two parts which fit together into eternity. Because I was delirious, it seemed to me to be like two hemispheres which ought to be put together, but the one was chipped and bent, a mere crock, and however much I tried it would not fit into the other one which, so perfect and smooth, was death. I must mend it, I kept saying to myself, so that the two will fit together: Well, now I belong to you.'

'After that, sister, I invented a life for myself. I say invented because much of it could not be pieced together, and had to be thrown away, while on the other side solid and complementary things were missing. With my youth there would also have been much to correct, but I did not bother myself with that much; the most important was, then, and still is, that in that real reality, that is in that that was not, and yet somehow did exist, not as a fact, but as a meaning—like a leaf torn from a book—God, what did I want to say?—that's owing to the fever. Yes, the most important thing is that in that real reality the things were different, quite different, do you understand? That is, they ought to have been different, that was essential; and that real story, as it really ought to have been, is—is—' His teeth chattered, but he controlled himself with an effort, 'You know, as I told you,' he chattered, 'as I told you, she was lying—and she said: "Well, now I belong to you." That is holy truth, sister, but what followed, what followed ought to have been different. Now I know because death and life have entered me. I ought to have said, You, yes, I should have said, that's it, thank God; You belong to me, and you will wait, wait, till I come back with life and death in my body. Don't you see that I'm not complete enough to live. I am not yet complete enough to endure, not brave enough to decide, not of one piece like you, like you. I ask you, what would you do with a heap like me? But I don't know myself what I shall become, I don't know where is my head and tail. As for you, you are eternal, you know everything that is to be known, you know that you belong; but I——'

A tremor ran through the whole of his body as he said this. 'Wait, I shall also come, and say: Well, now I belong to you. Ah, sister, do you understand, she knew it, she realized that even although I didn't say so. And so she said: No, wait till another time. That means that I am to return, doesn't it? Say, say yourself, that means that she will be waiting for me, doesn't it? And that's why she did not say even good-bye, that's why I didn't see her go away. I shall return, and both halves, like life and death, will fall into each other; well, now I belong to you. There is no proper and complete reality but what it is to be.' He sighed deeply, like a man with great relief. 'Love, death, life, everything that is in me, inevitable, and absolute, will all fall together into one another. Here you have me, only now am I in my true place; the only certain thing is to belong. Myself, my whole self I have found in that now I belong to somebody. Thank God, thank God, at last I have arrived.

'No, let me go, I can't wait, I'm going back. And she will only smile, Well, now I belong to you; I shall not be afraid any more, I shall not cover her over, I'm coming now, I'm coming now, I know that she's already tugging at the tapes and clasps of her dress. Do, quick, you know that I am to go back! You call this a storm?—get away, I know a hurricane when I see one, I have seen tornadoes and water-spouts; this breeze is not fresh enough to carry me. Don't you see, she flies into my arms, she bends forward, and flies, look out, we shall dash our heads together, and teeth, look out, you're falling on me, I shall fall on you, how passionate you are, how you snatch me into your arms!' Suddenly he began to wander feverishly. 'Why is that pilot flying into empty space? Sister, tell him that it's not there, tell him to come back! Or no, go to her, and tell her, let her know that I'm coming back! Don't you know that she's waiting! For God's sake, please tell her that I'm on the way, just till that pilot can find where to land; I couldn't write to her, I don't know where she is——' He raised his eyes, desperate and full of terror. 'What—what do you—Why don't you tell her? I must fly round, always round and round; and you only blink at me, and you don't want to tell anything, because——' Suddenly he began to change, on his head he had a mask of bandages, and he trembled frightfully; and I realized that he was scoffing at me. 'I know, you are an evil, envious, nasty nun; you are incensed with her because she loved. You needn't envy her; well, to tell you the truth, then even in that I lied a bit. Because of that, perhaps, do you see, I behaved so cowardly. So that you know, another time——'"

The sister of mercy sat still with quiet sad eyes. "Then he cursed and swore; it was as if Satan were talking in him. He vomited abuse and insults—God be merciful to me." She crossed herself. "The most terrible was that those words came from a chrysalis without either mouth or eyes. I was so frightened that I woke up. I know I should have taken my rosary to pray for his soul; but instead I went into number six to take his temperature. He was lying unconscious, a hundred and four point five, and he shook with fever."

CHAPTER X

Now he was only a hundred and one point six; he mumbled in his sleep, and his bandaged hands moved restlessly over the blanket. "Do you know, sister, what he says?" asked the surgeon. The sister of mercy shook her head, with her lips tightly pressed together.

"He says 'Yes'r,'" ' burst out the little man on the next bed. " 'Yes'r,' he says, 'Yes'r.' "

Yes, sir, guessed the surgeon. Well, English then.

"And said 'Mañana,' " the little old man remembered. "Mañaña, or mañana."

The old man crowed hoarsely. "Mañaña. Mañaña. Like a baby in swaddling clothes."

Somehow it struck him as extremely funny, he choked with laughter until he shook again, they had to make him be quiet.

And up till then no fresh information as to who he really was. Three times a day the poet rang up on the phone: "Hello, do you know anything further yet?"

"No, we don't know anything." And—"Please tell me how he is."—"Well, you can't shrug your shoulders through the phone —He's still alive."

During the afternoon his temperature fell further, but the patient (at least, what could be seen of him) seemed yellower than before, and began to hiccup. That points to some injury to the liver—or does it look like icterus; the surgeon grew doubtful, and for a second opinion he called in a famous visceral specialist.

The specialist was cheerful and pink, and an eminent old man, full of talk; he was so pleased that it was a wonder that he didn't embrace the sister of mercy, "Yes, yes, we two had some cases through our hands before they made a surgeon of you, eh?"

In a low voice, and more or less in Latin, the surgeon explained the case. The specialist blinked through his gold-rimmed spectacles at the figure made up of cotton-wool and bandages. "God bless you," he exclaimed with feeling and he sat down on the side of the bed. The sister of mercy silently removed the cover. The specialist sniffed and raised his eyes. "Sugar?"

"How do you know?" muttered the surgeon, "I had his water examined, of course . . . if there's no blood. Besides other things they did find sugar. You recognize it by the smell?"

"I'm not often mistaken," said the specialist. "You can tell acetone. Dear me, our *ars medica* is 50 per cent intuition."

"I don't put much on that," opined the surgeon. "I only . . . when I see someone for the first time I have a feeling at once: I shouldn't like to operate on this case, not even if it were only for corns. Something would go wrong with him, embolus, or something. But why—that I don't know."

The specialist gently passed his hands and fingers over the body of the unconscious man. "I should like to examine him," he said regretfully, "but we must leave him in peace, I suppose?" He carefully, almost tenderly, laid his pink ear on the patient's chest, his glasses pushed up onto his forehead. Silence followed, even a fly could be heard at the window. At last the specialist straightened himself up. "But his heart has had some wear," he muttered. "It could tell some stories. And his right lung isn't all right. Distended liver——"

"Why is he so yellow?" burst out the surgeon rather rashly.

"I should like to know that myself," said the specialist thoughtfully. "And his temperature has fallen so much, you say—Show me his water, sister." The sister silently handed him the tube: it had in it a few drops of thick brownish water. "I say," said the specialist, raising his eyebrows. "Where did you get him from? Ah, so you don't know where he was coming from when he fell out of the sky to you. Hadn't he got tremors when they brought him to you."

"He had," said the sister.

It seemed as if the specialist was counting up to five. "Five, at most six days," he murmured. "That's hardly possible. He might get here . . . from the West Indies . . . say, in five or six days?"

"Hardly," remarked the surgeon. "Almost impossible. Unless he came over the Canary Islands, or somehow by that way."

"So it's not impossible," remarked the specialist caustically. "Or where else could he get amaril fever?" (He pronounced amaril as if he were enjoying the taste of the word.)

"Where could he get what?" asked the surgeon, failing to catch his meaning.

"Typhus icteroides. Yellow fever. In all my life I've only seen one case before, that was thirty years ago, in America. Now he has got to the period of calm and is getting to the yellow stage."

The surgeon did not appear to be convinced. "Listen," he said dubiously, "mightn't it be Weil's disease?"

"Bravo, doctor," said the specialist. "It might. Do you want us to try it on guinea-pigs? That would be something for my hairy assistant; he's quite mad about tormenting guinea-pigs. If the guinea-pig keeps alive and well, then I'm right. And I should say," he added modestly, "that I am right."

"How do you know?"

The specialist made a gesture with his arms. "Intuition, my friend. To-morrow his temperature will go up, and he will develop black vomit. By all means I shall send that fellow here to make a blood smear for us."

The surgeon scratched his head in embarrassment; "And . . . listen, what is that red fever?"

"Red fever? Ah, *fièvre rouge*. That's the Antilles fever."

"Only in the Antilles!"

"The Antilles, West Indies, the Amazon. Why?"

"Only, well," mumbled the surgeon, looking uncertainly at the sister of mercy. "But yellow fever also occurs in Africa, doesn't it?"

"In Nigeria, and such places, but it's not indigenous there. When anyone says yellow fever, I think of Haiti, or Panama—just like a landscape, palms, and all that."

"But how could he get as far as here with it?" wondered the surgeon anxiously. "The incubation lasts five days, doesn't it? And in five days—Then he must have flown all the way."

"Well, so he did," replied the specialist as if that were nothing nowadays. "He must have been in a tremendous hurry. The devil only knows why he went at such a pace." He drummed quickly with his fingers on the bed-post. "I don't think he'll tell you much about what was driving him so hard. His heart is very bad, and he's gone through a lot."

The surgeon nodded slightly, and sent the sister of mercy away with a glance. "I'll show you something," he said as he uncovered the thighs of the unconscious man. Right on the groin in a semicircle there were four hard white scars, and one long one like a scratch. "You can feel how deep these scars go into the flesh," he said, "I've always wondered what could have made them——"

"Well, and?"

"If he'd been in the tropics it might have been a paw—a cat's paw. See how hard the claws clutched. But a tiger's paw would have been bigger; perhaps a jaguar—that would mean America."

"So you see," said the specialist, and blew victoriously into his handkerchief. "Here you have a nice piece of biography already. *Locus:* West Indies. *Curriculum vitae:* hunter and adventurer——"

"And a sailor as well. On his left wrist, under the bandage, he's got an anchor tattooed. By origin from the so-called better classes; comparatively long narrow feet——"

"By the body altogether, intelligent, I should say. *Anamnesis:* drinker, obviously alcoholic. An old lung trouble which broke out again some time ago, perhaps as the result of some fever. And you see red fever fits exactly." The specialist's eyes shone with pleasure. "And the scars of tropical framboesia. Ah, my friend, that nearly takes me back to the days of my youth. Far countries, Red Indians, jaguars, poisoned arrows, and such like things! What a story! A globe-trotter who goes to the West Indies—

why? Apparently without any object, if we are to judge by the luggage labels of life. He leads a strange and restless existence, for his age, his heart is terribly exhausted; he drinks from despair and owing to the thirst of diabetes—Man, I can almost see that life." The old gentleman thoughtfully scratched the tip of his nose. "And then that strange, headlong return, that mad chase after something—and somewhere before the goal he dies of yellow fever, which a miserable tiny *Stegomyia fasciata* squirted into him almost the last day of his wanderings there.

The surgeon shook his head. "He will die of concussion, and internal injuries. Leave him to me."

"Yellow fever is not so common with us," protested the specialist. "Don't grudge him a famous exit, let him go from this world like a unique and remarkable case. With that bandaged head of his, with no face and no name, doesn't he look like a mask to represent mystery?" The specialist gently covered the unconscious body. "Poor chap, you will tell us something or other when we have a look inside you; but then the story of your life will be already over."

CHAPTER XI

In the morning his temperature rose, about a hundred and one, and the bandages round his mouth were stained dark as if from vomited blood. The patient was yellow, according to rule, and as one says, was clearly sinking. "Well, what?" inquired the surgeon of the sister of mercy, "Nothing last night—you haven't dreamt of him again?"

The sister of mercy shook her head quickly. "No, I prayed, and it helped." And then she added, frowning, "Besides, to make sure, I took three doses of bromide."

Then another nurse appeared and announced that the patient in the general ward, the one with that abscess on his neck was feverish and hiccupped, he wouldn't say anything, and was getting weaker. Mumbling and upset, the surgeon rushed to the clairvoyant's room so fast that the tails of his white coat flapped behind him. The clairvoyant was lying with closed eyes, and his thin nose pointing pathetically at the ceiling.

"What business have you to get fever," shouted the surgeon. "Let me see." His temperature was about a hundred and one. Annoyed, the surgeon undid the bandage, but the wound was clean and nice, with no inflammation round it. And, altogether, there was nothing to show, only rather yellowish eyes, and the hiccup. The surgeon strolled along the corridor and dropped back again into number six; there bending over the bed of Case X the famous specialist was standing, surrounded by four young doctors in white coats, and announced, "Amaril fever," as if fondling the word. "My friend," he said, turning to the surgeon, "nothing can be done, you must let us visceral experts have this patient a bit. Such a rare, and beautiful case! Wait, the whole faculty will come to you here, with all the scientific luminaries; at least you ought to let him have a canopy over his bed, and an inscription crowned with laurels, 'Welcome to you,' or something like that." He blew into his handkerchief as if it were a war-trumpet. "With your leave we should like to take a small sample of his blood. Secundarius tell the assistant to take from the patient a sample of blood." When passing down the ranks, the message reached the assistant who stood at the left elbow of the great specialist, this long, hairy fellow bent over the fore-arm of the unconscious patient and wiped it with a swab of cotton.

"When you have finished," murmured the surgeon to the specialist, "I should like to speak to you for a moment." But the old doctor could not lose so quickly his enthusiasm for the yellow fever, and he was still talking of it when the surgeon hauled him into the clairvoyant's room. "Well," announced the surgeon, "now tell me, what's the matter with this one." The old gentleman snorted, and went for the patient with all the quick demands, and silent touches of his art. Breathe out, hold your breath, breathe out deeply, lie down, tell me if it hurts, and such familiar things. At last he stopped, doubtfully rubbed the tip of his nose, and looked suspiciously at the clairvoyant. "What can be the matter with him?" he said. "There's nothing amiss, that's quite clear. Very neurotic," he said peremptorily. "But what's behind that fever beats me."

"So you see," thundered the surgeon at the clairvoyant. "Now my man, tell us what you really think you're up to."

"Nothing," the clairvoyant made an effort to deny. "That's to say, it may have some connection with that case, don't you think so?"

"With what case?"

"With that man from the aeroplane. For he's in my mind all the time . . . Has he got fever again?"

"Have you seen him?"

"No, I haven't," mumbled the clairvoyant. "But I keep thinking of him . . . that is, I concentrate on him. You know what an experience that is. It exhausts me terribly."

"He's a clairvoyant, you know," remarked the surgeon quickly. "And you had no fever yesterday."

"I had," admitted the clairvoyant, "but . . . I kept it down from time to time, and my temperature went down. You can control that by your will."

The surgeon looked questioningly at the coryphaeus of abdominal medicine, but the latter rubbed his beard, and meditated. "And what pains?" he asked suddenly. "Didn't you feel any pains? I mean the pains that that other one has."

"I had," said the clairvoyant rather timidly and unwillingly. "That is, they were purely mental pains, even although they were localized in certain parts of my body. It is so difficult to say exactly," he apologized shyly. "I should call them mental pains."

"Where?" let fly the specialist.

"Here," pointed the clairvoyant.

"Aha, in the upper part of the abdomen. Right," muttered the specialist with satisfaction. "And here in the diaphragm?"

"Such a heavy pressure and a feeling as if I were sick."

"Quite right." The specialist felt pleased. "Nothing else?"

"An awful headache, here at the back—and in my back. As if I were broken in two."

"*Coup de barre*," crowed the old doctor. "Man, that's a *coup de barre*. You've hit on it perfectly! That's yellow fever, just as it is in the book."

The clairvoyant grew frightened. "But then . . . Do you think that I can get it?"

"Not at all," grinned the specialist. "You needn't worry, we haven't the right gnat here. Only suggestion," he replied to the questioning look of the surgeon, evidently feeling that with that word the matter had been solved to his complete satisfaction. "Suggestion. I shouldn't be surprised if he hadn't a bit of albumen and blood in his water. With neurotics," he said, "you mustn't be astonished at anything; they know some dodges—Turn to the light."

"But then my eyes run so," complained the clairvoyant. "I can't bear the light."

"All right, my man," said the specialist approvingly. "A perfect clinical picture, my friend. You are a complete diagnostic treasure and you can observe things nicely. I mean observe yourself. You would be a good patient. You wouldn't believe how some people are incapable of explaining what hurts them."

The clairvoyant was clearly flattered by this praise. "And here, doctor," he pointed shyly, "I feel such a strange anxiety."

"Epigastrium," said the specialist, approvingly, as if he were examining a diligent medical student. "Excellent."

"And in my mouth," recalled the clairvoyant, "a feeling as if everything was swollen up."

The old gentleman trumpeted victoriously and magnificently. "So you see," he announced to the surgeon, "here we've got together all the symptoms of yellow fever. My diagnosis is being confirmed. And when I think," he added sentimentally, "that for thirty years I haven't seen a case of yellow fever . . . Thirty years is a long time."

The surgeon felt less happy, and frowned at the clairvoyant, who was resting prostrate and exhausted. "But these experiments don't do you any good," he lectured severely. "I shall not let you stay here, off you go home. You might suggest for yourself illnesses from the whole hospital. In short, pack up your toothbrush and——" with his thumb he indicated the door.

The clairvoyant nodded gloomily in agreement. "I couldn't stand it," he admitted in a low voice. "I can't imagine why it exhausts one mentally. If he . . . that one, that X case, were conscious, then everything would be recognized clearly, definitely, and . . . as if it were in black and white. But with such complete unconsciousness." The clairvoyant shook his head. "A terrible, almost hopeless task. Nothing at all definite, no outline——" He made a gesture in the air with his thin fingers. "And besides those fevers of his, such a muddle even in the subconscious—all upside down, and incoherent. At the same time, everybody was—and is full of him here, everybody thinks about him, you, nurses, everyone."

On the clairvoyant's face the signs of a deep and intense agony appeared. "I must get away from here, or I shall go mad."

The specialist listened with interest, with his head to one side. "And," he inquired vaguely, "have you found out anything about him?"

The clairvoyant sat up and with trembling fingers began to light a cigarette. "Anything." He blew out smoke with relief. "In anything I find there are always gaps and uncertainties." He waved his hand. "To find out, that is to hit at some mystery. If you want to know if I have come across problems and uncertainties, then, yes; then I have found something out. I know you would like me to tell you, but you don't like to ask." He thought for a moment with closed eyes. "And I want to get rid of it. If I get it off my chest I shall be able to get away from it—to leave it alone as you would say. You never get rid of anything you keep silent."

CHAPTER XII

THE CLAIRVOYANT'S STORY

THE clairvoyant sat up on the bed, with his thin knees drawn up to his chin, gaunt and grotesque in his striped pyjamas, and looked into the void as if he were squinting. "I'd better outline to you the method, and introduce some notions," he began hesitatingly. "Let's say, imagine a circle—a circle of brass wire." Here he drew a circle in the air. "A circle is a visible thing. We can think of it abstractly, we can define it mathematically, but psychologically a circle is something we SEE. If I blindfolded you you could touch that wire, and you would say that it is a circle. You would have the SENSATION of a circle. And there are people who with closed eyes can discern with the ear what form the body has that is vibrating. In our case they would HEAR a circle if we hit that wire with a mallet. And if an intelligent fly wandered over that wire it would also acquire an absolutely definite SENSATION OF A CIRCLE. You must understand what a small step it is from these physical sensations to the mental state of a man who in complete darkness would have a sensation that somewhere here there is a circle. Without the aid of eyes, ears, or touch. A perfectly accurate sensation of a circle. I tell you that with the senses eliminated like this you would have a far stronger consciousness of the circle than of the material of which it is made; for form and not material is the spiritual medium. And if I say sensation, I don't mean some intuition, or guess, but an extremely accurate, penetrating, I might say painfully definite consciousness of something; but to give this consciousness a name, and express it as a part of knowledge is difficult, extremely difficult."

The clairvoyant stopped short. "Why," he mumbled, "why, indeed, have I taken a circle for an example? You see, I anticipated before I actually began. The feeling of a circle which closes in on itself. The shape of a tropic, and at the same time the shape of life." He shook his head in negation. "No, in this way we should not get anywhere. I know you both have your doubts about telepathy. And quite rightly. Telepathy is nonsense, we can't perceive things at a distance; we must approach them, approach the stars with number, matter with analysis, and the microscope; and when we have eliminated sensation and bodily presence we can approach anything by concentration. I admit that there may perhaps be premonitions, dreams, apparitions, and visions; I admit that, but on principle I do not want to have anything to do with it. I decline it, and reject it. I am no visionary, I am analytic; full reality does not disclose itself to us; it must be won with arduous labour, by means of analysis and concentration. You admit that the brain is the instrument of analysis, but you guard yourself from the conception that perhaps it is a lens which brings objects nearer to us, although we do not move from the spot, or open our eyes. A strange lens the power of which changes according to our attention and will. A strange bringing near which does not take place in space, or in time, and only manifests itself through the intensity of the sensations, and the scraps of knowledge that are in you. A strange will that brings to your consciousness objects independent of your will. You conceive ideas that did not arise in you, are not yours, and on which you have no influence. Yours is only the concentration. When you look, when you listen, you perceive through your sense-organs, in your nervous centres, objects and events which are external to you. In the same way you can have thoughts and feelings which are external to you, you can have recollections which are external to you, and are not in relation to yourself. It is as natural as seeing or hearing, but you do not possess the application and the practice."

The surgeon shifted himself uneasily, but apparently the clairvoyant took no notice; he continued his lecture with relish, he moved his nose, and hands, and croaked with a deep and satisfied conviction that he was singing. "Look out," he said, and put his finger on his nose, "I said, thoughts, recollections, images, feelings. That is a crude and inaccurate psychology, and I used these misleading ideas only because they are familiar to you. In reality, as far as I perceive in this way, I have the conception of a circle, and not of the material of which it is made; I have a sensation, I have a certain conception of a man, and not of his individual experiences, images and memory. Understand," he said, knitting his brows with the effort to express himself clearly, "of a man contracted in time, a man in whom it exists in the present, everything that ever he was, and what he ever did, but not as a sequence of events, but like—like——" With his hands he indicated in the air something comprehensive. "It is as if you made a film of a man's life from the moment he was born until now, and then placed all the pictures on the top of each other, and projected them all at once. You say, what a medley! Yes, for the present coalesces with the past, covers everything over, and only the form of the life remains as something indescribable, and immensely individual; something like a personal aura, in which everything is contained." His nose was fixed and tragic. "Everything, THE FUTURE AS WELL," he sighed. "That man won't live."

The surgeon snorted. He knew that, too. And for certain.

"I should like to tell it to you as objectively as I can," essayed the clairvoyant. "Let's suppose that a man came here highly gifted with the capacity of smell—there are such people. First he would detect a simultaneous, not very agreeable, and very complex odour; being capable of olfactory attention, he would begin to analyse it; he would recognize the smell of the hospital, of the surgery, tobacco, water, breakfast, of us three, and of our homes; perhaps he might even recognize that on this bed before me an old man died apparently after an operation on the kidneys.

The surgeon frowned. "Who told you that?"

"Nobody, but you don't know the sensitivity of smell. With a certain amount of concentration it is possible to analyse a given simultaneous impression into an objective or a temporal sequence. If your sensation of a certain personality is acute enough and

COMPLETE, you can with sufficient analytical and logical ability unravel it into an outspread picture of his life story. Out of the condensed form of his life you can deduce its individual events. If I told you that it is about the same kind of task as if you had been given the final sum of a long row of numbers, nothing but the sum, and you had to analyse it into its individual components, you would consider it to be quite hopeless. Yes, it is difficult, but not hopeless; for you must realize that in its inner character a four that has arisen from adding up two twos is not the same as a four that has arisen from the adding up of four ones, or of three and one."

He was sitting all hunched up, the points of his vertebrae sticking out like a bristling crest. "Dreadful," he groaned, "it was dreadful, that unconsciousness, and fever. Think of it, the more I concentrated on him, the more I became faint and delirious. That is, not me, I was awake, but I felt that unconsciousness and fever—in myself. Understand I must find it in myself, otherwise —otherwise it would not be, and I could not find out——" He shuddered, and his face was haggard with suffering, it was painful to watch him. "To make your way through that frightful unconsciousness, through that confused physical delirium in which bodily pains float like broken bits of ice—and at the same time to have always, always that supremely, definite, urgent, crushing feeling of the complete form of that life." He pressed his closed fists to his temples, his eyes were staring out, and he moaned: "Oh God, oh God, that was like going mad."

The specialist cleared his throat, and fished from his pocket a box of malted toffee. "Here you are, little man, have one," he mumbled. It was a special treat that was only given to a few, in fact, only to specially serious patients with perfect clinical symptoms.

CHAPTER XIII

THE clairvoyant brightened up, sucked the sweet, and settled down comfortably with crossed legs like a Turk, or a tailor. "I shall describe it to you in another way," he said, "but I warn you that even then it will be only a picture. When you strike a tuning-fork to give note A, the A string of a violin, or of a piano, also gives out a note, and everything begins to vibrate, even if it is inaudible to us, if it can vibrate at the A pitch. In much the same way we resound, we sing as we listen; and the musically receptive are those who know better how to listen to themselves. Think of life as of some sort of resounding, that a man resounds, that his mind, memory, and subconscious self are resounding; and his past, too, is also vibrating at this and at any other moment; it is a tremendously complex and infinitely multiple sound, in which the past is also present in an eternal progressive pianissimo, and it gives the dominant and minor notes; the whole past colours the sound of the present. Realize that also in us through transference from outside the same waves begin to vibrate, at any rate to the extent that we are in some kind of relation with the man who is transmitting into space his number of periods—like every one of us, every one of us; this resonance is weaker or stronger depending on our tuning, our sensitiveness, and alertness, and on the intensity of the particular relation. That resonance may be so weak and indistinct that we do not perceive it; or it may be so deep and strong that we hear nothing but it, nothing but the vibration that is transmitted to us. But even if we are not conscious of the response we are conscious of its emotional echo in our sympathies and antipathies, in the vague and inexplicable reactions with which we instinctively respond to people otherwise unknown to us."

The clairvoyant felt obviously pleased, and sucked energetically at his sweet, smacking his lips and gasping like a baby at the breast. "Yes, it is like that," he added with emphasis as if for himself. "We must listen to ourselves; we must perfect our own inner being so as to discern that silent and multiple message that some other person is sending out. There is no other second sight but to watch oneself; what is called telepathy is not reception from a distance, but from close at hand, the very shortest distance, and the most difficult to attain—from one's self. Just imagine that all at the same time you brought into action all the pipes, registers, and pedals of an organ, it would make a tremendous noise, but one in which you could recognize the breath, scope, strength, and perfection of that instrument. You would not be able by any kind of analysis to find out what had been played on that organ before, for (at least to your ears) the organ would have no memory to colour the sound. That first, that inarticulate resonance with which we respond to the life frequency of someone else, is also above all things the feeling of scope, life's space, strength, and nobility . . . a feeling of an absolutely definite and unique space formation, in which that life has evolved with its own particular atmosphere, and perspective——" The clairvoyant grew somewhat confused. "So you see what I am mixing up together: the organ and perspective, sight and hearing. It is frightfully difficult to express these things. Our words are the substitutes of sensations, they are derived from seeing, hearing, and touching; it is impossible to express with them ideas that are not accessible to these senses. Do be patient with me, gentlemen."

"It doesn't matter," said the specialist encouragingly. "This mixing of images, and interchange of the senses is a typical characteristic of certain mental disorders, akin to hallucinations. Go on, it gives a proper clinical picture."

"It is characteristic," the clairvoyant continued, "that through analysis of this complete sensation you get a picture of life completely different from what experience gives you. Experience synthesizes life out of individual moments; minutes and hours make up a day, days a year, hours and days are the masonry of life. A man is composed of his experiences, feelings, qualities, acts, and manifestations. Everything is made for us out of small pieces, which together give us something like a whole; but if we want to imagine this whole in some way or other we can only bring into present consciousness a bigger or smaller series of these pieces, only a sequence of episodes, only a pile of details. Let us say you," he turned suddenly to the specialist, "you are a widower, aren't you? Think of your late wife, whom you loved dearly, and with whom you lived for a quarter of a century in devotion and harmony, and I will enumerate the parts of her life that float up into your mind: her death; her great struggle, over which you stuck fast, helpless, cursing your science; her habit of cutting pages of books with a needle, against which you fought in vain; the day when you first met her; a happy day when you were together somewhere picking up shells by the sea."

"That was in Rimini," said the old gentleman softly, making a motion with his hand. "She was a good wife."

"She was. But if you tried to remember for hours nothing would come in your mind but a broken series of more and more episodes, a couple of phrases, a couple of tiny pictures—That's all. That is how your imagination views the whole life of some person nearest to you."

The old specialist removed his glasses, and cleaned them carefully; the surgeon made a strenuous effort to convey some sign to the clairvoyant with his eyes. "I say, not there, not there, turn round and follow another line."

"Yes," said the clairvoyant obediently turning, and driving at full speed in another direction. "Experience cannot give us another impression; we never comprehend through our senses a whole man, or a whole life, but only those discontinuous pieces and moments, and yet, thank God, we lose most of them. Vain glory, from that you cannot create, or work out the totality of life. But turn it round, I say, turn it round, Try to begin, begin logically, at the conception of a condensed and complete life, undivided into past and present. That's grand," he began to shout, and he almost tore his hair with enthusiasm. "If you imagine a river, a complete river, not as a meandering line on the map, but concisely, and completely, with all the water which ever flowed between its banks, your image will comprise the flowing river and the sea, all the seas of the world, the clouds, the snow, and the water vapour, the breath of the dead, and the rainbow in the sky, all that, the whole circulation of all the water in the world will be that river. How fine it is," he sobbed in ecstasy. "What a magnitude of reality it has! How beautiful and overwhelming it is to capture the conception of life, the sensation of life, the feeling of a man in his totality, and life's greatness! No, no, no," he waved his finger held erect, "you don't break that magnitude down into days and hours, or tear it into the litter of reminiscences; but you analyse it into essentials, into periods arching like vaults, into sequences which form the order of one's life; there is no chance, everything is determined, awesome, and beautiful, all causality appears in the simultaneity of cause and effect. There are no qualities, no events; only moulding forces," he gasped, "the interplay of which, and equilibrium, have determined the space of man."

There were flecks of foam in the corners of his mouth, he was terrible to look at as he grew gaunt with excitement. "Well, well," growled the specialist, taking out his watch. "And now, my little friend, lie down for five minutes and keep your chops shut. Close your eyes and breathe deeply and slowly."

CHAPTER XIV

THE clairvoyant opened his eyes, and breathed deeply. "Can I say something more? It's true that these things get on one's nerves." He rubbed his face. "Well, then, with regard to that man who fell from the sky—What shall I call him?"

"We call him Case X," observed the surgeon.

The clairvoyant sat up. "Case X, yes. If you are expecting me to tell you his name, who he really is, and what place he comes from, I must tell you in advance that I don't know. These are details which do not matter very much. For most of his life he didn't stick to what from time to time was his occupation. I have a feeling of tremendous life dimensions; in that man there is much space, much sea, but he was not a traveller. Understand that the life space of a traveller is measurable; but here—an objective is lacking here; there is no fixed point from which it would be possible to fix distances and directions."

The clairvoyant halted, silent and dissatisfied. "No, no, I must begin in a different way. In fact, I ought to begin with his death which is yet to be, and proceed backwards like a man spinning a rope. The life of Caesar began when a Caesar was born, and not a baby wrinkled and crying. We ought to begin at the last breath of the man to understand what was his life form, and what meaning pertains to anything he has experienced. Only with death is the youth and birth of a man complete." He shook his head. "But I can't, can't. How wretched is our conception in time!"

"For instance," he began again after a time. "If I tell you that he did not know his mother, it sounds like the beginning of a chronicle. But for me it was not a beginning but the end of a long strenuous line further back. He lies unconscious, and knows nothing any longer; but even under this unconsciousness, at the bottom of that darkness—deep, deep in him is solitude, and over his unconsciousness no one's shadow is falling. Where, and from what does this inner solitude continually spring? You must go back to the very beginning of things, back through the whole of his life to the source of his loneliness. He was the only child, and he did not know his mother. There was never a hand of which he could take hold, nobody said to him: 'That's nothing, I shall kiss it, and the pain's already gone.' Strange how this was missing in his life. The voice that assured him: 'That's nothing, that will pass; don't cry, don't fret about, go on playing. Here's my hand, hold it fast.' There never was a hand like that; and therefore never, understand, never could he clasp——" The clairvoyant made a helpless movement. "He was strong, but not patient. He had nothing to hold on to."

"Solitude," he said afterwards. "He sought out solitude so that there should not be such a discrepancy between himself and his surroundings. He tried to melt his inner destitution like a piece of ice in the immense solitude of the sea, or of foreign countries. He always had to forsake something to give an outward reason for his destination. Everywhere and always it was going on with him——" He frowned. "And where was the family? Why didn't his father make up for the mother's hand? We shall have to ask him about that. We must try to find out what was so irritable and touchy in him. He did not get on with people, and at once he sought out means of coming into conflict with them; he always had a feeling that he must defend himself, all the time he was up in arms. To turn back. To turn back to the child that had no mother, and who towards his father maintained a fierce and silent antagonism. The two could not understand each other. The widower wanted to wield the power and influence of two, he duplicated his authority, and overdid it in a petty and touchy manner with pedantic fussiness; inevitably the child became obstinate, and opposition grew in him like a permanent moral kink. For the whole of his life he has not been able to get rid of that conflict with society, order, discipline, constraint, and such like; until the time of his death he has continued to oppose his father." The clairvoyant was fretful and talked with clenched fists as if that relentless fight were taking place inside him. "Strange how these two opposite forces—loneliness, antagonism—have contended with each other during the whole life of this man. Solitude effaced the conflict, the conflict effaced the solitude; neither one nor the other ever attained fulfilment; with all his solitude he never became a hermit, he gained no victory from all his encounters and excitements; for always the feeling of loneliness overcame him. He was melancholy and quarrelsome, violent and perplexed; you might say inconsistent, but this inconstancy was an emotional balance of two forces set against each other.

Add together all that falls on the side that I have called solitude. Dreaming and desire for rest, resignation, indifference, lack of will, laziness and melancholy, aimlessness, passivity and dullness, enervation, yes. And now on the side of conflict: discontent, enterprise, a feverish and inventive spirit, vanity, obstinacy and pig-headedness, waywardness, acerbity, and so on. When you are building up a man out of qualities, well, put these two sides together somehow! A man may be either lazy or enterprising, or perhaps partly both, alternately one and the other, isn't that so? You can never understand a man if you keep on describing his qualities. It is not the qualities, it is the forces, forces which oppose each other, upset and check; and the man himself, living only in the present, is not aware that the small action which he is performing is the resultant of forces which run like lightning through the whole of his life, amounting to the tension between birth and death.

Imagine a man who wanders from place to place, from island to island, where God allows and chance directs; he does so out of laziness, and indolence, aimlessly seeking solitude and a refuge for his hazy dreams. But he could do the same from impatience, stamping his foot like a stallion in the stall; just to be somewhere else, try something else, and again let it drop and dash along after another goal. This map and the other may coincide exactly; but they are two different worlds, two different universes; different is the world of a man who fells trees, builds huts, and founds plantations from that of the loafer who gapes into the crowns of the trees, experiencing the delight and the nostalgia of his solitude. And I, who have been tracing backwards the footsteps of Case X, have found two worlds which do not resemble each other; they only come in like episodes in a dream. Through the one world, through the world in which one is busy building and getting into shape, the face of the other gazed at me, a sad and weak face which had discovered the vanity of all things; and again through it the first face forced its way in which one shouts, hurries and builds, argues and plans, God knows why, the devil knows what, and for what purpose. That—that was not reality," sighed the clairvoyant, "that was a nightmare, that was a grin; one reality a man can experience, but two he can only dream; and he who wanders through two worlds at the same time has no foundation under his feet, and he falls through a void in which there is nothing by which to measure his fall; for the stars fall too when a man is falling. Listen," he burst out, "that man was not quite real, and he lived most of his life in a dream."

CHAPTER XV

THE clairvoyant was silent, looking disconcerted and squinting at the tips of his fingers.

"Where did he live?" asked the surgeon.

"The tropics," mumbled the clairvoyant. "Islands. A dark brown feeling, something like roast coffee, asphalt, vanilla, or negroes' skin."

"Where was he born?"

"Here, somewhere here," indicated the clairvoyant indefinitely. "With us, in Europe."

"And what was he?"

"Surveyor, no? A man who shouts at people." He knitted his brows as if he were thinking. "But originally he was a chemist."

"Where?"

"In a sugar factory, of course," said the clairvoyant, as if it upset him to be asked something so obvious. "That's in keeping, isn't it? Those two incongruous worlds. In winter the campaign, bustle, shouting—and in summer, silence, the factory idle, and only in the laboratory a man working. Or dreaming." With his finger he drew a hexagon in the air. "You know, of course, how formulae are written in chemistry? Like a hexagonal figure, from the corners of which letters are sticking out. Or like lines which form a cross with branches——"

"Those are structural formulae," explained the specialist. "It is called stereochemistry. Those diagrams you know represent the arrangement of the atoms in the molecules."

The clairvoyant nodded with almost nothing but his nose. Yes. Imagine that those diagrams of his make a kind of network. He looks into the air to see how they combine and intercept, fit on to the next, and even intercross. He scribbles it down on paper, and breaks into a fury when anyone disturbs him. Not in winter, in winter it is activity, bustle, and impatience; but in summer—

in a factory laboratory like that, with a roasting sun, and a sugary smell like candy. Here he sits with an open mouth and gapes into the void at those diagrams; they look like a honeycomb in which one diagram links up with another to make a single system. But it's not in a plane, it's in a space of three, four dimensions; all the time it eludes him when he tries to draw it on a flat piece of paper. And the heat—even the buzzing of a fly can be heard against the window-pane.

The clairvoyant blinked thoughtfully with his head bent to one side. "That isn't just one moment, it's weeks and months—I don't know how many years. All the time he is constructing that chemical space made up of formulae, which become complete and link up with each other. They are no longer real known compounds, but possible and imaginary; non-existent and new combinations to fill up the empty gaps in chemical space; new and unknown isomers and polymers," he burst out uncertainly, "polymerization and multivalency, which lead him on to unsuspected combinations of atoms. He dreams of those imaginary compounds and their possible properties. They are drugs, rainbow colours, unknown scents, explosives, materials with which the face of the world might be changed. He covers one notebook after the other with formulae of aromatic compounds, acids, polysaccharides, and salts, which so far do not exist, but which will take their place in that crystallized space of chemical formulae. The longer he works the more he is led to believe that it is possible to imagine and work out unknown molecules of compounds, just as Mendeléeff worked out unknown atoms of elements. At the same time he is moved with pleasure because he is discrediting and breaking down current scientific ideas—always that motive of conflict and revolt. He begins on laboratory experiments with this or that supposed combination of matter; but the experiments are not successful, the factory laboratory is not sufficient for them. He chooses one or two formulae which seem to him quite obvious, they only need to be put into effect, and he travels in search of the international luminary of chemical science to present them to him, and to persuade that arch-priest that they deserve an exhaustive experimental trial."

The clairvoyant shrugged his angular shoulders. "Of course, it was shattering. In a few words the luminary of science reduced the suppositions of the young chemist to smithereens. Nonsense, impossible. Evidently you haven't seen the work of so-and-so, read this and that. And at the end a rare benignity: Besides, you can stay with me; I'll find some sort of a job for you, perhaps trim the lamps, or watch the filters. If you are patient, and when you have learned to work scientifically . . . Only Case X was not patient, and didn't want to learn to work scientifically; he went away stammering, and fled from the ruins of his chemical space in such a panic that—that he didn't halt till on the edge of the shadows, where good-naturedly and unscientifically the broad teeth of negroes glistened at him."

The clairvoyant raised his finger. "To make it quite clear: that scientific bonze did the right and honest thing, for he defended science against an intruder. He would have been willing to accept a verified fact, but on principle he rejected a hypothesis which at the beginning would create more disorder and uncertainty than anything else. He had to crush Case X; in the totality of life, things you know, don't occur accidentally and at random, but are directed by necessity."

It was clear that the surgeon was becoming afraid that the clairvoyant was turning again to abstract things, and therefore he hurriedly inquired: "Then he wasn't a chemist any longer?"

"No, he wasn't a chemist any longer. There was no voice in him to tell him: 'That's nothing, that will pass, go on playing.' Each of his shipwrecks was final and couldn't be undone. When with a few words his chemical edifice collapsed, that innate feeling of solitude and destitution welled up in him with great force—understand, almost a satisfaction that it was in such ruins, such dreadful rubble. He put away his notebooks without looking at them again, and went away even from the sugar factory to make the mess greater; he himself was almost horrified by that feeling of vanity and nothingness, and still more because he really felt at home in that debacle, and he took to flight."

"He was a young man," objected the surgeon. "Well, was there nobody——"

"There was."

"A girl, was it?"

"Yes."

"Did he like her?"

"He did."

There was silence. The clairvoyant, clasping his knees, kept his eyes down, and breathed through his teeth. "Surely I needn't tell you everything," he said in a thin voice at last. "I am no chronicler. For it's certain that in his love there was solitude, and obstinacy, and he certainly destroyed her as he destroyed everything—out of sheer obstinacy, and because he was going into solitude. What devastation! Now he can sit down and see how everything can be reduced to bits. As a child he used to crawl into the lumber-room; nobody found him there, he was alone, and his obstinacy melted in his solitude. Always the same manuscript of life." He outlined something in the air. "Obstinacy moved him and solitude released him. He would have liked to lie quiet, but revolt pricked him. Out of obstinacy he would have liked to stay settled, but solitude asked him what was the good, what was the good. It was only left for him to wander."

The clairvoyant raised his head. "Perhaps he was a chemist full of genius. Perhaps his ideas would have upset the world. But do you imagine that a man of his upbringing had the patience step by step, experiment by experiment, at the price of lousy mistakes and failures, scientifically to ferret out and verify his system of chemical ordinates? He stood at the threshold of something big, but the scientific drudgery that would have taken him an inch further terrified him. He was to be broken. That was his inner destiny, in fact something like a flight from a task which was beyond his strength. If he had remained a chemist, he would also have only wandered from one thing to another among experiments and phantasies, without an aim, losing himself in a space too large for him. He had to wander over the seas and islands so that the deep restlessness of his spirit was represented by it. You," he said, stabbing at the specialist with his finger, "you spoke of the interchange of ideas. You must realize that there is also a transference of fate, and that sometimes external events stand for a far deeper theme that is written inside us."

CHAPTER XVI

THE clairvoyant reached for a cigarette; the surgeon held up the burner and offered him a light. "Muchissimas gracias," mumbled the clairvoyant, bowing deeply; he didn't notice that the surgeon was watching the reaction of his pupils. "Strange," he said, sputtering away the shreds of tobacco. "Strange, how his surroundings stick to a man, well, what is called the outer world. Outside surroundings relate to his inner self much more strongly than as a sum of agents which condition his actions. Rather," he said hesitatingly, "as if these surroundings were flowing out from his inner self, or were conditioned by his life; as if they were simply . . . an unwinding of the fate that is in him. Yes, right, it is like that, if we take the life of a man as a whole, and not as a series of episodes."

"Let's take . . . Case X. An impression of unusual space; in him there is much sea, and many places—understand, purely extensively and numerically, a large amount of solitude, departures, and of that restlessness which mirrors itself in flitting from place to place. A man whose soul is complex lives in a complex and strange *milieu*. That factory laboratory, scorched by the sun, in which he wandered among his diagrams and visions, was a premonition of the scorching countries in which he was to wander, accompanied by the scent of roasted sugar. Where was he? I have a perfectly definite impression, peculiar and olfactory. Heat trembling over a brown field, a deep, eternal buzzing, cracking sound, gutteral bubbling, and shrieks like laughter, and vomiting. Countries made of lethargy, and feverish excitement. And always the sea, the sea, restless and phosphorescent; ships smelling of hot wood, tar, and chocolate. Guadeloupe, Haiti, and Trinidad."

"What do you say?" burst out the surgeon.

"What?" asked the clairvoyant distractedly.

"You said Guadeloupe, Haiti, and Trinidad."

"I?" exclaimed the clairvoyant. "I hardly know, I wasn't thinking of any names." He knitted his brows. "Strange that I said that. Hasn't it ever happened to you that you have become conscious of something only by saying it? It must be like that. Cuba, Jamaica, Haiti, Porto Rico," he enumerated like a schoolboy. "Martinque, Barbados, the Antilles, and B-Bahama Islands," he ran on happily with relief. "God, for how many years haven't I recalled those names," he rejoiced. "I used to like so much those exotic words. Antilles, antelopes, mantillas——" Suddenly he stopped, "Mantillas, mantillas, wait—Spanish ladies, Cuba. He must have been some time in Cuba," he gasped. "I've a kind of . . . Spanish feeling, I don't know how to express it; it's like a romance."

"A moment ago you said muchissimas gracias," reminded the surgeon.

"Did I? I was hardly aware." He glanced thoughtfully sideways. "You see, that also gives space . . . such a strange spaciousness. On one side those old Spanish families, aristocracy, sir, a world to itself, tradition and respectability, mantillas and crinolines; or American naval officers—how these worlds clash. How many races and riff-raff . . . down to those negroes in the clearing who tear to pieces a live chicken with their teeth, voodoo, voodoo—the bellowing and flopping of the mating frogs; the clatter of the wooden mill crushing the sugar-cane; the shrieks and guffaws of the mulattos kicking with their legs in the clasp of lust; teeth and shiny bodies—what a heat, what a heat," he murmured, soaking with sweat so much that his limp pyjamas stuck to his back. "The drone of a moth which crackles as it flies into the fire. And overhead the Southern Cross like a chemical formula, and thousands of starry constellations which outline in the sky the formulae of unknown and strongly smelling compounds."

"And again," he waved with his erect finger, "it was beyond him, and in him at the same time: laziness and hypertrophy—a blind creative force, and that drowsy lethargy, two fevers, a fire dying and fecund. In him, in him, everything was in him.

Again those frogs which mate together out of infinite boredom, a wooden mill of routine, animals roaring, bare fleet flopping in the dark in search of vain and sweaty satisfaction—and terribly flaming stars, and the man in the universe pinned down to the earth like a mounted beetle; and again the ship tossing at anchor, and rocking sluggishly in the slimy water of the harbour, an impatient desire to run away from those frogs, and from that mill; the feeling that everything ought to be different, but that it is not worth while. Pieces of the world, or lumps of the soul; there's no difference. It's all the same."

"He was alcoholic, wasn't he?" asked the specialist. "A heavy drinker, wasn't he?"

"How do we know," said the clairvoyant vaguely, "whether a man drinks out of solitude or out of obstinacy? What is he loosening and melting in him: the ice of destitution or a little ill-tempered, jumping flame? You're right, he had gone to pieces very much; he could have been a powerful gentleman with fat lips, instead of rolling about swollen with rum, or dried up with fever like that. Why didn't he provide himself with a ball of gold which would have tied him to one place? Property makes a man settled and cautious. He could have been rich and afraid of death."

"Nothing else?" asked the surgeon after a moment's silence.

The clairvoyant grinned. "You would like me to invent something, wouldn't you? A beautiful creole for him to fall in love with. Some erotic adventure in which his life would be at stake. Wild animals, and tornadoes. Interesting events in an active life. I'm sorry," he jeered, "but events aren't in my line; I look at life in its totality, and I can't provide you with chequered life stories." He seemed annoyed as if he had lost the thread. "I know," he mumbled, "you're interested in that scar on his leg. It was nothing, only an accident; he had no passion for hunting, and he didn't look for excitement in danger." He knitted his brows and swayed with the strain of remembering. "He fell foul of a wild beast that others were hunting," he burst out at last, glad that it was over. "It's true, he went through a lot; but that was because at first he was impatient and irritable; that is, he was prone to encounter situations that don't occur to people of a quiet disposition. Later on he became lazy, and dull, and without caring for it, wealth began to cling to him, his outward restlessness was succeeded by a drowsy and misguided kink in his mind. Most of the time he lay in his room, his mouth half open with the heat, listening to the buzzing of the flies against the mosquito netting; for hours at a time, for whole days he gaped at the ceiling, and at the wall stuck over with patterned wallpaper. It was covered with hexagonal pictures, like a honeycomb, and he put up with them without thought and without motion."

CHAPTER XVII

"STRANGE," exclaimed the clairvoyant, "how his life was closing in and becoming almost reconciled in that feeling of solitude. Apparently in his childhood he had been surrounded by walls covered with the same or a similar kind of design, and even then there was a feeling of solitude in him. If he had cried openly the nurse would have gone to ask what was the matter with him; but now it was an old negress with long breasts flapping like shiny plaice.

All his life might be only a dream amidst those regular diagrams; who knows how long a dream lasts, perhaps a second, perhaps an hour. All other things, in fact, only came to disturb that ingrained solitude of a lonely child: his father's reprimands, school, youth, the sugar factory, and his wanderings, Lord, that futile wandering! Some huge bug with orange and green dots running over the patterned wallpaper, not in a straight line as if it wished to get anywhere, but here there, here there, always stopping for a moment, and then off again somewhere else; he gazed at it for hours, too lazy to get up and throw it out. And then, yes, still that irritated buzzing of the fly hitting its head against the mosquito netting. That was everything; but what came from outside, the gabble of the negroes, the clacking of the mill, the dry rustling of the palm-trees, the rustle of the sheaves of sugar-cane, cracking in the heat of the sun, a thousand voices and murmurs, all that was nothing, only so much phantasy: he could half-close his eyes and listen to it flowing away into nothingness.

In that lethargy a scrap of a paper or a copy of a journal fell into his hands, the journal of some professional publication, or something like that; he turned over the pages without interest, and halted at a hexagonal diagram from the corners of which rays ran out with symbols of atoms. How about it, how about it, it was a very long time since such-like things had interested him. But the pictures on the wall changed into chemical formulae, they seemed to grin at him, again he took the bit of paper in his hand, and studied that diagram with contracted eyebrows, spelled out the letters, and struggled through the erudite text. Suddenly he sat up, sprang up, ran about in the room, and beat his head. Yes, yes, surely it was that very diagram, that damned chemical formula, with which more than twenty years ago, yes, Christ, what a long time, what a long time! with which he had gone to the arch-priest of chemistry, and, sir, if you gave permission for work in your laboratory—on a bigger scale—with this supposed compound. He raised his bristly eyebrows—what long hair; nonsense, impossible. Apparently you haven't heard of this and that authority, you haven't read this and that work: ages ago I showed scientifically that the benzole group, and so on. Case X ran round the room, and snorted excitedly. And here it's in black and white, signed by some American, of course; and unsuspected industrial possibilities, he says—Case X halted as if rooted to the ground. And that was only one link of a chain of possibilities, one stone in the vault; that formula would link up with another like the cells of a honeycomb in accordance with geometrical laws. And they don't know that, Case X sniggered, they haven't got to that; but it's written down, everything set out, and written down in those notebooks, put away in a box, in a lumber-room. With them are broken toys, and clothes from mother. Perhaps termites have already destroyed everything. No, there are no white ants there; everything is just as it was . . ."

The clairvoyant, sitting on the bed, began to sway with his body. "He sat on the bed, swaying to and fro, strenuously recalling what those formulae were like, and how they fitted together. But his mind was unbalanced through heavy drinking and indolence, flight and solitude; he beat at that learned paper with his fist as if he wanted to force it into compliance, but what could he do, what could he do with that dull and thick head. Instead of chemical formulae, the Southern Cross, Eridanus, Centaur, and Hydra stole into his mind. He still tried to brush it all away, but it weighed on him like a numb and dreadful strain; and suddenly it came—like a flash; I will go home and find those notebooks. It was as if everything fell away from him, such a peculiar and immense relaxation. Then he got up, opened the window for a fly which was buzzing madly and in desperation against the net, he also set free the bug helplessly wandering over the wall."

The clairvoyant with his head to one side seemed to enjoy the taste of this picture. "It's strange," he observed, "that it's possible to explain the same event in two entirely different and at the same time correct ways. If Case X decided so precipitously to return, you would say, and so would he: it was so, that they would not steal his spiritual property. He began to be terribly anxious about his notebooks when he realized that they might be of some value. Certainly it would be possible to draw from it a considerable sum of money—even that side of the business was of some interest to Case X, who was no longer a young fellow. But chiefly there was the motive that it was HIS business, that strong accent on the *I* which none of us men escapes. We defend OUR possessions, OUR rights, OUR work so instinctively and ferociously as if we were defending our own life.

"But on the other side," said the clairvoyant, bending his head over the other shoulder as if to gain a favourable point of view, "these are immediate or actual motives, I should say, mere pretexts on which an act or a decision could be arrived at. If we view Case X in the light of the totality of his life, the matter is different. Not only was the matter of his spiritual property at stake, but something bigger and more difficult; duty which he ran away from once by letting himself be defeated. He violated the task he wasn't equal to, and he let it slip out of his hands; from that time on he lived an odd, stray life that was not his own; one might say that he ran off his proper track. Yes, one may call it his tragic error, and it really was an error, even although he could not have acted differently. And then he returned—or was by his inner guidance turned back to the way which he had lost because he had not the patience and consistency to go on with it. He was returning, a man physically ruined, infected with the canker of lassitude, but mature. Then at last he realized the dreadful and inexorable constraint of life, for he felt it his duty to die. The circle was closing in, and necessity was being fulfilled."

"So he did want to come back?" reminded the surgeon after a while.

"Yes, but first he had to do this and that: to sell the property and suchlike things. The more those outside obstacles became involved the more violently his impatience accumulated; through the days of delay his haste almost became an affliction; he was beyond himself with the fury of return, every minute was for him a nagging torment; at last he disentangled and tore away everything, and back he dashed to where he had come from."

"By boat?" asked the surgeon.

"... I don't know. But if he had been borne by a ray of light, even that would have been intolerably slow for him, and he would have pressed his nails into his palms with insane impatience. Certainly his return was violent and infinite like a headlong fall."

"I looked at the map," observed the surgeon. "He might have come via Florida, Europe, or via Natal, Dakar, Europe. But wasn't it chance that he should have found an aeroplane ready!"

"Chance," mumbled the clairvoyant. "There is no such thing as chance. It was predestined that he should travel with such fury. He left behind a fiery trail like a meteor."

"And ... why did he crash?"

"He was at home then." The clairvoyant raised his eyes. "Understand, he had to crash. He could not do anything more. It was enough that he had come back."

CHAPTER XVIII

WHAT could be done, what could be done when his heart weakened; it beat quicker, always quicker, but his blood-pressure fell; how soon would that tattered heart stop with a faint hiccup? The end of Case X. Who put that nosegay by his bed?

"There's a new kind of serum for yellow fever, they say," the famous specialist was heard to say. "But where could we get it here, eh? Besides, he'll die of heart-failure, even God can't help him with that."

The nurse crossed herself.

"That clairvoyant of yours," went on the old coryphe, sitting on the edge of the bed, "that's a nice neurotic. But how he described the interconnection of those solitary and excited periods was quite interesting. It would correspond to the periodic succession of depression and excitation in a badly balanced man. That explains sufficiently well the story of Case X."

"As much as we know," said the surgeon, shrugging his shoulders.

"Something surely, my friend," said the specialist. "That body says a lot. For instance, that he was down there a long time, but that he was not born there; he caught any tropical disease that was going, *ergo* he was not acclimatized. I ask you, why did he run away to such lost places?"

"I don't know," muttered the surgeon. "I'm not a clairvoyant."

"Nor am I, but I'm a doctor," said the old gentleman with meaning.

"Look here, he was periodically neurotic, a dual personality, easily succumbing to fits of depression."

"That's what that clairvoyant explained to you," grinned the surgeon.

"Of course, but patellar reflexes also say something. Hum, what did I want to say?—Yes, a cyclothymic like that easily gets into conflict with his surroundings, or his employment, weariness comes over him, he lets everything go, and runs away. If he were physically weaker he might submit passively; but that chap was so physically developed—you've noticed that, haven't you?"

"Of course."

"His reactions must have been abnormally violent, almost throwing him off his line. As a doctor I ought not to say so, but physical weakness with many people is something like wise and gentle fetters; instinctively they put a brake on their reactions because they are afraid not to crack up. This one had no need to be careful with himself; and so he was not afraid of such a jump. As far as West Indies, what?"

"Via service in the navy," reminded the surgeon.

"That also shows a roving disposition, doesn't it. As you were good enough to remark, it is a body of an educated man; that Case X was not born a tramp, and if he became a sailor or an adventurer, it reveals the damnable cleavage in his life. What sort of a conflict was it? It's all the same; whether it was of one kind or another, it was conditioned simply by his constitution."

The specialist leaned over the sphygmometer fastened to the arm of the unconscious man. "It's bad," he sighed, "he's sinking; he won't last much longer." He rubbed his nose, and watched with regret the faint and irregular breathing of that immovable body. "Down there," he said, "I should think that there are quite good doctors, those in colonial service; I wonder why they let him be gnawed through with framboesia. He must have lived in some place where doctors were too far away; perhaps some negro magician on Haiti, or somewhere, rubbed some stuff on it for him. That was no civilized life. Oh dear." He blew into his handkerchief, and carefully rubbed it. "A life story. You can read many queer things." The old gentleman nodded his head thoughtfully. "And he drank, he must have drowned his wits in drink. Think of it in that climate, in that feverish and stewy heat—that was not even being alive, it was half-unconsciousness, deception, wandering away from reality——"

"What interests me most," said the surgeon suddenly becoming unusually communicative, "is why he was coming back—why he was coming back in such a dreadful hurry. First, that—that he flew in such a storm as if he couldn't wait. And then that he came back with yellow fever. Four or five days before the crash he must have been somewhere in the tropics, isn't that so? That means that he had . . . I don't know; apparently from one aeroplane to another—it's queer. I'm always wondering what a tremendously strong motive he must have had to come back with such a rush. And bang, in that flight he got killed."

The specialist raised his head. "Listen . . . he'd got to die all the same. Even if he hadn't crashed. . . . It was very nearly the end with him already."

"Why?"

"Sugar, liver—and especially the heart. There was nothing to be done. Eh, my friend, it wasn't so easy to come back. Too long a journey." The old gentleman raised himself. "Take that sphygmometer off him, sister. Well, he came back, and now he's nearly home. He's not wandering any further, he knows the way—isn't it true, my lad?"

"Dear Doctor,

When you have a free moment, read these few pages that I enclose. I want to explain that they are about the man who fell from the sky, and whom you in the hospital called Case X. You advised me not to think of him any more; I didn't obey, and the result is these pages. If he'd had his name on the report sheet over his head, or if anyone had known the slightest bit about him, it would probably not have occurred to me to think about him; but his fatal incognito would not let me rest. This shows you how accidental and casual are the causes which excite our minds.

From that moment I have been thinking of him, this in literary language means that I have been inventing a story about him, one of the thousand stories that I haven't written and shall not write. It is a bad habit to look at people and at things for possible stories. As soon as you open your mind to possibility, you are lost; you open, as they say, the door of your phantasy; nothing prevents you from inventing anything, for the sphere of possibility is inexhaustible, running from every face and event into infinity, with an agreeable and disturbing freedom. But look out, stop! As soon as you start on that line you discover that even by way of fiction you must travel with decision, examining the fitness of every step. Here we've got it! Now we have to split our heads deciding which possibility is possible and probable; we have to support it with our knowledge of facts and with reasons, we have to struggle with our own phantasy, nursing it so that it does not forsake that mysterious and proper path that is called truth. What folly to suck truth out of one's finger! what nonsense to invent people and stories, and then deal with them as if they were real! I will give you an axiom of metaphysical madness: that possibility which among all possibilities is the only one possible WOULD BE REALITY. See the fixed idea of men of fancy: to chase reality through the roundabout of phantoms. If you think that all we have to do is to manufacture illusions, you are mistaken; our mania is more monstrous: we attempt to achieve reality itself.

In short, for three whole days (also counting my sleep and dreams) I tried to create the reality of a life that I shamelessly invented from A to Z. I shall not write that story just as I have not written most of the others; but to get rid of it. Besides you more or less manufactured my hero out of calico and cotton-wool, and therefore I am returning him to you, not taking into account that you advised me to blow rainbow bubbles. This might have been very rainbowy; but they say that life is too serious for us to look at its flaming and changeable colours."

The surgeon was distrustfully counting the pages of the poet's manuscript when the door opened slightly; the sister of mercy appeared and made a silent motion with her head in the direction apparently of number six. The surgeon dropped the manuscript and ran. So it had come. He frowned a little, when he discovered the young, hairy assistant sitting on the side of Case X's bed (those people from the medical block are spreading themselves too much here), and holding in his fingers the wrist of the unconscious man. A very young, nice nurse (who also didn't belong to that department)—a novice very likely; she had eyes only for that hairy assistant's mane.

The surgeon wanted to say something not very pleasant, but the assistant, who hadn't noticed him, raised his head. "I can't feel his pulse. Bring the screen sister."

CHAPTER XIX

THE POET'S STORY

"Let us first recall the event that gave the impulse from which that further series of events was being developed; whether you like it or not, we must begin at this point if we are to construct our story.

On a hot, stormy day an aeroplane crashed; the pilot was burned to death, the passenger was gravely injured, and unconscious. You can't get away from the picture of the people who run together to that heap of ruins; they are excited because they are witnesses of a catastrophe, they ache with horror, giving advice one over the other as to what ought to be done; but bound with fear and squeamishness no one makes any effort to help the unconscious man. It is only when the police arrive that the heap of chaos begins to get straightened out; the police bark at the people, and send this one there, that one somewhere else; it's strange how, as a matter of course, unwillingly, but secretly glad, people obey orders with a sense of importance and relief. They run for firemen, for the doctor, to telephone for the ambulance, while the police write down the names of witnesses, and the crowd fidgets from one foot to the other in respectful silence, for it is present at an official act. I have never witnessed such a misfortune, but I am full of it, I am one of the onlookers myself, in heated agitation I run along the hedge, to be there as well, carefully avoiding some fields (for I am a country man), I am upset, I make suggestions, express my opinion that most probably the pilot hadn't switched off the engine, and that the fire ought to have been put out with sand; all these details I invent with an unsparing hand, in a disinterested manner, for they do not fit into this or any other story; I cannot even boast to my acquaintances that I saw a great accident. You haven't the slightest bit of phantasy; and so you said 'Poor fellow,' and in saying that the affair was settled for you (not taking into account what you did as a surgeon). What a proper and simple reaction, while I toss about with cruel and painful details which I imagine for myself. I often feel ashamed when I see you others react so simply and humanly to various incidents of life which for me are only themes round which to spin with my mulish cleverness. I don't know exactly whether in it there is an unruly playfulness, or, on the contrary, a strange and relentless thoroughness; (but to return to our case) I invested that man's fatal fall with so many pictures, horrible and grotesque, that out of shame and penitence, withdrawing contritely the gimcrack of all outside circumstance, in my story I should like to try to describe it as the fall of an archangel with broken wings. It's simpler with you; you say 'Poor fellow' as if making a holy mark on the scene of the disaster.

Perhaps this explanation strikes you as rather muddled. Phantasy for its own sake seems immoral and cruel, like a child; it indulges in horror and ridicule. How often have I led my fictitious beings along the paths of sorrow and humiliation so that I could pity them the more! Such are we, we creators of phantasy; to add glory or value to a man's life we interfere and bring in a portentous destiny, and we overburden him with trouble and adversity. But after all, doesn't it bring with it a special glory of its own? To show that he hasn't led a barren and empty life, a man nods his head and says: 'I've lived through a lot.' I say, doctor, let's share our tasks: you as becomes your profession, and out of love for the man, take away his pain, and heal his weaknesses; while I out of love for him, and as becomes my profession, will hedge him round with conflict and mortification, and poke about in his wounds without so much as a touch of Peru balsam. You stroke the scar which has beautifully and clearly healed, while I with amazement will probe the wound. In the end it may perhaps emerge that I also relieve suffering by explaining how it hurts.

I try to excuse literature for its pleasure in jeering and in dealing with tragedy. For both of these are detours that phantasy discovered by means of which, and along their unsubstantial paths, it created the illusion of reality. Reality in itself is neither tragic nor ridiculous; it is too serious and infinite for either the one or the other. Compassion and laughter are only shocks with which we accompany and comment upon the events around us. Evoke these actions by any sort of means, and you evoke the impression that beyond you something real had taken place, the more real it is the stronger is the emotional effect. My God, what tricks and dodges we invent, we professionals in phantasy, to agitate properly and mercilessly the encrusted soul of the reader! Dear doctor, in your honest and conscientious life there isn't much room for compassion and laughter. You don't wallow excitedly in the frightfulness of a man soaked in blood, but you wipe away the blood and do what is necessary. You take no pleasure in laughing at a man with soup on his clothes, but you advise him to get himself clean, at which the boisterous laughter of mankind is suppressed, and the event undone that gave rise to it. Well, we invent stories which you can't undo, against which you can do nothing, they are as irreparable and unchangeable as history. Throw away that book, or allow yourself to fall to the shocks that are set like snares for you, and look beyond them for the reality to which they correspond.

Here are some technical conclusions which can be drawn from the above explanation: If I proceed by way of phantasy I shall choose some striking and unusual event; like a butcher appraising a beast, I shall see if, as a sensation, it is duly plump and substantial. See, here we've got a crash, a dreadful headlong turmoil, at the sight of which you can't help but stop. Almighty God, what a hopeless heap of chaos it is! What can we make of these broken wings, and struts, how can we put it together so that it flies again, at least as a paper kite, whose string I can hold in my hand? At this one can only look, dithering with fright, or like a decent man say seriously and respectfully, 'Poor fellow.'"

CHAPTER XX

"ONE says of phantasy that it chops and changes; perhaps it does in some cases (which, however, aren't found in good prose), but far more frequently it runs smartly and attentively, like a dog with its nose on a fresh scent; she just gasps with eagerness, she tears along the line, and drags us here and there. You are a hunter, and you know that a setter on her zig-zag course doesn't run here and there, but on the contrary she sticks to the scent with sustained and passionate interest. I must tell you that well-developed phantasy is no uncertain dreaming, but an activity unusually relentless, and passionately determined; it is true that it halts and doubles, but only to make certain that that is not its prey. Where are you going you eager bitch; what are you after, what's the line of your aim? Aim, what an aim; I'm after something alive, and I don't know yet where I'm going to come across it.

Believe me, writing novels is more like hunting than, say, building a cathedral according to plans already drawn up. Until the very last moment we are continually surprised at what we come across; we get into unsuspected situations, but only because we are foolishly and persistently following that trail of ours of something alive. We are after a white stag, and while doing so, almost by accident, we discover new places in the world. To write is an adventure, and I shall say no more in praise of that occupation. We can't go astray so long as we are faithful to our trail; even if our pilgrimage leads to the Crystal Mountains, along the fiery track of a falling star, our direction is good, thank God, and we haven't lost the right way. (I'm not speaking here of our anxiety when we do lose the right scent; of our miserable and helpless attempts to get further; of our inglorious homecomings with that tired and ashamed cur crawling behind us, instead of running on ahead.)

By which in so many words is said: to the devil with phantasy;

it's no use to us, and it won't lead us even to the tips of our noses if her muscles are not quivering with the fever of interest. I say, let her lie down if she hasn't before. her already marked out an invisible trail, and if her tongue isn't hanging out with impatience to follow it to the end. What is called talent, is far the greater part interest or obsession, interest to follow something alive, the deer lost in the expanse of the world. Dear man, the world is wide, wider than our experience; it is made out of a handful of facts, and a whole universe of possibilities. Anything that we do not know of is a kind of possibility here, and every fact is a bead in the rosary of past and future eventualities. It's no use, if we follow a man we must enter that world of guess-work, we must scent out his possible steps, past and future; we must pursue him with our phantasy if he is to appear to us in his invisible aliveness. It is absolutely immaterial to us whether he has been completely invented, or is completely real; an Ariel or a hawker selling tape; both are spun out of the pure and infinite material of possibility, which is the depository of everything, even of what actually was. What is called a real story, or a real person, is for us no more than one possibility among a thousand, and perhaps not even the most consistent and important one. All reality is merely a casually opened page, or a word read at random in the sibylline books; and we desire to know more.

I am attempting to show you that if we are led by phantasy we cross a threshold into some sort of infinity; the threshold of a world not bounded by our experience, wider than our scraps of knowledge, and containing infinitely more than is known to us. I tell you that we should not dare to step into those limitless regions, if we did not blunder there blind and headlong in search of something that is eluding us. If the spirit of the tempter whispered to us: Now invent something, anything you like—we should feel embarrassed, and probably we should shrink back in terror at the vanity and senselessness of the task; we should be afraid to embark without aim and direction on that *Mare tenebrarum*. Let me put a question: What right has a man who does not want to be taken for a fool or an impostor to invent something that is non-existent? There is only one answer, luckily definite and certain: Let him, he must; he isn't doing so out of waywardness, he is being dragged into it, he dashes off after something, and his meandering course is the path of necessity. Ask not him, but God, what is necessity.

I am wondering why that man who fell from the sky got into my head; why not Ariel, or Hecuba? What is Hecuba to me! but it may happen to me that for a time she would be all for me that matters. I should fight with her until she would bless me like the angel blessed Jacob; and I might be given grace to find in myself the life and pain of an old despondent hag. God be with Hecuba; it is frivolous of me not to pay her more attention, but as I said I have on my mind a man who did not complete his flight. I think that you are to blame for that, for you said with that well-known cool manner of yours: Why the devil did he fly in such a wind? Yes, why the devil; why all the devils; why all the accursed did he fly in such a storm? What an overmastering and undeniable motive he must have had to undertake such a senseless flight! Isn't that something for meditation and wonder? Yes, it's a mere accident if a man gets killed; but it's not a mere accident if he flies in spite of everything. It's obvious that he HAD TO fly; and then over the ruins that looked nothing more than a broken toy, the huge edifice of an event arose made up of a mere accident and necessity. Necessity and mere accident, two legs of a tripod on which Pythia sits; the third is mystery.

You let me see him, the man without a face or a name, the man without consciousness; this is the last passport of life, and anyone who cannot prove his identity with it is Unknown in the severe and forbidding sense of the word. Hadn't you a tormenting feeling that we owe him his identity? I saw it in your eyes: to know who he was, and where he wanted to go in such a hurry; perhaps we might testify that he got as far as here, and so fulfil this human duty. I am not as human as you are; I did not think of his affairs of this world, I became obsessed with the passion of investigation. And now no one and nothing will detain me; fare you well, I must be after him. Since he is so unknown, I shall invent him, I shall search for him amongst his possibilities. You ask what business it is of mine? If only I knew! I only know that I became obsessed with it."

CHAPTER XXI

"I USED the phrase 'The passion of investigation,' and I feel that it is right; but that passion arose purely by accident, and through a circumstance so petty that I ought to feel ashamed of it. When they brought you that injured man you said that apparently his papers had been burnt, and that in his pockets there was nothing but a handful of small change, some French, English, and American money, and a Dutch dubbeltje. That collection of change surprised me; you may imagine that that man really had something to do in those different countries, and what was left in his pockets was the small change that he could not spend; but whenever I have travelled I have always tried in some way or other to get rid of all the small coins of the country which I was leaving, in the first place because I should no longer be able to change them, and secondly so that they wouldn't be in the way. It has occurred to me that that man was familiar with those currencies, and that he had lived in those regions where they are in circulation. And at the same time I said to myself: Antilles, Porto Rico, Martinque, Barbados, and Curaçao—American, British, Dutch, and French colonies with the currencies of their home lands.

If I try to explain psychologically that mental jump from the handful of money to the West Indies, I find in my memory the following:

1. A strong wind blew which reminded me of Orcan. Association with the Leeward Islands, and the famous Caribbean region of cyclones.

2. I was put out, discontented, furious with myself, and with my work. Wandering images arose in my mind, and a desire for escape. Nostalgia for far-off and exotic countries; with me usually for Cuba, the island of my nostalgia.

3. An overwhelming and rather envious notion, that that man had flown from somewhere a long way off; an auto-

matic connection of the present event with the previous disposition.

4. At last that event itself, that flying accident, an exciting and almost agreeable sensation, and at the same time the tendency to adorn it with romantic conjectures. It is a typical example, showing how strongly human catastrophies direct the course of our phantasy.

By means of all that the conjecture (as I realize now very superficial), arose in me that that handful of money pointed to the West Indies; just then I was almost enthusiastic about my perspicacity, and I felt that it was as clear as daylight that that man was coming straight from the Antilles; it satisfied and excited me greatly. When you took me to the bed of Case X, I went feeling certain that I was going to have a look at a man who had come from my emotional Antilles. I did not tell you of my discoveries because I was afraid that you might snort contemptuously, as is your disagreeable habit; I did not want you to doubt a notion with which I was just falling in love. That man was ghastly in his unconsciousness; he was inhuman and deeply mysterious in those bandages which lay on his face the mask of silence and the unknown; but chiefly for me he was a man from the Antilles, the man WHO HAD BEEN THERE. That was decisive. From that moment he was MY Case X, which I had to solve; I set out in pursuit of him, and it was, my friend, a long and devious trail.

Yes, now I am through with it. Now it is clear to me that what I felt to be a brilliant, and likely interpretation was, strictly speaking, a mere whim of mine that gave me pleasure; and therefore I cannot write any more of my story. It might be shown, if it has not already been done, that that man was a commercial traveller from Halle-an-der-Saale, or an ordinary American trying to make himself believe that an enterprising man of business like himself has not time to wait twenty-four hours for better weather. How deplorable! I can invent anything I like, but only on condition that I believe in it myself. As soon as my confidence that it really might have been like that is shaken, my phantasy appears to me as puerile and deplorable bungling. Well, and now you are called off, you silly and eager bitch; in vain you have romped along over the fallen leaves with your nose to the ground, pretending that you have a trail that doesn't exist, or which you lost long ago at the crossroads of possibility. You still pretend that you are on the scent, for dogs make a point of prestige; you still sniff at every mousehole, and you try to make me believe that our prey is still on the move. Well, leave it, it isn't here; you look up at me with your canine eyes as if to say: 'Is it my fault? you are the master, tell me where I am to go, show what you want!' And now I must look for the trail, look for the REASONS why he set out in this direction and not in that. Good Lord, reasons! motives! verisimilitudes! what a mess! even that dog no longer has any faith in me or in herself, and cannot understand what I want from her; this? here? or something else? Empty-handed master and dog return. Strange what a feeling of SOLITUDE there is in failure.

I will tell you this: a story has to fall to pieces if you are to know of what it is composed. While it is whole and living you might be intoxicated with the work and swear: All this is pure nature and no deceit, sir. I am writing it out of mere instinct, I myself don't know why; it is all imagination and intuition. Not until it has fallen to pieces will you discover how you aided her, how cunningly and secretly you pushed on your phantasy. God, what a conglomeration! but truly in every direction intellectual motives and intentional constructions stick out of it; what a little engine it is! Everything, almost everything, in some way is planned and surveyed, nothing but calculation and erection. I imagined that it all came of itself to me as if in a living dream, and, instead, it is a product of relentless engineering thought that tests and rejects, binds and predicts. When it is dead, and taken to pieces, all those wires, all that ingenuity, routine, and precision of intellectual work becomes visible. And I tell you that a broken machine is equally terrifying; it is the same chasm of emptiness like life in decomposition.

But even regret for fruitless work is not equal to the sadness of a story in ruins. Don't you know that a human life is buried in those ruins? Why make a fuss, you will say, for that life was only a fiction; a tale invented to pass the time. Ah, it is strange; it is not quite certain that that life was merely invented: and when I look at it I should say that it was MY OWN life. It is me. I am the sea and that man, that kiss blown from the dark shadow of the mouth belongs to me; that man sat by the lighthouse on the Hoe, because I sat under the lighthouse on the Hoe; and if he lived in Barbados, or Barbuda, so thank God, praise be to God, at last I have been there. All that was me; I don't invent anything, I only express what I am, and what is in me. And if I wrote of Hecuba, or of the Babylonian harlot, it would be myself; I should be the old woman who moans, and harrows her sagging and wrinkled breasts; I should be the woman crushed by lust in the hairy hands of the Assyrian, of a man with a greasy beard. Yes, man, woman, and child, to make it clear, it is me; I am the man who has not finished his flight."

CHAPTER XXII

"So enough for the introduction, and now we can roam along the paths by which our story began to take shape. We know that the DATA was only a man who had not finished his flight, and his fall, as was explained, was a pathetic event arising from mere accident and necessity. The accident and necessity were data; since our knowledge does not reach further, let us make of them the start or trail, along which we are going to set out; we shall attempt to construct that definite life out of two fundamental elements, out of mere accident and necessity, so that the final crash will emerge from them logically and lawfully.

Admit that the beginning holds out no little promise. Mere accident, which means freedom and adventure; a playful and unaccountable caprice, a germ of possibility and a magic carpet: what iridescent and ethereal material it is without weight or repetition, extensible, and gathered into mysterious folds, a material with which one can do anything; wings which will carry us anywhere; what is more poetical than chance? And its opposite is necessity, a shady park, a permanent force, and unchangeable necessity, which is order and system, as fine as a collonade, and as certain as a law.

And now it's like this; yes, this is what I want, and for which I am longing. For a chance that would bear me somewhere, the hesitating stay-at-home anchored by his seat to the table; for a chance, adventurous and rash, for a panting daredevil that would make me dance. We are growing old, my friend, and we accept life like a boring habit. Yes, but what about the other, the unconditioned and the certain? Would that my life had a meshwork of necessity, would that for once I could feel with certainty and without uneasiness that in everything I do an order is being fulfilled; praise be to God, I have not been doing anything but my task. Now see here, that man directed by necessity and chance will be myself; I shall be the one who will wander along the devious and inevitable road, and I shall pay for it with all the hardships that I can invent; for such a devious journey is no pleasure trip.

Well, then, in the name of God, let's begin; and when we do not know what is coming next let necessity or chance be our aid. How are we to begin? What shall we write as the first word of the story of a man from the Antilles? We will begin at the beginning: There was a boy who had no mother.

Bad, and you can't get any further that way. Case X, don't you know, has no face, and no name, has no identity, he is *Unknown*. If we give him a home we shall know him, so to speak, from his childhood up; he will cease to be unknown, and will lose what is now his strongest and most peculiar characteristic. If he is to stay as himself, he will have to keep his incognito; let him be a man without an origin, and without any papers. Let us stick to facts, proceed from what is given; he fell from the sky, and that is surely very characteristic of him. In our story also he ought somehow to fall from the sky, so that he emerges all of a sudden from the devil knows where, created by accident, completely finished, and perfectly unknown.

We have, then, a person and his arrival; the place where he emerges is decided for us beforehand; it is Cuba. It might be from any other of the Antilles, in fact it might be from any place in the world if only it were sufficiently remote. Distance is given us in that he flew, and that we do not know from what place; it is a far-away spot, and more or less exotic just because it is unknown to us. The money that you found in his pockets points to the Antilles; it is true that there is still another region where American, British, French, and Dutch colonies are all near together; that is along the sea-coast bounded by the Philippines, Annam, Singapore, and Sumatra, and I have found nothing that would exclude that possibility. I had to choose, and I decided on the Antilles from motives which are apparently purely personal; I told you that they have for me a particular charm. Briefly there somewhere is the goal of my ESCAPE; I may never get there, but it is the spot which exists for me more strongly than the countries in which I have been.

These, then, are roughly the beginnings of our story, and it is left to us to determine the terminus *ad quem*. This, of course, is the crash of the man who had not ended his flight; but here an important point arises: Was he flying somewhere on a new project, or was he coming home? I know only that he was in a tremendous hurry, for he was flying in a heavy storm. Generally we can expect that a man who is embarking upon something new, and in pursuit of things that are not familiar to him, would show a certain hesitation, an apprehension that would check his progress, while on the contrary, a man who is returning would be rather impatient; anticipating his goal he would undervalue the means that would bear him to it. I should say that that man was in such a haste because he was coming back, and I accept it as the most probable reality. Regardless of the fact that a man who flies is free to set off to any point of the compass, for infinite is the number of conceivable possibilities and objectives from which to choose; while, on the contrary, a man who is returning can only fly to one place, the only conceivable one of them all, in pursuit of an objective laid down from the beginning, determined and unchangeable. The way back is something exactly mapped out. By this alone the end of our story is fixed, and we can begin at the beginning.

The beginning is as confused and vague as chance. It was somewhere in Cuba, amidst the hedges of Bougainvillea; someone was being pursued, revolvers barked, and on a path that resembled the milky way an unknown man was left lying with a bleeding neck. The wound was inflicted with a knife with a broad blade that is used for cutting sugar-cane."

When the surgeon had read as far as this he snorted with disapproval, and threw the manuscript on the table. Nonsense. There's no scar on the neck; there's one just above the right breast, it couldn't have been inflicted by a broad knife, but by a sharp-pointed instrument. A shallow wound that only went as far as the rib.

CHAPTER XX

"SOMEWHERE in Cuba amidst the hedges of Bougainvillea someone was being pursued, revolvers barked, and on a path that resembled the milky way an unknown man was left lying with a bleeding neck. The wound was inflicted with a knife with a broad blade that is used for cutting sugar-cane. About ten yards further on someone else was lying, with arms and legs splayed out; this one was dead.

Cursing silently, three fellows bent over the one that had been stabbed; but he already began to raise himself and murmured: 'What—what do you want after all? Don't push me, Cavalier!' He felt the back of his neck, screwed up his mouth, and looked in amazement at his hand covered with blood, and at the three men. Mother of God, he was drunk!

'What business had that mule to get mixed up in this,' burst out one of the three in an angry mood, scratching his head. 'Que mierda! Take him to the house, chaps!'

They snatched him up by his arms and legs, and shuffled along; they didn't mind in the least that his backside was dragging along the road, leaving a trail in the dust like a sack of maize. They gasped and dragged that vagabond along the milky way. Let him bump his rump, the beast!

They put him down behind a door, an old hag flashed a light on his face, and cried to all the saints, and the master of the house, something of a bigwig if we are to go by his fierce blue mug, and evil eyebrows, bent down above it all and inquired why they had taken such a brute there.

The one who scratched his head blinked with all his might at the gentleman with knitted brows. 'So that he won't run away, your Grace. When that cavalier went away from here, we heard shooting outside; we ran to look and found this dago lying with this revolver in his hand. A few yards further on lies that unfortunate gentleman. He is dead, may God have mercy on him!'

The other two listened with open mouths as if they wanted to raise some objection; and the gentleman regarded them with inquiring eyes. 'Do you know for certain that he's dead?'

The tall peon crossed himself. 'Like a calf, your Grace. He must have got at least three bullets in the back of his head. He had a knife in his hand . . . Most likely he tried to defend himself with the knife when this bandit came across him. This cut-throat here wanted to run away, but we put a stop to that. You agree with me, don't you, boys? Well, then, moo you oxes!'

Only now did the other two grasp his meaning, and they began to grin broadly. 'As God is above us, your Grace, that's how it was, just like that, holy truth; he tried to do a bunk after he had shot that cavalier. And he had a pistol in his hand.'

'We ought to ask the police to take care of him,' observed the tall one, looking round for corroboration.

The gentleman stroked his blue chin, and frowned darkly as he meditated, 'No, Pedro (or Salvador—names hadn't been decided on), not that. If the police were after him——' he shrugged his shoulders. 'But I shall not do it without due reason. That wouldn't be fair. Lock him up somewhere in a room and give him a drink.'

The lanky one raised his hands. 'Your Grace, he's not in a state to worry about himself.'

'Give him a drink,' repeated the gentleman impatiently. 'And while you're about it, don't cackle about him any more than you need, do you understand?"

'We understand, your Grace, and we wish you good night. Pour some rum down his throat, so that he doesn't know which way up he is; what business has a tramp like that near the master's house, pushing his nose into other people's business? He doesn't look like a half-breed, but they're all the same, who knows what Hollander, or damned Yankee, to judge by the mess he's in. Slop, slop, there's still a little bit of room in him, let him have a pull so that we can knock out of him the last bit of his memory.'

It was delirium that came out of it, it shook the man worse than a fever; and the hag who had held the light brought water in an unglazed jug, and damped the bandages on the forehead and cheeks of the unconscious man. (The theme of unconsciousness at the beginning just as at the end; the circle closes.) She was a half-Indian from somewhere in Mexico; she had a dry and long face like a mare, and sad eyes which blinked anxiously and kindly. 'Poor fellow!' she said, wrapping that heavy head in cooling rags. She squatted on the floor and blinked her eyes, clap, clap, clap, like water dripping on a brick floor.

His unconsciousness or stupor lasted for thirty-six hours; the fellow was lying with his head wrapped in wet rags, and was not aware of himself. From time to time that lanky one came in and kicked him. 'Hi, get up, you damned corpse of a dog! We ought to take him somewhere in the night, sir, and leave him there. Let the devils, God pardon me, take him where they like.'

The master shook his head. 'That would be something. The police will get him, and wait till he can speak. No, no. When he wakes I'll have a talk with him myself, and then I'll see. Then I'll see.'

At last the hand moved, and tried to rub the forehead; he still had those rags on it, and when they slipped off something foreign and strange remained that could not be wiped away. The man sat up and rubbed his forehead hard. Tell master to come, master wants to talk to him.

Master, with thick eyebrows (according to all appearances, an important gentleman), carefully sized up that ragamuffin. No, he couldn't be a Spaniard, or he'd take more care of his shoes, even if, say, he'd only one sleeve to his shirt, his shoes would shine like an orange.

'Come va?' said the gentleman.

'Muchas gracias, señor.'

'Yankee.'

'Yes, sir. No, sir.'

'What's your name?'

The man rubbed his forehead, 'I don't know, sir.'

The Cuban wheezed with annoyance. 'And how did you get here?'

'I don't know, sir. I was drunk, wasn't I?'

'They found a revolver on you,' the gentleman challenged.

The man shook his head. 'I don't know, I don't know anything. I can't remember anything——' His face was screwed up with effort and uneasiness; he got up and made a few steps. 'No, I'm not drunk; I've only . . . like an iron band round my head.' He searched for something in his pockets; the Cuban offered him a cigarette. He only nodded his head, *gracias*; as if it were understood. No, this is no rat from a ship; say what you like, but he bears the signs of a gentleman. For instance, his hands; they're so dirty that they're a disgrace, but as he holds that cigarette—in short, a caballero. The Cuban knitted his brows. With a tramp it would be easier, and if it came to court what judge would believe a tramp?

The man eagerly smoked his cigarette, and tried to think. 'I can't remember anything,' he said, beginning to grin. 'It's a queer feeling, I tell you, to have a clear head, and yet empty at the same time. Like a whitewashed room into which someone is going to move."

'Perhaps you know at any rate what you used to be,' suggested the Cuban.

The man looked at his hands and clothes. 'I don't know, sir; but according to what I look like——' With the smoke from his cigarette he made a kind of zero. 'I don't know anything,' he said lightly. 'Nothing, nothing wants to come into my mind. Perhaps later I shall remember——'

The Cuban looked at him closely and suspiciously. The man's face was indifferent and slightly swollen, with an expression of amusement, and something like relief."

CHAPTER XXIV

"YES, you're right; another case of loss of memory, another case of literary amnesia, to which we owe so many romantic and touching stories. I shrug my shoulders with you over this already familiar plot, but I can't help it; if our hero is to remain Unknown we must abolish his identity, take away his papers, unpick the monograms, and especially, sir, remove his memory, for memory is the stuff out of which is woven our own identity. Root out your memory, and you will be the man who fell from the sky, who comes from nowhere, and doesn't know where he wants to go; you will be Case X. The man who lost his memory resembles a man who has lost his conscience; even if his brains remained clear and normal, it is as if he had lost the basis of reality, and lived outside it; without memory you see, there would be no reality for us either.

Certainly as a doctor you appreciated the fact that our case of loss of memory is the result of acute alcoholic poisoning, and of a physical shock caused by that nocturnal adventure. He fell down on the ground and hurt his head, and here we are; from a medical standpoint there can be no objections if he suffered mental injury; we have the factor of chance on which we cannot count; but the incident is too important to be left to chance, and to satisfy us it must occur is a matter of course and logically. Case X sustained a mental injury and lost, had to lose, his memory, for reasons which were in him; for him it was the only possible way, the only exit to get away from himself; it was something like an escape into another life. How it was in actual fact you will find further on; at this stage I only wished to remind you that there are deeper reasons, and more legitimate than chance.

But it is possible that even escape from one's own identity is in the nature of a normal human desire. To lose one's memory must indeed be like beginning everything again; to stop being what we are is, my friend, like a deliverance. Sometime, perhaps, you have had the experience of finding yourself in a foreign world in which you could not make yourself understood either by speech or money. It is true that you did not lose your identity, but that was of no avail; your education, social standing, name, and the other things that make up the ordinary I were of no use; you were merely an unknown man in the streets of a foreign town. Perhaps you will remember that in such circumstances you apprehended everything with a strange and almost dreamlike intensity; deprived of all accessories you were only a man, a being, an inner man, only eyes, and heart, only amazement, helplessness, and resignation. Nothing is more lyrical than to lose oneself. Case X, who lost himself so thoroughly that he doesn't even know who he is, will be such an astonished man; life for him will pass like a hallucination, all people unknown, all things new; but at the same time everything will be seen as if through a veil of remembering that he knows it already, and that it has passed at some time through his life, but where was it, my God, when was it? He will be as if in a dream whatever he does, in vain will he fish out pieces of reality from the eternal stream of phenomena; strange how the world becomes unsubstantial if memory is wiped away.

One thing I think needs explanation, and that is the special interest of the Cuban in Case X. I don't think that he kept him in his house as an interesting psychological case; I rather believe that he was not prepared to take him on trust as a mere onlooker at that nocturnal murder. Apparently at the beginning he suspected that loss of memory is an elegant form of exploitation: if someone will take care of me my memory can remain obscured, what was, was, and I don't know anything; but look out, and see, sir, that my memory doesn't come back. At the final end of all he might even think that Case X had done something against the law, and was interested in concealing his identity, or in having at hand evidence that he was something like a fool. So his dealings with him were cautious and circumspect; but even after he had made sure a hundred times that without doubt the man had lost his memory completely, he still was apprehensive in case he should suddenly wake from his dream and begin to talk; and so it was better to treat him well, particularly since day by day it became more and more obvious that he was a polite and obliging man. Let that stay as it is, a knowledge of languages comes handy if our business interests are widely scattered, thank God, from Caracas to Tampico; when you have to deal with Englishmen, Frenchmen, Dutchmen, and with those louts from the States, who, God curse them, won't learn Spanish all their lives; and those people from Hamburg almost expect you to correspond with them in some language of their own. The Cuban thought of this deeply while he chewed a black cigar, as thick as a banana; he had his own cigars, and he himself looked after the mulattos when they rolled them with the palms of their hands upon their round young thighs; he chose his cigars according to the girls, more strictly speaking, according to the length of their shanks; the longer the legs, the better the girls were grown, and the better the cigars rolled up. When he found, then, that the man whom he had taken into his house knew not only how to speak and write in those different languages, but even how to swear (various suspicious characters too frequently dropped into his house, and the Cuban was already tired of telling them what he thought of them when they didn't understand), he became enthusiastic about him, and offered him a post; from his own side the relation was something like a contract between crooks, that is hearty and almost humane. To avoid any misunderstanding, the Cuban was an old settler, of noble birth, from Camaguey, who was called Camagueyno, at one time a breeder of bulls on the savannahs; but when it became clear to him that in those miserable times it was no longer sufficient to be owner of herds and rule a house and family, he shrugged his shoulders, and went in for business something in the style of the old and famous buccaneers who played their antics among the islands. In short, *este hombre*, as he called our hero, was useful for negotiating with the victims in their own language, and for keeping up appearances, even if it were only a matter of stripping and sinking their ships. One must choose one's men as one chooses stud bulls, with care and with a touch of the prophetic spirit. This bull certainly limps a bit, but I wager, sir, that he will leave good stock. *Este hombre* was certainly somewhat strange and bewildered, but it seemed as if he knew quite a lot. And sighing deeply, the old pirate went to consult his wife, who sat with swollen legs somewhere at the back of the house, reading her fortune with cards while sweat ran down the wrinkles of her bloated face like eternal tears. Nobody ever saw her; only from time to time, her deep bass could be heard as she cursed the negresses.

It should be pointed out that the Cuban had not only business to do with sugar, pimento, molasses, and other blessings of the islands, but chiefly and above all with affairs of all kinds. People came to him, sometimes, it is true, rather suspicious looking, the devil knows what strange races there are in the world; this one, he said, to found an export company for ginger, angostura, nutmegs, and Malagetta pepper somewhere in Tobago; that one, he said, about a bed of asphalt on Haiti; that one, he said, to export kubavi, a wood as tough as armour-plate, pipiri that never rots, Santa Maria, or corkwood, lighter than cork from the Algerian oaks. Or to plant vanilla, cacao, sugar plantations, here and there, where labour was cheap. Or to produce starch in wholesale quantities from manihota, jams out of mombin, extract from Cassia bark. Some of them had already been in the islands for three months at least, and so they knew of all kinds of things with which one could do business, or what ought to be founded. The more experienced carried on negotiations for the import of labour, land speculation, limited companies confidentially supported by their Governments. Old Camagueyno listened with half-closed eyes, chewing his black cigar; he had a tropical liver that made him suspicious and irritable. By degrees on all the islands that the heavenly God had scattered around he had his interests, his sugar-cane and cacao plantations, his drying kilns, mills, distilleries, his square miles of forests which his associates acquired and then ran away, or went down with drink or fever. He himself hardly ever left the house, tormented as he was by his liver and lumbago; but many petty pirates, thieves, many Morenes and shameless half-breeds, sweated and bustled about, drinking hard, and practising fornication on his estates with all the demons and devils of this fiery world. In this cool and whitewashed house, where in the patio green water murmured in Toledo faience, little was heard of that struggle without; sometimes, it is true, someone arrived with feverish eyes as gaunt as a Cassia pod, and cried that he had been ruined; but for such purposes there were three mozos, erstwhile cowboys from the savannah, to show them the way out. Times were different when you rode on a horse through grass as tall as a man; there on a hillock stood an old spreading ceiba, and from its shade you could see for miles and miles; and on the slopes there were herds of black cattle. And now these people shouted for a couple of greasy dollars as if some big thing were afoot. Just the same kind of ruffians as those who had turned the savannah into a sugar factory. And instead of black bulls had introduced zebu, hunch-backed and lagging animals; zebu being cheaper. The old gentleman raised his bushy eyebrows as if he were astonished. And people like this imagine that you ought to make a tremendous fuss of them. It's all foreign, so what——"

CHAPTER XXV

"It was strange how it was coming out in the old lady's cards: heaps of money, and some misfortune; *este hombre* was from a rich and noble family, but then there was a woman, great vexation, and a letter. As for that woman, it was queer for in the Cuban house there was only herself and some mulattos, who, of course, didn't count. It wasn't respectable for a señora to prophesy and thus enter into contact with evil powers; and so an old negress was called in who knew her way about with incredibly dirty cards, rum, and incantations. When the cards were spread out, Morena began her patter so amazingly fast that the old lady hardly understood every tenth word, so that it was impossible to be certain of what was written in the heavens except again a large sum of money, a distant journey, a woman, and a dreadful misfortune, which the negress represented by pointing wildly to the floor. There was nothing there but a tiny beetle, with a metallic-looking coat, crawling slowly along; when the black prophetess pointed tragically to the floor, it drew up its tiny legs and seemed to be dead.

Nevertheless it was a warning; if the Cuban didn't mind, it was evident that even he was moved by a deeper necessity. First he produced private papers from some man who had died in hospital; *este hombre* had to have a name, and an identity, and he could raise no objection to being called Mr. George Kettelring. Kettelring was a good name; it might have been Yankee, German, or something else, and it looked businesslike and reliable. If George Kettelring, then George Kettelring; nobody would ask where he had come from, for he didn't lead one to think that he had only come to the islands yesterday. He was called *el secretario*, but that didn't mean anything in particular; chiefly his work was to translate and write letters. When he put down the first statement I should imagine that he started; and looked fixed at what he had written; most probably it reminded him of something deeply personal that he was unable to recall; perhaps it was his lost personality preserved in the characteristics of his handwriting. From that time on he only wrote on the typewriter, mildly amused by the extent and complexity of the Cuban's commercial interests. 'Mildly amused,' that is the right phrase; whether it was a matter of business, molasses, or the profit from tobacco-fields, or collective contracts with Ceylon coolies on Trinidad, or land in San Domingo, or on Martinique, or the sugar factory in Bermuda, or of the agency in Port au Prince, it seemed to him as if they weren't real people, real estates, real goods, real money, but as something rather funny in being so far away and unreal; as if you were telling him about the mortgage on Centauri, or the profit from the fields on Algola, or of the small gauge railway between the stars of the Boot, or of the Little Bear. From a commercial and human standpoint, it is certainly not pleasant to think of someone looking at your interests, investments, and mortgages from such an astral distance, and more than once old Camagueyno raised his irritated brows when *este hombre* Kettelring bared his teeth so strangely with pleasure on coming across some fresh name. It makes you anxious if someone treats your property with such disrespect as if it were a mere phantom or something. But the old filibuster discovered that it had its better side too. Mr. Kettelring never made the slightest sign whatever he wrote; say, to stop credits to a planter who was toiling in despair on Maria Galante, to dismiss hands, or to put a knife to someone's throat; sometimes the Cuban couldn't even get it out of his throat, he snorted, hesitated, and waited for some objection, but already the typewriter was rattling cheerfully, and *este hombre* merely raised amused eyes to inquire what further. Camagueyno once used to have an old scribe, a Spaniard; that old fellow always got into a frightful temper when he had to write a letter like that, he would begin to cry, and run away; he came back drunk and wrote it with a face like the damned, cursing his mother as the worst of all harlots. But now everything went smoothly, devilishly smoothly, it only clicked. The old Cuban felt, I imagine, uneasy because it went like greased lightning, he needn't dictate any more, it was sufficient if he shrugged his shoulders over the letter from a poor unfortunate whose orchards had been eaten by Lima mould, Mr. Kettelring wrote it, and the farmer could go and hang himself. It seemed as if Mr. Kettelring had no conscience. Most likely conscience goes lost with memory.

But as you can imagine, there was another point relating to his memory. As you know, it is true that *este hombre* Kettelring lost his memory, with everything in it, but in return a new one was born with which he might be exhibited. He remembered word for word letters, bills, and contracts that had passed through his hands. To So-and-so we wrote a month ago this and that, in this man's memorandum of agreement there is so-and-so. A complete living repository. Chewing his eternal cigar, Camagueyno looked thoughtfully at the inconceivable Mr. Kettelring. From time to time he pulled out of his safe in the depths of the house copies of old contracts, and commercial correspondence. Read it, he said, and Mr. Kettelring read it and remembered. The old Cuban did not set much store by such new-fangled ideas like order; besides, many of his interests were of a kind which he preferred not to commit to writing. There were some venerable pirates of equal standing with whom it was sufficient just to smoke a cigar, and then shake hands on it. But man grows old and never knows when his hour will come; and with some misgiving he began slowly to initiate Mr. Kettelring into his business, and confide to his memory what and how it was. We may take it for granted that it was not all commerce. The old country Camaguey, savannahs with herds, noble Cuban farmers of the times; the former races in Havana, the society, courtly and respectable, ladies in crinolines. Do you know that Cuban society was the most noble, and most exclusive in the world? There were only masters and servants, but no rabble. Old Cuba, Mr. Kettelring. And the old gentleman, mastering his rheumatism, showed how a cavalier used to bow to a lady, and how the lady very nearly used to kneel down before the cavalier, holding her skirts in both hands. And the dances, chaconne, or danzon—no, none of these rumbs and sones; they were danced by the negroes, that was the orgy of Morens, and Pards, but a Cuban, sir, wouldn't let himself go like that. Not till the Yankees turned us negro. Camagueyno's eyes flared up. Even those mulattos are no longer what they used to be. What small and round little backsides they used to have! To-day they're already spoiled by American blood, bones too coarse, *señor mio*, and wide mugs only for shouting. Now they do shout, but then they only cooed, yes, cooed when they'd got it. The old gentleman waved his hand. Altogether we holloa too much; that's what the Americans have introduced. Before, we were quieter, there was more dignity——

Mr. Kettelring listened, with his eyes half-shut, and with a slight distracted smile. As if into his empty inner self the remote and knightly past was flowing like a stream."

CHAPTER XXVI

"BUT otherwise one can well imagine that with Mr. Kettelring there could be little conversation; it seemed as if he tried to avoid people, as if he were afraid that someone might recognize him, and slap him on the shoulder. How do you do, Mr. So-and-so? When he drank, he certainly drank alone and heavily; he dropped in at the saloons where colorados went, gazed at the bespattered floor covered with fruit-stones, and fag-ends, and talked to himself in a language that suited his mood. I think that at times he jabbered a phrase which then long and thoughtfully he tried to examine like a wreck thrown up by the waters of Lethe; but because he must have been dreadfully drunk for such a word memory to have detached itself from the depths of his unconsciousness, he never came to any solution, and only shook his head half-falling asleep, mumbling something unintelligible even to himself. And in this the sound of the negroes' drums, tamtams, little bells, and a guitar, wild and sweaty music, a leaping cataract from which emerged a shrieking naked girl slapping her shiny hips, the neighing of a trumpet, and the soft texture of a violin, ah, as if you were stroking a smooth back, and shoulders, a back flexed and yielding just to stick your nails into it. Mr. Kettelring stuck his nails into his sweaty palms, and shook his head, but he couldn't keep up with the pace of the black musicians, not at all, his head would fall off and roll on the floor. And why do those musicians jump so much, wait, wait, I haven't drunk enough yet not to see clearly; wait, I shall close my eyes, and when I open them, mind that you are sitting quietly, I tell you, but don't you stop playing. Mr. Kettelring opened his eyes; black musicians jumped, and showed the whites of their eyes, that one with the blaring trumpet was standing up as if he were emerging out of the darkness, and on a tiny bit of the floor a brown chabine in a flowered dress was wriggling, the olive Cuban threw a red shawl round her hips, and pressed her to himself, belly to belly, they jostled each other in a violent and cramped rhythm, the Cuban with his mouth open, and the mulatto with leaden eyes, they shuffled and hissed, showed their teeth as if they wanted to bite one another; and then another couple; and a third, it was full of them, they wriggled between the tables, they staggered, and roared with laughter, they went for one another, glistening with sweat, and pomade; and above it all the trumpet blared and droned in its sexual triumph.

See how Mr. Kettelring drums on the table and shakes his head. God, what does it remind me of, what does it remind me of? Surely once before I was just as drunk, yes just so, yes, but how did it end? In vain he tried to grasp some picture that eluded him. The eyes and teeth of the mulatto sparkled, she had a hibiscus flower in her teeth, and she rocked from her hips; Yes, I know I might go with you, but think of it; girl, I can't remember—A young man leaned over Mr. Kettelring and said something to him. Mr. Kettelring's eyes bulged. Que vuole? The young man with the thin neck grinned and whispered confidently. I can take you, sir, to a beautiful girl. Beautiful, coloured, he rattled, and clicked his tongue. In Mr. Kettelring something suddenly gave way; he sprang up, and hit the young man so hard in the face that he flew back, and fell on the floor among the dancers. Mr. Kettelring roared and beat his forehead with his fist. Now I shall remember—He couldn't. There was a dreadful brawl, and a still more dreadful debauch followed with some Americans, who threw out the whole saloon together with the girls and the musicians, and occupied the conquered territory; they declared that the Cubans were a band of half-breeds and negroes, and they crowned themselves with paper roses, which in that land of flowers heightened the splendour of the Cuban saloon.

Then, arising from that, let us say, demonstrations of Cuban nationalists broke out against the Americans. The local students joined in, and waving flags striped with blue and white, they harangued fiercely against the States. Nothing could be done;

the whole affair had to be officially investigated. Old Camagueyno thundered irritably amidst his clouds of smoke; on the one hand, he admitted that young people in that climate needed something to keep their spirits up, by which he meant Mr. Kettelring and the hot-headed Cuban youths; but as a business man he was for order, and as a Camagueyno for final accounts with the foreigners. He would not like to lose *este hombre* Kettelring, and what he feared most was that his identity might be disclosed at the official investigation; who knew if the police might not again take an interest in that dead man with three bullets in his skull, which had been put down to unknown rowdies from the North (for local people, as was well known, settled their own affairs with a knife; not reckoning the peons, who had gained experience in New Mexico). Ay, hijos de vacas, cobardes, cojones! Did ever such things happen in Cuba? Everyone himself, and without official aid, looked after his own honour, there were no disputes and brawls, nobody was keen on getting stabbed. And what justice there was on Cuba! It paid due regard for property, rights, leases, and heritage settlements, and not for brawls of drunkards. The old gentleman frowned, his hairy brows deeply annoyed, and he spat brown saliva, while Mr. Kettelring, bruised and ruffled, tapped away at the typewriter. That Dutchman on Haiti is inquiring again about raising credit for building the sugar factory.

Mr. Kettelring raised bloodshot eyes. 'Last time he wrote that the erectors had nearly finished the presses; now he writes that the room for the presses hasn't got a roof on yet.'

The Cuban bit his cigar; had he not other worries now?

'Somebody ought to have a look at that building,' mumbled Kettelring, and again started rattling the machine.

The old Cuban began to snigger silently. 'That is an idea, Kettelring, Wouldn't you like to go there?'

Este hombre shrugged his shoulders, it was apparently all the same to him; but the Cuban veiled himself in smoke, and meditated, rocking with laughter.

'Excellent, sir, you go to Haiti. In the meantime things will cool down here, and we need someone to look after our affairs over there. There is the agency at Port au Prince, those things in Gonaiva, and in Samana—but you know about them.' The old Camagueyno was immensely amused. I should like to know what *este hombre* will do on Haiti; it's not like Cuba, *sabe?* Most likely he will drive himself to death with rum, as long as the negresses don't shake him out of his trousers; there people get so idiotic that they don't even steal. It's true we need an able man; there's money to be made there—The Cuban grew serious. Haiti isn't Cuba; there the Americanos haven't yet stolen it by bits, nobody can stick it there, no, nobody can stand the life, but a negro. All the same, you could buy and sell there—And this man hasn't got overmuch conscience. He may stick it there; a man can stand a lot when he's got no conscience.

'I'll go,' replied Mr. Kettelring indifferently.

The Camagueyno grew lively; dipping some sort of a pear into salt, he began with a full mouth to explain what information he wanted from there. 'Drink, Kettelring, your health; and mind the women, they're quite mad after fair hair. I'm looking for land that would do for sugar-cane. I put my money on sugar, Kettelring, for ten more years I put my money on sugar-cane, a la salud de usted! And beware of sorcerers, those cattle aren't even Christians. Yes, we shall want a warehouse in Gonaiva. I'm sending you as if you were my son, Kettelring, and I warn you, beware of those obeahos, those sorcerers. That, and see you bribe the officials, that's the chief thing.' The old Cuban sucked some dark wisdom from his cigar. 'Rather negresses than mulattos, man; a negress is at least a beast, but a mulatto is a devil. A devil, I tell you. Mind that agency in Port au Prince. Don't forget to take with you some stuff for the bugs, Kettelring, and write to me how it goes, and how it is there with the women.' "

CHAPTER XXVII

"Of course I went to have a look round the hothouse at the Botanical Gardens to give myself an idea of tropical vegetation. Now I should be able to describe sufficiently well the Crotons, whose leaves are streaked with red and yellow, so magnificent that you might think they're poisonous; Acalyphas with its bright red leaves, the velvet foliage of Anthurium hanging over the dark pools, and smelling sweetly of decay, the bushes of black pepper, and the hard cups of Bromelias, from which spring incredibly pink or ethereally blue sprays of flowers, Pandanus standing on the tips of its roots, sharply toothed like little saws, not to speak of the palms; amongst those an ordinary individual who doesn't walk about with his head tipped back, like Gulliver when he came from Brobdingnag, can't find his way about. But if I had to say concisely what I imagine a tropical country to be like, I should have to leave all that aside and burst out like Rimbaud into data geographically rather vague. 'I came to incredible Floridas, you know, where eyes of panthers, with human skins, mingle with flowers, and rainbows stretched like reins; I saw fermenting swamps where gigantic snakes, eaten by bugs, drop from crooked evil-smelling trees; I would like to show the children those golden countries. . . .'

Yes, something like that; but one would have to slash that festering jungle with the white-hot hatchet of the sun, set fire to the weeds, and beat out the sparks with a naked paw; plant batatas, or coffee trees, and build straw huts, and only then show the children these golden countries, where flowers and scents mingle, human skins and commercial agents, huge snakes, export, and labour, the blue sheen of the butterflies, and the international conventions about the supply of fruit. What an immense and exuberant bastardy, what a wild jungle; you must realize that I'm not wandering into a paradise where

I should rest in the shadow of the palms, and let Nature embrace me, cover me with purple blossoms, and the scent of jasmine: alas, alas, things aren't so simple for me! I should like to peep inside to see what a hellish and acrid sauce is stewing there, made up of the sun, conjuncture, human races, and business, of wilderness and credit, of basic instincts, and civilization; my friend, not even the devil would like to stir the spoon in that saucepan. I should like to see which is fiercer, the Green Snake to which the negroes bow, or the Laws of Economics to which we bend the knee; I know only that these two together make a jungle more fantastic than the groves of Equisetum, in which the Dinosaurs sat on eggs. There is the question whether that black chicken, scratching itself in the shadow of the sweet potatoes, will be sold at the market, or whether its head will be bitten off for the propitiation of the incensed and supreme Snake. I should like to see how the Green Snake, coiled up in his armchair, smiles into the telephone, and expedites his commercial affairs. What, the exchange in Amsterdam is weak? Well, we'll abolish the plantations on the Leeward Islands. The Green Snake is annoyed, and lashes his tail round the oceans of the world.

And I went to look up the statistics to have a whiff and see how that tropical sauce is being cooked. Taking the Antilles, you have all conceivable variations; beginning with Cuba, where only one-third are colorados and two-thirds are white (this is contrary to the classical tradition of slave countries; the right proportion is two coloured to one white), and finishing with the republic of Haiti, where in tropical despair a handful of whites live in agony among the shouting and neighing negroes. To heighten the effect, don't forget the Syrian usurers, Chinese, and coolies imported from India, Java, or Oceanea. What an excellent idea! an imported coolie is more easily managed than local labour; just wait till the Green Snake colonizes Europe, the workers will be taken from one country to another; they will obey better, and will be interested in nothing but work and copulation.

And this hot sauce is thoroughly savoured with the salt of the earth. Every colonial power sends there its chosen specimens to represent with dignity the message of the white races. Go out into the world and teach all nations what is State and Commerce; wherever your foot falls, set up offices, and commercial agencies. Show those poor savages the blessings of civilization in the form of the ill-tempered, irritated, unhealthy men, who feel themselves in exile, and count their days and money looking forward to the time when they can come back to their aunts and cousins. They must be made to believe that on their loins rests the Dignity of the State, or its Prosperity, so that they don't drink themselves to death through nostalgia and laziness, and still hang on marking time with questions of prestige, with gossip, and with changing their sweaty shirts. A man like Camagueyno, at least, made no pretence that he represented any higher interests; he was an honest pirate, and therefore we have dwelt on him with a certain pleasure.

So we have got it thoroughly mixed up in our saucepan; British, American, French, Dutch governors, lieutenants, commercial representatives, and warehouse-keepers; beautiful creoles, and old settlers, something like a colonial aristocracy; from here we can cheerfully jump down the steps of mankind from complexions nut brown, to tealike, light coffee, down to the whiteness of leprosy. In our wardrobe we have the sombreros of the Cubans and the orange shoes of the mulattos, the shiny nakedness of Yorubas and the variegated turbans of the girls from Guadeloupe, and all this brought together from everywhere, swept up and moved from the whole world; fabulous sweepings, in which it is possible to rummage; Spanish, African, British, and French traditions in a state of anachronous exclusiveness or grotesque bastardization. Only humming-birds, toads, jungle, and tobacco, not counting the weeds, and diseases are genuine there. Others sprang up on the rubbish-heap of the human business.

These are, then, the islands of my desire, this is how I imagine them; as you see, I do not hunt for rainbow-coloured butterflies, nor do I pretend to be a dreamer flying into virgin nature to worship the sun naked and garlanded. Nothing of the sort. If I call it an escape, then it is an escape into the very centre of things, where everything is in conflict, and where ages copulate in an addled medley of cultures. Here there is still orgy and violence, here gain is sought for convulsively and widely like fornication. Let it be, this is how mankind appears to us in the remarkable amplitude of its human . . . and inhuman qualities."

CHAPTER XXVIII

"THAT sugar factory on Haiti I imagine to have been near a negro village called on the maps, let us say, Les deux Maries; it consisted of some partly built walls, no machines, and three hundred acres of yellow, cracked soil, grown over with jungle weed and sugar-cane of the fourth ratoon, that is, the fifth year, one without juice or sugar. The Dutchman had already discreetly disappeared some time ago, and Mr. Kettelring moved into his hut after he had the centipedes killed off. On the whole he felt content; behind his back was the jungle, a thicket of chestnut trees, kaklines, and devil trees, the little bird keskidy sang to him, and in the evening, in the evening the shining beetles swarmed out from the thicket, and the bats flitted in a zig-zag course over the dry buzzing of the sugar-cane. From the village he could hear the negroes drumming and dancing, celebrating the arrival of their new master. Mr. Kettelring sighed with relief, here, my word, you needn't have a name, and as for a memory, what could you do with it, what could you do with it? You blink with heat, or sleepiness, and have no desire to wander in time along the footpaths of reminiscence. You are here, and that's enough; it's such a lasting, buzzing present.

He ought to have written a letter to Camagueyno to say what it looked like there, but he felt too lazy. Round the hut the convolvulus and hibiscus flourished, kasava and the mafafo banana; a hairy caterpillar crawled on a stalk, and an ant ran up and down across a huge leaf as if it had some business there. For a time it amused him to watch the lizards chasing one another on the factory wall; but then the lizards became stiff, and sat still, sat as if nailed down; if only there was a stone to throw—they would flash like lightning! But wait, I'll make you move. With his finger, Mr. Kettelring beckoned to a negro who was hiding behind a wall. It was the local mayor, labour contractor, surveyor, and altogether a dignitary. 'What state of affairs is this,' says Mr. Kettelring. 'You band of thieves, you toads, get a move on and build the factory; bring here thirty men, do you understand, compris? I'll make the bullets fly, you sluggards!' Yes, and then a score of negroes swarmed on to the plot, and made a show as if they were building something; the lizards had their rest cut short, and Mr. Kettelring blinked his eyes in the quivering heat. At least something was going on; at least it seemed to him as if he were doing something; at least he needn't look at an unfinished, miserable wall, on which a lizard sat immovable as if it were fixed to the spot. Something was going on, and days, weeks, months passed; and nights, well, at night there was palm wine, and sleep, at night there were the stars, you could exist through the night.

Now they were putting the rafters on; it was about time to begin inquiring for what purpose this huge edifice was being built. Around it nearly the whole village was messing about, old hags, young pigs, naked children, hens, every living thing, at least something was going on. But it won't be a sugar factory, there are no machines. Quick, laggards, quick, don't you see that in the corner a lizard had stopped again as if it didn't know what it was after? It might be, say, a drying-shed; a drying-shed is always handy for something.

Sometimes a neighbour came to see him on a mule, a young planter, his name was Pierre; a peasant son from Normandy, who wanted to make money there so that he could get married at home. He was gaunt, and heavy, tormented with swellings and fever, death looked out of his eyes. 'You Englishmen,' he used to say (for he took Mr. Kettelring for a Briton), 'you know how to command; but a man who saves will never learn. No, a man who saves can't make a master. When these negroes saw that I was working with these paws of mine—it was impossible to live with them any longer. Do you think that I can order them to do something? They laugh in my face, and they do all kinds of things to me on purpose—and lazy, my God!'—He trembled with hatred and disgust—'This year they let seven acres of young coffee trees perish—I couldn't weed it myself, could I?'—He was so embittered, he nearly cried—'And when I go to Port au Prince to those gentlemen in white shoes who call themselves commercial representatives, and I say, I have coffee, I have ginger, I can deliver nutmegs—"We don't want anything." Say, Kettelring, well, why do they stay here, if they don't want anything? Not that they're catching flies. They behave as if I weren't even there. And then they say: "What do you want after all? We can give you so much and so much"—a ridiculous price. And they're Frenchmen too, Kettelring. If you knew what it is to be up there——'

Pierre swallowed heavily, and his Adam's apple ran up and down; he scratched all over his body where the red mite itched him. 'But this is hell,' he growled. 'These mulattos—they think that they're as good as me. "My father was an American agent, I am no nigger," these loafers say, puffing themselves up. And I slave—I have a girl in le Havre, a good girl, she's a typist in a shop; if only, sir, I could sell out and have a thousand or two francs left.' With his head in his hands, Pierre remembered how it was in his old home; he didn't even notice that Mr. Kettelring never told him any reminiscences in return, for recollection is selfish. He complained of sweat and weariness; they advised him to eat elephant lice, nuts of kashu trees, these, they said, drive weariness away, and sharpen the wits. After that, poor Pierre always had his pockets full of them, and he chewed them continually; he didn't realize that besides other things they were also aphrodisiac, and he was pining with desire for his girl. Besides, he was frightened of the negresses because he thought they were diseased, and he loathed them because he hated negroes; hadn't they ruined his seven acres of coffee? 'Say, Kettelring,' he mumbled feverishly, 'say, do you sleep with them? I couldn't——'

Once when he hadn't appeared for ten days Mr. Kettelring went to look him up. Pierre was down with pneumonia, and couldn't recognize him. 'Mon amant,' boasted the negress in the hut, a horrid woman, covered with scabs. 'Moi, sa femme, eh? Since last night.' She neighed and slapped her thighs, while her breasts dangled.

A few days afterwards Pierre died.

Strange how people begin to be interested in a man when he's dead. Two days afterwards a couple of gentlemen arrived from below, from Port au Prince. And what will happen to the plantations of Mr. Pierre. They also called on Mr. Kettelring. They sat with him, they smeared their sores with palm olive and simaruba ointment, and cursed the whole lousy region. 'You could make money here if those nigger scum weren't as lazy as lice; how is it here with labour conditions? and what are you building, Mr. Kettelring—sugar factory, or what?' Mr. Kettelring waved his hand contemptuously. 'Sugar, here? The country is too dry, sir. Grow cotton-wool here, that would be something. Well, to set your minds at rest, this will be a drying-shed for cotton.'

Both gentlemen stopped for a bit to smear themselves, and to kill mosquitoes on their sweaty shanks. 'Well, look here, a drying-shed for cotton—why, we're interested in cotton. A planter from New Orleans, but labour's too dear there now. Those lousy niggers up there have already got their trade unions, would you believe it? And how much arable land is there here?'

Mr. Kettelring pictured to them three hundred acres of cultivated land; it was, however, mostly a jungle, but in any case it was all the same, nobody would come to look at it. Besides, he didn't believe in any American planter who was interested in cotton, and why cotton, anyhow? The Haitian Cotton Plantation Society would be founded, and shares would be sold; the deuce take the cotton, business doesn't want any cotton; a drying-shed and land is enough for throwing on the market nicely printed shares with which a meritorious piece of work of commercial and political enterprise would be done. At the top of the shares there would be a picture of happy negroes with a perspective view of the new drying-shed in the background. Poor Mr. Pierre; his coffee trees will now be choked with weeds for good.

God knows, I should like to describe something else, the flowers of frangipans, the blossoms of marhaniks, and the brilliancy of butterfly wings; why, indeed, do I surround myself with that dreadful wall of yellow and muddy brick? Where have I got to, this is a nice tropical country for me! I might go down into my garden and enjoy campanulas in flower, and the morning freshness of the bushes; instead, I blink my eyes in the midday glare at the yellow wall of the drying-shed lined with banana skins, excrement, and rotting stalks, and I can't deny myself a deep satisfaction. Now, at last we're here, so far, that we can prop our elbows on our knees, and laze. Well, that's how it looks, and this is reality; this wall, long and dirty yellow, baked by the sun. And so we have, praise be to God, escaped to the other side of the world.

There we left Mr. Kettelring; he was sitting in front of his hut, chewing pig plums, and frowning at the lizards fixed motionless on the wall of the drying-shed. A huge nigger from Port au Prince arrived, carrying a letter on his head. It was old Camagueyno writing, muy amigo mio, and so on; in short, he was rubbing his hands because he had just sold three hundred and sixty acres of cotton land near Deux Maries, a fully equipped gin-house and the drying-house included. That affair is not settled yet, wrote the Cuban; the political parties are attacking the officials and saying that they haven't yet investigated the affair. Wouldn't Señor Kettelring have a look round Gonaiva for a time.

To Kettelring it was all the same; he left the half-completed rafters standing, and had a look round Gonaiva for a time, from Gonaiva to San Domingo, he didn't care, then perhaps to Porto Rico, and after that, quicker still from one island to another, to so many places that they didn't seem real."

CHAPTER XXIX

"I'M only giving you an outline of the story of Case X, indeed, it isn't even an outline; I couldn't give a connected account of what happened to him from one year to the next. Besides, his life didn't consist of events; events necessitate will, or something, at least, that isn't indifference; but having lost his memory, Case X undoubtedly lost most of the motives that influence people. You can't conceive what an alert force our memory is; we look at the world through eyes of previous experience, we greet things like old acquaintances, and our attention is held by what captivated it once; the greater part of our relations with everything around us is tied by the fine and invisible hands of reminiscence. A man without memory would be a man without relations; he would be surrounded by strangeness, and the sound which would reach him would not contain any answers.

And yet we think of Mr. Kettelring wandering from place to place as if he were seeking something. Don't be deceived by that; he was not interested enough to be after anything, and if he had been left to himself perhaps he would have stayed sitting permanently by that cracking wall at Deux Maries, gazing at the lizards, darting or motionless. He merely accepted the commercial interests of the Cuban Don as his own; and he was led on by them. Everywhere there was some step, or stump, where he could sit down; he followed the path of a drop of sweat running down his back; he listened to the dry rustling of the palms, or of the lebbek pods, and he was mildly amused to see how lazy people moved. It was like a kaleidoscope, and he turned it round to make them move quicker. Well then, you niggers, get a move on so that something is being done, that something is moving before my eyes; load the ships with coconuts, carry baskets on your heads, roll barrels with pimento rum; a bit faster so that I don't put pepper on your tails. On the water in the harbour oil and dirt made rainbow colours, rainbow rings; what beautiful putrefaction, what phosphorescent corruption! And get a move on you black pigs, march into that sugar-cane and make it wave, make it ripple, that rustling field, and make it flash with naked loins among the tawny litter.

And with all this a strange thing: without caring about it, doing it all just to fill out his laziness and inertia with something, he was very likely accompanied by what in business is called success; people were afraid of his indifferent eyes, his commands were definite, and not to be argued away, his reports to Camagueyno were a model of commercial reliability. He gave orders as if used to it from birth, and urged people in a way that made them submit with a dark and powerless rage. If they could have seen that he was enjoying his command, and that he was glorying in his power and superiority, it would have been, God knows, more tolerable, but fear and hatred merely settled on his broad and indifferent shoulders, always as if ready to shrug. Tear your guts out, or get out, it's not my affair. But quite deep down, deep down below everything, a tiny and pained astonishment was stirring, a kind of eternal numbness. Perhaps I also carried loads, or rowed in a boat, scratched my back, and ate a dirty pancake in the sand; maybe I was also a sweaty storekeeper, running with papers in my hand, or I had white breeches, and a panama hat, like I have now, and I looked after men and saw that they sweated for the sake of some other Cuban. All that was equally far away and equally unreal; it was possible to look at it as if through the wrong end of a telescope—so far it was, and so ridiculous to look at; how they all struggled, the coolies, typists, storekeepers, and gentlemen in white shoes playing tennis behind the net.

Or various gentlemen came: Camagueyno's agents, and representatives, planters laden down with mortgages, directors of sugar factories, small and robust farmers; Hello, Mr. Kettelring, my wife would feel honoured to invite you, and, Mr. Kettelring, what about a cocktail. Soon their tongues faltered before the indifferent eyes of Mr. Kettelring; short crops, they said, bad markets, those thieves the mulattos, and such like. Mr. Kettelring didn't even wait to let them finish, he was bored. You will do so-and-so, sir, bring me a report, I will go and look for myself. They shuffled before him from one foot to the other, perspired humbly, and convulsively, intensely hating this their lord, who, without long harangues in the Cuban's name, put the knife to their necks. And all the time Mr. Kettelring was exploring in himself such a strange and uneasy possibility. Perhaps this was my previous, my real, self. Perhaps I was a slave-driver with a whip, a planter, or something, a man in charge of property, and therefore also of people; how could I manage them like this if it weren't in me? Perhaps it will come out stronger if I try it on others; perhaps it will hurt inside me sometimes when I strike a man, and I shall realize suddenly that I was like that.

If we pay no attention to external events, he led a double life, of boredom and intoxication, and there was nothing more, nothing else; only boredom passed over to intoxication, and intoxication to boredom. Boredom which is the most dreadful and the ugliest prose; boredom which almost with satisfaction pastures on everything that is repulsive, monotonous, stale, and hopeless, which lets slip no stench, and decay, which follows the way of the bed-bug, the juice of corruption, sneaking cracks in the ceiling, and the vanity or foulness of life. And intoxication. Whether it be intoxication by rum, boredom, lust, or heat, if only it all mixes up, let the senses run into one another, let us be governed by an enraged enthusiasm; let us take it in all at once, all at once into our mouths and into our hands, so that we can gorge on it greedily, and squeeze out the juice till it runs over our chins—breasts and fruit, cooling foliage, and red-hot fire; when nothing has limits we have none, and everything that moves moves in us—in us the swaying of the palm-trees and of the hips, in us the dazzling sun, and the eternal weeping of water; out of the way, make room for the man who is so great and drunk that everything is in him. The stars, and the rustling of the tree-tops, and the open gates of the night. What landscapes are they pictured by intoxication, or boredom; dead landscapes stuck with dryness, with rotting fermentation, flies, stench, sticky dirt and decomposition, or again reeling landscapes, heaped with suns, rut, smells, and fiery tastes, sultry flowers, water, and dizziness. Listen, with boredom, and intoxication, a decent hell with all it contains can be circumscribed, so vast that even paradise is inside—paradise with all its wonder and brilliance, with all the delights, but that is the deepest hell, for it is just from there that disgust and boredom arise."

CHAPTER XXX

"Let us take at random: Haiti, Porto Rico, Barbuda, Guadeloupe, Barbados, Tobago, Curaçao, Trinidad, Dutch agents, British colonial cream of society, naval officers from the States, sceptical and untidy French bureaucrats; and everywhere creoles chattering in patois, negroes, *filles de couleur*, many brutal people, more unhappy ones, and most of those who in some way or other tried to preserve their respectability against drink, prurience, and sexual mesalliances. Case X, as far as possible, preferred to stick to the trodden paths; in spite of which there were perhaps weeks and months when he lived under a straw roof, in a hut supported on beams like a dovecot, to keep away from crabs and centipedes, on the edge of a forest which creaked in the wind, or smoked after a sultry downpour: here, enthroned on the wooden steps, he had the sand lice picked out from the soles of his feet and he took steps to see that another hundred acres of virgin nature were ready to bear the pith and fruit of the plant called Prosperity. Then blessings would settle on the country in the shape of negroes, who would have to work harder than before, but still remain as miserable as ever in return, in some other part of the world, the pith and fruit of the fields would cease to pay the peasants. That is the way of things, and to Mr. Kettelring it was all the same; if sugar-cane, then sugar-cane; let the axes ring, then gnats buzz, and the negroes bray, and at the end all this will be nicely sifted, and straightened out to the clicking of the typewriters. No, these aren't typewriters, they're frogs, cicadas, it's a bird hammering with his beak on a tree. No, it is not a bird, or rustling of stalks, it's the sound of a typewriter, and Mr. Kettelring sat on the floor and hammered with his finger at a rusty typewriter. Only a buisness letter, Cubans, nothing else, but that miserable machine was so eaten with damp and rust—somehow Kettelring felt relieved. What is one to do, I can't type this letter, all right, I'm coming back.

So he was coming back to Cuba, having done well over the profit from sugar-cane on the islands; he was returning on a big-bellied boat, laden with vanilla, pimento, and cacao, mace and tangerines, angostura and ginger, on a boat full of odours, trusty like a shop with colonial goods; it was a Dutch boat puffing from one port to another like a gossipy aunt who stops in front of every shop and has too much to say. No hurry, sir, hands in your pockets, and have a look. At what? Well, at the water, at the sea, at the track of the sun that is drawn on it; or at the islands with their blue shadows, at the clouds lined with gold, at the flying fishes as they splash about the sparkling water. Or in the evening at the stars; then the bellied captain would appear, offer a fat cigar; he also had not too much to say. After all, it would not be so bad to remain just Mr. Kettelring.

All the time there was some kind of a storm on the horizon, at night there were broad red flashes of lightning behind a veil of rain; or the sea became iridescent with pale and bluish stripes that ran apart and suddenly faded away; and below in that black seething water something was phosphorescent all the time with its own light. Mr. Kettelring leaned against the rail and was filled with a feeling that was neither boredom nor intoxication. Yes, that at least was certain; he had sailed once before just like that, and felt just as happy and free. Now he was storing it up in himself so that he would not forget it again. To spread out his arms with longing. With that immense feeling of love, freedom, or something.

Camagueyno welcomed him with open arms; the old pirate knew how to show acknowledgment when a vessel was returning laden with booty. He no longer sat with Mr. Kettelring in the office, but in a shady room at a table covered with damask, English glass, and jugs with heavy silver heads, he poured out red wine for him, and—apparently out of respect—he tried to talk to him in English. The room opened with slender arches and small columns into a patio inlaid with majolica; in the middle a fountain murmured, surrounded by small palms and myrtles in faience pots, like somewhere in Seville. Señor Kettelring was now a valued guest. 'My house belongs to you,' said the Cuban with old Spanish grandeur, and inquired after his travels and return as if they were the rambles of a nobleman just for pleasure. Mr. Kettelring, of course, had not sufficient tradition for those formalities, and he talked business. There and there it looks like this, that debtor is bad, that concern there may have a future, and is worth watching. Camagueyno nodded. 'Very well, sir, we will talk about that again,' and he waved his hand. 'Well, well, there's time enough.' He had grown much older, more respectable, more foolish than he used to be; his bushy eyebrows run up and down on his forehead. 'And your health, my dear Kettelring, your health.' He giggled excitedly, 'And what about the women, how is it there with the women?'

Kettelring was astonished. 'Thanks for asking, it wasn't so bad. With regard to that land on Trinidad, it's a damned swamp; but if it were drained——'

'Is it true,' wheezed the Cuban. 'Is it true that on Haiti the negresses are as if they were mad when—when those pagan fiestas of theirs are on? Eh?'

'It is,' said Kettelring. 'Absolutely mad, sir. But the best chabines are on Guadeloupe.'

Camagueyno bent towards him. 'And what about the Hindoo women, what are the Hindoo women like? Are they muy lascivas? They have, they say—some secret cults, is it true? You must tell me everything, my dear Kettelring.'

A girl entered the room in a white dress. The Cuban got up, raising his eyebrows impatiently almost to his hair. 'This is my daughter, Maria Dolores, Mary; for she has been to a university in the States.' It was as if he wanted to apologize for her; for a Spanish girl would never enter a room where there was a foreign caballero. But Mary was already shaking hands in the American fashion. 'How do you do, Mr. Kettelring?' She pretended to be more bony and angular than she really was, she wanted to look

English; at the same time she was pale olive, and black like pitch, her brows joined together, and there was down under her nose—a genuine and good Cuban maiden.

'Well, Mary,' said Camagueyno, to indicate that she might go; but Mary was an independent American girl, she sat down and crossed her legs, and shot at Mr. Kettelring one question after the other. What is it like on the islands? What about the social conditions of the negroes? How do they live, what are their children like, what of the health conditions? Mr. Kettelring was silently amused by her schoolgirl energy, while Camagueyno raised shocked eyebrows like two huge hairy caterpillars. And Mr. Kettelring lied like a school book: Lovely islands, Miss Mary, perfect paradise; all virgin forest with colibrees fufu, vanilla grows there by itself, you have only to pick it; and as for the negroes, one can't complain, they have a good time like children. . . .

The American girl listened, holding her knees, and never took her eyes away from that man who had come straight from paradise."

CHAPTER XXXI

"In the evening Camagueyno soon excused himself, tormented by pain in his gall-bladder; he really looked miserable, and his eyes sank deep with pain. Mr. Kettelring went out into the garden to smoke a cigar; there was a smell of nutmeg, acacias, and volcameria, and big moths fluttered as if they were drunk. A white girl was sitting on a majolica seat breathing the unbearably sweet air through her half-closed lips. Mr. Kettelring avoided her in a respectable curve, he knew what was seemly. And suddenly the cigar flew into a thicket of oleanders. 'Señorita,' said Kettelring quickly, and almost roughly, 'I am ashamed of myself; I was lying to you, it is like hell down there, and don't let them make you believe that a man can remain a man there.'

'And you will go back?' she inquired in a low voice; night softens the voice.

'Yes. Where else should I go?' She made room for him beside her. 'Perhaps you know that I have . . . no home anywhere. I have nowhere to go back to unless it is there.' He waved his hand. 'I'm sorry to have spoiled your picture of a paradise. But no, it is not so bad.' He tried to think of something beautiful. Once I saw a Morphos butterfly; just a yard in front of me, he was fluttering with those blue wings of his, he was a beauty. He was sitting on a dead rat, full of maggots.'

The university girl straightened herself up severely. 'Mr. Kettelring——'

'I am not Mr. Kettelring. Why, why should I always lie, I'm nobody. I think that a man who has no name has no soul either. That's why I could stand it there, *sabe?*'

And suddenly it wasn't a university girl, but a small Cuban, blinking her long lashes in pity. *Ay de mi*, what to say to him, what can I say nice to him? Best run home, for he's so strange; cross myself and get up—No, an American girl can't do that, an American girl would be his comrade; didn't we study psychology.

I can help him to find his lost memory, to bring out his suppressed notions; but first I must win his confidence—In a friendly manner the American girl held his hand. 'Mr. Kettelring—or what shall I call you?'

'I don't know, I am that man.'

She squeezed his hand to give him a lead. 'Try, try to think of your childhood. You MUST remember something—at least your mother, don't you. You are remembering, aren't you?'

'Once I . . . I had a fever. That was on Barbuda. An old negress treated me with compresses of black pepper cooked with pimento. She put my head on her lap, and hunted for lice. Her hand was as wrinkled as a monkey's. I had the feeling then that she was like my mother.'

The little Cuban felt like tearing her fingers away from his. He had such a warm hand; but that perhaps wouldn't be right, it was dreadful how uncertain one was about such things. 'So you do remember your mother!"

'No, I don't know. I think I never had one.'

The American girl was firmly determined to help him. 'You must try a bit more. Remember something about when you were a boy. Some games, friends, any little thing——'

He shook his head doubtfully. 'I can't remember.'

'Something at least,' she urged. 'Children have such strong impressions!'

He tried to do as she said. 'Always when I look at the horizon it seems to me that there must be something beautiful beyond it. That's a childish idea, isn't it?'

'You thought of that at home?'

'No, here on the islands. But at the time I felt . . . as if I were a boy.'

He held her by the hand, and ventured further. 'Listen, I have . . . stolen a ball.'

'What ball?'

'. . . A child's,' he mumbled in confusion. 'It was in Port of Spain, in the harbour. It rolled under my feet. . . . A red and green ball. As a child I must have had one like it. Ever since then I've carried it about with me——'

Tears came into her eyes. God how stupid I am! 'So you see, Mr. . . . Mr. Kettelring,' she breathed excitedly, 'it will come, you'll see. Close your eyes and think, will you? Try to remember terribly hard—but you must close your eyes to concentrate.'

Obediently he closed his eyes, and sat motionless as if he had even been told to do that. And there was silence, only the hum of drunken moths could be heard, and in the distance the squeal of a mulatto.

'Are you thinking?'

'Yes.'

Holding her breath, the little Cuban leaned towards his face. How strange he was, how severe he looked with his eyes closed; tormented and dreadful. Suddenly his face relaxed.

'Have you remembered anything?'

He sighed with deep relief. 'It's so beautiful here!'

She had to fight with an absurd impulse; and still it burst out of her, although she didn't want to say it: 'Here . . . it's not like hell here?'

'It's not like hell here,' he whispered. He was afraid to move his hand, or to open his eyes. 'It is so new to me. Do you understand, I didn't like THEM.'

God knows which understood first, the American girl, or the small black Cuban; but she pulled away her hand, and felt a hot wave sweep over her face. What a good thing that it was so dark.

'Did you . . . like anyone BEFORE?' God, how dark it is!

He shrugged his heavy shoulders.

'You couldn't help remembering THAT. . . .' This was said by the American girl for the Cuban knew that it wasn't right to talk like that with a stranger. But even the big American student was puzzled; up there, in the girls' college, didn't they talk about everything; and with young men you could talk openly about anything—God knows why it was so difficult now.

She cooled her cheeks with the back of her hand, and she bit her lips.

'Mr. Kettelring?'

'Yes.'

'You must have loved a woman. Can you remember?'

He was silent, leaning forward over his knees. Now it was the little Cuban who so anxiously blinked her long eyelashes. 'Never,' he said slowly, 'have I felt what I do now. That I know, that I know for certain.'

The little Cuban could not breathe, her heart was beating so, her knees were trembling so. That is how it is, gracious God, and it is so beautiful that you feel like crying. But the American brains snatched at that sentence, and quickly turned it over. Yes, it is like this, and I realized it at once, as soon as he said: 'Señorita, I lied to you.'

'I am so glad,' she said, and her teeth chattered slightly, 'that' (well, what?)—'that you like it here.' (No, it's not that, but it's almost the same.) 'I like this garden so much, I sit here every evening——' (God, that was stupid!) The American girl tried to get on top. 'Look here, Mr. Kettelring, I will help you to remember, do you want to? It must be dreadful if you can't remember who you are.' Mr. Kettelring jumped as if he had been struck. 'I mean,' said the American girl trying to cover herself, 'that I should be so glad if I could help you! Please——' She touched his sleeve with her finger. (Only to flirt a bit before I go! Just to go home better!)

He got up. 'I beg your pardon. I will accompany you.'

She stood before him, as close as if she were holding him with both hands. 'Promise me that you will remember!' He smiled. At that moment he seemed so beautiful to her that she nearly cried out with happiness.

She leaned from the window into the scented night; on the balcony above the red-hot fire of a cigar was glowing.

'Hello, Mr. Kettelring!'

'Yes?'

'You're not asleep?'

'No.'

'I'm not either,' she communicated happily, and leaned out with her bare arms into the night. Take, stroke, press my shoulders, here I am; feel here how my heart beats.

No, I'm not looking, I daren't; see I even throw my cigar away into the darkness so that you won't see how my teeth chatter. Damn, Mary don't stroke your shoulders, for it's as if I were doing it.

. . . I know, I feel it. You have burning hands as if they were lying in the sun. Why is it that my fingers tremble so much? And yet I'm quiet, quite quiet. I KNEW that it would come. When did I find it out? You needn't know everything. As soon as I came into the room, and you got up—so tall, and he doesn't even know who he is.

The man above on the balcony sighed.

Oh, Mr. Kettelring, please, don't be silly; but this is very fine of you. One might take you by the hand, and say: Dear lil' boy, whose are you? I should have kissed you on the spot, or something. Maternal instinct, I guess.

Thanks—politely.

No, don't you believe it. I was afraid of you. You are so mysterious and dreadful—as if you wore a mask. Altogether exciting. I very nearly ran away when you spoke to me in the garden; it was a fright.

I beg your pardon. I didn't mean, in fact——

But I wanted you to come; you didn't realize? These Spanish customs are stupid that won't let me sit with you at dinner. We have almost to steal a meeting . . . and at once it's so strange; my heart beats as if it were a sin or something. Hello, are you still there?

Yes, here I am, here. Don't look, or I shall jump down, Maria Dolores.

Quickly she covered her arms with a silk shawl; now again

she was a black Cuban, sweetly blinking her long eyelashes into the darkness; she didn't think of anything, merely waited.

Do you realize that a man meets very few white women down there; you don't know what a miracle it is to have suddenly that fine and dreadful feeling of respect. The desire to kneel down, and not even dare to raise your eyes. Ah, señorita, what wouldn't I do if you gave me your handkerchief, I should fall on my knees, and be happy to the end of my days.

The Cuban girl's eyes sparkled, and slowly, slowly, the shawl slid from one shoulder, only a narrow strip of a dim arm, but it was more than ever—Perhaps a bat had fanned her in its zig-zag flight; she shivered, crossed her hands on her breast, and was gone.

And then, already day was breaking, in the garden God's birds peeped, still from sleep; the American student stole silently, cautiously to the window, and looked towards the balcony. Yes, the little red fire of the cigar is glowing there too, that man was standing there motionless, clutching the rail in his hand; and the girl's heart ached with happiness.

After that she sat for a long time on the edge of her bed, and smiled in ecstasy down at her white round legs."

CHAPTER XXXII

"I CAN'T think it out in any other way; she didn't see him at all next day, it was as if on purpose; Camagueyno dragged him away to the office and somewhere to dinner. He vaguely reported this and that; and now it was the Cuban who had to ask questions to make him talk business, and even then he mixed up one thing with another, and Barbuda with Trinidad. The Cuban fixed on him his hollow scrutinizing eyes and laughed lightly, although he was tormented with pain. Again the two of them had supper alone; the Cuban was quite yellow with pain, but he showed no inclination to get up, he only kept on pouring out the rum. Drink, Kettelring, the devil, do drink! And how is it with sugar on Haiti? Kettelring's memory wasn't as good as it had been before, he paused, and stammered—Well, drink, man! At the end, Kettelring got up, taking care not to stagger. 'I'm going into the garden, sir., My head aches.'

Camagueyno raised his eyebrows. 'Into the garden? As you please.' Again that splendid gesture as if it all belonged to the valued guest.

'By the way, Kettelring, how is your memory?'

'My memory, sir?'

The Cuban's eyes narrowed. 'Can't you still say—who you really are?'

Kettelring spun round quickly. 'I think, sir, that I'm known well enough . . . as Mr. Kettelring.'

'True,' mumbled the Cuban, gazing thoughtfully at his cigar. 'Stupid that you don't even know if you haven't . . . say . . . been married already a long time, isn't it?' He raised himself with difficulty, and pressed his hand to his side. 'Good night, Mr. Kettelring, I wish you good night.'

Kettelring did stagger a little as he stepped into the garden. A pale and excited girl, wrapped in a shawl, was waiting for him; behind her in the shadow stood that old Mexican Indian, whose eyes blinked anxiously and kindly. Oh, duena, understood Mr. Kettelring, but otherwise everything danced before his eyes: huge shadows, the pink inundation of the flowering corallitas, an intense scent, and the girl in a folded shawl. She took him by the arm, and dragged him into the lower part of the garden. 'Think of it,' she chattered excitedly. 'They wanted to STOP me from coming here!' She was immensely offended like an American girl, but her clenched fists were Cuban. 'I shall do what I like,' she threatened fiercely, but it wasn't true. This, at least, she didn't want to do, she did not intend: that in the deepest shade, in the shade of the hibiscus, her shawl should fall to the ground, and that she should hang on the neck of that man who staggered with despair. She raised her face to his, her mouth painfully open with the desire for a kiss. 'Señorita, India,' he murmured warningly, and pressed her in his arms, but she only shook her head; she offered him her mouth, the damp shadow of her mouth to drink of her; stiff, beyond herself, with glazed eyes. Suddenly she collapsed in his embrace, exhausted, with limp arms. He let her go; she staggered, her face in her hands, defenceless, urrendered. He picked up her shawl, and put it round her shoulders. 'Mary,' he said, 'you must go home now; and I—I shall come back. Not as Mr. Kettelring, but as someone who will have the right to come for you. Did you understand?'

She stood with her head bowed. 'Take me with you—now, at once!'

He put his hand on her shoulder. 'Go home, God knows how much more difficult it is for me than it is for you.' She let herself be led back, if only she could feel that heavy hot hand on her shoulder.

A tall peon stepped out from the thicket. 'Va adentro, señorita,' he commanded hoarsely. 'Pronto!'

She turned her face to Kettelring: her eyes shone, God knows with what. 'Adios,' she said silently, and gave him her hand.

'I shall come back, Mary,' murmured *este hombre* desperately, fumbling her fingers. She bent down quickly and kissed the back of his hand with moist lips; he could have shrieked with terror and love.

'Va, va, señorita,' said the peon huskily, and stepped back. She pressed that hand strongly to her heart, and offered her face. 'Adios,' she whispered, and kissed him with her mouth and face full of tears.

The old Indian took her by the waist. 'Ay, ay, señorita, va a la casa, va a la casa.'

She let herself be led away as if blind, trailing the fringe of her shawl on the ground.

Kettelring stood motionless like a black post and pressed in his hand a small lace handkerchief, with a penetrating scent. 'Va, señor,' growled the vaquero almost soothingly.

'Where is Camagueyno?'

'He is waiting for you, sir.' The peon struck a match on his trousers to light Kettelring's cigar. 'This way, sir.'

The old Cuban was sitting at the table, adding up money. Mr. Kettelring looked at him for a while, and then grinned. 'That is for me, isn't it?'

Camagueyno raised his eyes. 'That is for you, Kettelring.'

'Salary, or a share of the profits?'

'Both. You can add it up.'

Kettelring stuffed the money into his pocket. 'But to let you know, Camagueyno,' he said as distinctly as he could, 'I shall come back for her.'

The Cuban drummed with his fingers on the table. 'Unfortunately in Kettelring's papers it states that he is married. What is one to do?'

'Kettelring won't come back again,'' said *este hombre* slowly.

Camagueyno winked at him with amusement. 'Well, sure, personal papers aren't expensive, they can be bought, can't they? For a couple of dollars——'

Este hombre sat down without invitation, and poured himself a drink, he was more sober now than ever. 'Let's suppose, Camagueyno. Let's suppose that it won't go any other way.

But a very good estate would be like a very good name, don't you think so?'

The Cuban shook his head. 'With us in Cuba, a good name is worth too much.'

'About how much?'

The Cuban smiled. 'Eh, Kettelring—I can still call you that?—you know how much MY estate amounts to.'

Kettelring whistled. 'Do talk sense, Camagueyno. Of course, I can't earn as much as that in all my life.'

'Of course not,' agreed the Cuban, and sniggered. 'Those times are not any longer, and they won't be.'

Kettelring again poured himself a drink, and thought deeply. 'That's true, sir. But if it happened that your estate got a good deal smaller in a couple of years—then it would be easier to catch up, wouldn't it?''

They both looked closely at one another. So now the cards were on the table.

'Let's suppose, Camagueyno, that somebody knows your affairs and contracts through and through—many things could be done with that.'

The Cuban reached for the bottle of aguardiente, not minding his liver. 'Without money,' he said, 'nothing can be done.'

Kettelring pointed to his pocket. 'This will be enough for the beginning, sir.'

Camagueyno laughed and showed his long yellow teeth: but his eyes had narrowed to evil and deep loopholes. 'I wish you great success, Kettelring. I gave you a lot of money, didn't I? Well, what's to be done. A la salud!'

Kettelring got up. 'I shall come back, Camagueyno.'

'Adios, muy señor mio.' Camagueyno bowed in the old Cuban fashion when a valued guest was being taken to the door. 'Good night, sir, good night.'

The tall peon banged the rails behind Kettelring. 'Good night, sir.' And Case X walked away among the flowering hedges of bougainvilleas, along the path that glittered in the starry night like the milky way.''

CHAPTER XXXIII

"Now it was no longer an indifferent man whose indolent eyes gazed at the changing kaleidoscope of harbours and plantations; but a man who went to conquer, a pugnacious fellow with his head held erect; his spirit on fire, and his taut muscles almost humming. As if he had been born afresh. But isn't this the supreme sexual element in love? Aren't we really born from the breasts and lap of the woman we love, and doesn't this womb cry out for us because it desires to bear us. Now you are mine because in tremors I gave you birth, young and beautiful. And isn't the attainment of love like the beginning of a new and complete life? You call it illusion; but has illusion a source less deep than disappointment?

And so let us go on with him, first to Haiti: there was a swamp there in which it was said there were deposits of black bitumen; but that swamp, they said, smelt so strongly that not a bird, toad, or negro could bear to stay near it. He rode there on a horse —say, from Gonaiva, but he had to leave the horse behind, and with his niggers hacked his way, lacerated with thorns, and cut with the high grass which was as sharp as a razor. The negroes ran away, he had to fetch them back, and pay them double; in spite of the attractive wage two fell out on the way, one bitten by a snake, and the other, the deuce knows. He was all screwed up with cramp, and he breathed his last with a yellow scum on his mouth; some poison maybe, but the negroes thought that *djambios* had done it, and they didn't want to go any further. At last he reached the swamp, and saw that it was not so bad; there were clouds of gnats, so a living creature could exist there. It was a dreadful place, black and close, roasting in the glare of the sun; in places it bubbled forth a yellow foamy pus, and there the smell was unbearable. He went back to Gonaiva, bought the land, and made a contract with some thievish mulatto to build for him a road to the 'Asphalt lake,' as he called it rather ostentatiously; and after that he went away, say, to Porto Rico.

Well, and now he got down to it: he decided to go for Camagueyno, that is for sugar. Before he used to write to the old Cuban and say that sugar would go down, but Camagueyno wouldn't believe it. The great conjecture in sugar has had its day; let me tell you that it will make the old fox tremble. He knew of people who would gladly buy Camagueyno's lands, shares, or this or that concern; he went to them, and asked how much they would like to give. All right, I give you my word that you will get it for half if you will pay me so much commission. The Cuban is up to his ears in sugar-cane, and he will have to sell helter skelter to scramble out; but we must work him down yet. And then he rushed, let us say, to Barbuda, Terre-Basse, Barbados, Trinidad; he found that the Cuban was already getting the wind up, and was beginning to sell to save his cash. Kettelring threw himself into the fray with his chin stuck out and his sleeves rolled up. Wait, you wait; offer him one quarter, terminate your contracts, tell him to lick your feet; what is ahead is nothing but a crash worse than ever before. You will be able to buy a sugar factory for the price of scrap iron, and plantations for a handful of pig beans. And the price of sugar is falling, a third of last year's crop is still in store; what can they do with it, they can't even use it for fuel, only sweeten the Atlantic Ocean with it; it will be a nice sweet mash, gentlemen.

It was like an avalanche, every man jack began to run away from sugar (they really did), and sell what they had, or what they hadn't. Well, now old Camagueyno could look for buyers for his sugar factories, and plantations. It is true the old man defended himself well, but in his offers you could also sense a panic; I should like to see how his bushy brows jumped up and down. Well, it'll pull down a lot of other people with it, but it can't be helped; did anyone think of poor Pierre? Old planters went about with long faces, not understanding what was going on; nobody would give them anything for their cane, for their coffee, vanilla went for a mere song, bananas perished with Panama disease; and they couldn't even turn their backs on the islands because there was no one interested in the land either to hire or to buy it. And some years ago this was called the Golden Antilles.

In the end Camagueyno gave up the fight; he had a nose good enough not to wait for the worst, and he sold, as they say, at any price.

The beast, he still got away with a third of his fortune, Mr. Kettelring sighed with satisfaction; little was left of the commissions that he had negotiated, for a life like that is expensive and showy, and here and there he had to be lavish in helping on the course of events. Now the turn of the asphalt was coming. Everybody can't grow asphalt like sugar-cane, or cacao. You can put your money on asphalt. I'm putting my money on black against white.

And he ordered retorts and barrels, he bought an old light railway complete, and moved back to Haiti.

Dear doctor, I shall feel happier when I'm at home again—the scent of thyme, the smell of juniper, and Carthusian pinks in my hand; strange how foreign lands fill you with disquiet. I certainly should be revolutionary if I didn't live on my native soil; here (I mean on the islands) I feel the injustice, and horror of things, stronger . . . or at least with more hatred than at home. If I were really to write my story, a man with an open shirt, and with a gun slung on his shoulder, wouldn't be missing, that partisan, that avenger, that passionate antagonist of all Kettelrings, would be myself. It's no use, I must give it up; and when I sit at home again on a bank with flowers, and rub in my fingers the sweet scent of resignation, horror and hatred will melt away, and I shall drop the wild flower, the northern flower, over the grave of a half-breed in an open shirt who fell somewhere on the islands fighting against the Laws of Economics."

CHAPTER XXXIV

"THEN the destiny of Case X got mixed up. Suppose that the mulatto contractor left the road unfinished, and ran away, enticed by the star of a variety dancer. Mr. Kettelring began to build the road himself, and spent a lot of money on it because he was in a hurry. He couldn't make the negroes carry stones in wheelbarrows, those black longshanks put the boulders on their heads and carried them as if they were baskets of pineapples; and the wheelbarrows were only good for giving a ride to shrieking wenches kicking their legs. Oh, to punch their faces and make them realize that life isn't just for their cackling guffaw! Behind the columns of workers moved crowds of girls, at night they swayed with their buttocks to the sound of guitars and tamtams, while Kettelring was gnawed with desperate impatience. He daren't even urge those louts on as much as he would have liked; the ecomonic crisis hit Haiti too, with the strange result that the negroes indulged to an unprecedented extent in fetishes, and each week they brayed and raved in the clearings in the forest; they came back like shadows exhausted and wild, and Kettelring never let his revolver go from his hand, even at night, as he listened to the tapping of their bare paws. Not far away two or three children went lost, and Kettelring was careful not to try to get to the bottom of the affair; and the black police from Gonaiva, barefooted, and with golden epaulettes, who came to investigate the case, were also careful not to discover a certain stone altar in the jungle to which led well-trodden paths.

Month after month slipped by, and with them Kettelring's funds and health melted away; he suffered from boils and fever, but he didn't go away to get better lest the band of negroes should disperse. He watched over them with evil eyes, sunken with hatred, and he only hissed out his commands. The road was still unfinished when he settled down at the asphalt swamp in a hut, built on piles, to direct the building of the light railway; but in the meantime people had stolen the rails lying in the harbour at Gonaiva, God knows what use anyone could make of them. The whole place smelt of sulphuretted hydrogen, and it fermented with a yellow suppuration like an immense distintegrating ulcer; it exuded heat like a kettle of boiling tar, and every step hung with the semi-fluid, trembling, squelching bitumen.

At last the road dragged itself to the swamp, and Kettelring went to Port au Prince to hunt for credit, get the lorries, and barrels, hire drivers and overseers. When he came back there wasn't a single soul alive on the spot; the devil himself, they said, had appeared in the middle of the swamp, and lashed up all the slush until it had boiled like jam. With great trouble he got together a handful of mangy sickly negroes with inflamed eyes, full of flies, and they began to dig the asphalt. It was a glossy black glance-pitch of first-rate quality. It was worse with the lorries; one was ruined by a mulatto who was bringing retorts and barrels from Gonaiva; the other ran into the swamp, and in a few days it disappeared under the surface; only one was left to transport the asphalt to the harbour. Kettelring took charge of the retorts to see that the pitch was well boiled up; he was black and dirty like a stoker, and he shivered with malaria by that hellish fire; they all had it there, so what about it. He didn't even take in his hands that little lace handkerchief so as not to make it dirty; he thought of nothing but the barrels full of asphalt. Well, now things were on the move, and with eyes scorched by the heat and with his feverish finger Kettelring outlined in the air the factories that were going to stand there. Haiti Lake Asphalt Works, or something like that.

Of course there were vexations. That mulatto who takes the barrels to Gonaiva. Always breaking down, and yet he bares his teeth at your face. A bad car, sir, and a bad road. Kettelring threw him out, and then he drove himself, he rattled to the harbour with full barrels, and was pleased to see how they were piling up. Hundreds of barrels, hundreds, and more hundreds, how lovely! But that mulatto who had been given the sack was not just anybody, he had seen a bit of the world; he prowled round the Haiti Lake Asphalt Works with an open shirt and held discussions about labour conditions and impudent foreigners, until one day four niggers came to Kettelring, they nudged one another, and shuffled—in short, either he must take that multato back to work, or——

Kettelring reddened. 'Or what?' This question he asked while he moved the safety-catch on his revolver.

A strike followed. An organized strike as well as cannibalistic rites, but that's how it is to-day. Only a few people stayed there, so ill that they couldn't get home on foot. It seems that Kettelring went mad; he snatched up a pickaxe and, up to his knees in mud, he began himself to hack out chunks of asphalt, and hissing and wheezing with the strain he dragged them to the retorts, while the sick ones gazed at him with open mouths, and were too afraid to take a spade in their hands. When he had hauled out sufficient to fill a retort he broke into tears. 'Pierre, Pierre!' he sobbed, and beat his head. Then the sick ones ran away too.

For two days longer Kettelring sat by the deserted lake of asphalt, and watched how slowly the excavated pits filled up again. Thousands, hundreds of thousands of tons of asphalt. Hundreds and hundreds of barrels waiting for a buyer. Then in that lace handkerchief he wrapped a chip of raw asphalt and a bit of the refined, shining like anthracite, and he rattled with the empty lorry down to Port au Prince. There he slept for forty-eight hours as if he were dead.

And again he came in front of the wrought-iron railings of the Cuban's house, and knocked; Open, open! The tall peon stood behind the railings, but he didn't open the door. 'Que desea, señor?'

'I want to speak with Camagueyno, but at once,' wheezed Kettelring, 'Open, man!'

'No, señor,' murmured the old peon. 'I have been ordered not to let you in.'

'Tell him,' gasped Kettelring, 'tell him that I have business for him, a tremendous business.' And he rattled the two bits of asphalt in his pocket.

'Tell him——'

'No, señor.'

Kettelring rubbed his forehead. 'Could you—deliver a letter——'

'No, señor.'

There was silence. In the evening air there was the scent of corallita in flower.

'Buenas noches, señor.'

And down again, down round the islands: Porto Rico, Barbuda, Guadeloupe, Barbados, Trinidad, and Curaçao: Yankees, British, French, and Dutch, creoles and half-breeds; everywhere he had his commercial relations, men on whose necks he had once laid the knife, or with whom he had helped to make sugar go smash; at least they knew with whom they had the honour. In front of them he pulled two bits of asphalt out of a lace handkerchief. Look, what asphalt, black and glossy like the pupil of your eye. Thousands, hundreds of thousands of tons, a whole lake. Millions can be made out of it. So, well, will you join me?

They scratched their hair, and sighed. Bad times, Mr. Kettelring; think of it, even ashpalt's no good now; they're sacking men in Trinidad, they say. It seemed as if when they lost faith in sugar, all their faith in anything was shaken. No, no, sir, nothing can be done; not a penny, not a cent will I put again in those damned islands. (What a grand invention are colonies! To discover countries which aren't a home for a man, but only land for exploitation! How it must give scope for commercial ability!)

Kettelring dragged himself in the boat from one port to the other. During the day he slept, and at night he stood in the bows like a post, they could have tied a cable to him. That huge, blue-black night, shot with lightning, blazing with stars; the soughing sea, phosphorescent, sparkling, black like anthracite; all asphalt, sir, milliards and milliards of tons, millions could be made from it. The boat dragged itself, jerked, quivered as if it couldn't move from the spot; perhaps the propeller was turning in something thick and oily that stuck to its blades; it was dark like heavy black naphtha; and the black boat slowly made its way through the asphalt lake which closed behind it like batter. Good night, señor. There above . . . that was the milky way similar to the path in the night, the light path among the purple bougainvilleas, and the blue grapes of petrea. What a scent, what a scent it had of heavy roses, and jasmine; Kettelring pressed to his lips a little creased lace handkerchief; it smelt of asphalt, and of something immensely remote. I shall come back, Mary, I shall come back!

And all shook their heads doubtfully. We can do nothing, Mr. Kettelring, no credit anywhere, no interest in anything; on Dominica they've also stopped extracting asphalt; but if you waited twenty years, that would be something different; these blasted times can't last for ever.

Now there was only one thing left, go to those gentry from the Trinidad Lake Asphalt Company; on Trinidad the funicular was still creaking, which took barrels of asphalt from the lake straight into the boats, but even it creaked rather rustily. Those gentlemen let him stand like a suppliant while with a perspiring forehead he unwrapped his two bits of asphalt from out of the lace handkerchief; they wouldn't even look at them. What can we do with it, Mr. . . . Mr. . . . you said Cattlering, didn't you? We've got enough asphalt here for at least fifty years, and we can cope quite easily with the world consumption. There's so much money invested here—why should we develop another deposit?

But my asphalt is better; it's not got as much water in it, or clay—and a thick naphtha comes up there.

They laughed at him. Worse and worse, Mr. . . . Mr. Cattle. Couldn't you, say, flood it with water, so that it disappears for good? In that case we might buy it, perhaps—of course, for the current price of land on Haiti. Good-bye, Mr. Kling.

(Good-bye, good-bye! At last I'm out of it, and I feel a good deal easier; I didn't feel at home in that world of business transactions, it was stranger to me than a swamp with alligators, but what of it, I found myself in it as if I were in a forest. And I was losing Kettelring in it; well, and now we've found ourselves again. You know, even he will find himself again; nobody comes to himself so intensely as one who is unhappy. Praise be to God, now we're at home, and this is MY return; this man with empty hands, who stands for nothing else but a man who has lived.)

That evening Case X sat in a room of a hotel for half-breeds at Port of Spain, full of bed-bugs, and pestering flies: through the thin walls he could hear how someone was talking and complaining in his dream, and a sailor embracing a mulatto; the whole hotel resounded with the clatter of plates, drunken brawls, guffaws, with hot snoring, and wheezing, as if somebody were dying.

Case X put into the typewriter a sheet of paper bearing the imprint of the Haiti Lake Asphalt Works, and began to tap out slowly: 'Dear Miss Mary.'

No, it was impossible to write this letter on a typewriter. Kettelring sat hunchbacked over the sheet of paper, and sucked the pencil. It is desperately difficult to begin when for such a long time, when we have, as far as one's memory goes, never written anything like this, making and joining the letters according to some infinitely refined laws and customs. On the typewriter it would be easier to write, it wouldn't hurt so much, it wouldn't swim in front of one's eyes. Kettelring was screwing up his back like a tiny scholar writing out his first effort. Oh—oh—ho—o—oh, gasped the mulatto behind the wall, and somebody was suffocating with nightmare, as if his last hour had come.

Dear, dearest, my only one, this is my first and last letter. I promised to come back, to come back like a man who has a name, and property; now I have nothing, I am shipwrecked, and I am going away. Where? I don't know yet. This life of mine is at an end, and I have had enough not to begin again. The only thing that is certain is that there is no longer a Kettelring, and that it would be useless to remember now who he really was. If I knew of a place in this world where it would be possible to live without a name I should go there; but even to beg one must have a name.

My only love, what madness it is that I still call you my love, and say you are mine. Now you will know that I am not coming back; but you must also know that I still love you as I did the first day, indeed infinitely more, for the more I have suffered the more I have loved you.

Kettelring grew thoughtful. Who knows if she is still waiting. It's three years since I went away; perhaps she's married to a Yankee in white shoes . . . Well, let her be happy.

I don't know, if I really believe in God, but I clasp my hands, and I pray that you will be happy. There must be a wise God if only because he did not bind up your fate with mine. Good-bye, good-bye, we shall not see each other again.

Kettelring had to bend right over the paper because he couldn't see, and he quickly scrawled his signature. At that instant he stiffened as if something had struck him on the head. He didn't sign his name George Kettelring. Unable to see for tears, blindly, unconsciously he wrote the real name which for so many years had escaped his memory."

CHAPTER XXXV

"He couldn't stand it in the hotel, he had to go out into the night; he sat by the harbour on a pile of sleepers guarded by a negro policeman; and, leaning with his elbows on his knees, he gazed into the black rippling water. Now he knew everything, and he needn't try to remember; he tidied it up inside himself as if straightening up a pack of cards, and he turned over this and that. Yes, it's there, and nothing is missing. Such a queer feeling —was it relief, or was he painfully overwhelmed?

Let us say home. A home without a mother, big rooms with heavy curtains, and black respectable furniture. Father who had no time for the child, big, strange, and severe. A timid anxious aunt. Mind, baby don't sit down there, don't put it in your mouth, you mustn't play with dirty children. A red and green ball, the most treasured toy because it was stolen in the street from a bawling urchin, one of those lucky ones who could run about with dirty noses, and bare feet, and make mud pies, or sit squatting in the sand. The former Mr. Kettelring smiled, and his eyes glinted. So you see, aunt, and yet in the end I did run about barefoot, and dirty like a coal-heaver. I have eaten chuchu cucumbers which a negress had wiped with her dirty skirt, and unripe guavas picked up from the dust of the road. The late Kettelring had almost a feeling of sated revenge. After all, I did do as I liked.

And now the restless boy whose natural wildness had been suppressed by so-called education. He began to understand the craft of his father. That craft was wealth. That craft was factories, to force the greatest possible number of people to work as hard as possible, and as cheap as possible. The boy saw those crowds of workers who streamed out from the gates of the factories with their peculiar sour smell, and he had a feeling that they all hated him. The father used to shout and give orders; God knows what vexation it costs to win such a fortune. You'd think that it isn't worth the bother; but no matter, property isn't just dead material, it wants its grub so that it doesn't peg out, and it must be fed properly. You, my boy, one day this property will be entrusted to you, not to have it, but to add to it; therefore learn to save, and get down to it if one day you are going to make others sweat and make ends meet. I'm bringing you up for a practical life; I'm bringing you up for my property. The former Kettelring grinned broadly. So that's where it comes from, from my father, that I can order people about and make them slave; well, some inheritance at any rate. Then, yes, at that time the young boy didn't care for it; he was rather easygoing and lazy—perhaps that was only out of spite against something that had already been fixed as his future. We're not here for our own sakes, but to serve property; who doesn't serve his own will slave for a stranger—something like that is the law of life. And you, my boy, will follow in my footsteps.

The former Kettelring shook with silent laughter. No, certainly he hadn't followed in them. He was only an heir-apparent, who was waiting one day to give it a turn. And just on purpose—bad society, and such like things. Debts, of course, silly, it's true, and not particularly honourable. Father quivered with agitation and made inquiries. What does it mean, why have you spent it, and such like things? You rascal, do you imagine that I slave for that, earn and save my money to pay for your infamies? And then it broke out in the stripling—of course, only spite, only waywardness, only such a passionate temper; with clenched fists he stormed at his father: 'Keep your money, stick it down your throat, I don't want it; I spit on it, I loathe it; don't think that I shall be such a slave to money as you are!' Father became purple, strange that he didn't have a stroke; he showed him the door, and hissed: 'Get out!' Then the door banged, that was the end, exit the son.

The former Mr. Kettelring shook his head. God, such a stupid thing! As if there were only a few thunderstorms like that in a family, may the devil take them. But that time two particularly tough and obstinate people fell foul of each other. The stripling never returned, and didn't even present himself when father's legal adviser invited him to see him; in the end the respectable legal friend found the prodigal son in bed with a theoretical and practical anarchist; and because the young gentleman made no move, he had to explain to him his mission in that shocking situation. He managed it quite nicely; on one side he put on a reprimanding frown, and on the other he beamed with tactful and mild good will, for youth must sow its wild oats, particularly the youth of so promising an heir. 'Your father wishes me to tell you that he doesn't want to see you till you have come to reason, my young friend,' he said heartily. 'I have no doubt that you will try, and that you will succeed, haha, isn't that so? Between us,' he said, with his head bent piously to one side, 'the property (he very nearly said Mr. Property) of your father is now put at thirty, thirty-five millions; young man, SUCH a property is no joking matter.' At that moment he really did look immensely solemn and serious, but he cheered up again. 'Your father asked me to tell you that through me he is willing to make you a certain allowance until you come of age.' And he named a sum almost miserable—the old miser kept faith with himself even in his righteous anger. 'Of course, if after that you don't see reason——' the solicitor gave his shoulders an eloquent shrug. 'But I hope that it will be a healthy and hard school of life for you.'

'Well, give me the dibs,' replied the heir of thirty millions, 'and tell the old man that I wish him a real long life while he's waiting for me.'

The anarchist clapped her hands enthusiastically.

The respectable solicitor playfully shook his fat finger at her. 'You, you, don't you turn our young friend's head. Let him enjoy himself, that's all right, but nothing more, do you understand?'

The girl stuck her tongue out at him; but the benevolent solicitor beamed and warmly pressed the hand of the prodigal son. 'My dear, dear friend,' he said touchingly, 'we shall all look forward to your speedy return.'

The prodigal son was eighteen then; until his coming of age he roamed about as is the way of young people, that is, he himself wouldn't be able to say how, and to whom he chiefly owed the money for it. Of course: Paris, Marseilles, Algiers, Paris, Brussels, Amsterdam, Seville, Madrid, and back again to Paris. As far as he was aware, with the breaking up of the family his father had lost all his inner inhibitions and plunged pathologically into making money, and into miserable senile stinginess. God bless him, it will be a pile of money that grows up there! Exactly on the day when he came of age the miserable pittance stopped. The prodigal son became furious: 'Do you expect me to crawl back on my knees? Not on your life!'—He tried to work; but strange, not until he began to work did want and misery oppress him, and when he tried to return to his former easy way of life, it wasn't the same any longer, he already carried some mark that made him suspicious of poverty. Then he took to a girl who was ill and had lost her job. He was sorry for her, and wanted to help her; he wrote to his father's legal friend that circumstances had arisen in which for a short time he needed a couple of thousand francs. He got to the centime as much as the journey cost from Paris third class, and with it a letter that his father was willing to pardon him if he showed that he wanted to work sensibly at home, and so on. It was really only then that he clenched his teeth, with no blithe swagger any longer, and he said to himself: 'I'd rather peg out with hunger.'

The former Mr. Kettelring, sitting on the beams at Port of Spain in Trinidad, almost grew frightened. He said it aloud, as he had done then, but now he shook his head."

CHAPTER XXXVI

"THE former Kettelring saw it now in an astonishingly clear light: If he had been genuinely and honestly poor, he would certainly have settled down somewhere; he had not lacked opportunities. Perhaps a book-keeper in Casa Blanca, or in Marseilles as a commercial traveller in mother-of-pearl buttons. But just realize, if you please, that I'm actually heir to thirty, forty, fifty millions, or as many as the old fellow has sucked up in the meantime; how am I to have the patience or resignation to argue with a blustering vulgar market dealer over the sale of twenty dozen buttons? At times he was seized with the absurdity of his position, he couldn't take it seriously, but he wasn't up to haggling with a sweaty and eager face for a couple of francs or pesetas; suddenly it was clear in his eyes that he was only playing at it, or something—people were offended, and from time to time he himself let off steam with an escapade so provocative that nothing was left but to change his post as quickly as possible. The former Mr. Kettelring remembered it with a certain relish. I didn't make it clear for you, you boobies, and perhaps even to-day your mugs are bitter and dry with rage when you remember that impudent bounder who treated you in this and that with so much disrespect, and then—Good-bye, please lick my shoes.

But on meditating over it—after all it was so half-unreal, and no matter what he did, he couldn't get rid of the feeling that in some way it was only provisory, and didn't really happen, but only as a matter of chance, and tentatively. The only thing real was that spite which led him on through thick and thin, and especially the thin; even in the utmost misery those millions were within his reach, easy to grasp, if only he had wished to end it all. Well, he could let them tinkle in his pocket when he took a stroll in the street, an individual without domicile or employment, his eyes could smile maliciously at all people who got out of the way of a suspicious-looking tramp, if only they knew who he was! Millions in his pocket, and he wouldn't even buy them a glass of beer. Five coppers in your pocket, and you can buy a red rose. It was in fact a perpetual occasion for jeering occupation; he mustn't forget the wild delight with which he first began to beg; it was on the Rambla in Barcelona amidst swarms of sparrows—how that old lady, with a rosary round her hand, looked terrified at the fellow baring his teeth, 'Por Dios misericordia, señora.'

The former Mr. Kettelring rubbed his forehead. No, I couldn't have borne it if it had been—real; but it was, you know, a kind of game with the unreal. As if I were trying to see how long I could stand it before I stretched out my hand, and begin to cry for help. The thrilling agony of standing on the side of the pavement and looking hungrily at the most beautiful and splendid women—only to say the word, and you would be mine, but now, of course, you won't even look at me, you beasts. That beautiful rage, that liberating scorn of everything. Yes, of course, of what is called morals as well; for there are the virtues of the poor, and the virtues of the wealthy, but there are no morals for the lousy ones who don't want to get rich. And they don't let themselves become attached to one place, the rascals. Not speaking of the ties of family, and customs, it is property and being dependent that makes one settle, and a man who doesn't mind misery, or care for money, is like a balloon without anchoring ropes, and ballasts, and he is led where God permits and the devil blows. Yes, wandering is certainly madness, it is a derangement of the property centres, something like losing one's sense of stability. And so reel about, you fool, if you can't help it——

Wait, there's something there that ought to be looked into. No, it was just mooncalf stupidity. In fact, no—well, say silliness. At the time I was something on a boat, that was in Plymouth; in the evening we used to sit on the Hoe, under the striped lighthouse, with a girl from Barbican. Such a thin, tiny English woman—she was seventeen. She held my hand, and tried to point out the good way of life to a big rotten sailor. The former

Mr. Kettelring's teeth chattered. But that was almost like . . . like . . . when Mary, Maria Dolores, held my hand, and wanted to bring me to myself! O God, there are signs in life that we don't understand. The former sailor gazed aghast into the black water, but he saw a blue, transparent evening on the Hoe, the red and green lights of the buoys, and the distance, Christ, that nice, even distance. She held my hand, and whispered quickly, 'Promise me, promise me, that you'll be good—and that sometime you'll settle here.' She worked in some kind of a factory. To tell her about those millions within my reach, wouldn't it have been like the Thousand and One Nights? It had been on the tip of his tongue, but he swallowed it somehow in a hurry and with too much effort. She kissed him good-bye furtively and clumsily, and he said, 'I shall come back.'

That boat went to the West Indies, and he had never gone back.

So, and now he was there, having arrived in good health, and that was all—No, that wasn't all, prompts some severe and undeviating voice. Do you remember what followed—Well, what would follow; I ran away from the boat, that was there on Trinidad, just there at Port of Spain, wasn't it?—Yes, and what next, what came after that?

Then I went downhill; when once a man begins to go downhill, it's too late to stop. How far down? Out with it—Well, I was a docker in the harbour, and a tallyman who ran about with papers in his hands—and nothing further? I was an overseer over the negroes at the asphalt lake to see that they didn't even wipe off the sweat with the back of their hands—And there was something else, wasn't there? Yes, I was a waiter on Guadelope, and in Matanzas, and I served mulattos with cocktails and ice.

And nothing worse than that?

The former Mr. Kettelring covered his face with his hot hands, and sighed. Let it be, there was something to say for it. It was revenge, it was revenge that they let me fall so low. To make it clear, I gloated over my abasement. You beasts, you beasts, here you have it, stick your millions down your throats; all of you look what the only son and heir of a millionaire looks like!

Yes, let's look into it.

Yes, look into it: he was being kept by a mulatto; so now you know. He loved her passionately, and touted for her among the drunken fellows, for the most perverse of them all, and he waited outside for his share.

So that's how it was—The former Kettelring's head fell low on his chest. In the café a Yankee was sitting, and I grinned idiotically: 'Can I, Sir, take you to a beautiful girl—beautiful——' the American turned crimson, and sprang up, perhaps he couldn't bear this ignominy of the white man; then he struck me in the face, on this cheek—A red spot appeared on the former Kettelring's face—He threw on the floor a creased five-dollar note, while they pushed me into the street. I came back for those five dollars, and I crawled on the ground like a dog.

The former Kettelring raised his horrified eyes. Will such a thing ever be forgotten?

Perhaps in the end, try, try to forget.

Yes, I drank like a beast, and yet I couldn't forget; I reeled, and I didn't know where and which way—along the path like the milky way, between the bougainvilleas in flower.

Yes, yes, there; I heard a revolver bark, and somebody ran and knocked into me. And then, then, at last, I forgot it all."

CHAPTER XXXVII

"The former Kettelring sighed with relief. So—now it's all out, and do what you like, you can't make it any worse. And see here, even when I crawled on all fours like a dog I didn't give in, it didn't cry inside me. Enough, I'm giving up, and this is my return, begging for pardon, my homecoming. I only drank, and howled over my degradation. It was . . . in fact . . . some sort of a victory.

And you will give in.

Yes, now I will give in, and gladly, God, how gladly! If they wanted me to spit into my face, or crawl again on all fours, I'll do it. I know why. It's for her, for the Cuban's daughter.

Or for getting the better of old Camagueyno.

Shut up, it's a lie. For her sake it is. Didn't I tell her that I should come back, didn't I give her my word of honour?

Your word of honour, pimp, pimp!

Yes, and perhaps even a pimp; if only I knew who I am. What do you want, a man is complete only when he is defeated. Then he realizes that it is unmistakable and real, that it is an undeviating reality.

The defeat.

Yes, the defeat. It is an immense relief to be able to give in; to put your hands on your breast, and give in——

To what?

To love. To love, in defeat and humiliation—a man knows then what love is. You are no longer a hero, but an insulted and battered pimp; you have crawled on the ground like a beast, and yet you will be dressed in the most beautiful garment and a ring will be put on your finger. That is the miracle. I know, I know that she is waiting for me; and now I can go to her. Christ, I am happy!

Happy, really?

Immensely happy, it freezes me—feel, feel how my cheeks burn.

Only the left cheek. That's the blow burning on it.

No, it's not a blow. Don't you know that she kissed me on that cheek? Yes, kissed, and damped it with her tears, don't you know? Everything is redeemed—as if it had cost so little pain! But what longing I had, and the hell I went through, that terrible work—was all for her.

And that blow?

—Yes, and that blow was for her, too. That the miracle could take place. And I shall go to her: she will be waiting in the garden as she was then——

—And she will put her hand in yours.

For God's sake, don't mention her hand! One says hand, and already my fingers and chin tremble. How she took me then by the hand—I am thinking of her smooth fingers, stop! stop!

Are you immensely happy?

Yes, no, wait, it will pass. Damn these tears! How is it possible that a man can love someone so absurdly! If she were waiting for me there—there at that crane, I should be horrified. God, how far, when shall I reach her! And if I held her by the hands, by the arms—God, how far!

Are you happy, then?

Nonsense, don't you see that I may go mad! When shall I see her? First I must go home, mustn't I? I must bow my head and beg for pardon. I must stand for a name and a man; and then again over the sea. No, but that's impossible. I shall not be able to endure it, it's impossible, such a time!

That you would go first to her, and tell her——?

No, I can't do that, I mustn't, that's not right. I told her that I shouldn't come for her until I had a right to. I mustn't disappoint her. I must go home, first go home, and only then—I shall knock at that gate as one who has a right to knock. Open, I am coming for her.

The black policeman who for a long time had been watching the man talking to himself and waving his arms about, drew nearer. Eh, sir!

The former Kettelring raised his eyes. 'Do you understand,' he said quickly. 'First I must go home. I don't know whether my father is still alive, but if he is, God knows, I will kiss his hand, and say, bless, father, bless, thy prodigal son who was glad to eat the husks thrown to the sows. I have sinned against heaven and before thee, and am no more worthy to be called thy son. And he, the old miser, will be pleased, and will say: This son of mine was dead, and is alive again; he was lost, and is found. So it's written, brother, in the Scriptures.'

'Amen,' said the policeman, and wanted to go away.

'But wait, that means, doesn't it, that the prodigal son will be pardoned? His profligacy will be pardoned, and his piggish hunger, and that blow will be wiped away. Bring forth the best robe, and put it on him, and put a ring on his hand.' The former Kettelring got up, and tears were flowing from the eyes. 'But I can only guess that my father is alive, and is waiting for me in his old age to make out of me a rich man and a miser as he was himself. You don't know, you don't know what the prodigal son gave up. You don't know what he sacrificed—But no, she is waiting; I will come; Mary, I will come back, but first I must go home.'

'I will take you, sir,' said the black policeman. 'Where are you going?' 'There,' and with his hand he pointed across the sky, to the horizon where silent lightning flashed.

I am obsessed by the idea that he did not return by boat; travel by boat is too tedious and soothing, its tempo is not brisk enough. I went to the air companies to inquire if there is a connection by aeroplane to Trinidad. It seems that there is a regular air line from Europe to Natal, and from there to Para; but they could not tell me if there is any further connection by air from Para to Trinidad, or to any other place in the Antilles. It is possible, and I assume on no other grounds that Case X chose this quicker route. He had to choose it because in the end we have seen him fall head first, enveloped in the flames, to reach the end of his journey, like a meteor, with the most terrible speed. He had to fly with his impatient eyes fixed on the horizon; the pilot sitting motionless as if he were asleep. Oh, to give him a whack on the back of his head to wake him up and make him fly faster. And from one aeroplane into another, deafened and dulled by the roar of the engines, only conscious of one thing, of the haste. At the last aerodrome, almost within sight of home, that rattling train of speed suddenly stopped short. They could not fly, there was a storm. He raged with foam at his lips. You call this a storm? You dogs, you mangy dogs, if you knew what the hurricanes down there are like! Alright, then a private aeroplane, whatever it costs; and once more that convulsive, mad agony of impatience, clenched fists, and teeth set into the lace handkerchief—then the end: whirling, flames, the smell of naptha, and the black lake of unconsciousness which closed thickly round him.

Dear doctor, I should like to pay you the honour, and sketch you, your honest and broad shoulders bent over the dead body of Case X. I saw you by the bed, and yet I can't visualize you very well. Please don't object if once more I break away from plain reality. I shall place by his bed that hairy, not very agreeable fellow; he holds the patient by the wrist, and bends attentively his cocksure, bristly pate. The pretty nurse can rest her eyes on those blond feathers, for she is up to her ears in love with the young doctor. Ah, to run through them with my fingers, and tear, comb them through, gently like breath—The young fellow raises his head. 'I can't feel his pulse. Fetch the screen, sister.' "

CHAPTER XXXVIII

The surgeon finished the manuscript, and mechanically he straightened it up so that no page was out of place.

The old specialist came to see him. "It's a pity you didn't come and have a look at the post-mortem. An interesting case. That man had gone through a lot—I should like you to see his heart."

"Big?"

"Big. Do you know that they've already got some information? A telegraph from Paris. It was a private aeroplane."

The surgeon raised his eyes. "Well, and?"

"I don't know his name, the name came muddled; but he was entered as a Cuban."

AN ORDINARY LIFE

"Is that so?" exclaimed old Mr. Popel. "So he's dead now? And what was wrong with him then?"

"Arterio sclerosis," said the doctor curtly; he wanted to add something about the man's age, but he looked sideways at the old gentleman, and kept silent.

For a little while Mr. Popel reflected that with him, thank God, everything was at present in order; no, he didn't feel anything that might somehow point to this or that. "So he's dead now?" he repeated absent-mindedly. "But he couldn't have been seventy? He was just a bit younger than me. I knew him . . . I knew him when we were lads at school together. After that I didn't see him for years and years, till he came to Prague, to the Ministry. Now and again I used to meet him . . . once or twice a year. Such a downright man he was!"

"A good man," said the doctor, proceeding to tie a little rose to a stick. "I was here in the garden when I first saw him. Once someone spoke to me over the fence: 'Excuse me, but which kind of Malus is the one that you have in flower over there?' 'Oh, that's Malus Halliana,' I said, and I invited him to come inside. You know when two gardeners get together. Sometimes he used to drop in when he saw that I had nothing else to do, and always about flowers. I didn't even know who, and what he really was till he sent for me. Then he was already in a very bad way. But it was a nice little garden he had."

"That sounds like him," reflected Mr. Popel. "All the time I knew him he was such a regular and conscientious man. A good civil servant and so on. In fact, we know terribly little about decent people like that, isn't it true?"

"He wrote it down," said the doctor suddenly.

"What did he write down?"

"His own life. Last year in my house he came across some

famous biography, and he said that someone ought to write the life of an ordinary man. And when his health began to fail he sat down to write his own life. When . . . when he got worse, he gave it to me. Perhaps there was no one for him to leave it to." The doctor hesitated a moment. "Since you were a pal of his I might let you have a look at it."

Old Mr. Popel was somewhat moved. "That would be very good of you. You know I should like to do it for him. . . ." Apparently it seemed to him like rendering a service for the dead. "So, poor chap, he wrote his own biography!"

"I'll fetch it straight away," said the doctor, carefully breaking off a sucker from a rose. "Look how this stem would like to be a briar. All the time we must keep down that other rose, the wild one." The doctor straightened himself up. "Ah, I've promised you that manuscript," he said, absent-mindedly, and he glanced round his garden before he went, as if unwillingly.

So he's dead, mused the old gentleman pensively. It must be quite an ordinary thing to die, then, when even such a regular man knows how to do it. But surely he didn't want to go—perhaps that's why he wrote his own life, because he was fond of it. Who'd have thought of it: such an ordinary man, and bang, he's dead.

"Well, here it is," said the doctor. It was a tidy, carefully arranged pile of sheets neatly tied with tape like a fascicle of completed deeds. Mr. Popel's hands trembled as he took them, and turned over the first few pages. "How neatly it's written," he whispered almost piously. "You can recognize an old bureaucrat; in his days, sir, there weren't any typewriters, everything had to be written by hand; in those days they thought a great deal of a nice clean manuscript."

"Farther on it's not written so well," mumbled the doctor. "By then he was in a hurry and crossed out a lot. Even the handwriting isn't so smooth and regular."

It's queer, thought Mr. Popel; to read the handwriting of

someone who's dead, it's like touching a dead hand. Even in that writing there is something dead. I oughtn't to take it home. I shouldn't have said that I would read it.

"Is it all worth reading?" he inquired uncertainly.

The doctor shrugged his shoulders.

CHAPTER I

THREE days ago I knelt down in my little garden beside a group of alum root in flower to get the weeds out; I felt a bit giddy, but that used to come quite often with me. Perhaps it was the giddiness that made the spot seem to me more beautiful than ever before: the little bright red leaves of the alum root and behind them the white cool panicles of the spiraeas—it was so beautiful and almost myserious that it turned my head. Two yards away from me a finch sat on a stone, her head cocked to one side, and she looked at me with one eye: Well, who are you? I didn't even breathe, I was afraid that I should frighten her away; I could feel how my heart throbbed. And suddenly it came. I don't know how to describe it, but it was a terribly strong and certain FEELING OF DEATH.

Really I can't express it in any other way; I think that I struggled for breath or something, but the one thing that I was conscious of was a tremendous anxiety. When it began to grow less I was still on my knees, but my hands were full of torn leaves. It passed away like a wave, and left me with a sadness that was not unpleasant. I felt my legs trembling beneath me in an absurd fashion, I went cautiously to sit down, and with my eyes shut I said to myself: Well, now you've got it, it's here already. But there was no horror, only surprise, and the consciousness that we have to settle it somehow. Then I had the courage to open my eyes and move my head; Lord, how beautiful that garden seemed to me, like never before, never before; I didn't want anything, only to sit like that, and look at the light and shade, at the full flowers of the spiraeas, and at a blackbird who was struggling with an earthworm. A long time ago, the day before, I had made up my mind that next spring I should take out two clumps of larkspurs, damaged by mildew, and replace them by others. Very likely I shall never do any more, and next year the plants will be disfigured as if with leprosy. I felt sorry for that, I felt sorry for many things; somehow I was softly moved because I had to go.

I am worried that perhaps I ought to tell my housekeeper. She is a good lady, but she gets excited like a clucking hen; she would run about in terror, her face swollen with crying, and she would let everything drop. But no fuss and no upset; the smoother it is settled the better. I must put my things in order, I said to myself with relief; thank God that I've got something to do for a couple of days. Not much of a job for a man who is a widower and retired like me to get his chattels into order, is it? Very likely I shall not ever move the larkspurs again, and shall not cut out the cankered wood of the barberry in the winter; but my drawers will be tidy, and there'll be nothing that might suggest an unfinished act.

I am writing down the details of that moment to make it clear how and why that urge arose in me TO PUT MY THINGS IN ORDER. I had a feeling that I had already had a similar experience before, and not only once. Whenever in my official career I was moved to somewhere else, I tidied up my desk so as not to leave in it anything unfinished and muddled; the last time was when I retired; a dozen times I rearranged and went through everything, page after page, and still I lingered, and then again I wanted to go through everything in case some chit had slipped in that didn't belong there, or should have been finished with. I was giving up to take a rest after so many years of service; but my heart was heavy, and for a long time afterwards I used to worry in case I had mislaid something, God knows where, and left it behind, or not checked it by the last initialling.

This, then, I have experienced a number of times, and so this last time I felt relieved that I could do something familiar; I ceased to be frightened, and the surprise which the sense of death had caused me passed over into relief which came from familiarity and intimacy. It seems to me that because of that people talk of death like sleep, or rest, to give it a semblance of something they know; therefore they hope to meet their friends who have passed away so that they are not afraid of that step into the unknown; perhaps also they make their last wills and testaments because by that the death of a man becomes an important financial event. See, it's nothing to be frightened of; what is in front of us has the likeness of things with which we are personally well familiar. I shall put my things in order, nothing more, nothing less; well, thank God, that won't be difficult for me.

For two days I have been going through my papers; now they're in order, and tied up with tape. There are all my certificates from the first standard in the elementary school; good Lord, how many firsts did I victoriously bring home, for which my father used to pat my head with his fat hand and say with some emotion, Go on, my boy! Certificates of christening and domicile, marriage certificate, appointments, all filed and nothing missing; it's a wonder I haven't given them numbers and letters for filing. All the letters from my late wife; they are only a few, for we were seldom apart, and only for short periods. A couple of letters from friends—and that's all. Just a few bundles tied up in the drawer of my desk. The only thing still to do is to write on a sheet of paper a fair copy of my petition: A B, the retired State official, requests to be transferred to the other world. See documents A to Z.

They were quiet and almost dear, those two days when I was busy with my papers; except for that pain in my heart I felt easier—perhaps the quietness did it, a shady and cool room, outside the twittering of the birds, and in front of me on the desk old and rather touching papers: the calligraphic school certificates, the maiden handwriting of my wife, the stiff paper of the official documents—I should have liked to have had more to read through and tidy up, but my life was simple; I was always fond of order, and never kept any unnecessary papers. My God, there's nothing to put straight, such an uncomplicated and ordinary life it was.

There's nothing more to put straight, but still there is in me—what shall I say?—a mania for order. It's unnecessary for me to wind up the clock which I already wound up a moment ago, and useless to open the drawers to see if there is still something that I've overlooked. I am thinking of the offices where I worked: has anything been left there that I should not have finished, and tied up with tape? No longer do I think of the finch that cocked one eye at me as if to say: Well, who are you? Yes, everything is ready as if I were going on a journey, and waiting for the taxi; suddenly in some way you feel desolate, you don't know what to do next, and you look round full of uncertainty in case you've forgotten something. Yes, that's it, restlessness. I was looking for something more to put straight, and there was nothing left: only that uneasiness in case I had overlooked something important; such a fatuous thing, but it swells like anxiety, like a physical depression in the heart. Right, there is nothing more to arrange; but what next? And then it occurred to me: I'll put my life straight, and that's it. Well and good, I'll write it down so as to file it and tie it up with tape.

At first it almost made me laugh; for God's sake, I ask you, what for, and what to do with it? For whom am I to write it? Such an ordinary life: what is there to write? But I already knew then that I was going to write it, I only put it off somehow out of modesty, or something. As a child I saw an old woman die who lived near us, my mother used to send me there to fetch and carry things for her if she wanted anything. She was a solitary old hag, you never saw her in the street or talking with anyone; children were a bit frightened of her because she was so much alone. Once my mother said to me: "Now you mustn't go in, the priest is with her, for her confession." I couldn't imagine what such a lonely old woman could confess; I felt like pressing my nose to the glass of her window to watch her confessing. The priest was there an endless and mysteriously long time. When I went there afterwards she lay with her eyes closed, and her face had such a peaceful and festive expression that I felt uneasy. "Do you want anything?" I burst out; she only shook her head. I know now that she also had PUT IN ORDER her life, and in that is the last sacrament of the dying.

CHAPTER II

TRUE: why shouldn't there be a biography of quite an ordinary life? In the first place it's my own personal affair; perhaps I needn't write it down if there were someone to tell it to. Now and again a reminiscence of something long past crops up in your conversation, even if it's only what mother used to cook. Each time I mention something like this my housekeeper nods her head compassionately as if to say: Yes, yes, you had a lot to go through; I know, I had a hard life, too. With her you can't talk about such ordinary things; her temperament is too doleful, and in everything she looks for what is emotional. Others again listen to reminiscences with only half their mind, and impatiently, so as to interrupt the conversation with: Well, with us, and in my young days, it was like so and so. I have the impression that people somehow boast with their reminiscences; they assert that when they were young there was diphtheria, or that they lived through that big storm, as if it were part of their personal merit. Perhaps every man has the need to see in his life something remarkable, important, and almost dramatic; and so he likes to call attention to singular events that he's experienced, and he expects that because of them he will become the object of heightened interest and admiration.

In my life nothing has occurred that was extraordinary and dramatic; if I have anything to remember then it is only a quiet, obvious, and almost a mechanical sequence of days and years until the final stage that is in front of me, and which will be, I hope, equally as undramatic as the rest. I must say that glancing back I almost find pleasure in the straight and clear path that is behind me; it has its beauty, like a good, straight road, on which it is impossible to go astray. I am almost proud that it is such a direct and comfortable road; I can compass it in one glance right back to childhood, and again enjoy its distinctness. What a beautiful, ordinary, and uninteresting life! Never any adventure, no great struggle, nothing extraordinary, or tragic. Looking at it gives one a pleasant and even strong impression like a smoothly running machine. It will stop without rattling; nothing will squeak, it will run down silently and resignedly. So it ought to be.

My whole life long I have been a reader of books. What a lot of remarkable adventures have I read of, what numbers of tragic and strange characters have I met—as if there was nothing else to talk about, and to write of but unusual, exceptional, and singular cases and chances! But really life is no extraordinary adventure but a common law; what is unusual and extraordinary is only the rattling in its wheels. In fact, ought we not to celebrate life for being normal and ordinary? Is it, perchance, less of a life because it didn't rattle or moan, and didn't threaten to fly to pieces? Instead, we have got through a pile of work, and fulfilled all proprieties from birth to death. On the whole, it has been a happy life, and I'm not ashamed of that small and regular happiness that I used to find in the pedantic idyll of my life.

I recollect the funerals in the little town where I was born. In front the acolyte in a surplice and with a cross; then the musicians, the shiny bugle, French horn, clarinet, and the helicon, the most beautiful of them all; then the curate in a white rochet, and with his calotte, the coffin with its six bearers, and the black host, all serious, solemn, and somehow looking like puppets. And above it all waved the funeral march, the clamour of the bugle, the wailing of the clarinet, and the deep lament of the angelic trumpets; the street was full of it, and the town, it vaulted as high as the sky. Everyone stopped working and went out in front of their houses with bowed heads to pay homage to a man who was departing. Who is it who died? Is it some king or duke, was he some hero that they carry him so solemnly and high? No, he was a grocer. God give him eternal glory; a good man, and just; well, his time has come.

Or it was a wheelwright, a furrier; now they have finished their labour and this is their last journey. I, a lad, would have liked most to be that acolyte at the head of the procession, or no, rather be the one whom they carry in the coffin. Surely it's as glorious as if they were carrying a king; the whole world with lowered head pays homage to the triumphal progress of a righteous man and neighbour, the bells ring out his praise, and the bugle weeps victoriously; you would like to fall on your knees before the holy and great being that is called man.

CHAPTER III

My father was a joiner. My oldest remembrance is of sitting in the warm sawdust in the yard next to the workshop and playing with the twisted curls of the shavings; father's assistant, Frank, grinned at me and came up to me with a spokeshave in his hand: Come here, I'll cut your head off. I must have begun to whimper because mother ran out and took me in her arms. That pleasant, noisy tumult of a joiner's workshop envelops my whole childhood: the banging of the planks, the whizz of the plane running against the knots, the dry rustling of the shavings, and the biting coarseness of the saw; the smell of the wood, glue, and varnish; the workmen with their shirt sleeves rolled up, father marking out something on the planks with fat fingers and with a fat carpenter's pencil. His shirt sticking to his broad back, he puffs and bends over his work. What will it be? Why, a cupboard; don't you see, one plank will be joined to the other, the grooves will fit together, and it will be a cupboard; with a professional thumb father runs over the finished piece along the edges and on the wrong side; it's good, as smooth as a mirror. Or it's a coffin, but that isn't such a thorough job, only just knocked together, ornaments stuck on it, and now, my lads, paint it and varnish it so that it shines a lot. Father doesn't run his hand over a coffin unless it's one of the better ones, of oak, as heavy as a grand piano.

High up on a pile of planks a little chap is sitting. Oh, no, other lads can't sit so high, and they haven't got blocks of wood to play with or shavings shiny like silk. A glazier's boy, for instance, has nothing because you can't play with glass. Leave those bits alone, you'll cut yourself, mammy would say. Or with a house-painter, that's nothing either; unless you were to take the brush and smear the wall with paint; but then varnish is better, it sticks better. But that's nothing, we've got a blue colour, boasts the painter's boy, and all the colours in the world;

but the joiner's son won't let himself be outdone. What's colours? they're only powder in paper bags. Yes, it's true, painters sing at their job, but a joiner's work is cleaner. In the next yard there is a potter, but he has no children; making pots is nice work, too. There is something to look at when the wheel is spinning, and the potter fashions the damp clay with his thumb until it becomes a pot; they stand in his yard in a long row, still soft, and when he's not looking a lad can leave his finger-marks on them. But stone-cutting, on the contrary, is not nearly so interesting: for an hour you watch the stone-mason tap his chisel with a wooden mallet, and still you can't see anything, still you don't know how he'll make the statue of a kneeling angel with a broken palm leaf out of that stone.

High up on the pile of planks a little chap is sitting; the planks are piled up as high as the tops of old plum-trees, you can catch them with your hands and in a moment you are sitting in the forked branches. This is higher still, somehow it is a dizzy height; now the little chap doesn't belong to that joiner's yard, he has a world to himself, which is connected with that other world by a single stem. It's slightly intoxicating; daddy and mammy can't come here, not even Frank the workman; and the little chap sips for the first time the wine of solitude. There are still other worlds that the child has for himself alone; for instance, somewhere among the longer planks there are shorter ones, too, and a tiny cave is formed, it has its ceiling and walls, it smells of resin and warm wood; nobody would squeeze himself in there, but there is room enough for the little chap and his mysterious world. Or chips are stuck into the ground like a fence, the enclosure is strewn with sawdust, and into it a small handful of coloured beans are stuck; these are hens, and the biggest bean, the speckled one, that's the cock. It's true that behind the joiner's yard there is a real fence, and behind it real hens cluck with a real golden cock who stands on one leg and looks round with flaming eyes, but that's not the thing; the little fellow crouches over his tiny heap of illusions, sprinkles sawdust about, and cries in a low voice: Chuck, chuck, chuck! That is his farmyard, and you grown-ups must make believe that you don't see it; you would destroy its charm if you looked.

But the grown-ups are good for something after all: for instance, when midday rings out from the church tower the workmen stop cutting, pull out the saw from the half-cut plank, and sit down squarely on a pile of planks to eat. Then the little fellow scrambles up Frank's strong workman's back and sits down astride on his damp nape; and that is his presumptive right, and it is part of the glory of the day. Frank is a dangerous fighter, and once in a row he bit somebody's ear, but the little fellow doesn't know that; he adores him for his strength and for the right to be enthroned on his neck in his midday triumph. There is another workman, he's called Mr. Martinek; he is quiet and thin, his moustache hangs down and he has beautiful large eyes; the little chap is not allowed to play with him because they say that he has consumption; the lad doesn't know what that is, and he feels some sort of embarrassment, or fear, when Mr. Martinek looks at him in a friendly and beautiful way.

And there are expeditions into THEIR world, too. Mother says: "Sonny, run and fetch some bread from the baker for me." The baker is a fat man, sprinkled with flour; sometimes one can see him through the glass in the shop running round the tub, mixing and kneading the dough. Who would have thought that of him, such a big, fat man, and he runs round and round till his slippers smack on his heels. The youngster takes the loaf home, still warm, like a sacrament, his bare feet sinking into the warm dust of the road, and he sniffs in rapture the golden aroma of a loaf of bread. Or to go to the butcher's for meat; terrible gory pieces of flesh hang from hooks; the butcher and his wife have shiny faces; they hack through pink bones with a cleaver and smack goes the meat on to the weighing machine it's a wonder they don't cut their fingers off! But it's quite different at the grocer's: there it smells of ginger, gingerbread, and of suchlike things; his wife talks gently in a low voice, and she measures out spices with tiny weights, and for one's trouble you get a couple of walnuts, one of which is usually bad and shrivelled up, but that's all the same, if only it has two shells—at least you can stamp on it and make it bang.

I remember these people, now a long time dead, and I should like to see them once again as I used to see them then. Each one had his own particular world, and in it his own mysterious work; every craft was as if a world for itself, each of different material, and with a different ritual. Sunday was a strange day because then the people didn't wear their working clothes or have their sleeves rolled up, but they had black clothes and they all looked almost like one another; they seemed to me somehow strange and unfamiliar. Sometimes father used to send me with a jug for beer; while the landlord filled the misty jug with froth, I glanced furtively into the corner; there at the table the butcher, the baker, the barber, sometimes the gendarme, fat, with his coat unbuttoned and his gun leaning against the wall, were sitting and talking with loud voices and much noise. It was strange for me to see them away from their yards and shops; it struck me as rather indecent and untidy. Now I should say that I was troubled and mystified when I saw their closed worlds intercross. Perhaps that is why they made such a noise, because they were disturbing some order.

Everyone had his own world, the world of his craft. Some of them were taboo, like Mr. Martinek, like the parish idiot who bellowed in the street, like the stone-mason who lived in silent isolation because he was a spiritualist and reticent. And among those worlds of the grown-ups the youngster had tiny reserved worlds of his own; he had his tree, his enclosure of chips, his corner between the planks; these were the mysterious places of his deepest happiness, which he shared with no one. Squatting on his heels and holding his breath—and now it all merges into one great and agreeable roar; the banging of the planks and the damped tumult of the crafts, there is tapping at the stonemason's, cans rattle at the tinker's, the anvil rings at the smithy, someone is hammering a scythe, and somewhere there is a baby wailing, shouts of children in the distance, the hens cluck excitedly, and mother calls from the doorstep: "Where are you?" You call it a small town, and yet it is a mass of life, like a big river; jump into your little boat and don't make a sound, let it rock you, let it carry you till your head turns round and you will feel almost afraid. To hide from everyone—even that is an expedition into the world.

CHAPTER IV

The common world of children, that is something entirely different. A lonely child in his game forgets himself and everything that is round him, and his oblivion is beyond time. Into the common game of children wider spheres are drawn, and their mutual world is governed by the laws of the seasons. No amount of boredom will make boys play marbles in summer. You play marbles in spring when the frost goes; that is a grave and indisputable law, like that which commands the snowdrops to flower, or mothers to make Easter cakes. Only later can you play at touch or hide and seek, while the school holidays are the time for adventure and escapades: into the field to catch grasshoppers, or to bathe on the sly in the river. No self-respecting fellow will ever feel in summer the urge to make a bonfire; that's not done until towards the autumn, at the time when kites are flown. Easter, summer holidays, and Christmas, fairs, village wakes, and feasts, these are important dates and big watersheds in time. The year of children has its routine, its ritual is governed by the seasons; a lonely child plays with eternity, while a pack of children play with time.

In that pack the joiner's little son was not an outstanding personality; he was somewhat overlooked, and they reproached him that he was a mother's darling and that he was afraid. But at Easter didn't he have a rattle that Mr. Martinek had made for him, couldn't he provide wooden chips for swords, and have as many blocks as he liked? With the painter's son it was something different; once he smeared celestial blue all over his face, and after that he basked in special esteem. But in the joiner's yard there were planks on which you could swing seriously and silently; wasn't that a kind of detachment from the earth and therefore an act that fulfils all desire? Let the painter's boy smear his face with blue: he was never invited to have a swing.

A game is a game, a serious thing, a matter of honour; there is no equality in sport, there is either excelling or submitting. Let it be said that I did not excel; I was neither the strongest nor the most daring of the pack, and I believe I suffered for it. It was of little avail that the local policeman touched his hat to my father, but not to the painter and decorator. When my father put on his long black coat to go to a meeting of the parish council, I grasped his fat finger and I tried to make as long strides as he did; don't you see, boys, what a gentleman my dad is—he even carries one pole of the canopy over the curate at the Resurrection and in the evening of his birthday the local musicians come and play in his honour. Dad stands on the doorstep, this time without an apron, and with dignity he acknowledges the celebration of his feast. And I, drunk with the sweet torment of pride, am looking round at my friends who listen attentively; with a tremor I experience this summit of terrestrial glory, and I hold on to my father for everybody to see that I belong to him. The next day the boys had no wish to be conscious of my glory; again I was the one who did not excel in anything and one that nobody wished to obey unless I invited him to swing in our yard. And on purpose not, I would rather not swing myself; and out of grief and spite I made up my mind at least to excel at school.

. . . . .

School, that again is quite another world. There children differ no longer according to their fathers, but by their names; they are no longer distinguished by one being the glazier's and the other the shoemaker's, but by one being called Adamec and the other Beran. For the joiner's little boy it was a shock and for a long time he could not get used to it. Up to that time he had belonged to his family, to the workshop, to the house, and to his pack of boys; now he sat there terribly alone among forty little chaps, most of whom he did not know and with whom he had no common world. If daddy, or mammy, or at least the apprentice Frank, or even the sad Mr. Martinek, had been sitting with him it would have been something different; he would have held them by the lapel of their coat, and he would not have lost continuity with his world, he would have felt it behind him like a protection. He would have liked to burst into tears, but he was afraid that those others would laugh at him. He never merged into his class. Those others soon became friends and nudged each other under the forms, but it was easy for them; at home they had no joiner's shop, or enclosure of chips strewn with sawdust, or the strong man Frank, or Mr. Martinek; they had nothing about which to feel so terribly lonely. The joiner's little boy sat in the swarm of the class, self-conscious, and with a lump in his throat. The teacher bent over him. "You are a good, quiet boy," he said approvingly. The little chap blushed, and his eyes filled with tears of happiness never known before. From that time on in school he became the good and quiet boy, which, of course, separated him still farther from the others.

But in a child's life school means still another new and greater experience: there for the first time he comes in contact with the hieratic order of life. Up to that time, it's true, he has had many to obey; mother gives orders, but mother is ours, mother is here to cook, and mother also kisses and strokes; sometimes father loses his temper, but at others you can scramble on to his knees or hold his fat finger. Other grown-ups sometimes snap or swear, but you don't mind that very much and you run away. But the teacher is something different; he is here only to command and admonish. And you can't run away and hide somewhere, you can only blush and be horrified of your shame. And you will never scramble on to his knees, never clutch his well-washed finger; he is always above you, inaccessible and untouchable. And the curate, he is more still; when he pats you on the head you are not only patted but distinguished and raised above all the others, and it is a hard job in your pride and gratitude to keep your eyes from watering.

So far the little fellow has had a world of his own, and round him has been a multitude of closed, mysterious worlds. The baker's, the stonemason's, and those others. Now the whole world splits into two distinct grades: into a higher one, in which there is the teacher, the curate, and those who talk with them; the apothecary, the doctor, the public prosecutor, and the magistrate; and then that ordinary world in which there are fathers and their children. Fathers live in workrooms and shops and only come out on to their doorsteps as if they had to hold to their houses; those from the higher world meet in the middle of the square, they greet with a long bow, and they stand together for a while or they accompany each other for a bit of the way. And for them in the public-house on the square there is a table covered with a white cloth, while the other table-cloths are red or with blue checks; it almost looks like an altar. Now I know that that table-cloth was not so amazingly white, that the curate was snuffy, fat, and good-natured, and the teacher a country bachelor with a red nose; but then for me he was the embodiment of something higher, and almost superhuman; it was the first articulation of the world according to dignity and power.

I was a quiet and industrious little scholar, pointed out to others as an example; but in secret I nursed a tremulous admiration for the painter's boy, a hangman's rascal who drove the teacher insane by his roguery, and bit the curate's thumb. They were almost afraid of him and were quite helpless with him. If they thrashed him as hard as they could, the fellow laughed in their face; it was beneath his savage dignity to cry, whatever happened.

Who knows? Perhaps it was one of the most decisive things in my life that the painter's boy would not have me for his pal. I would have given, I can't say how much, if he had gone with me. Once, Satan knows what he had been up to, a beam crushed his fingers; other children began to cry, but he not, he only turned pale and bit his teeth. I saw him when he was going home carrying that bleeding hand in the other like a trophy. The other boys in a crowd round him, screaming: "A beam fell on him!" I was beyond myself with terror and sympathy, my legs quivered, I felt sick. "Does it hurt you?" I gasped out in terror. He looked at me with proud, flaming, mocking eyes. "It's not your business," he trickled through his teeth. I stood there rejected and snubbed You wait, I'll show you, I'll show you what I can stand! I went into the workshop and pushed my left hand into the vice which holds the planks together; I tightened the screw, you will see! Tears burst from my eyes, well, now it hurts me as much as it does him; I'll show him! I tightened the screw more, more yet, I no longer felt any pain but rapture. They found me in the workshop in a dead faint with my fingers held in the vice; to this day the last joints of the fingers on my left hand are stiff. Now that hand is crabbed and dry like a turkey's claw, but still remembrance is written on it—of what? Of revengeful childish hatred, or of passionate friendship?

CHAPTER V

THAT was the time when the railway got to our little town. They had been building it for a long time, but now it was quite near; in the joiner's yard you could hear them blasting out the rocks for the cutting. There were strict orders that children like us must not go there, partly because they were using dynamite and partly because there were some queer people; the devil wouldn't trust that riff-raff, they used to say. The first time my father took me there, so that I could see, he said, how a railway is built, I clutched his finger, I was afraid of "those people"; they lived in wooden huts, between which ragged underwear hung on lines, and the biggest hut was a canteen with a paunchy, evil woman who swore continuously. On the track half-naked men were digging with pickaxes in their hands; they shouted something at my father, but he made no answer. Then there was one with a red flag in his hand. "Look there, that's where they'll fire a charge," said my father, and I clutched him still more convulsively. "Don't get frightened, I'm here," said father reassuringly, and with a blessed sigh I felt how powerful he was, and strong; nothing could happen while he was there.

Once beyond the fence of our workshop a little ragged girl stopped, she pushed her nose through the bars and jabbered something. "What do you say?" asked Frank. The little girl stuck out her tongue in a temper, and went on jabbering. Then Frank called my father. Father leant against the fence and said: "What do you want?" The child went on still faster. "I can't understand what you say," said father gravely, "who knows what nation you belong to. Wait here!" And he shouted for mother. "Look at that child's eyes." She had large dark eyes with very long lashes. "She's beautiful," exclaimed mother with amazement. "Are you hungry?" The little girl said nothing, she only gazed at her with those eyes. Mother brought her a slice of bread and butter, but the little one shook her head. "Perhaps she's Italian, or Magyar," suggested father uncertainly. "Or a Rumanian. Who knows what she wants." And he went on with his job. When he had gone Mr. Martinek took out a penny from his pocket and without a word gave it to the girl.

The next day when I came from school she was sitting on our fence. "She's after you," laughed Frank, and I was terribly annoyed; I didn't pay any attention to her at all, although from something that might have been a pocket she fished out a shiny penny, and she looked at it to catch my attention. On a pile of planks I put one across to make a see-saw and I sat down on one end; the other could stick into the air, that was no business of mine, I turned my back to the whole world, frowning and somehow vexed. And suddenly the board with me on it began to move mysteriously; I didn't turn round, but an infinite, almost painful happiness came over me. It swung me up to the top, dizzy with bliss; I leaned back to bring the swing down on my side to the ground, the other end responded lightly in rhythm, a little girl was sitting there; she said nothing, she swung with silent joy, on the other end a boy with silent joy; they didn't look at each other and they began to see-saw body and soul, for they loved each other; at least the boy did, even if he could not give it that name he was full of it, it was beautiful and tormenting at the same time; and so they swung without a word, almost like a ritual, as slow as possible to give it greater glory.

She was bigger and older than I was, with black hair, and as dark as a black cat; I don't know what her name was or her nationality. I showed her my enclosure of chips, but she didn't even look at it, perhaps she didn't recognize that the beans were hens; it hurt me frightfully, and from that day on my enclosure gave me no more pleasure. Instead she snatched up the neighbour's kitten and pressed it, all terror-struck and with staring eyes, to herself; and she knew with her fingers how to make a piece of string into such a star that it was like a charm. A boy can't keep on adoring continually, love is a feeling too heavy and tormenting; at times one must temper it down to comradeship. The boys jeered at me for being pally with girls, it was beneath their dignity; I bore it bravely, but the chasm widened between them and me. Once she scratched the saddler's son, it was a regular fight, but the painter's boy intervened and hissed contemptuously through his teeth: "Let her be, it's a girl!" And he spat like an apprentice. If after that he had beckoned to me I should have followed him instead of that black little minx; but he turned his back on me and led his gang to other triumphs. I was beyond myself with pique and jealousy. "Don't you worry," I threatened, "if they came for us, I'd let them have it!" But in any case she didn't understand what I said; she stuck her tongue out after them and altogether behaved as if I were under her protection.

Then it was the holidays and sometimes we were together all the day long, until towards evening Mr. Martinek used to lead her by the hand back to the wooden huts on the other side of the river. Sometimes she didn't come, and then in desperation I didn't know what to do; I crawled with a book into my hiding-place between the boards and pretended that I was reading. From the distance I could hear the war-cries of boys to whom I no longer belonged, and the firing of shots in the rocks. Mr. Martinek bent down, as if to count the boards, and he murmured compassionately: "Why is it that she hasn't come to-day?" I made as if I hadn't heard, I only read on furiously; but I could feel almost with bliss how my heart was bleeding and that Mr. Martinek knew it. Once I couldn't bear it any longer and I set out after her; it was a terrible adventure; I had to cross the foot-bridge to the other side of the river, which on that day seemed to me more terrifying and wild than ever before. My heart thumped and I went, as in a dream, to the hut which seemed destitute; only the voice of the fat canteen woman could be heard somewhere, and a woman in a shirt and skirt was hanging out washing and yawning loudly like the butcher's big dog. The dark girl was sitting on a box in front of a hut and she was sewing some rags together; she blinked with her long eyelashes and in her concentration she kept sticking out the end of her tongue.

Without any fuss she made a place for me beside her, and she began to talk quickly and pleasantly in her foreign tongue. I never had the feeling before that I was so immensely far from home; as if I were in another world, as if I never should go home again; it was a desperate and heroic feeling. She put her thin, bare arm round my neck, and for a long time she whispered, damply, ticklishly into my ear; perhaps she was telling me in her strange tongue that she liked me, and I was so happy that I could have died. She showed me the hut in which apparently she lived; the sun had warmed it up to suffocation and it smelt like a dog-kennel; a man's coat hung on a nail, rags on the floor, and some boxes instead of furniture. It was dark in there and her eyes were fixed on me so near and beautifully that I could have cried without knowing what for: love, helplessness, or terror. She sat down on a box with her knees under her chin, she whispered something like a little song, and she looked at me with those fixed wide eyes; it was as if she were performing magic. The wind banged the door to and suddenly it was quite dark; it was terrible, my heart jumped into my throat, I didn't know what would happen next; there was a light rustling in the dark and the door opened, she stood against the light and looked out, quite still. Then again there was the rumble of a shot in the cutting, and she repeated: "Bang." Suddenly she was cheerful again and showed me what she could make with string; God knows why she began to behave towards me like a mother, a little nurse; she even took my hand and wanted to take me home, as if I were a baby. I tore myself away and began to whistle as loud as I could so that she could see what I was like; I even stopped on the foot-bridge and spat into the water, just to show her that I was big and that I was not frightened of anything. At home they asked me where I had been to; I told a lie, but although I lied easily and often like every child, I felt that this time my lie was somehow greater and heavier; therefore I lied with overmuch zeal and haste—I wonder that they didn't find me out.

The day after she came as if nothing had happened, and she

tried to whistle with pouting lips; I taught her, generously letting her have a bit of my superiority; friendship is big. On the other hand, it was easier for me to set out on a pilgrimage to the huts; we whistled to each other from a distance and that greatly strengthened our friendship. We scrambled up the slopes from where one could see the navvies at work; she basked on the stones in the sun like a viper, while I looked at the roofs of the little town, and at the onion dome of the church. How far it was. That one there with the tarred roof is the joiner's shop; daddy puffs and measures something out on the boards, Mr. Martinek coughs, and mammy is on the doorstep and shakes her head: What is that rascal up to again? Here, nowhere, you can't see me; here on a sunny slope where mullein and viper's bugloss are in flower; here on the other side of the river where pickaxes ring and dynamite goes bang and where everything is quite different. This is such a secret place: from here you can see everything and nobody sees you. And below they have already laid the little rails and they carry away stone and soil in trucks; someone jumps up on the wagon and it goes by itself on the rails; I should like that, too, and to have on my head a kind of turban made out of a red handkerchief. And to live in a wooden hut, Mr. Martinek would make it for me. The little dark girl looks at me steadily, it is silly that I can't tell her anything. I tried to talk to her in a secret language: "Javra tivri nevrecovro povrovivrim," but she couldn't even understand that. All we can do is to stick our tongues out at each other and one after the other make the most dreadful grimaces to express the harmony in our minds. Or to throw stones together. Just now it's the time to stick out our tongues; hers is active and thin, like a little red snake; altogether a tongue is a queer thing, from near it is as if it were made out of lots of little pink lumps. Down below we can hear people shouting, but someone is always shouting there. And who can look longest into the other's eyes? That's strange, her eyes look black, but from near they've got green and gold things; and that little head in the middle, that's me. And suddenly her eyes opened wide with terror, she jumped up, screamed something, and ran down the hill.

Below on the track a confused little group of people moved towards the canteen. Only their scattered pickaxes were left behind.

In the evening there was animated talk that one of "those people" had stabbed a foreman in a row; the gendarmes had taken him away, they said, he had chains on his hands and his child ran after him.

Mr. Martinek turned and looked at me with his big, beautiful eyes, and he shrugged his shoulders. "Oh, well, who knows which of them it was," he murmured. "People like this may be anywhere."

I never saw her again. In sadness and solitude I read anything that fell into my hands, hidden between the planks. "You have got a good boy!" the neighbours used to say, while dad, with a paternal modesty, replied: "Let's hope that he's some good!"

CHAPTER VI

I LIKED my father because he was strong and simple. To touch him gave me a feeling like leaning against a wall or a strong pillar. I thought that he was stronger than anyone else; he smelt of cheap tobacco, beer, and sweat, and his powerful build filled me with a pleasant sense of safety, reliability, and strength. At times he was cross and then he was terrible, he thundered like a storm; but sweeter was the touch of terror with which I climbed up on to his knee. He didn't talk much, and when he did it was never about himself; I never got rid of the feeling that if he liked he could talk about great and heroic deeds that he had done, and I would put my hands on his powerful, hairy chest to feel it resound. He was deeply and thoroughly immersed in his work; and he was very economical, for he measured money by the work which he had done for it. I remember how sometimes on Sundays he took the bank book out of his drawer and looked into it; it was as if he were looking with satisfaction at properly made piles of good, sound planks; there it is, my boy, heaps of labour and sweat. To squander money is like ruining a finished job, it's a sin. And what is it for, dad, this money you save? For my old age, perhaps father would say; but that isn't it, people only say so; money is to show work, life's virtue of industry and self-denial. Here you can see for yourself, this is the result of a life's work; here it is written that I have worked and saved, as is seemly and proper. And as economically as is seemly. The time came when father was already very old; for a long time mother had been asleep in the churchyard below a little marble monument (but it had cost lots of money, daddy used to say with piety) and I had a good position; but dad still shuffled on his heavy, swollen legs to the joiner's yard in which there was almost nothing more to do, saved, counted, and on Sundays, quite alone in the late family nest, he took out his savings book and looked at the numerical total of his honest life.

Mother was not so simple; she was far more sensitive, emotional, and overflowing with love for me; there were moments when she pressed me convulsively to herself and sighed: My only one, I would die for you! Later on, when I was a lad, these bursts of love somehow embarrassed me; I was ashamed that my pals might see when my mother kissed me so passionately; but when I was quite small her fervent love placed me in a state of subjection, or subjugation, I loved her enormously. When I whimpered and she took me in her arms I had a feeling as if I were dissolving; I liked tremendously to sob on her soft neck, wet with tears and a dribbling child's mouth; I pressed gulps out of myself as much as I could until everything melted in a blessed, sleepy mumbling: Mummy! Mummy! Altogether mother was for me combined with an over-sensitive urge to enjoy my pain. Not until I became a little five-year-old man did aversion to such feminine manifestations of feeling grow in me; I turned my head away when she pressed me to her breast and I wondered what she got from it; daddy was better, he smelt of tobacco and strength.

Because she was supremely emotional she somehow dramatized everything; small family disputes ended with swollen eyes and tragic silence; daddy banged the doors and set to work with fierce tenacity, while from the kitchen an awful repining silence rose to the heavens. She cherished the idea that I was a weak child, that some misfortune might happen to me, or that I might die. (Her first baby had died, my unknown little brother.) Therefore she was always rushing out to see where I was and what I was doing; later on I frowned manfully when she watched me like that and I gave her sullen and obstinate answers. And all the time she kept asking: Are you all right? haven't you got tummy ache? At first I felt flattered by it; you feel so important when you are ill and are put to bed; and mammy convulsively presses you to her breast. You darling, you mustn't die! Or she used to take me by hand to a miraculous place of pilgrimage to pray for my health; she sacrificed to the Virgin Mary a little wax bust because she said my lungs were weak. I was deeply ashamed that she had sacrificed a woman's bust for my sake, it humiliated my manly pride; altogether it was a strange pilgrimage, mammy prayed silently or sighed with her eyes fixed and full of tears; I felt dimly and painfully that it was not all for me. Then she bought me a bun which, of course, was much better and finer than those at home; but in spite of that I didn't care for going on those pilgrimages. That feeling has remained with me all my life: my mother was something that had to do with illness and pain. Even now I think I would rather rely on father with his smell of tobacco and manliness. Father was like a pillar.

There is no one for whom I might wish to make the home of my childhood more beautiful than it was. It was commonplace and good, like thousands of other homes; I honoured my father and loved my mother, and my days were long upon the land. They made a decent man out of me to their image; I was not so strong as father, not as great in loving as mother, but at least I was industrious and honest, sensitive, and, to a certain extent, ambitious—that ambition is certainly an heritage of my mother's liveliness; altogether what used to be wounded in me most is very likely from my mother. And see here, even that was in order and to some good; as well as one who was prepared to take pains, there was in me a man of dreams. For instance, it is certainly not from my father that I am looking into my past as into a mirror; father was so absolutely objective; he had no time for anything but for the present because he was absorbed in his work. Remembrance and the future belong to those who have an inclination to dream and who are more absorbed in themselves. That was mammy's share in my life. And as I look back now on what in me came from my father and what from my mother, I find that both have accompanied me all my life, that my home never came to an end, that even to-day I am a child who has his own mysterious world while daddy works and counts, and mammy follows me with a look of fear and love.

CHAPTER VII

BECAUSE I learned quickly, and because out of solitude and aloofness I soaked myself in books, father let me study; besides, it was somehow understood from the very beginning because he had a great respect for gentlemen and because material and social advancement was for him the holiest and most obvious task of a righteous man and of his progeny. I have noticed that the most able children (in the sense of life's career) come as a rule from those industrious middle strata which have only just begun by modesty and self-denial to lay the foundations of something like a claim to a better life; our advancement is pushed onwards by the labours of our fathers. In those days I had no idea of what I should like to be; except something grand like the tight-rope walker who swung one evening over our little square, or the mounted dragoon who once stopped at our fence and asked something in German; mammy gave him a glass of water, the dragoon saluted, the horse pranced, and my mother blushed like a rose. I should have liked to be a dragoon, or perhaps a guard who slams carriage doors and then, with infinite elegance, swings up on to his step when the train has begun to move. But you don't know how people manage to become conductors or dragoons. One day my father announced in an awed voice that he would let me study after the holidays; mother cried, the teacher told me to appreciate what it would mean if I became an educated man, and the parson began to say to me: "Servus, student." I turned crimson with pride, it was all so glorious; it was already beneath my dignity to play, and with a book in hand I painfully and in solitude ripened into adolescent seriousness.

. . . . .

It is strange how the following eight years at the gymnasium seem to me so irrelevant—at least in comparison with my childhood at home. A child lives a full life, it doesn't take its own childhood, the present moment as something temporal and transitive; and it is at home that it is an important person with a place to fill that belongs to it by the laws of property. And one day they take a country lad and put him in a school in the town. Eight years among strange people, it might be called, for there he won't be at home any longer, he will be a little outsider and never will he have the reassuring feeling that he belongs there. He will feel terribly unimportant among those strange people, he will always be reminded that he STILL is nothing; the school and the unusual surroundings will create a feeling in him of humiliated smallness, paralysis, and inferiority, a feeling which he will try to overcome with cramming, or—in some cases and not till later—with a mad revolt against the authorities and school discipline. And at school it is continually being rubbed into him that it is all merely a PREPARATION for what is to come; the first year is nothing more than a preparation for the second, while in his fourth year a boy is only getting ready for his fifth if, of course, he is sufficiently attentive and studious. And all those long eight years are again only a preparation for the leaving certificate, and only then, my boys, does real learning begin for you. We prepare you for life, the masters lecture, as if what was wriggling on the forms in front of them was no life worth the name. Life is what will not come until after the certificate: that is roughly the most powerful notion that the secondary school cultivates in us; and therefore we leave it as if we are set free instead of feeling rather upset because we are saying good-bye to our boyhood.

Perhaps because of that our reminiscences of school consist only of fragments, disjointed; and yet how keen is our perception in those years! How well and clearly do I remember the masters, the ridiculous, half-mad pedants, the good fellows who in vain tried to tame the wild swarm of rascals, and the few noble scholars at whose feet even a boy had a vague feeling, almost with tremors, that it is not a matter of preparation but of knowledge and that at that very moment he is in a process of becoming something and somebody. I can also see my colleagues, the battered forms, the corridors of the old building *scholarum piarum*, a thousand reminiscences as clear as a vivid dream; but all that time at school, those eight years, taken together, are strangely without a face and almost without a sense; they were fleeting years of youth lived impatiently to get them over.

And again: in those years how ardently and keenly does a boy appreciate the things that do not belong to school; anything that is not a "preparation for life," but IS life itself: whether it be friendship or the so-called first love, troubles, reading, religious crises, or romping about. This is something to which he may give himself heart and soul, and what is his now and not till after the certificate, or until, as one says at school, "when he has finished." Most of the inner conflicts and follies of youth, lived with tragic seriousness, are, I think, the result of that period of suspense in which our adolescence takes place. It is something like a revenge that we are not taken seriously. In revolt against that chronic feeling of unreality we long at least in some way to experience something positive. And that's why it is like this; that's why in adolescence a silly rascality and a tragic, surprising seriousness so confusedly and sometimes so painfully are mixed together. The progress of life is not such that out of a child a man develops gradually and almost imperceptibly; suddenly there appears in a child terribly complete and devilishly mature lumps of manhood; the parts will not fit together, they are disorganized, they clash in him so incongruously and illogically that it almost seems like madness. Fortunately, we older ones have learned to take this state leniently, and we soothe and make these boys understand who begin to take life with deadly seriousness that they will grow out of it.

(What crudity when we talk of happy youth! Apparently we are thinking of our healthy teeth and healthy stomachs; what does it matter if everything else made our souls ache! If we had in front of us as much life as we had then: I know that we should change at once, whatever we are. I know with me it was the time when I was least happy, the time of longing and loneliness! But I know that even I wished to change, with both hands I should try to snatch that constrained youth—what would it matter if my soul again would ache so infinitely, so desperately?)

CHAPTER VIII

ALL that happened with me as it does with every boy, but perhaps less tempestuously, not so markedly as with most others. In the first place, much of that ferment of youth was in me wiped away by the continual longing for my home, in the loneliness of a country boy in strange and, to some extent, superior surroundings. My father was thrifty, he found me a lodging with the worried family of a tailor; for the first time I had the feeling that after all I was an indigent and almost poor little scholar who was destined to have to stint himself and to keep aloof. And I was a shy country lad who felt that he cut a poor figure with the audacious little masters from the town; how they felt at home there, how much they knew and had in common! Because I could not find any approach to them I made up my mind to excel in school; I became the book-worm who found some sort of sense of life, some revenge, some triumph, in that I proceeded from class to class *summa cum laude* accompanied by the ill will of my colleagues who, in my lonely and serious industry, observed disgusting ambition. The more I became hardened, and pored over my lessons with my fists on my brows in the dry, close atmosphere of the tailor's irons, in the smell from the kitchen where his sighing wife prepared a pale and eternally sour meal. I grew dull with learning; wherever I walked my lips moved in a continual repetition of my lessons, but how great was my secret and deep triumph when at school I KNEW the answer and sat down amidst the annoyed and unfriendly silence of the class! I didn't even turn round, but I could feel how they all were looking at me with animosity. And this petty ambition carried me through the crises and fundamental changes of youth; I escaped them by learning by heart the Sund islands or Greek irregular verbs. That was my father in me bent over his work until he gasped with concentration and zeal; my father running his thumb over the finished work. It's good, no gap anywhere. And it is dusk, you can't any longer read the lessons; through the open window you can hear the retreat sounded from the barracks; a boy stands at the window with burning eyes and his heart aches with a beautiful and desperate melancholy. What for? There is no name for it, it is so vast and deep that those sharp little needles of petty offences, humiliations, failures, and disappointments which everywhere goad the shy boy, dissolve away. Yes, that's my mother again, this overflowing with pain and love. That concentrated drudgery is my father, this that is sentimental and passionately tender is my mother: how is one to contain and straighten out these two in a boy's narrow chest?

At one time I had a pal to whom I was drawn with passionate friendship; he was a country boy, older than I, with a light down on his lip, amazingly untalented and gentle; his mother had promised him to God as a sacrifice of thanksgiving for his father's recovery, and he was to study for the priesthood. When he was asked a question in school there was a complete tragedy of good-will and panic; he trembled like a leaf and couldn't stammer out a single word. In a strenuous endeavour to help him I taught him myself; he listened with an open mouth and gazed at me with beautiful, adoring eyes. When they examined him I suffered terribly and inexpressibly; the whole class tried to prompt and help him, they even took me into grace and prodded me: you, what is it? Then he sat down, crimson and ruined; I went to him with my eyes full of tears and comforted him. Look, you're already doing a bit better, you could nearly answer it, just wait, and it'll go! During lessons in school I sent him the answers on screwed-up bits of paper. He sat in the opposite corner of the room; my message passed from hand to hand and nobody opened it, it was for him; youth is usually callous, but it is chivalrous. With our combined forces we got him as far as the third year, then he failed inevitably and went home; I was told that he had hanged himself at home. That boy was perhaps the biggest and most passionate love of my life. I used to think back on it later on when I read stories of the sexual motives in youthful friendships. Good Lord, what nonsense! We hardly ever got to shaking hands with each other in a clumsy fashion; almost crushed and overwhelmed we lived the amazing fact that we were souls; we were filled with happiness in being able to look at the same things. I had the feeling that I was learning for his sake so that I could help him; that was the only time when I really liked my lessons and when they all had a positive and glorious meaning. Even to this day I can hear my own entreating, eager voice: "Look here, say it after me: Phanerogams are divided into monocotyledons, dicotyledons, and acotyledons." "Monograms are divided into," my big pal would mumble with a voice already masculine, gazing at me like a dog with clear, faithful, and devoted eyes.

A little later I had another love affair; she was fourteen and I fifteen. She was the sister of one of my schoolfellows who had failed in Latin and Greek, an awful rascal and good-for-nothing. One day a shabby, melancholy, and mildly drunk gentleman was waiting for me in the school corridor. He took his hat off and introduced himself as an official, so and so, his voice trembled at the mention of it; and seeing that I was such an excellent student, he said, and would I be kind enough and help his son a little in Latin and Greek. "I can't afford a tutor for him," he stammered, "but if you would be so exceedingly kind, sir——" He said "sir" to me, that was enough; could I ask anything more? I took up my new task with enthusiasm and tried to teach that bristly urchin. It was a strange kind of family; the father was eternally at the office or drunk, and the mother did sewing work with families or something; they lived in a narrow, notorious little street where as evening came on fat and faded ladies used to stand in front of the houses, swaying like ducks. At home there were, or perhaps were not, the young rascal and his little sister, clean, shy, with a narrow face, and light eyes bulging with myopia, with which she eternally bent over some embroidery or needlework. The progress of the coaching was deplorably slow, the rascal had no wish to learn and that was that; instead I fell head over heels in love, and painfully, with that shy girl who used to sit very silent on a little stool with the embroidery right up to her eyes. She always raised them suddenly, and as if terrified, and then somehow she apologized with a trembling smile. As time went on the rascal wouldn't repeat my statements any longer, he magnanimously allowed me to do his exercises and went his way. I sat hunch-backed over his notebooks as if they were giving me God knows how much trouble; whenever I raised my head she quickly lowered hers, crimson to the roots of her hair; when I spoke her eyes almost shrieked with agitation and a miserably timid smile trembled on her lips. We had nothing to say to each other, it was all terribly embarrassing; the clock ticked on the wall and rattled instead of striking; sometimes I never know how I sensed that all of a sudden she was breathing more rapidly and pulling the thread quicker through the embroidery; then my own heart began to throb and I didn't even dare to raise my head, I only began unnecessarily to turn over the pages in the rascal's notebooks so that at least something happened. I was utterly ashamed of my embarrassment and I used to make up my mind: To-morrow I will say something to her, something that will make her start talking with me. I thought out hundreds of remarks and also what she might say; for instance: Show me that embroidery, and what will it be, or something like that. But when I was there and wanted to say it, my heart began to beat faster, my throat turned dry, and I couldn't get one word out; she raised her frightened eyes, and I sat hunch-backed over the notebook murmuring with a man's voice that there were hundreds of mistakes. And all the time, on the way home, at home, at school, my head was full of it: what I would say to her, what I would do; I would stroke her hair, I would take up paid coaching and buy a ring, I would save her somehow from that home of hers; I should sit down beside her, put my arm around her neck, and I don't know what else. The more I thought it out the more my heart throbbed, and the more hopelessly I sank into a panic of embarrassment. And the rascal left us alone with intent almost striking. You will prompt me, he commanded, and dropped out of the house. And once, Yes; now I will kiss her, now I will kiss her; I will go to her and will do it; now I will get up and go to her. And suddenly in confusion, almost with terror, I became conscious that I really was getting up and going to her. And she rose, her hands on the embroidery trembled, her mouth was half open with fright; our foreheads knocked together, nothing more; she turned away and began to sob: "I like you so much, I like you so much!" I also wanted to cry, I was lost. Good Lord, what shall I do now? "Somebody's coming," I blurted out stupidly; she stopped sobbing, but that was the end of a great moment; I returned to the table crimson and embarrassed, and began to put the notebooks together. She sat with the embroidery close to her eyes, her knees shook. "Well, I must go," I stammered, and on her lips a humble and timid smile appeared.

The next day the rascal said to me, expertly and out of the corner of his mouth: "Don't I know what you are doing with my sister!" And he winked knowingly. Youth is strangely without compromise and consequence. I never went there again.

CHAPTER IX

After all, the course of life is moved forwards chiefly by two forces: by habit and chance. When I had taken my certificate (almost disappointed that it was so easy) I had no fixed idea of what I should really like to be; but because twice before I had already taught somebody (and in each case those were the times when I felt important and big), that was the single thing in front of me that had at least a suspicion of a habit: to teach others; therefore I decided to study philosophy. Father was well pleased with the idea: to be a schoolmaster; after all that is a profession and comes under a pension scheme. By then I was a tall and serious youth; I was allowed to sit at the white-covered table with the curate, attorney, and other big-wigs, and I puffed myself up immensely; now life was in front of me. Suddenly I realized how local, provincial, and rural those big-wigs were; I felt myself called upon to achieve something greater, and I looked mysteriously like a man who has big plans; but even that was only uncertainty and a certain amount of trepidation before that step into the unknown.

I think that it was the most painful moment in my life when I stepped out of the train with my box in Prague, and suddenly lost my head: what now, and where to go? I felt as if all the people were turning round and laughing as they saw me standing helplessly there with my box at my feet; I was in the way of the porters, people pushed into me, cabmen shouted at me: Where do you want to go, sir? I snatched up my box in panic and began to wander through the streets. Hi, get off the pavement with that luggage, the policeman shouted at me. I fled into the side streets, lost and aimless, changing the box from one hand to the other. Well, where was I going? I didn't know and therefore I had to run; if I had stopped it would have been still worse. At last the box fell from my fingers stiff with cramp and pain. It was a quiet street, grass pushed its way up on the pavement like it did at home on the square; and just in front of my eyes on the front gate a notice was nailed: A room to let for a single gentleman. I sighed with an infinite relief: Well, see, I did find it after all.

I hired that room from an old, close-tongued hag; there was a bed and a sofa; it smelt gloomily, but what did that matter? At least I was safe. I was in a fever of excitement, I could not eat anything; but to save appearances I made as if I were going to eat somewhere, and I wandered through the streets, in fear and trembling lest I should lose my bearings. That night my nervous fever muddled and crumbled my dreams; towards morning I woke and on the side of my bed a fat youth was sitting; he smelt of tobacco and recited some verses. "You are astonished, aren't you?" he said and went on reciting. I thought that it was still part of my dream and I closed my eyes. "Good Lord, this is a loony," said the youth, and began to undress himself. I sat up in the bed; the youth sat on the side and began to take his shoes off. "Again I have to get used to another ox," he lamented. "What trouble I had to silence the one who was here before you, and you will sleep like a log," he complained bitterly. I was immensely glad that someone was talking to me: "What verses were they?" I asked. The youth flew into a rage. "Verses! You talk to me about verses, you cabbage! Listen," he stammered, "if you want to get on with me then may the Lord protect you if you start bringing in that daft Parnassism. You know darn little about poetry." He sat with one shoe in his hand, with a far-away look in his eyes; he began to recite some poem in a low voice and rapturously. I shivered in fascination, it was for me so infinitely new and strange. The poet threw his shoe at the door as a sign that he had finished and got up. "Misery," he sighed. "Misery." He blew out the oil lamp and lay down heavily on the sofa; I could still hear him whispering something. "You," he inquired from the darkness after a while, "how does it go on: Gentle Jesus, meek and mild——You don't know it either? When you are such a pig as I am you will miss it as well; you wait, you will see how you will miss it——"

In the morning he was still asleep, swollen and dishevelled. When he woke, he weighed me up with cloudy eyes. "To study philosophy? What for? Man, to think you care for it!" In spite of that he took me under his wing and showed me the university. Here you have this, here that, and may the deuce take you. I was confused and fascinated. This, then, is Prague, and people like this are here; very likely it's part of the thing, and I must act accordingly. In a few days I got accustomed to the routine of the university lectures; I scribbled into my notebook learned expositions which at the time I couldn't understand, and at night I argued with the drunken poet about poetry, women, and life as a whole; this and that turned my country head and gave it some sort of dizziness which was not unpleasant. Besides, there was much to look at. Altogether there was too much at once, it filled my mind until it was chaotic and turbulent; perhaps I should have crawled back again into my steady and lonely drudgery if there hadn't been that fat, drunken poet with his stimulating sermons. It's all muck, he used to say with assurance, and the matter was dismissed; only poetry was partially exempt from his ruthless contempt. I readily contracted his cynical superiority to the things of life; he helped me to master victoriously that mass of new impressions and inaccessible things; I could reflect with pride and contentment on how much I scoffed. Did it not give me a terrific feeling of ascendancy over anything that I repudiated it? Did it not liberate me from the romantic and painful dreaming about life which in spite of all my glorious freedom and officially legalized maturity still escaped me? A young man desires everything that he sees, and is annoyed if he can't have it; therefore he takes his revenge on the world and on the people, and searches for the things in which he can repudiate them. And then he tries to test his own disquiet; nights of loafing begin, expeditions to the fringes of life, endless wordy debates, and haste for the experiences of love as if they were the most famous trophies of the male.

Perhaps it was different: perhaps savagery and nonsense had

accumulated during those eight cramped schoolboy years, and now they must break out. Perhaps it is simply a part of youth, like the growth of a beard and the atrophy of the thymus. It was obviously necessary and natural to live through it; but measured by the sum of life it was a strange and deranged period, a grand waste of time, giving something like pleasure because we had succeeded in violating the sense of life. I was no longer an undergraduate of the university; I wrote verses, bad ones, I imagine; in spite of that they were published in periodicals of which for a long time now nobody has known anything. I'm glad that I didn't keep them and that no trace even of them is left in my memory.

Of course it all went bang. My father came after me and made a terrible scene; and if it was like that he wouldn't be such a fool as to send his boy money to throw away. I puffed myself up, offended, obviously with a bad conscience; I'll show him that I can support myself. I sent an application to the Ministry of Railways to take me on an as official probationer and, to my astonishment, I got a positive answer.

CHAPTER X

I WAS officially appointed to the Franz Joseph Station at Prague in the dispatch department: in an office that had a window looking out on to a dark platform and where we had to have artificial light all the day long; a dreadful and hopeless den, where I looked through transit fees and such-like things. People flitted past the window waiting for someone or to travel somewhere; it had its nervous, almost pathetic, atmosphere of departure and arrival, while behind the window I scribbled down the idiotic and completely bald figures. But never mind, there was something in it. And from time to time I could stretch my legs on the platform with an indifferent face, for I was at home there, you know. Otherwise it was an immense, dull and colossal bore; the only deep satisfaction it gave me was that I was already a man who could support himself alone. Yes, I sat hunch-backed below a lamp as I did when I was doing my mathematical exercises; but that was only a preparation for life, while this now it was life itself. That's a tremendous difference, sir. I began to despise the fellows with whom I had been squandering the past year; they were unripe, dependent chaps, while I had become a man who was already standing on his own feet. Altogether I avoided them; I preferred to drop into a quiet and respectable pub where steady, middle-aged men expounded their worries and arguments. Gentlemen, I'm not here just as you see me; I'm a mature and adult man who supports himself by a wearisome and boring job. But it is dreadful what I must do to keep myself alive; all through the day the only light comes from a hissing gas lamp, that's intolerable; probationer or no, gentlemen, I already know what life is like. Why did I take it up? It was like this, family feeling, and such things. When I was a child they built a railway near my home and I wanted to be a conductor, or that chap who takes and dumps the loosened stones. You know, a boy's ideal; that's why I'm writing out notices and things like that. Nobody took any notice of me, every mature man has each his own worries; I was just scared to go home because out of weariness I should have to lie down in bed, and then again I should develop a temperature and that absurd sweat would break out over me. It comes from that dark office, you know. Nobody must know about it, a probationer must never be ill or they would sack him; he must keep to himself what happens to him at night. It's a good thing that I've already experienced enough to have, at least, something to dream about. And what heavy dreams: everything runs together and gets muddled; it's monstrous. This is such a real and serious life, gentlemen, that I'm pegging out with it. Somehow a man must throw his life away to understand its value.

That period of my life was a kind of continuous monologue; a monologue is a dreadful thing, a bit like self-annihilation, something like sawing through the fetters that bind us to life; a man who holds a monologue is not only lonely, but he is discarded or lost. God knows what sort of obstinacy or something there was in me: in the office I got a sort of savage pleasure from the fact that it was ruining me; besides that agitated haste of arrival and departure, always that rush, always that disorder; a station, particularly a big station, is congested, a little like a festering ganglion —the devil knows why so much riff-raff, petty thieves, pimps, wenches, and queer individuals collect there; perhaps because people who are coming or going are already de-railed from their lines of habit and become, so to speak, a favourable spot upon which all kinds of vice can sprout. I sniffed with satisfaction that faint odour of decomposition, it suited my feverish mood, that revengeful feeling of annihilation and petering out. And then, you know, there was another victorious satisfaction; there on that same platform I had got out a little more than a year before, a startled country bumpkin with a wooden box, not knowing where to go; and now I was crossing the rails, waiving the notice, nonchalant and blasé; how far had I gone in that time, where had I left my stupid and bashful years? How far, almost at the end!

One day I coughed up over my papers into my handkerchief

a lump of blood, and while I was looking at it in astonishment a bigger and terrible portion came up. They crowded together round me, frightened and helpless, one old clerk wiped my sweaty forehead with a towel; I seemed to myself like Mr. Martinek at home; it used to come over him while he was at work, and then he sat on a pile of planks, terribly pale and perspiring, with his face in the palms of his hands; I used to look at him from a distance, dreadfully perplexed and frightened—now I had an equally strong feeling of terror and of distance. That old clerk with spectacles, like a slow, black beetle, took me home and put me to bed; he even came to visit me because he saw that I was afraid. After a few days I got up, but God knows what happened with me: I had a terrible desire to live, even if it were as silently and slowly as that old clerk; a desire to sit at a table and turn over the papers while the gas lamp hissed silently and stubbornly.

"Above" in the office there was someone very sensible; they didn't make much fuss over the investigation into the state of my health, and they moved me officially to a small railway station in the mountains.

CHAPTER XI

In its way it was the end of the world; the line ended there; a little bit past the station were the buffers where the last rusty metals were overgrown with shepherd's-purse and hair-grass. You didn't go any farther; beyond a green mountain river murmured in the bend of a narrow valley. Well, it was like being at the bottom of a pocket there, the end, nothing beyond. I think that the railway was built there merely to carry planks from the sawmill and long, straight trunks tied with a chain. In addition to the station and the sawmill there was a pub, a few wooden houses—Germans like logs—and forests murmuring in the wind like an organ.

The station-master was a grumpy man like a walrus; he weighed me up suspiciously. Who knows why they've moved this youngster here from Prague, very likely as a punishment; I shall have to watch his fingers. Twice a day a passenger train arrived, consisting of two carriages from which a group of hairy men got out with saws and hatchets, wearing green hats on ginger-haired pates; when the signal bell had stopped ringing, bim, bim, bim, bim, bim, bim, you walked out on to the platform to assist with the great event of the day. The station-master, with his hands on the back, chatted with the chief guard, the engine-driver went for a drink of beer, the stoker made as if he were wiping the engine with a dirty rag, and again there was silence; only a bit farther on the planks banged as they were being loaded on to the wagons.

In the tiny, shady office the telegraph apparatus would tick, that was some gentleman from the sawmill announcing his arrival; in the evening a little cab would wait in front of the station while the unshaven driver thoughtfully flicked away the flies from the shaggy horse's shoulder with the point of his whip. "Na prr," he would say at times in a thin voice, the horse would shuffle from one foot to the other, and there was silence again.

Then a little train would come puffing up with two carriages, the station-master somewhat respectfully and somewhat intimately would salute the magnate from the sawmill, who would take his seat in the cab, talking conspicuously and loudly; the other mortals would only exchange remarks under their breath with snuffling voices. And that was the end of the day; there was nothing else but to go to the pub, where one table was spread with a white tablecloth for the gentlemen from the station, from the sawmill, and from the forest management; or to take a stroll for a bit along the rails to where they were grown over with grass and shepherd's-purse, sit down on the pile of planks, and breathe the keen air. High up a little fellow is sitting—no, it's no longer so high, and out of the little chap has emerged a gentleman in a tight official blouse, with an official cap on the head, and with an interesting little moustache on an interestingly pale face; the devil knows why they've sent him here, thinks the station-master of the last station in the world. I beg to state, sir, that they've sent him for this; to sit on the planks as he used to sit at home. You have to go a long way to get back home again. You must learn a lot and commit many stupidities, you must cough up part of your life to find yourself again on the planks smelling of wood and resin. It's healthy for the lungs, they say. And already it's dark, stars peeping through in the sky; there were stars at home, too, but not in the town. How many there are, no, how many, it's almost impossible to believe. And then one thinks how much it matters who knows how much one has gone through; and yet there are such masses of stars! And this is really the last station in the world: the line runs to its end in the grass and shepherd's-purse, and then comes the universe. Right behind those buffers. You might say that the wood and the river are murmuring, and instead it's the universe, the stars rustle like the alder leaves and the mountain breeze blows between the worlds: Lord, it's good to fill your lungs!

Or to go with a rod to catch trout, to sit by a swiftly flowing river and make as if we were fishing, and instead we're only looking into the water to see how quickly it flows away; it is always the same ripple, and always new, always the same and new, and never an end; man, how much flows away with that water! as if something in you were detaching itself, something were swimming away from you, and the water carries it off. Where does it come from in man? All the time it's taking away with it some of his impurities and sadness, and always there's enough left for the next time. Even from that solitude how much has flown away and never an end. The young man sits over the water and sighs with loneliness. That's good, something says in him, only sigh a lot, and very deeply; it's good for the lungs. And the trout fisherman sighs greatly and deeply.

But be it said: he didn't give in easily, and he didn't just become reconciled with the last station in the world. First he had to show them that he had come from Prague and that he was not just anybody; it did him good to be a little mysterious, and he put on airs in front of the forestry probationers and the red-nosed, beardy men from the woods, like a man who has much behind him; but look what deep and ironic lines life had etched out round his mouth. They couldn't understand it very well, they were too healthy; they bragged about their adventures with girls picking raspberries, or at village dances; and they could be absorbed in a game of skittles for a whole Sunday afternoon. As time went on the interestingly pale man found that he was mildly and quietly interested in watching the run of the ball and the fall of the skittles, always the same and always new, like the ripples on the river. The line grown over with hair-grass and shepherd's-purse. The piles of planks sent away, and again there were new ones. Always the same, and always new. And, gentlemen, I caught five trout. Where? Just behind the station, such fellows. Sometimes I became horrified: Is this life? Yes, it is life: two tiny trains a day, a blind line grown over with grass, and just behind the universe like a wall.

And the interesting young man sitting on the pile of planks stooped down with satisfaction for a tiny stone to throw at the signalman's hen. So, and now get excited, you silly; I'm already a level-headed man.

CHAPTER XII

Rails / Links

Now I understand it; all that squealing and rattling was only a crossing; I thought I should fly to pieces as it shook inside me, and instead I was already running on to the proper and long line of my life. Something adjusts itself in man when his life is getting on to its proper line: up till then he had an uncertain possibility of being this, or that, to go here or there, but now it's to be determined by a higher validity than his own will. Therefore his inner self jibs and tosses about, not knowing that these tremors of his are just the rattle of the wheels of fate as they run on to the right rail.

Now I understand how it is all rolled out nicely and continuously right from childhood; nothing, almost nothing, was due to mere chance, but a link in a chain of necessity. I should say that my fate was decided when in the place of my childhood they began to build a railway; the tiny world of a little old town was suddenly linked with space, the little town was putting on seven-league boots; it has changed tremendously since then, factories have sprung up, money and misery—in short, it was its historical re-birth. Even if I didn't understand it then, I was fascinated by those new, noisy, manly things that invaded the closed world of a child, those rowdy troops of ruffians, scourings of the whole world, bangs of dynamite, and riddled slopes. I think that that child's great attachment to a strange little girl was mainly an expression of that fascination. It remained with me subconsciously and inevitably. Why otherwise should I have jumped at the first opportunity to apply for a post on the railways?

Those years of study, I know, they were another rail; but wasn't I homesick enough, and lost? But instead I found satisfaction and certainty in performing my duties; it was a relief to stick to the prescribed line of lessons and tasks; it was some sort of order, yes, it was a fixed rail along which I could run. I am apparently a bureaucrat by nature; to give me a feeling that I am working fully and well, my life must be directed by a sense of duty. Therefore I suffered such a catastrophe when, on going to Prague, I ran off the straight and safe lines that would have guided me. Suddenly I was not governed by any schedule or by any task that must be done by to-morrow morning. Because no authority had taken me up I gave myself to the wild leadership of the fat, drunken poet. God, how simple it all is, and I thought then what experiences I was having. I even wrote poems like every other student in those days, and I thought that at last I had found myself. When I applied for the post on the railways I did it out of spite, to show my father; in reality, unconsciously and blindly, I was already feeling for MY own firm line under my feet.

And there's another thing, apparently a mere detail, perhaps I am making too much of it: my derailment began at the moment when, with my box in my hand, I stood on the platform, helpless and miserable, almost crying with embarrassment and shame. For a very long time I felt ashamed of that defeat. Who knows: perhaps I became a young gentleman on the railways and later on a rather bigger cog in the railways, also to efface and redeem for myself that painful and humiliating moment on the platform.

. . . . .

These explanations, it's true, are retrospective; but at times I used to have an intense and strange sensation that that particular moment CORRESPONDED to something in my life that happened long ago; that something was being accomplished that I had already experienced before. Perhaps it was when under a hissing lamp I sat bent over the notice: Good Lord, but it was just like the time when I sweated, gnawing my pen over my school exercises, urged on by the awful realization that they must be done. Or the feeling of the conscientious pupil which I never lost all my life: that I have done all my lessons. It is strange that those moments when I was conscious of this remote and strangely clear connection with something long ago moved me like a revelation of something mysterious and great; in them life was revealed to me as a vast, determined whole linked by invisible relations which we comprehend but rarely. When at the last station in the world I sat on the planks which reminded me of father's joiner's yard I began for the first time, with amazement and resignation, to live the beautiful and simple order of life.

CHAPTER XIII

In due time I was moved to a more important station. It was, it's true, not big, but it was on the main line; six times a day big express trains passed through, without stopping, of course. The station-master was a German, and very good-natured; the whole day long he smoked his clay pipe, but when an express was signalled he put it down in a corner, brushed himself, and went on the platform to pay due honour to the international connection. The station was very tidy, petunias in all the windows, everywhere baskets of lobelias and nasturtiums; the garden full of lilac, jasmine, and roses, and then by the storehouse and signal-box nothing but flower beds, marigolds in flower, forget-me-nots, and antirrhinums. And everything had to shine—windows, lamps, green-painted pumps—otherwise the old gentleman was terribly annoyed: "What's this," he grumbled, "international expresses pass through here, and you leave muck about like this!" The muck might be a bit of waste paper, but it could not be tolerated, for a great moment was approaching: over there behind the bend with a dull roar the powerful, high chest of an express locomotive was emerging, the old gentleman took three steps forward, and already it was thundering past him: the engine-driver greeted with his hand, on the steps of the express the conductors saluted, the old gentleman stood to attention, heels together, shoes polished like a mirror, and raised with dignity his hand to his red cap. (Five paces behind, that interestingly pale official with a high cap, in trousers polished on the seat, saluting a bit more casually, that was me.) Then the old gentleman, with a wide, proprietary eye, looked at the blue sky, clean windows, flowering petunias, raked sand, his polished shoes, and the metals which glistened as if he had had them specially polished for the purpose, he contentedly rubbed his nose; well, that was all right, and went to light his pipe again. That ceremony took place six times a day, always with the same pomp and the same solemnity. Railway people throughout the whole monarchy knew of the old gentleman and his model station; that festive transit was a pleasant and serious game that they all looked forward to. Every Sunday afternoon, on the covered platform, there was a holiday corso; the local people, dressed up and starched, promenaded politely and silently under the baskets of lobelias, while the old gentleman walked up and down with his hands behind his back, looking at the lines, like the chef of an establishment having a look to see if everything is in order. It was his station, his household; and if miracles could happen so that recompense and glory might be given to righteous souls, one day an international express (the 12.17) would have stopped at the platform, and the Emperor would have stepped out; he would have raised two fingers to his cap and said: "You've made it very nice here, Mr. Station-master. Your station has often caught my eye."

He liked his station, he liked everything to do with railways, and, best of all, he liked engines; he knew them all by their series numbers and their good points. That one there doesn't go very well uphill, but, sir, what lines she's got! And this, look, what length, by Jove, that's a boiler for you! He talked about them as if they were girls, with appreciation and chivalry. Yes, it's true, you laugh at this short and stumpy thirty-six one with her squat chimney, but think how old she is, you chicken! For express engines he had an admiration absolutely passionate. That short, robust chimney, that deep chest, and those wheels, my friend, she's a beauty! His life was almost pathetic in that beauty passed him flying like lightning; and yet for its sake he polished his shoes, for its sake he decorated the windows with petunias, and saw to it that there was no tiny blemish anywhere. God, how simple is the prescription for a happy life: to do what we have to out of love for the thing.

And God knows by what miracle on that station such a collection of good-hearted fellows had been brought together.

The telegraphist, a shy and bashful youth who collected stamps and felt terribly ashamed of it; he always hid them quickly in a drawer, red to the roots of his hair; we all pretended that we didn't know anything about it, and we dropped secretly on his desk, among his papers, between the pages of the book he was reading, whatever stamp we could lay our hands on. Those stamps the train postmen let us have. Most likely they detached them from all the letters from abroad that passed through their hands; because it was against the regulations, the old gentleman behaved as if he hadn't the slightest suspicion of it, and it fell to me to perform the forbidden part of our secret undertaking; after that with fine enthusiasm he assisted in playing pranks on the timid telegraphist. That unhappy youth found stamps from Persia in an old coat pocket, or from the Congo in crumpled paper in which he had brought his lunch; under the lamp he found a Chinese stamp with a dragon, and out from his handkerchief he shook a blue one from Bolivia. He always blushed frightfully and his eyes filled with the tears of emotion and amazement; he squinted towards us, but we made no sign, no sign at all; we had no inkling there might be someone among us who collected stamps. Happy grown-ups at play.

The porter who grumbled eternally and ten times a day sprinkled the platform with a dribble of water and scolded those who at the station represented the incorrigible element of disorder and confusion. If it were possible he wouldn't have let anybody in; but what can one do with those old women, with their hampers and bags? He always struck terror, and yet no one was ever afraid of him; his life was weary and disturbed, and only when the international express rattled through the station did he stop grumbling and throw out his chest. Just to let you know it's my job to keep things straight here.

The old man who tended the lamps, a melancholy and passionate reader; beautiful, moving eyes like Mr. Martinek had at home, or my late chum at school; altogether he reminded me of them, and therefore I used to drop in to see him occasionally in the wooden lamp-room, sit down on the narrow bench, and without wasting words enter into long and distracted meditations: why, for instance, women are like that, or what may come after death. I used to end with a resigned sigh: and, after all, who knows, but even that was somehow soothing and peaceful; I tell you, a poor man has got to accept the things of this earth and those beyond the grave, whether they are like this or that.

The man who looked after the stores, the father of about nine children or so; his children were also mostly in the storehouse, and when anyone came in they disappeared quickly behind the boxes like mice. It was not supposed to be allowed, but what can one do with such a blessed paternity? At midday they used to sit on the ledge of the storehouse according to size, one fairer than the next, and eat jam pastries, apparently just to have a jam moustache reaching from one ear to the other. I can't remember what their father looked like and what sort of man he was; I can only see his loose trousers with deep creases that seemed to express all his paternal care. And so on: the whole lot of them were such conscientious, sympathetic people—it was clearly part of the ordinariness of my life that I have come across so many good people.

Once I stood behind a train made up ready; on the other side a signalman was walking with the lamp attendant, they didn't notice me, and they were discussing me.

". . . a good chap," said the signalman.

"Such a good-hearted man," mumbled the slow lamp attendant.

Well then. So now we have it, and already we are at home. And get away from the people to turn it over in my mind that I really am a happy and simple man.

CHAPTER XIV

A STATION like that is a world to itself; it is more in touch with all the stations on the line than with the world on the other side of the fence. But the space in front of the station where the yellow mail coach is waiting belongs a little bit to us, but you go into town as if into a foreign region; there we are no longer on our own ground and with it we have almost nothing in common. Here is a notice, "Unauthorized persons not allowed," and what is behind that board is only for us; you others be glad that we permit you to come on to the platform and get into the trains. At the entrance to a town you can't put a notice "Unauthorized persons not allowed," to you is not given such an exclusive and closed domain. We are like an island suspended on the iron rails, on which more and more other islands and eyots are strung; all this is ours and it is severed from the other world with fences, crossing gates, notices, and prohibitions.

Therefore observe that on this our own preserve we walk differently from other people, with more importance, and a nonchalance that greatly differs from your confused rush. If you ask us something we bend our heads a little as if we were astonished that a creature from a different milieu were talking to us. Yes, we say, train number sixty-two is seven minutes late. Would you like to know what the station-master is discussing with the chief guard who is leaning out from the luggage van? Would you like to know why the station-master sometimes standing on the platform with his hands behind his back suddenly turns and, with long, rapid, determined strides, goes away into his office? Every closed world becomes somewhat mysterious; to a certain extent it is conscious of it and accepts it with deep satisfaction.

When I think back on that time I see that station as if from above, like a small and clean toy; that other block is the storehouse, that is the lamp-room, these are the sheds and the plate-layers' houses; here in the middle the toy lines run, and those little boxes, you know, are wagons and trains. Sh-sh-sh, sh-sh-sh, along the toy lines minute engines run. That tiny, squat little figure is the station-master, he has just come out of his office and stands by those miniature lines. And that other one with a pointed cap, with his legs stretched right out, that's me, that blue one is a porter, and that one in the tunic is the lamp attendant; they are all good and pleasant and they stand out with nice distinctness. Sh-sh-sh, sh-sh-sh, look out, now the express is coming. Where have I had that experience before? But that is like when I was a little chap in daddy's yard; I stuck chips into the ground to make a fence, covered the enclosure with clean sawdust, and put a few coloured beans in it; these are hens and the biggest bean, that speckled one, is the cock. The little chap bends over his enclosure, over his tiny world, he holds his breath in concentration, and he whispers: Chuck, chuck, chuck! But the little chap couldn't take other people to his enclosure, the big ones; each of them had his own game, a game of making things, keeping house, a little town; but now when we're grown up and serious, we all play together, the game on our station. And therefore we have decorated it so that it is ours still more, and still more a toy; and therefore, yes; everything hangs together, even that it was such a closed world shut in with a fence and prohibitions. Every closed world becomes something of a game; therefore we form exclusive, ours only, jealously guarded regions of our pastimes and hobbies to be able to give ourselves up to our favourite game.

A game is a serious matter, it has its rules and its binding order. A game is an absorbed, tender, or passionate concentration on something, on something ONLY; therefore, let that on which we concentrate be isolated from everything else, separated by its rules, and removed from the reality around. And, therefore, I think a game likes to be on a reduced scale;

if something is made small and tiny it is removed from that other reality, to a greater extent and deeper it is a world of its own, our world, in which we can forget that there still is another. Well, and now we have succeeded in tearing ourselves away from that other world, now we are in the middle of a magic circle which separates us; there is a child's world, school, the Bohemian poet's party, there is the last station in the world, the prim station sprinkled with sand and all trimmed with flowers, and so on, till at the end there is the little garden of the retired man, the last thing isolated from the world, the last silent and concentrated game; the red ears of alum root, the cool panicles of spiraeas, and two steps farther a finch on a stone, his little head to one side, looking with one eye: Well, who are you?

The enclosure made of chips stuck up in the earth toy lines which run apart and come together again, the little cubes for storehouses and signal-box; the toy signals, and points, of coloured lamps, and pumps; the little boxes for wagons, and the smoking engines; the little grumbling blue figure sprinkling the platform, the fat gentleman with a red cap; that little man with the legs stretched right out, that's me. Above in the windows behind petunias in flower, a doll for a little maiden, that is the daughter of the old gentleman. The little man salutes, the maiden quickly nods her head, and that's all. In the evening the maiden goes out and sits down on the green bench under the flowering lilac and jasmine. That one with the pointed cap stands by her, his legs stretched right out. It is getting dark, red and green lights shine on the lines, railwaymen swing over the platforms with lamps alight, there is a hoarse whistle from the bend of the rails, that is already the evening express, and it scuttles through with all its windows alight. The one in the pointed cap doesn't even look round, there is something more important for him here; but it passes the two young people strangely and excitedly, like distance and adventure, even the eyes of the pale maiden light up in the dark. Yes, already she must go home, and to the one in the pointed cap she gives her fingers which tremble and are a bit damp. From the lamp-room the old lamp attendant comes out and mumbles something very likely: and altogether, who knows? On the platform that one in the pointed cap is standing and is looking up into a window. Why wonder, for she is the only girl on this island, the only young woman in the closed domain; that already gives her a terrific and dangerous rarity. She is pretty with youth and cleanliness; her father is such a good fellow and her mother dignified and almost aristocratic, smelling as if of sugar and vanilla. The maiden is German, but that makes her a bit exotic. Good Lord, but even that has happened before, when that little imp with an unknown tongue—well, is it really true that the whole of life is made as if it were of one piece?

And then those two sit on the bench side by side and talk mostly about themselves; the jasmine is no longer in flower, but the autumnal dahlias are. All pretend that they can't see those two at the back; the old gentleman prefers not to go in that direction, and the lamp attendant, when he has to pass that way, coughs from a distance: Look out, it's me. Oh, you good-natured ones, why such fuss? as if it were something unusual and rare that one is up to his ears in love with the daughter of one's chief! That does happen, it already belongs to that ordinary and conventional life; but it is as if it were in fairy tales for children, to try to win the hand of the princess. Everything is as simple and clear as the palm of one's hand; but even that is part of the poetry of the case, to dally excitedly, and not to dare as if something inaccessible were at stake. The maiden is also in it up to her ears, but in her she has deeply written the rules of the game; at first to give only the tips of her restless fingers, to look out through the petunias, and then do nothing. Then it comes out that the other one was seriously, terribly, gravely ill; if it was like that, she can hold him maternally by the hand and remonstrate with him eagerly and anxiously: You must take care of yourself, you must not fall ill; I should like so much to look after you! And already there is a bridge over which from one side to the other groups of excited, generous, and intimate feelings can pass; now even that bridge isn't enough, one must hold hands so as to communicate also without words. Wait, when did that happen before, when have I experienced this delight of being coddled and commiserated with in my pain? Yes, it was when my mother picked up her howling child. You, my cherub, you, my only one in the world! If I fell ill now no elderly clerk would come who had no neck and who looked like a black beetle; I should lie pale and feverish, into the room a maiden would slip with tearful eyes, and I should pretend that I was asleep; and she, leaning over me, would sob suddenly: You, my only one, you must not die! Yes, like my mother. For the little maiden it is also good somehow to be a mother and weave round the other one her sentimental care; with eyes full of tears she is thinking, If he fell ill how well I should look after him! She doesn't realize how much by that she appropriates him, how much she tries to make him submit to her; she wants him to be hers, to be unable to defend himself, and to give in to the terrible immolation of her love.

We say love, but it is a whole host of feelings; we can't even discern them all. For instance, not only the need to impress, but also the need to be regretted. See, maiden, I am a strong and dark fellow; strong and dreadful like life. You are so pure and naïve, you don't know what it is. And one black evening which covers everything, the man on the bench begins to confess. Does he brag or is he humbly prostrate before the angelic purity of the maiden whom he holds by the hand? I don't know, but it must all be told. Loves which were. The waster, and the shameful life there in Prague, wenches, waitresses, and such experiences. The maiden does not even say a word, she snatches her hand from the other one and sits perfectly motionless; God knows what hosts of feelings she has. And that is all, my soul clean and redeemed; what shall you say to me, you pure little girl, what shall you say to that? She did not say anything, only quickly, convulsively as if in sharp pain, she pressed my hand and ran away. The next day, no maiden behind the petunias in the window. All is lost, I am a dirty and rude pig. And again it is such a black night, the white figure on the bench beneath the jasmine is the maiden; the one in the pointed cap daren't even sit down beside her, and he murmurs imploringly; she turns her head away, she may have tear-washed eyes, and she makes a place beside her. Her hand is as if dead, you can't get a word out of her. Oh, Lord, what is one to do? Please, please, can't you forget what I told you yesterday? Suddenly she turns to me, our foreheads hit together (as it was with the girl with the frightened eyes), but somehow I find her cramped and tightly held lips. Someone is moving on the platform, but now it's all the same; the maiden takes me by the hand, she lays it on her small, soft breasts and presses it to them almost desperately—here you have me, here, and IF EVEN THIS MUST BE, let it be! there are no other women, here I am; I don't want you to think about others. I am beyond myself with compunction and love. God forbear, maiden, that I should accept such a sacrifice; there need be nothing of the sort, it is enough to kiss tearful eyes, to smudge the tears, and to be terribly and solemnly moved. The maiden is immensely touched by this chivalry, she is grateful for it, so grateful that out of sheer enthusiastic gratefulness and trust, she would be able to give herself still more. God Almighty, it can't go on like this; she knows it, too, but in her the order of things is written deeper; she takes me wisely by the hand and says: When shall we get married?

That evening she doesn't even say that she ought to go home; why, now we are quiet and sensible; from that moment there is in our feelings a perfect and beautiful order. It is taken for granted that I accompany her as far as the door, we linger yet and are in no hurry to part. The grumbling porter disappears in some other door and we two are left alone, everything is ours: the station, metals, red and green lights, and the lines of sleeping wagons. No more will the maiden hide behind the petunias; she will always show herself there when from the office on to the platform the one in the pointed cap will come, wink into the window, and, holding himself together happy and reliable, will do what is called his duty.

But turn it round, turn it round; it wasn't just fun, it wasn't fun at all; great and heavy is love, and even the happiest love is horrible and crushing in over-measure. We can't love without pain, let us die of love, let us measure its vastness in suffering, for no pleasure plumbs the bottom. We are immeasurably happy, and we clench our hands almost desperately; you save me, I love too much. It is good that there are stars above us, good that there is space enough for something as big as love. We only talk so that silence will not crush us by the vastness of things. Good night, good night, how difficult it is to tear eternity into bits of time! We shall not sleep, we shall feel heavy, and our throats will ache with crying for love. If only it were day, God, if only it were day so that I could greet her at the window!

CHAPTER XV

SOON after the wedding I was transferred to a big station; perhaps the old gentleman had a hand in it, for willingly, and almost with a healthy appetite, he had taken me under his paternal care. Now you are ours, and that was the end of it. His wife was more reserved; she came from an old civil service dynasty, and she would evidently have liked to marry her daughter into a higher grade; she cried a bit with disappointment, but since she was romantic and sentimental she became reconciled because it was such a great love.

The station to which I went was as gloomy and noisy as a factory; an important junction, miles of track, storehouses, and engine sheds, a heavy goods transit; coal-dust and soot, a finger thick, over everything, whole herds of smoking engines, an old and crowded station; several times a day it got into a knot and one had to undo it in a hurry, as when, with fingers already chafed and bleeding, you undo a knotted cable. Nervous and irritated officials, grumbling staff, altogether something a bit like hell. You went into it like a collier going down a mine in which cracks are forming; any moment it might collapse, but it's man's work; here at any rate he feels a man, he shouts, decides, and carries his responsibility.

And then home, to scrub oneself down to the waist and to roar with delight from the clean water; my wife was already waiting with a towel in her hand and smiling. This was no longer a pale and interesting youth; it was a well-set worker, weary and hairy, with a chest, sir, like a cupboard; each time she used to pat him on his wet back like a big and good animal. So, now we're washed, now we shall not make our clean wife dirty; still we must wipe our face so that nothing remains on it that was said between the rails, and then, decently and decorously, we kiss the lady wife. So, and now tell me about it. Well, there were some troubles, this and that, the whole station ought to be pulled down, or at least those storehouses at the back; that would make space for six new lines and it would be easier to manage; I told so and so that to-day, but he only just gave me a look. You tell us something, and you've hardly been here a couple of months. She nodded her head with understanding; it is the only person with whom it is possible to talk about everything. And what were you doing, darling? She smiles, such a stupid man's question! What do women do? This and that, and then they are waiting for their man. I know, my dear, it is not visible, all pettiness, here a few stitches and there to buy something for supper, but it all makes a home; if I kissed your fingers I could tell by my lips that you had been sewing. And how nice she is when she gives me supper; the supper is frugal, it's true, German, but she herself, she has her head in the half-shadow and only her hands move prettily and kindly in the golden circle of the home light. If I kissed her on the forearm she would shrink back, and perhaps she would blush because it is not seemly; and so I only squint at her good, feminine hands and mumble praises of the supper.

We did not want to have any children until later. There, she used to say, it was too smoky, it would not be good for a child's lungs. How long ago was it since she was an inexperienced and pathetically helpless maiden? And now she was such a sensible and quiet wife who knew what to do; even in her conjugal love she was as quiet and kind as when she gave me supper with nice bare arms. She had heard, or read, somewhere that tuberculous people are very passionate: so she used to watch anxiously for any signs of excessive passion in me. Sometimes she frowned and said: You mustn't do it so often. But not really! She laughed pleasantly into my ear: You wouldn't be able to concentrate on your work to-morrow, and it's not healthy. Sleep, just sleep. I pretended that I was asleep, while she, anxious and worried, gazed into the dark and thought about my health and about my work. Sometimes—I don't know how to express it—sometimes I could have wished very much that she would not think of me alone. It's not only for me, darling, it's for you, too; if only you would whisper into my ear, My only one, how I have been longing for you! And then again she was asleep, and I awake. I kept thinking how well and safe I felt with her, never had I had such a reliable friend.

It was a good, strong time; I had my heavy, responsible work in which I could prove my worth; and I had my home, again a shut-up world only for the two of us. We, that no longer meant the station, it didn't mean men in joint service, it meant just we two, wife and I. Our table, our lamp, our supper, our bed: that "ours" was like an agreeable light, which fell on the fittings of our home and made them different, nicer, and rarer than all the others. Look, darling, curtains like that would look nice in our house, don't you think? And so that's how love proceeds: at the beginning to acquire one another is enough for us, it is the only thing in the world that matters; and when we have acquired one another body and soul, we acquire objects for our joint world; we are immensely pleased when we make something else our own, and we make plans to get something more some day to add to the things that are ours. Suddenly we find unprecedented joy in property; I like to economize, to be thrifty, and to put something aside; but it's for us, and it's my duty. In the office, too, my elbows are growing, and I push upwards with all my might; the others look askance at me, and almost with hostility, they are evil and unsociable, but what does that matter? But then, one has his home and a sensible wife, one has his own private world of trust, sympathy, and well-being, and the devil take the others. Here you sit in the golden gloriole of the home lamp, look at the white, agreeable hands of your wife, and readily talk about those envious, evil-minded, and incompetent people in the office; you know, they would like to get in my way. My wife nods her head in appreciative agreement; with her you can talk about everything, and she will understand; she knows that it is all for us. Here a man feels strong and good. If only she would whisper sometimes at night, confused and confusing: My dear, I've been longing for you so much!

CHAPTER XVI

AND then I was moved to a nice, good station; I was rather young to be a station-master, but wasn't I thought well of by those above me? Perhaps my father-in-law also helped a bit, but that I don't quite know; I was my own master now. I had my station, and when I moved there with my wife I felt with deep and solemn satisfaction: We've done well, and now, with God's will, we can settle down for life.

It was a good station, a junction mainly for passenger traffic; a nice country, meadows in deep valleys, the clatter of mills, and vast estate woods with shooting boxes. In the evening there was the smell of hay from the meadows, and estate carriages rattled in chestnut avenues. With the autumn gentlemen came to shoot, ladies in tweed dresses, gentlemen in hunting kit with piebald hounds and with guns in waterproof cases; a Duke, a couple of Counts, and here and there a guest from some ruling house. And then in front of the station carriages with white horses were waiting with grooms, lackeys, and stiff, erect coachmen. In the winter there were bony foresters with moustaches as big as foxes' tails and mighty agents from the estates who went to town from time to time to carouse gloriously and splendidly. In short, it was a station in which everything had to clatter without a hitch; no longer such a garlanded democratic festival as the station of the old gentleman, but a respectable and quiet station, where expresses came to a halt noiselessly to set down one or two gentlemen with chamois brushes at the back of their hats, and where even the conductors shut the carriage doors silently and respectfully. There the naïve and gay flower-beds of the old gentleman would have been out of place; that station had another soul, something like the courtyard of a castle; so that there had to be strict order, clean sand everywhere, and no domestic clatter of life.

It gave me plenty of labour and touching up before I had

made the station a work of my own. Up to that time it had been orderly, but characterless; it had not possessed, so to speak, any inspiration; but round about there were beautiful old trees and the smell of meadows. And I decided to make it into a clean and silent station, like a chapel, like a severe courtyard in a castle. There were hundreds of small problems, such as how to arrange the service, how to change the order of things, where to put empty carriages, and such-like things; I didn't make my station beautiful with flowers, like the old gentleman, but with system, a beautiful order, a smooth and silent circulation. Everything is beautiful if it is in its proper place; but there is only one such place, and it is not given everyone to find it. And suddenly it comes as if it were a bigger and freer space, things have a clearer outline and acquire something like nobility. Yes, now it's the right thing. I built my station without masons, merely out of what was already there. The old gentleman came to have a look, he raised his eyebrows and rubbed his nose almost with astonishment. "Well, it looks very nice here," he murmured, and squinted at me doubtfully; it looked as if, at that moment he wasn't certain if his flower-pots were the right thing.

Yes, now it really was MY station, and for the first time in my life I had the feeling of something genuinely mine, the strong and good feeling of my own self. My wife felt that I was getting away from her and that what I was doing was only for myself; but she was sensible and let me go my way with a smile, Well, get on with it, it's your work, it is for you, and I shall guard what is ours. You're right, darling, perhaps I have estranged myself a bit from what used to be ours; I feel it myself, and that is why perhaps I'm so terribly considerate to you when I have a moment to spare; but you see how busy I am! She used to treat me kindly and with maternal leniency. Go on, but I know that with you men it can't be different, you get absorbed in your work like—like children when they are playing, isn't that so? Yes, like a child at play. We know all this without having to say it, it's not necessary to talk about it; vainglory, something of ours has been sacrificed for something that is only mine. My work, my ambition, my station. And she doesn't even sigh, only folds her hands at times in her lap, and looks at me kindly but anxiously. "You"—she hesitates—"perhaps you ought not to work so MUCH; surely you haven't got to." I frown slightly. What do you know about the things that have to be done to make a model station here? You might say sometimes: You are a fine man, and you do a good job well; and not always: Take care of yourself, and so on. At times like that I used to take a stroll outside just to make sure once more that everything was in order, and that it was worth the labour; but it took some time before I could again enjoy my work.

But never mind; it WAS a model station, people walked about almost on tiptoes, as if in a castle; everything so tidy and straightforward. The gentry in green hats most probably thought that I was doing it for their sake; they used to shake my hand, as if I were a landlord with whom they are very, very satisfied, and the ladies, too, in their tweeds waved pleasantly and appreciatively to me; even the piebald hounds wagged their tails politely when the gentleman in the official cap passed by. Ah, you people, don't deceive yourselves. I'm doing it for myself, you know. What do the stupid guests from the noble houses matter to me? If need be I salute, pull myself up, and that's all. Do you really know what railways are, stations, order, and smoothly-working transit? The old gentleman understands something, his praise means something; that's like the times when father passed his hand over a piece of furniture. It's good. None of you can appreciate what my station is and what I have put into it. Even my own wife doesn't understand it; she wants to have me for herself, and therefore she says, Take care of yourself. She is self-sacrificing, no doubt about that; she is able to sacrifice herself to man, but not to find, big things. Now, she thinks, if there were children, my man wouldn't be so wrapped up in his work and he would be more at home. And look, like a curse: no children. I know how much it is on your mind; and that's why you're always after me: so that I don't overwork myself, and you rush here and there and feed me like a woodman. I'm putting on weight, I'm big and strong, and still nothing. And then you sit with dry eyes and the sewing falls into your lap—like my mother, but mother's eyes always had tears on the brim. It's like a gap between us; no good now it's you who press convulsively to me, but the gap still remains. Then you lie in bed and don't sleep, neither do I, but we do not speak in case we might suggest that something is lacking. I know, my dear, it is a bit hard; I have my work, my station; it is enough for me, but not for you.

And the gentleman in the official cap walking up and down the platform throws his arms out a bit: Well, what can I do?—at least the station is really mine, it is in excellent order and clean, and it functions like a perfect engine, running silently in well-oiled bearings. What can I do? In the end, a man is most at home in his work.

CHAPTER XVII

WELL, everything changes with time; after all, time is the greatest force in life. My wife grew accustomed to and reconciled with our lot, no longer did she hope for children, but instead she hit on another mission in life. As if she had said to herself: My husband has his work, and I have my husband; he keeps a piece of the world in order, and I keep him. She found out a lot of things which for some reason unknown to me she took to be my habits and rights. This thing my man likes to eat, and that disagrees with him; he wants to have the table spread like this, and not in any other way; to have water and a towel ready here, his slippers ought to be there; he likes to have the pillow like this, and his night-shirt like this and not otherwise. My man likes to have everything ready at hand, he is used to his own system, and so on. And when I came home I was at once surrounded by a pedantic order of my own habits; she thought them out, but I had to fulfil them to satisfy her fancy that I wanted it like that. Not knowing myself how I was falling into that system of habits prepared for me; unconsciously I felt terribly important and noble, for everything centred round my own self; I would raise astonished brows if my slippers were waiting even an inch away from their usual place. I was conscious that my wife was getting hold of me through my habits and dominating me more through them; I gave in to it gladly, partly out of comfort and partly because it really flattered my self-esteem. And most probably I was also getting older, for I was beginning to feel established and well at home in my habits.

And my wife was glad that she could reign like that on the first floor behind the windows full of white petunias. Every day had its fixed and almost sacred routine; I knew by heart all the small, everyday, agreeable noises: my wife getting up quietly, putting on her dressing-gown, and going on tiptoes into the kitchen. Then the coffee-mill rattled, orders were given in a whisper, somebody's hands lay my brushed clothes on the back of my chair: I obediently used to pretend that I was still asleep until the moment when my wife came, neat and tidy, and pulled the blinds up. If I opened my eyes a bit too soon she became upset and would say: "Did I wake you?" And so it went on day after day, year after year; it was called "my order," but she created it and she watched over it with eager eyes; she was mistress there, but everything was done for me—an honest conjugal division. I was in my official cap downstairs, walking round the station from one set of points to the other—that was my household; I felt very much like an important and exacting overlord, for they were extremely careful and zealous when I was in sight; just to look was my chief task. Then I used to shake hands with the bearded foresters; they were experienced men who knew what order meant. The gentry in green hats by then felt that it was their duty to shake hands with the station-master; by now he belonged to the place like a curate or the local doctor, and so it was good form to talk with him about one's health or the weather. And in the evening one used to remark: "Count so and so was here, he looks very badly." My wife used to nod her head and observe that it was due to his age. "Age," I used to protest, with the offended air of a man who is approaching fifty, "but he's ONLY sixty." She used to smile and look at me as if to say: What, you, you're just in your prime; that's due to a quiet life. And then silence reigned, the lamp buzzed, I read the newspaper and my wife a German novel. I knew that it was something touching about a great and pure love; she was still extremely fond of reading about such things, and it made no difference to her that in life it is different. Conjugal love is something quite different; it is part of an order, and it is healthy.

I am writing this while she, poor thing, has already been a long time in the grave. I still remember her, God knows, how many times a day; but least during those months before her death when she was so very ill—I prefer to avoid that; strangely little of our love, and of the first years of our married life; but most of all just this quiet and regular period at our station. Now I have a good housekeeper who does her best to look after me; but when I am looking even for a handkerchief or fishing under the bed for a slipper, it comes home to me, Good Lord, how much love and attention was in the order of those things, and I feel myself terribly an orphan, and a lump wells up in my throat.

CHAPTER XVIII

THEN came the War. My station was quite an important little point for the transport of troops and material, and so they placed there an army commandant, a drunken captain, half mad. From early morning he roared, as long as he was in his senses; he interfered with my arrangements and drew his sabre to the foreman; I asked headquarters to send me someone, if possible, less out of his senses, but that didn't help matters, and all I could do was to shrug my shoulders. My model station wasted away, it was saddening to see it; the waste and disorder of the War swept over it: the smell of the hospital trains, piled-up transports, and the detestable mess of dirt and filth. Families from the evacuated front and their belongings on the platforms, in the waiting-rooms, on the benches, on the bespattered floors the soldiers slept as if dead. And all the time hoarse, irate gendarmes patrolled and kept their eyes open for deserters, or poor fellows with bags in which were a few potatoes, people continually crying and shouting, bawling at each other irritably, or being pushed somewhere like sheep, in the middle of that confusion a long and terribly silent train carrying wounded men overshadowed everything, and from somewhere you could hear the drunken captain vomiting as he leant against a wagon.

God, how I began to hate it! War, the railways, my station—everything. I was sick of wagons smelling of dirt and disinfection, with broken windows, and scribbling on the walls; I was sick of that useless running about and waiting, lines eternally blocked, fat Samaritans, and altogether everything that had to do with war. I detested it madly and helplessly; I crawled between the wagons and very nearly cried with hatred and horror, Jesus Christ, I really cannot bear it, nobody could bear it. At home I could not talk about it, for my wife, with shining and enthusiastic eyes, had faith in the victory of the emperor. With us, as everywhere during the War, children of the poor went to get coal from the passing trains; one day a little chap fell down and the train ran over his leg; I heard his shriek of terror and saw the smashed bone in the bleeding flesh. When I told my wife about that she turned rather pale and burst out vehemently: "It was God's punishment!" From that moment I didn't talk to her about things that had any connection with the War. Well, can't you see how tired I am, and my nerves all are gone?

One day a man presented himself to me whom I couldn't recognize at first; we found that we had been together at the gymnasium and that he was something in Prague. I had to get it out of me, I couldn't talk with anyone about it at the station. "Man, we shall lose this war," I wheezed into his ear; "let me tell you, here we have our finger on the pulse." He listened to me for a while and then whispered mysteriously that he would like to talk to me about something. That night, behind the station, we came to an understanding, it was almost romantic. He said that he and a few other Czech people were in touch with the other side, they wanted to get hold of regular information about the transport of troops, the condition of supplies, and such-like things. "I'll do that for you," I burst out. It made me terribly afraid and at the same time I was immensely relieved of that convulsive hatred that was suffocating me. I know that this is high treason and that I might get hanged for it, but I shall let you have the information, and that's that.

It was a queer time; I was as if beyond myself, and at the same time like a clairvoyant; I had the feeling that it was not myself but something powerful and strange inside me that made plans, dropped hints, and thought of everything. I could almost have said: It's not me, it's the other one. In a jiffy everything was fixed up, it was a pleasure; it was as if everything had been waiting for someone to make a start; after all, we Czechs had to do something. With my hands behind my back and under the eyes of the gendarmes and of the hiccoughing commandant, I received reports from the chief guards, postmen, and conductors as to where the munitions were going and the guns, what units were on the move, and things like that. In my head was the whole of the transport network, and with half-closed eyes, walking up and down the platform, I pieced it together. There was a brake man, the father of five children, a sad, silent man; I always gave him the message to take farther, this he repeated to his brother in Prague who was a bookbinder, and how it went then, I never knew. It was thrilling to do this sort of thing under the eyes of everyone, and, at the same time, to have it so well organized; at any moment our plot might have failed, and every one of us, elderly men and fathers of families, would have been in it up to the neck; my friends, that would have been a crash! We knew it, and it was on our minds when we crawled to our wives in our feather beds; but what do women know about a man? Thank goodness, our thoughts aren't visible on our faces. For example, what causes a stoppage on the line at a station? Suddenly everybody shouts and gets worked up, and it takes a couple of days before it is straightened out again. Or lubrication in war time is bad; whose fault is it when axle boxes run-hot? Our station was full of abandoned wagons and engines out of use; it's no good getting worked up and sending telegrams, nothing can be done, we can't get things through faster. Holding our breath we listened how it was falling to pieces.

There was an accident at the old gentleman's station, there was a block on the line, and a train with the cattle for the front ran into it; nothing big, a few injured, and the cattle had to be slaughtered on the spot, but the old gentleman was so keen on the railways that it turned his head, and he died shortly afterwards. My wife cried on my shoulder at night; I stroked her, and I was very sad. You see, I can't tell you about my thoughts and about what I am doing; we have lived so well together and now we are so damnably far from each other. How is it that people can become so estranged!

CHAPTER XIX

THE end of the War, the end of the Monarchy; while my wife sniffed and wept (it was in her family, that loyalty to the Emperor), I received a summons from Prague to join the new Ministry of Railways and give my great experience to the task of organizing the railways of the young state. Because of that "great experience" I accepted; besides, during the War my station had suffered so much that it was not difficult for me to part from it.

This is, then, the last paragraph of an ordinary life. From my twentieth year I have been associated with the railways and I have enjoyed it; there I found my world, my home, and chiefly a deep satisfaction in that I was doing something that I could do well and capably. And now I was called upon to make use again of the whole of that experience. Well, see, that hasn't been in vain. I knew it all so well from the blasting of the rocks and building of the track, from the last station in the world and the wooden shed of the lamp attendant, to the confusion and bustle of the big stations; I had met with station buildings like glass palaces, and little stations in the fields smelling of camomile and yarrow; red and green lights, the steaming bodies of the engines, signals, points, and the tapping of the wheels on the points; nothing had been in vain, it all was added up and fused into one single and vast experience; I understand the railways, and that understanding is me, it is my life. Now there is everything that I have lived, it is together in my experience; I can again make use of it, and to the full, and that is as if I lived my life again in its totality. In my office I felt—I can't say happy, for there was too much disorder, but in my place. It was an ordinary but of its kind a complete life; and as I look back on it I see that in everything that happened some kind of order was realized, or . . .

CHAPTER XX

FOR three weeks I haven't written a word; again these heart attacks have come over me as I was sitting at the desk, just in the middle of a word (should it have been law, or purpose? I can't say any longer). Then they sent for a doctor for me; on the whole he didn't say much, some change in my arteries. You must take this, and mainly rest, sir, rest. And so here I lie and think—I don't know if this is a real rest, but I have nothing else to do. It is better again now, and so I wish to finish what I began; there is not much left, and I never left anything unfinished. My pen fell from my hand, just when I was about to write a big untruth; I deserved that attack. Surely I have no one whom I need deceive.

Yes, I liked the railways; but I could not like them any longer when they were messed up by war, when I made plans to sabotage them, and chiefly when I came to the Ministry. Sickened and disgusted by that paper and, for the most part, futile work called the reorganization of the railways; on one side I appreciated too well the various troubles below, and above, which offended my bureaucratic conscience; on the other side I began to sense something more inevitable, the tragedy of railway transport, which awaits the fate of the coaches and coachmen; vainglory, the great days of the railways are over. In short, this kind of work did not suit me at all; the only pleasure it gave me was that I was a rather important bureaucratic creature, that I had some sort of a title, and that I could throw my weight about: for in the end that is the proper and the only purpose in life: to rise as high as possible and enjoy one's honour and position. Yes, and that's the whole truth.

. . . . .

As I read what I have just written I feel rather flustered. How is it, the whole truth?

Well, yes, the whole truth about what we call the purpose of life. It was no pleasure to sit in that office; that was only the sense of satisfaction that I had scrambled up to something, and a jealous envy that those more able or politically more artful had got farther still. And that is the whole story of an ordinary life.

Wait, wait, that isn't a complete story. (There are two voices arguing, I can discern them quite clearly; the voice which is talking now as if it were defending something.) Surely I wasn't bent in life—on some career, and such-like things!

Weren't you really?

I wasn't. I was too ordinary to be ambitious. I never wanted to excel; I lived my work and did my work.

Why?

Because I wanted to do it well. To run my thumb down the front and the back, see if it's good. That's the real ordinary life.

Ha, and that's why in the end we sat in that office, not to work for anything more than our own position.

That—that was something else; in fact, it had no connection with what took place before. A man changes as he grows old.

Or he gives himself away in old age, is that it?

Nonsense. It must have been evident a long time ago that I was pushing myself to the front or something.

All right, then. And who was the little fellow who was worried because he couldn't beat the others? Who hated the painter's son so violently and painfully because he was stronger and more daring—do you remember?

Wait, it wasn't quite like that; but surely that little chap mostly played alone; he discovered his own tiny world, his little courtyard of chips, and his corner among the planks; that was quite enough for him, and there he forgot everything. Don't I know that?

And why did he play alone?

Because it was in him. His whole life long he has been making his small and shut-up world. A corner for his solitude and for his everyday happiness. His enclosure of chips, his little station, his home: surely you can see that it was always in him!

You mean that need to fence off his life?

Yes, that urge to have a world of his own.

Then do you know why he had his enclosure of chips? Because he couldn't excel among the other fellows. That was spite, that was the escape of a little boy who wasn't strong and daring enough to match himself against the others; he made his own world out of sadness and weakness, he felt that in the wider, open world he would never be anything big and daring as he wanted to be. An ambitious little poltroon, that's all. Do read carefully what you've written about him!

There's nothing of the sort!

There is, and quite a lot; only you stuck it in between the lines to hide it from yourself. For instance, that good and industrious little pupil in the elementary school: how he couldn't mix with his class, how he was nervous and timid; he was good because he was lonely and because he wanted to distinguish himself. And how that exemplary little boy nearly burst with pride when the teacher or curate praised him! Then tears of happiness never known before welled into his eyes; later on there will be no tears, but how his chest will puff out when he reads of his appointments. Do you remember with what unspeakable pleasure you took home your good reports?

That's because they pleased my father so much.

Well, then, let's have a look at your father. He was so big and strong, the strongest of them all, wasn't he? But he "had great respect for gentlemen"; more precisely, he greeted them humbly, so humbly that it even made his little son blush. And all the time he was eagerly hammering it in, if only you become something, boy, some day, that's the only thing in life, to become something. You must drudge, save, and grow rich so that the others will respect you and so that you will be somebody. Well and truly, the little chap had an example at home; that comes from his father, all that.

Never mind about my father! Father, that was quite a different example; to be strong and live for one's work.

Yes; and on Sunday to see in the bank-book—how far we've got already. Some day the little chap will sit in an office and measure himself by the dignity into which he has grown. Now my poor father would be pleased with me; now I am more than the attorney and those other big-wigs. At last the little chap has lived to see that he is something; at last he has found himself, and "a great and new experience" has come true which he discovered when he was a child: that there are two worlds, a higher one in which there are gentlemen, and then the humble world of ordinary people. At last I am something like a gentleman; but at the same moment it seems that above me there are still greater gentlemen sitting at still nobler tables and that I am again a small, ordinary man to whom it is not decreed to excel. Vainglory: it is a defeat, a damned and final defeat.

CHAPTER XXI

AND always it is as if you could distinguish two voices which quarrel; as if two people were tugging in opposite directions over my past, and each wanted to appropriate the biggest bit.

And what about those years at the gymnasium—do you remember?

Yes, and if you like, I will leave them to you. In any case they weren't worth much; that immaturity and that aching feeling of inferiority, all that drudgery of a country student—you're welcome, you can keep it!

Well, well, you needn't talk: as if that pot-hunting were nothing; that delight in being first in the class, always to have the exercises finished, always to know the answer; in something at any rate to be better than the others, better than the livelier and more daring ones, isn't that true? And for those successes to sit up at night with your head in your hands and cram—but it took eight full years!

Not full, don't say that; there were other things, too; deeper ones.

For instance?

For instance that friendship with that little friend who was hard up.

Oh, that one; I know, that lumbering, stupid boy. A fine opportunity to feel superior to somebody and to know that it's acknowledged. That wasn't friendship, man; that was a burning and passionate gratitude that somebody in the world humbly acknowledged your ability.

No, it wasn't like that! And what about love for that shy, short-sighted girl?

Nothing, stupidity; just puberty!

That wasn't just puberty!

Besides, it was lack of courage. The others, my lad, they got on better with girls, you envied them a lot for their courage;

and you, well, what else could you do but crawl into a corner and make your own enclosure of chips, your own shut-off world? Because in the open one you wouldn't have won, don't you know. Either among the boys or among the girls. It's always the same story with you; always the disappointed child who has his own world, and intently whispers: Chuck, chuck, chuck!

Stop!

. . . . .

Well, then, do explain that year in Prague, that futile and absurd year in Prague. That year when I loafed around with the poet's group and wrote verses and despised everything.

. . . I don't know. That year doesn't fit in very well. It doesn't with me either.

Wait, there's something I can explain. Here we have an industrious stripling; he's finished school and he thinks, Now the world belongs to him. At home he could behave like a somebody and feel important and big; but as soon as he comes to town, oh my gosh, he falls right bang into it, into that panic of inferiority, humiliation, and I don't know what else. If he'd had time to build an idyllic enclosure of chips round himself he'd have saved himself from it.

Only, unfortunately, the poet had taken him up.

Yes. But do remember how it was. But surely this also was a shut-up corner; those little pubs, that little circle of five or so people—man, it was damned small, smaller than a joiner's yard. And scoff at everything, that at least is an illusion of ability.

And write verses?

They were bad. He wrote verses to be able to stand on tiptoes. That was only a mask of a wounded and unsatisfied self-consciousness. He ought to have studied properly, and he would have been all right; he would have passed his examinations with success and would have felt like a little god.

But then I shouldn't have got on to the railways; I had to slip away somehow from the university so as to look for a post on the railways. Surely I had to get on to the railways, hadn't I?

There was no need.

I beg your pardon, that's absurd, what else could I have done?

All sorts of things. A man with elbows takes root everywhere.

. . . . .

Why, then, did I look for a post on the railways?

I don't know, perhaps by accident.

Well, I'll tell you: from affection. Because the building of the railway was the greatest event in my childhood.

. . . . .

And when I was at the gymnasium, it was my favourite walk in the evening: to stand on the bridge which spanned the station and to look down at the red and green lights, at the rails, and engines.

I know. Over that bridge an old, hideous prostitute used to walk; she always rubbed against you when she passed.

That, of course, doesn't seem to belong here.

Of course not, it's not nice.

. . . . .

Upon my honour: that was my predestined fate; I liked the railways, that's all. That's why I joined them.

Or because someone at the station in Prague had such a humiliating experience, do you remember? My dear fellow, a piqued self-consciousness is a terrible force, especially, you know, with some pushing and ambitious people.

No, it wasn't like that! I know, I know that it was from the love of the thing. Otherwise, could I have been so happy with my job?

. . . I don't know about happiness.

I say, who are you after all?

I'm the one with the elbows, you know.

. . . . .

In any case: you must at least admit that in my work I found myself and my real life.

There's something in that.

So you see.

Only it wasn't so simple, my friend. What came before? Poetry and women, an immense intoxication with life, is that it? Altogether, guzzling, poetry, bestiality, and megalomania, reaction against I don't know what, and a drunken feeling that something in us, God knows what, grand and unfettered, was boiling over. Do try to remember.

I know.

And that's the reason, that's how it was, you know.

Wait, how was it?

It's clear, isn't it? Surely you felt that your poetry wasn't worth much and that you couldn't succeed in anything like that. That you hadn't enough talent for it, or personality. That you weren't equal to your pals in drinking, contempt, women, or anything. They were stronger and more daring, and you, you tried to imitate them; I know how much it cost you, you ass. You tried hard, it's true, but that was only from a sort of ambition: so I was a maligned poet, with everything that goes with it. And all the time in you there was a sober, faint-hearted, and cautious little voice: Look out, it's more than you can manage. Then your vain little self-esteem began to prick, then your eagerness to be somebody was balked. That was defeat, my friend. After that all you could do was to look for a way out to save yourself; well, thank God, you found a little place on the railways, and the sobered poet was very glad that he could turn his back on his admittedly short but sufficiently lost Bohemian past.

That's not true! To get on to the railways, that was my inner necessity.

So it was. That defeat was also an inner necessity, and that flight was also an inner necessity. And how that former poet was pleased that at last he had become a complete and mature man.

With how much superiority and compassion did he suddenly look down on his pals of yesterday, at those immature bunglers who hadn't yet learned what proper serious life is like. He didn't even mix with them, and he dropped with old cronies into little pubs where steady fathers of families expanded their worries and wisdom. All of a sudden he tried to get on a level with those small, cautious people; of course, he made a virtue of his retreat: no longer any megalomania, only to show off a bit with bitter, sarcastic resignation; still giving vent to his gall, but in time even that passed. Since then he hadn't looked at a single verse; he despised it and almost hated it because he considered it to be something unworthy of adult, practical, and genuine men.

Hated, that's rather a strong word.

Well, say: felt aversion to it. For it reminded him of his defeat.

. . . . .

And now you're at the end. From then on it was a real, modest, and thorough life.

But for the last station in the world.

That was convalescence, that was in connection with his lungs. Let it be, a man doesn't grow up so quickly. But there, and then at the station of the old gentleman, then I did run on to my real line of life.

Listen, why did you make advances to the station-master's daughter?

Because I fell in love with her.

I know; but I (the other one—you know?)—I courted her because she was the station-master's daughter. It's called a career *per vaginam*, isn't it? To marry an heiress, or the daughter of one's superior, we know that; "to woo a princess a little bit," eh? By that you increase your value somehow.

That's a lie! I never thought of that, not even dreamed of it!

But I did, and not with my eyes shut. The old gentleman's popular, and could help his son-in-law; it wouldn't be bad to marry into his family.

That isn't true! You don't realize, man, how fond I was of her; she was a perfect wife, good, sensible, and loving; I couldn't have been happier with anyone else.

Yes, but; a sensible wife who took a keen interest in her husband's advancement—yes, a keen interest; she understood extremely well his ambition and industry, you must grant her that. And she helped him when she could. You wrote so sweetly and innocently of your first little step upwards: "perhaps the old gentleman had helped a bit." And again the second time: "perhaps my father-in-law helped me a bit, I don't know much about that." But I know very well, my dear fellow; the old gentleman knew what was expected of him.

That may be so; he was a very good man, and he cared for me as if I were his own son; but between my wife and myself there was nothing of the sort; only love, only trust, just a strong and good feeling of fidelity. No, leave my marriage out of it!

What of that, it was a good marriage; now there were two of them, for that endeavour to scramble a bit higher. As soon as he got married he discovered in himself an "unprecedented joy in property"; he was very glad that he had a decent and proper pretext for it: "it's for us," wasn't it? And straight away "he grows elbows in the office"; he struggled upwards with all his might, some he tried to surpass at all cost, and with the others, those above, to ingratiate himself zealously—why not?—all this is "for us," and it's quite in order. And that's why he felt so happy; he could follow his own natural inclinations without having to be ashamed of them. Marriage is a good institution.

Was my wife—also like that?

. . . She was a good wife.

. . . . .

In the end you'll say that that station of mine, that work of art of mine, I had nursed it into a model—well, why? Because of my career? To win the favour of those above? If it hadn't been for the War I should most likely have stayed there until I died.

That was partly for the sake of the gentry.

Which gentry?

Those counts in green hats. To pull yourself together before them and show them what you were like. As if the station-master hadn't waited often and looked sideways to see if those gentlemen would notice what a fine station it was! And see they did; even duke so and so, count this and that condescended to shake hands with him. You know, it cheered him somehow even if the station-master pretended to himself that he didn't care a jot. So really, counts, and the Lord knows who besides; after all, they are the higher world, you didn't even have them with you at home. And this, if you please, isn't patronage; through his own work and merit the station-master has got so far. Now his work is more than his wife, she can't help him any farther, she is no longer necessary; he made her feel it, and so their relations began to grow cool at home.

That's not true!

Why not? It's there written above, just read it. "I had the feeling of something genuinely mine, the strong and good feeling of my own self. . . . My wife felt that I was getting away from her. . . . Vainglory, something of ours has been sacrificed for what is only mine." And so on. "It lies between us like a gap." Now the man follows his own bent, he has now detached himself; he only feels that it's a nuisance that his wife still tries to keep him for herself. Fortunately she's a sensible lady; she makes no scenes, and she cries it away with dry eyes; after that "she grew accustomed to and reconciled with our lot," that is, she submits and begins to serve her husband.

She wanted that herself!

I know; but what else could she have done? Either they had to part or hate each other, as married people can hate each other, secretly and madly; or she accepts HIS rules of the game and agrees that HE should be master, and everything revolve round him. When no mutual bonds are left she tries to keep him by what is his: his comfort, his habits, and needs. Now it's only himself, nothing else but himself; his home, the rule of life and conjugal love only serve his comfort and greatness; he is the master of the station and of the family—it's a small and shut-off world, it's true, but it's his and it worships him. After all, that was the happiest part of his life; so that when one day he will think back on his late wife it will be just at that time which so "strongly and well" pandered to his pride.

. . . . .

And what came next?

During the War?

Yes. That also sprang from my ambition?

It's not easy to say. It's just possible; one might count on the emperor's losing, but it was too risky. It doesn't fit into my case. Of course it doesn't fit into your story either.

Why not?

Look here, that idyllic station-master was no hero; it wasn't in his line. But I'll tell you why that story of yours had to be written.

Just because of that War episode. Perhaps someone will read it and discover, see, here there was a station-master who acted like this. He even risked his own life for his nation. Only a bit, only half a bite, and unobtrusively to call attention to one's merits—isn't that the reason why memoirs are written?

That's a lie, a lie! I wrote the reminiscences of an ordinary life!

And that heroism——?

Just that is also part of an ordinary life.

Quite. It's a pity that that isn't the last word. My dear fellow, it wasn't any longer a hero who sat up there in that office. It was me sitting there, my friend. There just a zealous, vain, and servile person sat there, who wanted to get somewhere. Just a small person who wanted to be bigger.

Don't mention that, even there he was a good, conscientious worker.

Nonsense. He did everything possible just to win respect and to scramble a bit higher. All his life long he thought only of himself, of nothing but himself. What solid drudgery have I done for it, Jesus Christ! a model pupil, a model official—how much have I had to swallow! Really it has cost me my whole life, I have sacrificed everything for it; and at the end one sees the cute fellows who are still a step higher—why? Only because they were stronger and more daring! They needn't even wear their trousers through in the service, they needn't sweat, and look how far they've got; you have to get up politely when they come into the office! Then why was it that even in the elementary school they pointed to me as an example for the others, and again afterwards, and brought one another to see my station, what was it for? The world is for the stronger ones and the more daring, and I lost it. You know this was the final culmination of an ordinary life: that I could look at my defeat. For that a man has to get a bit higher to see it.

And now you are having your revenge.

Yes, now I am having my revenge; now I see that it was in vain and therefore small, pitiable, and humiliating. As for you, you're different, you are in clover; you can play with little flowers, with the garden, with your enclosure of chips; you can forget yourself for that game, but I can't, I can't. I'm the one who was beaten, and this is MY ordinary life. Yes, I'm having my revenge; and haven't I reason? Didn't I give up almost with shame? Christ, but they did question me! Of course, I knew that there were awful irregularities—in the supplies, and so on; but that was the work of others, the braver ones—I knew that, but I held my tongue; I've got you under my thumb, my lads, and if need be these things will come to light! And then there was a scandal, and they interrogated me, me, I ask you: the blameless and model official! Of course, they had to admit—but I went into retirement. Defeat, man, and then I ought not to avenge myself! Of course, that's why I'm writing these memoirs——

Only because of that?

Yes. So that it will be said that I was not to blame. It ought to be in full detail, and not always just: an ordinary life, an idyll, and nonsense like that. This was the only thing which mattered; that dreadful and unjust defeat. It wasn't a happy life, it was terrible, don't you see that it was terrible?

CHAPTER XXII

I CAN'T go on like this, I must stop; it gets on my nerves too much, or something—when those two voices argue my heart begins to flutter and then I feel such a sharp oppressing pain here in my chest. The doctor came, he measured my blood pressure, and frowned. "What are you up to?" he grumbled; "your blood pressure's going up. You must keep quiet, absolutely quiet." I tried to stop writing, and just lie down; but then fragments of a dialogue spring up in my mind, again they squabble about some trifle, and I must again expostulate with myself: Keep quiet, you there, and don't quarrel; this and that is true, it was like that; but isn't there in man, isn't there even in the most ordinary life, scope enough for various motives? But it's quite simple: a man can think selfishly and stubbornly of his own profit; after a while he forgets it, forgets his own self, and nothing exists for him but the work that he is doing.

Stop, it isn't as simple as that: these are two completely different lives, aren't they? That's what matters, that's what matters!

What does?

Which of them is THE RIGHT ONE?

. . . . .

Well, enough of that, it doesn't do me any good. I've been accustomed to looking after myself; from that time at the station when I began to spit blood, I said to myself, Look out. Almost all my life I have been looking into my handkerchief to see if I hadn't brought up a tiny thread of blood; I began doing that at the last station in the world, and since then that continual worry about my health has stuck to me as it if were the most important principle in life.

The most important principle in life; and what if it really was? When I look back at my whole life—that was really the greatest shock when red blood spurted out of me at the station, and I sat there in misery; I felt extremely weak and wretched, and the terrified clerk wiped my forehead with a wet towel. It was dreadful. Yes, that was the greatest and the most astounding experience of my life: that dreadful amazement, and horror, and afterwards that desperate longing to live, even if it were the most insignificant and the most humble life; for the first time I had a conscious and completely overwhelming longing for life. In fact at that moment, my life changed completely, and somehow I became another man. Up to then I had only squandered my days, or almost casually lived them through; but suddenly I appreciated immensely the fact that I was alive, and I began to look quite differently at myself, and at everything around me. It was enough for me to sit on the planks, to gaze at the rusty line grown over with shepherd's-purse and hair-grass; or watch the ripples in the little river for hours, and see that they were always the same and always new. And at the same time to repeat a hundred times to myself: breathe deeply, it's healthy. Then I began to like all the small, regular things, and the silent course of life; I still boasted a bit with Bohemian cynicism; and I grinned at many things, but then I wasn't yet sure that I was going to live; it was still a wild and frosty prank of despair. I began to cling to life silently and contentedly, to enjoy nice, intimate things, and look after myself. In this way, in fact, the idyllic part of my life began: in convalescence. That was the important and decisive crossing.

. . . . .

But it wasn't even a crossing. Now I can see it better, now I see it quite clearly. I should have to start again from my childhood: with mother, who rushed to the door every second moment to see if nothing had happened to me; with Mr. Martinek, to whom I had not to get too near because they said he had consumption, and of whom I therefore was frightened. Mother was obsessed with the notion that I was in danger, that I was a weak and ailing child; she was, poor dear, so pathetic and passionate; when I fell ill she pressed me to herself as if she wanted to protect me, at night she bent over me in terror, she used to fall on her knees and pray loudly for my health. To be ill, that was an important and solemn thing; everything centred on the little fellow, the saws even, and the hammers in the yard, seemed to have been damped somehow, and father was only allowed to grumble under his breath. By all her love she fostered in me the idea that I was something delicate, more delicate than other children, something that must be specially protected; and so I didn't attempt any boyish pranks; I was under the impression that I MUSTN'T run about so wildly, mustn't jump into the river, mustn't fight because I was weak and delicate. I should have even liked to boast about it, I seemed to myself in some way finer and more precious than they were, but lads are too much like men for that, they like the idea of being strong and brave. That, then, was my mother; it was mother who had fostered in me that timidity towards life and distrust in myself, that physical feeling of inferiority with which I grew up; it was mother's pathological love which developed in me the inclination to regard myself as the object of endless nursing and coddling, an inclination in which I nestled almost with pleasure when the first tap of a real illness gave me the opportunity. Then, yes, then I discovered in myself that cautious, hypochondriacal being which with grave attention examines its sputum, measures its pulse, loves a safe order in life, and clings to a good, comfortable state of things. This, then, was —I will not say my whole life, but an important and constant component of it. Now I realize it.

Father was something different; he was strong and firm, like a pillar, and in that he impressed me tremendously. If he chose he could have stood up against everybody in the world. At that time, of course, I did not fully understand his cautious economy —in fact, stinginess; I realized it for the first time when Mr. Martinek, who was only a workman, gave that little girl a penny, but father didn't, he pretended that he hadn't noticed it; then something strange and terrible like scorn shook the little boy. Now I see that he, poor man, was not so strong, that he really was frightened of life; to economize is a defensive virtue; it is a desire for a protected life, it is fear of the future, of risks, and chances; avarice is terribly similar to some form of hypochondria. Do study, my boy, he used to say, in a solemn and trembling voice, you will go into an office, and you will have it settled. That is about the limit of what we can expect from life: certainty and safety, the faith that nothing can happen to us. If my father, who was as big and strong as a tree, felt like this, how could his weak and coddled son feel brave? I realize that it had already been thoroughly laid down for me in my childhood; the first physical shock was enough, and the man, with fear crawling into himself, discovered that defensive concern for life and made of it his rule of life.

. . . . .

God knows it must have stuck in me deeper than I realized; surely it guided me in life almost like an instinct, so blindly, and so certain. I am thinking now of my late wife: how strange it is that I should have found her, a woman who was almost born just to nurse somebody. Perhaps it arose from the fact that she was sentimental, and, at the same time, very sensible; to look after somebody is such a sensible, sober, and practical form of love. Didn't she fall for me ardently the very moment that she learned that I had come from the threshold of death, and that my interesting paleness had its deeper causes? Then suddenly charity, love, and motherhood broke out in her and a precipitant maturing of feelings began; it was all there together: a terrified little girl, feminine compassion, and a mother's zeal, erotic reverie and a terribly realistic and urgent concern that I should eat a lot and gain weight. It was equally as important and beautiful to talk of love as to get fat; she pressed my hand convulsively in the shadow of the night and whispered with eyes full of tears: Please, please, you must eat TERRIBLY much; do promise me that you will look after yourself! I can't smile at it even to-day; it had its sweet and even pathetic poetry . . . for the two of us. I had the feeling that I was getting better only for her sake, for her pleasure, and that it was fine and magnanimous of me; I struggled for my health to make her happy. And she believed that she was saving me and giving me my life back again; wasn't I hers by right and by fate? God, I know: surely it was only an accident that I was appointed to that particular station; but it is strange and somehow amazing how inevitably and deeply the order of my life worked out. Up to that time I had to conceal my hypochondriacal anguish and be ashamed of it as if of a weakness; now no longer, now it was a common and terribly important affair between two people, now it was part of our love and intimacy; it was no longer a defect or a derangement, but something positive and important that gave sense and order to life.

I am thinking of our marriage and how it emerged from it silently and self-evident. From the very first moment my wife took upon herself that concern for my health, as if she had said: That's a woman's job; you needn't worry about it, leave it to me. Yes, it was like that; I could pretend to myself, Myself nothing, it's her; she is so scrupulous and hygienic, well, let her be, if she likes to; and at the same time to revel silently and indulge in that feeling of security that one is being provided for and that so much is being done for one's health. When she waited for me with a towel, before I had finished scrubbing myself, to dry my wet back—it, you know, looked so agreeably conjugal, but it was a daily health inspection; we never said as much to each other, but we both knew it, and I always looked sideways at her, so what? She used to smile and nod her head, It's good. And her temperate, abstinent love that was also part of it: she made certain rules for me so that I was not driven to lay them down out of fear for myself. Don't get so excited, she used to say, almost like a mother, and sleep nicely; no rings round your eyes, and such-like things. Sometimes I was angry, but in the depths of my soul I was grateful to her, for I had to confess that it was better for me like that. I had not any longer to watch so anxiously over my physical state, she took that under her own care; instead she nourished my ambition—even that apparently is healthy and sharpens interest in life; it seems that a male can't breathe without it. Tell me what you have been doing all the day; you enjoy your work better then. Or let's make plans for the future; optimism is also healthy and forms part of a good mode of life. All that was plainly so self-evident, conjugal, and intimate; now I see it differently, now there is no one to shoulder for me that dreadful and impotent fear. Don't be afraid, you're at home here, you have everything that you need, you are protected and safe.

Then later on at my station, as was most likely I felt as healthy as a turnip; I imagine that that's why I didn't need her any longer so much, and in that lay that touch of estrangement. She felt it, and tried to keep me for herself; and therefore so sedulously: You ought to take more care of yourself, and so on. Now she would even have liked to bear me children, for it's good to be a father; well, no children came. When in the end she could not do otherwise she began despotically to look after my comfort and my routine; she created a BIG LAW out of it, that I should eat well, that I should sleep well, and have everything in its right place. A life which becomes a habit is somehow safe and deeply rooted; to cultivate one's habits, that is also some kind of caring for oneself. And, again, it was she who took it on herself: she looked after my habits and I, only indulgently and good-humouredly, accepted them; I, only for your sake, old girl, because you get it ready so nicely. Thank God, you needn't be an egoist when someone looks after you so well; you have an honest and masculine consciousness that you are not looking after your own comfort, but only after your work. And then at the end of your days you will say: I lived only for my work, and I had a good wife; it was an ordinary good life.

. . . . .

So now we've got a third one, said the cantankerous voice inside me.

Which third?

Well, the first was that ordinary, happy man; the second was the one with elbows who wanted to scramble up; and that hypochondriac, he's the third. Pardon me, man, these are three lives, and each one is different. Absolutely, diametrally, and in principle.

And see here, taking all together it was a plain and simple life.

I don't know. The one with the elbows was never happy; that hypochondriac was not stubborn enough to scramble upwards; and a happy man couldn't be a hypochondriac; that's obvious. Nonsense, here are three different beings.

And only one life.

That's it. If they were three independent lives, it would be simpler. Then each would be complete, with a nice sequence, each would have its own law and meaning. But as you've got it it's as if those three lives intersected, at one moment this, and at another that.

No, wait, not that! When something intersects it's like a fever. I know, I used to have nightmares—Lord, how everything in my dreams was an awful mess, and intersected! But surely that ended long ago, I have recovered now; I have no nightmares, have I, have I any nightmares?

Aha, that's the hypochondriac again. Man, that one's lost it!

Lost what?

Everything. I'll ask you when a hypochondriac is about to die. But stop that!

CHAPTER XXIII

For three days I haven't written anything: something has happened over which on the third day I am still shaking my head. It wasn't a great and solemn event—such things don't happen in my life, on the contrary, it was very nearly an awkward situation in which I think I cut rather a ridiculous figure. The other day my housekeeper announced that some young gentleman wanted to speak to me. I was annoyed. What business have I with him? You could have told him that I wasn't at home, or something like that; well, now let him in.

It was a youth, one of the kind I've always disliked, unnecessarily tall, self-assured, and hairy—in short a swell; he threw his mane back and trumpeted some name which, of course, I forgot at once. I felt ashamed for not being shaved, for being without a collar, and for sitting here in carpet slippers and in an old dressing-gown, shrivelled up like a pouch; so I inquired as grumpily as possible what he wanted with me.

He explained a bit hastily that he was just writing a thesis. The subject was the rise of the schools of poetry in the nineties. This is a tremendously interesting period, he assured me sententiously. (He had big red hands, and his arms were like logs: definitely disagreeable.) He said that he was collecting material, and therefore he had allowed himself to come.

I looked at him with some suspicion: My dear fellow, you must have made a mistake or something; what has your material to do with me?

And so, he said, in two reviews from that period he had found some poems signed with my name. With a name which in the history of literature had fallen into oblivion, he said victoriously. That is my discovery, sir! He had searched for that forgotten author; one old stager, so and so, had told him that as far as he could remember the author became a railway official. He followed up that trail until at the Ministry he found out my address. And suddenly he demanded straight out: Please, is it you?

Well, then, now it's out! I felt a strong desire to raise my eyebrows in surprise and say that he must have been mistaken; what, I, and poetry! But no, I won't lie any more. I shrugged my shoulders and mumbled something about its being only a trifle; I gave it up, sir, long ago.

The youth beamed and shook his mane victoriously. "That's superb," he trumpeted. And could I tell him if I had written for other reviews, too? And where had I published my poems in later years?

I shook my head. Nothing further, sir, not a line. I'm sorry, sir, I can't help you.

He choked with enthusiasm, he ran his finger round his collar as if he were being strangled, and his forehead glistened with sweat. "That's magnificent," he shouted at me. "That's like Arthur Rimbaud! Poetry that flares up like a meteor! And nobody has come across it! Sir, it's a discovery, a great discovery," he shouted, and ran his red paw through his tufts of hair.

I was annoyed; as a whole I don't care for noisy young people, somehow there's no order, nothing solid in them. "Nonsense, sir," I said dryly. "They were bad verses, they weren't worth anything, and it's better that no one knows about them."

He smiled at me compassionately and almost from above, as if he were putting me in my right place. "Oh, no, sir," he protested. "It's a matter of literary history. I should prefer to call it a Czech Rimbaud. In my opinion it's the most interesting phenomenon of the nineties. Not that it could originate any sort of school," he said, winking his eyes expertly. "With regard to development it meant little, it hasn't left any deeper influence. But as a personal manifestation it's amazing, something so personal and intense. For instance, that poem which begins: 'Come to the cocos palms when the drums are rolling——' " He rolled out with rapt eyes. "Surely you remember how it goes on!"

It touched me almost like an agonizing and disagreeable

reminiscence. "So you see," I murmured. "Never in my life have I seen cocos palms. Such rubbish!"

He almost lost his temper. "But it doesn't matter," he stammered, "if you hadn't seen any palms! You've got a completely wrong idea of poetry!"

"And how," I said, "can the drums roll in the palm trees?"

He was very nearly offended by my denseness. "But these are the coconuts," he blurted out, incited like somebody who is compelled to explain obvious things. "It's like the nuts tapping in the wind. Come to the cocos palms when the drums are rolling—can't you hear it? Those three c's, they're the knocks; then it dissolves into music—the drums are rolling. And then there are lines accidentally more beautiful." He became silent, nonplussed, and he threw his mane back; he looked as if in those verses he was defending his own and most precious property; but after a while he took me into his grace—youth is magnanimous. "No, seriously," he said, "these are stupendous lines. Strange, strong, stupendous new things—of course for that period," he added with conscious superiority. "Not so much in form, but those pictures, sir! For you, sir, toyed with the classical form," he started eagerly, "but you violated it from an inner urge. In form faultless, disciplined, regular verses, but loaded inside with terrible phantasy." He clenched his red fists to reproduce it somehow. "It looks as if you wanted to scoff at that disciplined and correct form. Such regular verse, but inside it is phosphorescent—like carrion or something. Or it glows so frightfully that you feel it will have to burst. It's like a dangerous game, that regular form, and that hell inside. In fact, there's a conflict there, a terrible inner tension, or how shall I describe it—can you follow? That phantasy would like to escape, but instead it's pressed into something so regular and enclosed. That's why it escaped those oxen, because at first sight it's such classical verse; but if they'd noticed how under that inner pressure caesuras are shifted——" Suddenly he was no longer so self-assured, he perspired with effort and looked at me with dog's eyes. "I wonder if I've expressed myself clearly, sir," he stammered, and blushed; but I blushed still more, I was immensely ashamed, and I blinked at him, I think, somewhat upset.

"But after all," I chattered on in confusion, "those verses were bad . . . that's why I gave it up, and altogether——"

He shook his head. "It's not like that," he said, and all the time he fixed his eyes on me so. "You . . . you were BOUND to give it up. If . . . you had gone on creating, you'd have had to break the form, to smash it—I feel it so strongly," he sighed with relief, for it's always easier for young people to talk about themselves. "It was a terrific experience for me, those eight poems. Then I told my girl . . . after all that's a minor point," he mumbled in confusion, and ran both his hands through his hair. "I'm not a poet, but . . . I can imagine what it's like. Only a young man can write poems like that . . . and only once in his life. If he wrote more that conflict would be settled in some way. In fact, that's the most amazing fate of a poet: to express himself once so terribly strongly, out of such an exuberance, and then finis. In fact, I imagined you to be quite different," he blurted out unexpectedly.

I was immensely anxious to hear something more about those poems: if only that blockhead had quoted one! But I was ashamed to ask him, and from sheer embarrassment I began stupidly and conventionally to inquire from where the stripling came, and things like that. He sat as if he had been boiled, evidently realized that I was talking to him as if to a schoolboy. Well, well, you can frown; I certainly won't ask you what was in those poems, and this and that. As if you couldn't start on it yourself; don't I leave enough long and awkward pauses in the conversation?

At last he got up with relief, again so unnecessarily tall. "Well, I must fly," he gasped, and looked for his hat. Well, fly; I know youth can't just come or go. Outside a girl was waiting for him, they took each other by the arm, and dashed off to the town. Why is it that the young are always in a hurry? I couldn't even tell him to call again sometime; so impetuous, I don't even know who he is——

That was all.

CHAPTER XXIV

THAT was all, and now you can shake your head off if you like. Well, look here, poet; who would have thought that? For a stripling to say it, that doesn't mean anything, may the deuce take him; youth exaggerates, and must exaggerate as soon as it opens its mouth. You ought to go to the university library and look it up for yourself; but the doctor said rest, rest; well, then, stay at home and shake your head. Vainglory, you can't remember a single verse, what's past is gone; how could it vanish so completely? "Come to the cocos palms when the drums are rolling——" You can't get much out of that; but to shake one's head—God Almighty, man, where did you get the palms from, and what business had you with the cocos palms? Who knows, perhaps in that, just in that, lies poetry, that all of a sudden the cocos palms, or let's say Queen Mab, is somebody's business. Perhaps they are bad verses and the stripling is an ass, but the fact is that there were cocos palms and God knows what else. "A terrible phantasy," said the youth; so there must have been heaps of things, and what strange ones, phosphorescent and glowing. It doesn't matter whether those verses were good or bad, but to know what was in them, because those things were myself. At one time there was a life in which there were cocos palms and strange things, phosphorescent and glowing. Here you have it, man, and now see what you can do with it; you wanted to put your life straight; well, then, tucked away somewhere there are those cocos palms, somewhere at the bottom of the drawer where they wouldn't be in the way, and where you wouldn't see them; isn't that it?

So you see, so you see; now it won't do any longer. You can't just wave them away with your hand. Rubbish! They were bad verses, and I'm glad I don't remember anything more about them. It's no use, there were cocos palms and drums rolling, and God knows what besides. And even if you waved both your hands and shouted that those verses were no good, you wouldn't get rid of those palms and you wouldn't take away from your life things that were phosphorescent and glowing. You know that they were, and the stripling didn't lie; the stripling isn't an ass, even if he knows darned little about poetry. I knew, then I knew extremely well what it is. The fat poet knew, too, although he couldn't write it; that's why he jeered so desperately. But I knew; and now, man, shake your head off, where did you find it in you? Nobody understood it, not even the fat poet; he read my poems with pig's eyes and shouted: You damned swine, where did you get this from? And then he went and got drunk for the glory of poetry, and cried: Look at that idiot, and he's a poet! Such a muff and what things he can write! Once he went raving mad and went for me with a kitchen knife: Now tell me how it's done! How would it be done! Poetry isn't done, poetry simply IS; it's so simple and self-evident, like night or day. It's not inspiration, it's only such a widespread reality. Things just are. It's whatever you're thinking about; perhaps cocos palms, or an angel fluttering its wings; and you, you only give names to things like Adam in the Garden of Eden. It's terribly simple, except that there's too much of it. There are innumerable things, they have their front and back, there's a myriad of lives; in that there's the whole of poetry, that's all it is, and who knows that is a poet. Look at him, as if he were making magic, the rascal: he happens to think of cocos palms, and here they are, they sway in the wind and shake with brown nuts; but it is equally self-evident, like looking at a burning lamp. What magic: he takes what's there and he toys with phosphorescent and glowing things for the divinely simple reason that they're here; they're in him, or somewhere outside, it's just the same. This, then, is absolutely simple and self-evident, but only on one condition: that you're in that peculiar world that is called poetry. As soon as you're out of it, it all disappears in a moment; the devil took it; there are no cocos palms, no things that glow and are phosphorescent. "Come to the cocos palms when the drums are rolling——"

God, what about it? such nonsense! There never were any palms, or drums, and nothing glowing. And wave them away with your hand—Jesus Christ, what rubbish!

You see, that's it: now you're sorry that the devil took it. You can't even remember any longer what there was besides those cocos palms; and you never will think out what else there MIGHT have been there and what other things you might have seen in you but which you will never see now. You saw them then because you were a poet, and you saw strange and dreadful things: carrion in decomposition, a seething furnace, and God knows what else; you might yet have seen perhaps a believing angel or a burning bush out of which a voice spoke. It was possible then because you were a poet, and you saw what was in you, and you could give it names. Then you saw things which were; now there's an end to it, there are no palms any longer and you can't hear the coconuts tapping. Who knows, man, who knows what might be found in you even TO-DAY if still for a while you were a poet. Dreadful things, or angelic ones, man, things from the Lord, innumerable and inexpressible things, of which you have no inkling; how many things, how many lives and relations would emerge if upon you once more descended the terrible blessing of poetry! It's no good, you'll know nothing more of it; it sank down in you, it's all over. Only to know why, to know why at that time somehow you rushed precipitately away from all that was in you; what terrified you so much? Perhaps there was too much of it, or it was too glowing and it began to burn your fingers; it phosphoresced too suspiciously, or—who knows?—perhaps the burning bush began to catch fire and you were afraid of the voice that might speak. It was something in you which you became frightened of; and you showed it a clean pair of heels, and didn't stop till—well, where in fact? At the last station in the world? No, it still phosphoresced a bit there. Not till at your station where you struck the right order of things. It wasn't there any longer, thank God, there you had peace. You were afraid of it as if of . . . say, death; and who knows, perhaps it was death, perhaps you felt. Look out, a few more steps farther along this road and I should go mad, I should destroy myself, I should die. Fly, man, from the fire that consumes you. High time; in a few months the red thing spurted out of you, and you had your work cut out to make that half-broken thing whole. And then hold fast to that good, solid, regular life which does not consume one away. Already to choose only that which is needful for life, and not see all that is, for in that is death, too; it was in you along with those terrible and dangerous things to which you gave names. Well, now it's covered with a lid, and it can't get out any more, whether it be called life or death. It's covered, it's gone, and it's no more; quite candidly you did get rid of it thoroughly, and you were right to shrug your shoulders over it: rubbish, what palms; it's not even proper for an adult, active man.

And now you shake your head, think of it, who'd have said so; perhaps those verses weren't so bad and it wasn't at all stupid of you. Perhaps you might even be pleased and a bit puffed up, think of that; I wrote verses, too, and they weren't so bad. But you, such sadness. Even that cantankerous voice is silent, it mightn't suit his purpose; he had an idea that it was a defeat and that you gave it up because you hadn't the means for it, neither the talent nor the personality. You see, now it looks quite different, something like a flight from one's self, like fear, lest you should succumb to what was in you. Wall it in like a burning pit, let the evil smother itself out. Perhaps it's gone already, who knows; now you won't burn your fingers any more, now you won't warm your hands any more. To keep your own self out of sight you began to busy yourself with things and make out of them your calling and your life; you did very well, you escaped from yourself, and you became a respectable man who conscientiously and contentedly has lived his ordinary life. What do you want? It was good; why, then, I ask you, that regret?

CHAPTER XXV

No, I wasn't quite a complete success. Let the poet be, may the deuce take the poet; but there was something very innocent and harmless that I never got rid of, and apparently didn't even want to. It was present a long time before the poet, in fact from childhood, it was already in that enclosure of chips; nothing special, only such dreaminess, such romanticism, enchantment with fictions, or what is one to call it? All right, with a child it's natural; it's more peculiar that it's equally natural with a grown-up and serious man. The child has his little beans in which he sees treasures, hens, and whatever he likes; he believes that daddy is a hero and that in the river there's something wild and dreadful that it's best to avoid. But look at the station-master; he walks with energetic, rather negligent strides over the platform and looks right and left as if he were aware of everything; instead he's thinking what it would be like if a princess, that one in the tweed suit that came for the hunting, were to fall passionately in love with him at first sight. Surely the station-master has a good wife whom he loves sincerely, but at the moment it doesn't matter; at the moment it's more agreeable for him to talk to the princess, to keep the most respectable reserve, and at the same time to suffer just a little bit the torments of love. Or if two expresses ran into one another: what would he do, how would he intervene, how would he master, with clear, dictatorial commands, that confusion and horror: Quick, here, there's a woman under the wreckage! And alone in front of them all to smash open the carriage sides, strange to think where that gigantic strength in him comes from! The stranger thanks her rescuer, she wants to kiss his hand, but he, not at all! It's only my duty, Madam, and already he's leading the rescue work again, like a captain on the bridge. Or he's going on long journeys, he's a soldier, at the railway he finds a crumpled chit on which is written in hurried hand: Save me. You slip into it without knowing how; suddenly you're in it, you perform great deeds and go through strange adventures; not till you have to wake up from it and then it almost drags you down, and it creaks disagreeably as if you'd fallen from somewhere; you feel fagged out and grumpy and you feel slightly ashamed.

And see, over these stupidities the station-master doesn't shrug his shoulders and he doesn't try to defend himself; it's true he doesn't take them seriously; for instance, he wouldn't confess them to his wife, but he almost looks forward to them. One may say that barring the time when he was in love, every day he dreams some story of his life; to some he returns with special predilection, he spins them out anew, with fresh details, and he lives them somehow in instalments. He has a whole series of collateral and fictitious lives, mainly erotic, heroic, and adventurous, in which he himself is everlastingly young, strong, and chivalrous; sometimes he dies, but always from bravery and self-sacrifice; after having excelled in some way he withdraws into the background, touched by his own unselfish and generous action. In spite of this modesty he wakes reluctantly to that other, real life in which he has not the means to distinguish himself, but also nothing to renounce generously and with self-sacrifice.

Well, yes, romanticism; but just because of that I liked the railways, because the romantic was in me; it was because of that peculiar, slightly exotic mist that railways possess, for that sense of distance, for the everyday adventure of arrivals and departures. Yes, that was something for me, that was just the fabric for my eternal dreaming. That other, that real life, was more or less a routine, a well-running mechanism; the more perfectly it clicked, the less it disturbed me in my day-dreams. Do you understand, you cantankerous voice? For that reason, only for that very reason, did I provide myself with that model, perfectly functioning station, so that in between the ringing of the bells and ticking of the telegraph, between the arrivals and departures of people, I could spin the fiction of my life. You look how the lines are running, they fascinate you somehow, and by itself it starts you off into the distance; and already you're off on the infinite journey of adventure always the same and always different. I know, I know; that's why my wife felt that I was slipping away from her, that down there, between the lines, I was living some life of my own, in which there was no room for her, and which I kept secret from her. Could I tell her about princesses in tweed suits, of beautiful strangers, and such-like things? Well, I couldn't; what can one do, my dear? You have my body to look after, but my mind is elsewhere. You married a station-master, but not a romantic, you can never have the romantic.

I know that romantic in me, it was my mother. Mother used to sing, mother lost herself in day-dreams, mother had had some secret unknown life; and how beautiful she was when she offered the dragoon a drink, so beautiful that my little childish heart stood still. They always said that I took after her. Then I wanted to be like my father, strong like him, big, and reliable like daddy. Perhaps I haven't turned out well. It isn't after him, that poet, that romantic, and who knows what else.

CHAPTER XXVI

WHO knows what else? But you know all right WHAT ELSE, don't you?

No, I don't know anything more, cantankerous voice. I don't know anything more to add.

Because you don't want to know, do you?

No, I don't; there's enough of it already for such an ordinary and simple life. Didn't I let you have that romantic into the bargain, didn't I? Well, look here, it was to be a quite simple yarn, the story of an ordinary and happy man; and now, look, all sorts of people are crowding in: the ordinary man, the one with elbows, the hypochondriac, the former poet, and the Lord knows what else; there's a whole pile of them, and everyone says of himself: That's me. Isn't that enough? Didn't I break my life into many pieces just by looking at it?

Wait, here and there you've left something out.

I haven't!

You have. Shall I remind you of this and that?

No, it's not necessary. They're casual things that don't mean anything. They simply don't fit into the whole and they have no continuity. That's the word: continuity. A man's life must have some continuity after all.

And so many odd things must be thrown aside, mustn't they?

It's like taking a fly out of a glass of water. Could I have ordered a new life to be brought me on a tray! Something falls into it that has no business to be there; well, yes, you take it out, and that's all.

Or at least you don't talk about it.

Yes, one doesn't talk about it. Pray, tell me what you are really after, and who you really are?

That doesn't matter; I'm always the other one, the one with whom you are annoyed. Do you know when it began?

What began and when?

That about which one doesn't talk.

I don't know.

It must have been some time a long time ago, wasn't it?

I don't know.

A terribly long time ago. Strange what experiences a child sometimes has. But shut up!

I, nothing. I only remember that little dark girl. She was older than you, wasn't she? Do you remember her sitting on the little box and combing her hair? she squashed the lice in her comb with her little tongue half stuck out, lup, lup, they did pop. You rascal, you felt a bit disgusted, and a bit—no, it wasn't disgust; rather a longing to have lice or something. A longing to have lice, isn't it strange? Never mind, man, people have such longings.

I ask you, in childhood!

I'm not talking about childhood. And once when you looked what the foreman was doing behind the canteen with that slut of a canteen woman. When you saw them throwing themselves about you thought that he was strangling her; you wanted to shout with fear; but the little girl was prodding you in the back, and how her eyes shone!—do you remember? You crouched behind that fence breathless, and your eyes nearly fell out of your head. She was such a horrid hag, her breasts rolled on her belly, and she bawled wherever she went; but she was quiet then, she only wheezed.

Well enough!

I, nothing. Only how once on a Sunday you went to see the little girl. It was as if life was extinct there, everyone was in the canteen or snoring in the huts. There was nobody in the hut, it only stank like a dog-kennel. Then somebody passed and you hid there behind a box; then the little girl came in and behind her a man, and he fastened the door with a hasp.

That was her father!

I know. A nice father indeed. He shut the door, and it was dark inside; you couldn't see anything, but you could hear, man, you could hear, how the little girl moaned, and the male voice was soothing and snapping; you couldn't imagine what was happening, and you pressed your little fist to your mouth to stop yourself from shrieking with desperate terror. Then the man got up and went away; for a long time after that you crouched behind that box and your heart thumped terribly; then you went silently up to that little girl, who lay on rags, sobbing. You were very perplexed, you would have liked to be big, to have lice, and to know what it meant after all. After a little while you played in front of the hut with clothes-pegs; but it was an experience, man, such an experience—I don't know how you can leave it out of your life.

Yes. No. I can't.

I know that you can't. But your games afterwards weren't so innocent—do you remember? And you weren't even eight years old then.

Yes, eight.

And she was about nine, but she as corrupt as a demon. Some sort of a gipsy or something. My dear fellow, an experience like that in childhood sticks in a man.

Yes, it does.

How you looked afterwards at your mother—almost with curiosity if she were like that, too. Like that canteen woman, or that little Romany. And if father was also so strange and disgusting. You began to watch them, what, and how. Listen, somehow it wasn't quite all right between them.

Mother was—I don't know; unhappy, or something.

And dad was a weakling, a lamentable weakling. Sometimes he got into a rage, but otherwise—it was dreadful how much he used to put up with from mother. God knows of what he must have been guilty to let himself be so humiliated and tormented by her. She liked you, but him—man, she did hate him! At times they began to quarrel about some stupid thing—and they pushed you out of doors, Go and play. And then mother spoke and afterwards dad ran out; crimson and furious, he slammed the door and began to work like someone under a curse, without a word, he only snorted. And at home mother wept victoriously and desperately, like someone who had broken everything; well, now it's over. And it wasn't over.

That was hell!

That WAS hell! Father was a good man, but he had been guilty of something. Mother was right, but she was evil. And the little boy knew it, it's dreadful how much a child like that finds out; only he doesn't know why. And so he only looks perplexed that something strange and evil is going on that the grown-ups are hiding from him. Perhaps the worst was when the little fellow was going with that young Romany; he used to sit at the table, father didn't speak, and ate; suddenly mother began such quick and jerky movements, she rattled the plates, and cried in a choking voice, Go, sonny, go and play. And those two were picking a bone with each other, God knows how many times, and God knows how serious and spiteful it was; and the little fellow, forsaken and helpless, with tears in his eyes, wandered on the other side of the river where that little gipsy girl lived. They would play in the dirty shanty, white hot with the sun's heat and smelling like a dog-kennel; while they played they would fasten the door with the hasp. It was a black darkness, and the children played a damnably strange game; it wasn't any longer so dark, a light came through a gap between the planks; at any rate one could see how those children's eyes were glowing. At the same time father at home set out to work like someone under a curse, and out of mother's eyes ran victorious and desperate tears. And the little fellow almost felt relieved. Ugh, now I have my secret, too, something strange and evil to hide. No more does it torment him so much that the grown-ups have something secret before which they push him out of doors. Now he himself has something secret of which they in their turn are ignorant; now he is all square with them and in a way has taken his revenge on them. That was the first time.

What?

That was the first time you tasted the delight of evil. Afterwards you went after that gipsy as if dazed; sometimes she beat you and tore your hair, sometimes she bit your ears like a little dog till your back shivered with delight; she depraved you through and through, an eight-year-old rascal, and ever afterwards it was in you.

Yes.

For how long?

. . . All my life.

CHAPTER XXVII

AND what came next?

Next, nothing. Afterwards I was an intimidated, shy little pupil, who crammed with his head in his hands. That was nothing, that was absolutely nothing.

You used to go somewhere in the evening.

On a bridge, on a bridge over the railway.

Why?

Because a woman walked there. A whore. She was old, and had a head like death.

And you were frightened of her.

Terribly. I looked down over the railings and she brushed her skirt against me. When I turned—when she saw that I was only a boy, she went on.

And that's why you used to go there.

Yes. Because I was frightened of her. Because I always waited till she touched me with her skirts.

Hm. That's not much.

It is. Didn't I say that she was terrible?

And how was it with that pal of yours?

Nothing, it was nothing of that sort. My word of honour.

I know. But why did you take away his faith in God when he was going to be a priest?

Because—because I wanted to save him from it!

Save! How was he to learn when you had taken away his faith? His mother promised him to God, and you kept on proving to him that there wasn't one. Nice, wasn't it . . .? Poor beggar, it turned his head! No wonder that he couldn't stammer a word! You did help your pal, indeed; he hanged himself in his sixteenth year——

Stop!

Please. And how was it with that short-sighted girl?

But you know. That was such a perfect feeling, almost

stupidly clean, almost—well, almost transcendental, or something.

But to get there you went through a little alley where whores stood in the doorways and whispered: Come to me, my dear!

That's a minor point. That had nothing to do with it!

Why not? But you could have gone the other way, couldn't you? It would have been nearer; but you, you strolled through the alley with your heart thumping dreadfully.

Well, and what? I never went TO THEM.

No, of course you daren't have done that. But it was such a strange, damnable pleasure, that perfect love and that cheap, dirty vice—to carry one's angelic heart through a street of harlots, that was it. Those were the phosphorescent and glowing things, I know. Let it be, it looked very queer in you.

. . . Yes, it was like that.

So you see. And then you became a poet, didn't you? That chapter also has something about which one doesn't talk.

Yes.

Don't you know what it was?

What would it be? There were girls. That waitress with green eyes and that girl who was tuberculous—how she fell to pieces with desire and her teeth chattered, that was dreadful.

Go on! Go on!

And that girl—God, what was her name?—the one that passed from hand to hand.

Go on!

Do you mean the one who was like a devil?

No. Do you know what was strange about it? That fat poet, he could stand something; he was a pig and a cynic, of which there are few; don't you know why sometimes he looked at you with terror?

That was not because of what I was doing!

No, it was for what was in you. Do you remember how he once quivered with nausea and said: You beast, if you weren't such a poet I'd drown you in a sewer!

That was—I was drunk then, and I was only saying something.

Yes, something that was in you. That's it, man: the worst and most depraved thing has remained in you. It must have been—something damnable which couldn't even get out. Who knows, who knows, if you hadn't reformed them. But you got terrified of it yourself, and "headlong you ran away from what was in you." "You covered it over with a lid"; but these weren't cocos palms, dear fellow, they were something worse. Perhaps an angel with wings, but hell, too, man. Hell, too.

But that was the end!

Well, yes, in a way that was an end. Then you only looked to see how to save yourself. A good job that blood spitting came on; a tremendous opportunity to start a new life, wasn't it? To stick to life, to investigate one's sputum, and to catch trout. To watch with a mild and sedate interest how the young foresters play skittles and at the same time to infect them a tiny bit with that deeply suspicious thing that was in you. The universe especially had a good effect; in face of the universe even all evil evaporates, that is in man. The universe is a good institution.

CHAPTER XXVIII

AND then at the station of the old gentleman, when I fell in love —was it still in me there, I mean that evil?

Look here, not at all. That's strange. It was a completely happy and ordinary life.

But making love to the maiden—how near was I to seducing her?

That's nothing, that may happen.

I know that I behaved towards her . . . decently on the whole; but my desire was not—was not—well, was not entirely under control——

Go on, that's part of the thing.

Did I marry her to scramble upward?

That's again another story. Now it's a case of those deeper things, you know? For instance, why did you hate your wife so much?

I? Didn't I marry her for love?

You did.

And didn't I love her all my life?

You did. And at the same time you loathed her. Remember how many times you lay beside her, she slept, and you kept thinking: God, to throttle her like this! To grasp that neck in both my hands, and squeeze, squeeze. Only what to do with the corpse afterwards, that's the problem.

Nonsense! It wasn't like that at all—and if it were! How can a man be blamed for such fancies? Maybe he can't go off, and is annoyed because she sleeps so quietly. I ask you, why should I have hated her?

That's just it. Perhaps because she wasn't like that little gipsy, or like that waitress, you know. That marshy brute with green eyes. Because she was so quiet and composed. With her everything was so sensible and simple—like a duty. Conjugal love is quite proper and hygienic, like eating or washing one's mouth. Nay, even like an ordinary and serious sacrament. Such a clean, decent, domestic affair. And you, man, at those moments you loathed her convulsively and madly.

. . . Yes.

Yes. In you, after all, was the longing to have lice, and to play in a stinking hut a deep and breathless game. That it would be unclean and wild and terrible. A fearful desire for something that would ruin you. If only her teeth had chattered, if she had pulled your hair, if her eyes had burned darkly and madly! But she—nothing, she only set her teeth on her lower lip and sighed, and then went off like a log, like someone, who, thank God, has done her duty. And you yourself—just a yawn; no longing for something evil, something that ought not to be. God, to grasp that neck with both my hands—would she at least shudder like a beast and produce one inhuman shriek?

Christ, how I loathed her at times!

So you see. And that was not only because of that. That was because on the whole she was so orderly and prudent. As if she had married only what was sensible and respectable in you, capable of bureaucratic progress and responsive to exemplary and domestic care. Perhaps she even had no inkling that there was something else in you—something different, by George! She didn't even know that she was helping to drive it into a corner. And now this was tearing itself as if on a leash, and silently, hatefully, spitefully it howled. To grasp that neck in both my hands, and things like that. Some day to set out along the lines, and go, go as far as where rock is being torn out; naked to the waist, with a handkerchief on my head, and to break stones with a pickaxe; to sleep in a filthy shanty which smells like a dog-kennel; a fat canteen woman whose breasts flop on her belly, sluts in petticoats, a lousy little girl biting like a puppy; to fasten oneself in there with a hasp. Don't cry, little pet, keep your mouth shut, or I shall kill you! And instead, here silently, regularly, a model wife to an honest and slightly hypochondriac station-master is breathing: what about squeezing her neck so——

Stop!

And you weren't unfaithful to her, you weren't rude to her, nothing; only in secret, and persistently, you hated her. A nice family life, eh? Only once did you have your little revenge on her: when you worked against the Emperor. I'll give you something, you German! But otherwise—an exemplary marriage, and everything; that was already characteristic of you: to be evil and depraved in secret; to be able to conceal it even from oneself—and only relish the idea that perhaps it MIGHT have been. Wait, what was it when you were up there at the Ministry?

There was nothing.

I know, nothing at all. Only to say with awe, but with quite agreeable awe, God in Heaven, one could make a mess here! It might cost millions, man, millions! It would be enough just to suggest that we were ready to listen——

And did I do that?

God forbid. A blameless official. Absolutely clean conscience in that respect. It was only such a delightful image of what might have been and how it might have been done. A complete and ingenious plan in full detail: it would have to be done in this way, and so on; if the time comes. And then not to do it, to carry one's official integrity without censure through temptations left and right. It was similar to the time when you wandered after your clean love through the street of brothels, Come to me, my dear! There wasn't a single official crime you wouldn't have invented which you haven't committed in your mind; you exhausted all the possibilities, and didn't accomplish one. Well, it's true, in reality you couldn't even make so much mischief, you would have to limit yourself to such and such cases; but while you are only thinking about it there are no limits, and you could do everything. Only don't forget those typists!

That is a lie!

Steady. Steady. Never mind, you were a big enough boss in that Ministry; you only had to frown and those girls' knees did tremble. To call for one and say, See here, miss, it's full of mistakes, I'm not satisfied with you; I don't know, I don't know, I OUGHT to demand your dismissal. And so on; you could try it on them all. And with that to have those mad millions within the reach of your hand! What wouldn't a girl do now for her small salary and for a few silk rags! They're young and they're dependent——

Did I do that?

Not at all! But because of that you cowed them down, I'm not satisfied with you, miss, and so on. As if their knees only shook a little before you, as if they didn't turn their eyes to you for mercy! Just to pat them kindly, and there it would be. It was only just a possibility with which the old rake toyed voluptuously. There was such a lot of those typists, he hadn't even added them up; it's best to make a job of it: to take them all in turn, one after the other. To hire somewhere in the suburbs a little room, rather loathsome and not too clean. Or if it had been possible, to have a wooden shanty, heated white hot with the sun and smelling like a dog-kennel; to shut oneself in with a hasp, it's as dark as hell there; you can only hear a voice moaning, and a voice that is threatening and soothing.

There's nothing more you know?

Nothing more. It didn't happen, altogether nothing happened; such an ordinary life. Only once it was absolutely real; that was when you were eight years old with that little gipsy girl; then something did fall into your life that perhaps really didn't belong to it. And from that time, well: all the time you kept throwing it out, and all the time it was still there. All the time you wanted to have it once more, and it never happened again. Man, this is ALSO a continuous life story, don't you think so?

CHAPTER XXIX

A CONTINUOUS life story. My God, what am I to do with it now? But, after all, it is true that I was an ordinary and on the whole a happy man, one of those who do their work conscientiously; that's the chief thing. But this life had been forming in me from my infancy; in it father, in his blue smock, has left his trace, bending over the planks and running his hand over the finished work; and all those round about, the stonemason, the potter, the grocer, glazier, and baker, seriously and attentively absorbed in their work as if nothing else had ever been in the world. And when something heavy and painful took place, you slammed the door and went to work more zealously than ever. Life, it isn't happenings, it's work, our continuous work. Yes, it's like this; my life was a kind of a task in which I became absorbed up to my ears. I should have been at a loss without some sort of thing to potter about with; even when I had to retire I bought this little house here and the garden, so as to have something to do; I broke up and planted the soil, I weeded it and watered it —thank God, it was a job in which you get absorbed until you don't know of yourself, and of nothing but what you're doing; yes, it was a bit of the tiny enclosure of chips in which I used to crouch when I was a child; but I lived to find great pleasure in it, even to find a finch that peeped at me with one eye as if to say: Well, who are you? I'm just an ordinary man, finch, like the others who live just beyond the fence; now I'm a gardener, but the old gentleman taught me that—almost nothing is in vain, in everything there is such a strange and wise order, it's such a straight and necessary road. From infancy right to here. Yes, that's the continuous story of a man. This simple and orderly idyll, yes.

Amen, and yes, it is true. But there is still another story which is also continuous and also true. That's the story of somebody who wanted somehow to rise above the small circle in which he was born, above those joiners and stonemasons, above his pals, above his school form, always and always. That also comes from infancy, and it reaches to the end. And it's a life made out of completely different stuff, unsatisfied and puffed up, which always wants more space for itself. This man doesn't think of work any longer, but of himself, and of being better than the others. He doesn't learn because he enjoys it, but because he wants to be first. Even when he walks with the station-master's maiden he is puffing himself up with the thought that he's got something better than the telegraphist or the cashier. Always self, only self. But even in marriage it eats up almost more and more space until it is only himself, and everything turns round him. Well, now he's got enough, hasn't he? It's just that he hasn't; when he's got everything that he wished for he must find a new and bigger space where he may again slowly and surely expand. But once it comes to an end, that's the sad thing about it, and it's ended badly; all of a sudden he's an old man and good for nothing and lonely, and all the time he makes a smaller heap. Yes, that was the whole life, finch, and I don't know if it was made of happy stuff.

That's the truth; then there is a third story, also continuous and also beginning in infancy; that's the one about the hypochondriac. There's mother in that story, I know; it was she who coddled me so and filled me with fear about myself. This man was like a weak and ailing little brother of the one with the elbows; both egoists, upon my word, but the one with the elbows was offensive, and the hypochondriac defensive; this one only feared for himself and wanted to let it be modest, if only it was safe. He didn't force his way anywhere, he only looked for a harbour, the leeward side—apparently that was why he became an official and got married, and set limits to himself. He got on best with that first man, with the ordinary and good one; work with its regularity gave him a nice feeling of security and almost of shelter. The one with the elbows was good in that he provided for some sort of prosperity, even if his unsatisfied ambition sometimes disturbed the cautious comfort of the hypochondriac. On the whole, these three lives agreed pretty well with each other, even if they didn't coalesce; the ordinary man did his job without worrying about anything else; the one with the elbows knew how to sell it, but also prompted, do this, and don't do that, nothing is to be got from that; well, and the hypochondriac, he usually scowled with worry; only not to overdo it, and everything in moderation. Three different natures, and on the whole there were no bickerings among them; they came to terms silently and perhaps they even had a certain amount of consideration for each of them.

These three persons, they were, so to speak, my legitimate and hereditary lives, my wife shared them and entered with them into a faithful and loyal bond. Then there was a further story, that was the romantic. I should say: the hypochondriac's pal. A very essential personality to compensate somehow for what the hypochondriac denied himself: adventure and magnanimity. With those others it was out of question; the one with the elbows was too sober and matter-of-fact, while that ordinary man was —well, so ordinary, and had no imagination. The hypochondriac, on the other hand, loved it immensely; something to be experienced, something fascinating and dangerous and yet at the same time one is safe at home; it's good to have such an adventurous and chivalrous person in reserve. It has been with me from my childhood, it was essentially and deeply rooted in my life, but not in my marriage; of that personality my wife must not know. Perhaps she also had her other self which had nothing to do with her domestic life, nor with her conjugal love; but I know nothing of that.

But then there is that fifth aspect, and that story is also continuous and true; it began right in my boyhood. It was that shameful life with which none of the others wanted to have anything in common. You mustn't even know about it, but sometimes . . . in strictest solitude, and almost in the dark, secretly and surreptitiously, you could recall it just a little bit;

but it was present all the time, evil and lousy and infinitely cursed, and it lived on by itself. That was no longer myself or some being (like that romantic was), but some sort of THING, something so degraded and suppressed that it no longer could have any personality. Everything that contained a bit of self avoided that thing with disgust; perhaps was even horrified of it—as if of something that was antagonistic to my own self, something destructive or making for self-annihilation, I don't know how to say it. I don't know anything more, I don't know anything more; even I don't know about it, I never saw it whole, always only like something groping blindly and in the dark. Well, yes, as if in a hut fastened with a hasp, and dirty, smelling of a beast.

And then there was—not a complete story, but only a fragment. The poet's case, I can't help it: I feel that that poet had more to do with that depraved and suppressed thing than with anything else what was in me. In him, of course, there was something higher—he stood on THAT side and not on mine. God, if I could only say it! As if he wanted to release something, as if he were trying to make a man out of it, or something more than a man. But for that perhaps there must be some divine grace, or miracle—why do I think all the time of an angel with beating wings? Perhaps because that unredeemed thing was fighting with some angel of mercy; sometimes it rolled the angel in the mire, and sometimes it looked as if perhaps that evil and cursed thing might be cleansed. As if through the chinks into that darkness some kind of intense and dazzling light were penetrating, so beautiful that even that uncleanliness appeared to shine intensely and amazingly with something. Perhaps it was that that unredeemed thing was to become a soul in me, I don't know, I only know that it didn't; the accursed remained accursed, and the deuce took the poet who had nothing to do with that which was my acknowledged and legitimate self; there was no place for it in the other stories.

This then is the inventory of my life.

CHAPTER XXX

AND not yet by any means. There's still one story left—or rather, a bit of a story. An episode which doesn't fit in to any other continuous story and which stands by itself, let its origin be what it may. Good Lord, what fuss, I won't hide my light under a bushel all the time. That work that I did during the War needed some damned courage—perhaps even heroism. Wasn't there a court martial for it, and a rope, that was as plain as a pikestaff, and I knew it quite well. I didn't even take very great precautions, except for not putting anything in writing; I talked about those things with lots of conductors, engine-drivers, and postmen—if one of them had blabbed or let the cat out, it would have been bad for me and for the others. At the same time I didn't feel in any way heroic or elated, I had no sense of duty, no feeling of sacrificing my life, or other such sublime thoughts; I only said to myself that something like that OUGHT to be done; well, and so it was done, as if it were obvious. I even felt rather ashamed for not having started on it earlier; I saw that the others, those fathers, those conductors, and stokers had only been waiting to do something themselves. For instance, that guard, he had five children, and he only said: "O.K., sir, don't you worry, I'll look after it." He might have been hanged, and he knew it. I hadn't any longer even to tell our people, they came themselves, I hardly knew them. "Munitions going to Italy, sir, something will happen there." And that was it. Now I see how risky it was—for them and for me, but at the time it somehow did not occur to us at all. I call it heroism because these people WERE heroes; I was no better than they were, I only gave it a bit of organization.

We blocked every station where it was possible, including the old gentleman's station. There was an accident there, and the old gentleman went mad and died. I knew that I was the cause of it; I loved him sincerely, but at that moment it was all the same to me. What is called heroism is no great feeling, enthusiasm, or anything like that; it's kind of a self-evident and almost blind necessity, such a terribly objective state; motives here, motives there, you go forwards, and that's that. It's not even a matter of the will, it's as if you are led on by it and prefer not to think much about it. And my wife mustn't know about it; it's not for women. Well, then, all that's quite simple and I needn't refer to it; but now the problem is how it fits together with those other lives that I led.

That idyllic station-master, no, he was no hero; it surely was very disagreeable for him to direct something like the sabotage of his beloved railways. Of course by that time the idyllic station-master was almost lost; the atrocious captain had reduced his model station to the state of a filthy madhouse; there was no more room in this world for a conscientious station-master. That one with the elbows, no; he wouldn't have risked so much, and he would have said, What shall I get out of it? it might, you know, end badly, and for most of the time it looked as if the Emperor might win. And then, in that a man could not and must not think of himself; if he had begun to think of what was in store for him his heart would have sunk to his boots and that would have been the end. Instead it was rather a feeling, The devil can have me, what the dickens does my life matter; only in this way could I bear it. No, that one with the elbows had nothing to do with it. And the hypochondriac, who was eternally frightened for his life, still less; strange that he didn't try to shield himself from that undertaking. The romantic, no. It wasn't a bit romantic, not a whiff of any visions or adventure; so absolutely sober and matter-of-fact, only just a little bit wild, only just enough to make me want to drink rum; but that perhaps came from the fellow-feeling that united us. I should have liked to hold those guards and conductors round the neck, to drink with them, and shout, Boys, my lads, let's sing! I who have been lonely all my life long! That was the finest thing about the whole affair that unity with others, that manly love for one's comrades. No solo heroism, but joy for that magnificent party: Damn it all, we railwaymen, we'll show them! Not that we ever spoke about it, but I felt it, and I think that we all did. Well, look here, what was lacking in my childhood was now made up; I didn't sit any longer in my enclosure of chips; I'm with you, boys, I'm with you, comrades, never mind what it is! My loneliness melted, there was our common cause; no more only self, and that was travelling, sir, that was the easiest part of the way. Yes, easier and finer than love.

That life seems to me to have had no connection at all with the others.

. . . . .

Lord, and there's still another life which I should have forgotten completely. Different and almost contrary to this and all the others; in fact, only such strange moments, as if they belonged to a completely different life. For instance, a longing to be something like a beggar at a church door; the desire not to wish to be anything, and to give up everything; to be poor and alone and in that to find peculiar pleasure or holiness—I don't know how to express it. For instance, as a child, that corner among the planks; I loved that place immensely because it was so small and forsaken, and it gave me a fine and good feeling. At home every Friday beggars used to go together from house to house; I used to go with them, I don't know why, and I prayed like them and like them I snuffled, Thank you, God bless you, at every door. Or that shy, short-sighted girl—in that, too, there was the need for something humble, poor, and forsaken, and that strange, almost pious, joy. And it was always like that: like those buffers at the last station in the world, nothing but rusty rails, shepherd's-purse, and hair-grass, nothing but just the end of the world, a forsaken place, and good for nothing; there I felt best. Or those talks in the lamp attendant's hut: it was so small and cramped, God, how well one could live! At my own station, too, I had such a corner, it was between the storehouse and the fence; nothing but rust, old rubbish, and nettles—nobody went there any longer except God, and it was sad and reconciled, like the vanity of everything. And the station-master used to stand and look at it sometimes for an hour at a time with his hands behind his back and realize the vanity of everything. The workmen would come running—perhaps we ought to clear it away? No, let it stay as it is. That day I didn't look any longer left and right, at what people were doing. Why always do this or that? Simply be, and nothing more: that is such a quiet and wise death. I know that in its way it was the negation of life; and so it had no connection with anything else; it only was, in it nothing happened, for there are no happenings where all is vanity.

CHAPTER XXXI

So how many are there of life's aspects: four, five, eight? Eight lives which compose my own; and I know that if I had more time and a clearer head I should discover a whole row of them, perhaps completely disconnected ones, maybe of those which only happened once and lasted only for a moment. And perhaps there are still more that never had their turn; if my life had run on a different line, if I had been somebody else, or had met with other adventures, perhaps quite different—persons, I should say, would have emerged in me able to act in a different manner. If, say, I had had another wife, a cantankerous and irritable man might have developed in me; or in some circumstances I might perhaps have behaved frivolously; I can't rule out that; I can't rule out anything.

At the same time, I know quite well that I am not some interesting and complex double, or God knows what, personality; I think that nobody could ever have thought that about me. What I was I was entirely, and what I did I did, so to speak, with all my heart. I never meditated about myself, I had no cause to; it's only a few weeks since I began to write this, and I was thinking myself what a nice and simple story it would be, as if made of one piece. Then I found out that I was contributing to that simplicity and compactness, even if unwittingly. . . . A man has a definite idea about himself and about his life, and according to it he selects or even arranges facts a little to fit in with his idea. I think that at first I intended to write something like an apology for the lot of an ordinary man, just as the famous and extraordinary people write in their memoirs apologies for their extraordinary and prominent destinies; I should say that in their various ways they also contribute to their own life-stories to make of them consistent and probable pictures; it looks MORE POSSIBLE when one gives it a connecting thread. Now I understand that: what a possibility! The life of man is a mass of various possible aspects out of which only one is realized, or only a few, while the others only manifest themselves incompletely for a time, or never at all. Somehow this is how I imagine the story of EVERY man.

Let us take my case—and I certainly am nothing special. There were several aspects which continually intertwined; sometimes one predominated, somethimes another; then there were some which were not so stable and only seemed to be like islands or episodes in that total collective life—as, for instance, the poet's case, or the heroic story. And again, there were others which were only a permanent and vague glimmer of possibility, like that romantic or that—what should I call him?—that beggar at the church door. But at the same time, whatever of those lives I lived or whichever of those figures I was, it always was myself, and that self was always the same, and never changed from the beginning to the end. That is what is so strange about it. For that self is something that is ABOVE those figures and their lives, something higher, single, and unifying—is it perhaps what we call a soul? But surely that self had no content of ITS own, at one time it was that hypochondriac and at another that hero, and it was nothing which floated above them! Surely it was empty in itself, and in order to exist in SOME way it had to borrow one of those figures and its life! It was something like the time when, as a little chap, I climbed up on to the shoulders of Frank, the apprentice, and then felt big and strong like him; or when I went with father, hand in hand, and felt serious and dignified like him. It's most probable that self was only riding on those lives; so much did it desire and need to be SOMEBODY that it had to acquire this or that life.

No, it's still different. Admit that a man is something like a crowd of people. In that crowd he wanders, perhaps, say, an ordinary man, a hypochondriac, a hero, that one with the elbows, and God knows what else; it is a muddled swarm, but it has a common path. One of them is always in front and leads for part of the way; and to make it clear that he is in charge let us imagine that he carries a standard on which is written *myself.* Yes, now he is me. It's only a word, but such a powerful and domineering word; while he is that self he is the master of the crowd. Then, again, another member of the crowd elbows his way to the front; well, and now he bears the standard and is the leading self. Let us suppose that that self is only just a dummy and the flag is only so that the little band has something in front of it to represent its unity. Except for the crowd even that common badge wouldn't be needed. An animal perhaps has no self because it is simple and only lives its single possibility; but the more complicated we are the more we must assert the self in us, raise it highest; look out, this is me.

. . . . .

Look at that, a crowd; a crowd that has its unity, its inner tension, and conflicts. Perhaps in it somebody is the strongest, so strong that he rises above all the others. He will bear that self from the beginning to the end, and will not let it fall into other hands. A man like that will appear all his life as if made of one piece. Or perhaps in that crowd there is someone better suited than the rest for the vocation or *milieu* in which the person lives, and that will then be the leading self. At other times the one of the crowd who looks most respectable and somehow representative; then one says pleasantly, see how noble and manly I am! Or, again, in that crowd there is such a vain, obstinate, egoistic little being which will see to it that IT bears the standard, and it will chafe and puff itself up just to have the upper hand; and then one thinks, I am so and so, I am a proper official, or I am a man of principle. Some of the crowd don't like each other; some, again, band together and form a clique or majority which then shares the self and will not admit the others to power. With me it used to be that ordinary man, that one with the elbows, and the hypochondriac who associated into some kind of a gang and passed myself from hand to hand among them; they had it well in hand and they kept the lead for most of my days. Sometimes the one with the elbows was disappointed, sometimes the ordinary man let go out of goodness, or embarrassment, sometimes the hypochondriac failed from weakness of will; then my standard passed for a while into other hands. The ordinary man was the strongest and most persistent, just a beast of burden, and so he was myself oftenest and longest. That low and evil being never became myself: when its moment arrived the standard, so to speak, was lowered to the ground; there was no self, it was only chaos without guidance or a name.

I know it is ONLY an image; but it is the only image in which I can see my whole life, not enrolled in time, but complete as it stands, with everything that was, and yet with infinitely much that perhaps MIGHT have been.

. . . . .

My Lord, such a crowd—in fact it's a drama! All the time they are fighting inside us and settling their eternal disputes. Each of those leading persons would like to seize the whole life, want to be in charge, and become that acknowledged self. The ordinary man wanted to take charge of the whole of my life, as well as the one with the elbows and that hypochondriac; that was a tussle, that was a silent and fierce struggle over what I was to be. Such a strange drama where people don't shout at each other and don't go for one another with knives; they sit at one table and discuss current and indifferent things; but how it lies between them! Christ, how tensely and hatefully it lies between them! The ordinary good fellow suffers silently and helplessly; he can't cry out for he is rather servile by nature; he is glad when he can become absorbed in his work and forget the others. The hypochondriac only gets mixed up at times; he thinks too much about himself, he is annoyed that there are other interests besides himself; God, what a bore those others with their silly worries! And the one with the elbows acts as if he weren't conscious of that hostile and close atmosphere; he gives himself airs, is ironical, and knows everything better, this ought to be like this and that like that, this isn't necessary and that ought to be done because it shows promise. And the romantic, he doesn't listen at all, he thinks of some beautiful stranger and doesn't know what's going on. Then in disfavour there is the poor and humble relation, one of God's beggars; he doesn't want anything and doesn't say anything, he only whispers to himself—who knows what he whispers so mysteriously and silently? Perhaps he might look after the hypochondriac and whisper it into his ear, but those gentlemen pay no need to him, nothing of the kind, such a feeble-minded and passive simpleton! And still there's something that one doesn't mention; sometimes it rustles and jolts somewhere like a ghost, but the gentlemen at the table only frown slightly and go on talking about their affairs as if nothing had happened; they only peer at each other a bit more irritably and spitefully as if they were accusing each other for something spectral that jolts. A strange household. Once somebody forced his way in, that was the poet; he turned everything upside down and haunted this place worse than that ghost; but the others, those self-respecting people, somehow squeezed him out from that decent and almost venerable household—that was already a long time ago, a terribly long time ago. And once a fellow came there, he was the hero; he made no fuss, and began to give orders as if in a fortress, You must get on, boys, and so on. And look, what a crew it was: that one with the elbows was beside himself with all the frenzy, and the ordinary man was strong enough for two, and the hypochondriac suddenly felt, with relief, my life doesn't matter a brass farthing: That was a time, boys, that was a time for men! And then the War ended and the hero had nothing left to do. Crikey, those other three were relieved when that intruder had gone! Well, thank God, now it's here, ours again.

To me it's like a picture, so lively and definite. This, then, is the whole of life, this drama without action, and now already it's moving slowly to the end; even that eternal dispute has been settled somehow. I see it like a scene. The one with the elbows doesn't talk any longer so haughtily and doesn't preach about what ought to be done, he holds his head in his hands and looks down at the ground. Jesus Christ, Jesus Christ! That ordinary good fellow doesn't know what to say; he is terribly sorry for the man, for that ambitious egoist who has spoiled his life; well, what can one do?—it wasn't a success, and don't think about it any longer. But on the other hand, God's little beggar sits at the table, he holds the hypochondriac by the hand, and whispers something as if he were praying.

FF

CHAPTER XXXII

THERE were some things in me of which I knew, this is my father, and others in which I felt, this is my mother. But in father and mother again their fathers and mothers existed, of which I knew almost nothing; only one grandfather who they said used to be a great spark, all women and pals; and one grandmother, a saintly and pious woman. Perhaps to some extent they are also present in me, and some member of that crowd bears their features. Perhaps that multitude that is in us is our ancestors for God knows how many generations. That romantic, I know, he was my mother, and that beggar at the church door might have been that pious grandmother, and the hero perhaps the grandfather, a good drinker and a ruffian, who knows? I'm sorry now that I don't know anything more about my ancestors; if only I knew what they had been and who they married—from that you might learn all sorts of things. Perhaps each of us is a sum of people which increases from generation to generation. And perhaps we now feel perplexed because of that infinite differentiation, and so we want to escape from it and we accept some mass self to make us less complex.

God knows why I must think of my little brother who died as soon as he was born. The thought worries me as to what he might have been like. Surely quite different from me; brothers are never the same. And yet he was of the same parents and under the same hereditary conditions as I was. He would have grown up in the same joiner's yard with the same apprentice, Frank, and with Mr. Martinek. All the same he might have been more talented than I, or more obstinate, he might have gone farther or done less, who can tell? Apparently he would have chosen others from the multitude of possibilities with which we come into this world, and he would have been quite a different man. Perhaps in a biological sense we are born a plurality, like that crowd, and only afterwards, through development, environment, and circumstance, one man is more or less fashioned out of us. Surely my little brother would have realized possibilities which were then too much for me, and perhaps I should also have recognized in them many things that are in me.

It is dreadful when one thinks of that uncertainty in life. Two others of the millions of germ cells might have met, and then it would have been another man; it would not then have been myself but some unknown brother, and God can say what a strange fellow he would have been. Another of those thousands, or millions, of possible brothers might have been born; well, it was I who drew the right lot, and they were in a fix; what was to be done? we couldn't all be born. And what if that plurality of lives that is in us is the crowd of those possible and unborn brothers? Perhaps one of them would have been a joiner and another a hero; one would have gone far and another would have lived like a beggar at the church door; and they weren't just my own, but THEIR possibilities, too! Perhaps what I took simply to be MY life was OURS; of us who lived and died long ago, and of us who weren't even born and only MIGHT have been. God, it's a dreadful thought, dreadful and beautiful; that ordinary course of life which I know so well and by heart suddenly looks to me quite different, it seems immensely big and mysterious. It wasn't me, it was us. You don't even know, man, how much you lived!

• • • • •

Yes, now we're all here and we fill the whole space. So look here, our whole race; and how is it that you all remembered me?

Well, we came to say good-bye; you know——

What?

Well, before we part. You've got it very nice here.

Well, well. My friends, my friends! You must forgive me for not expecting you——

Nice furniture, my boy. It must have cost a lot of money.

It did, daddy.

I can see, my lad, that you have done quite well. I'm very pleased with you.

My only one, my little chap, how badly you look! What ails you?

Ah that's mother! Mum, Mummy, I've got something wrong with my heart, you know.

Oh, God, with your heart? You see, I also had something wrong with my heart. That's from my father.

And he's not here?

He is. He, you know is that bad grandfather. It was he, poor chap, whose spectre used to haunt here, it's in our family.

Let me see you, confounded grandfather! So it was you, that sinner? Who would have thought it of you!

Well, never mind. Who would have thought it of you! It was in you, too.

But not in mother.

I ask you, in a woman! That's not for women, is it? What can one do? a fellow must sow his wild oats.

Oh, it's simple with you, grandfather!

Yes. I was a real fellow, my lad. Well, what, I had my fun sometimes.

And you dragged grandmother by the hair on the floor.

Yes, I did.

So you see; and then they reproach me for wanting to strangle my late wife! That comes from you, grandfather.

But you haven't got my strength, my boy. You have rather got your nature from women. That's why it was in you . . . so strange and secretive.

You may be right in that. So just look at it, from women! Was it you who had that pious and saintly grandmother for his wife?

Not at all. I had that jolly grandmother. Haven't you heard of her?

Now I know! She was that jolly grandmother who was full of fun.

I am that jolly grandmother. Do you remember how you teased that telegraphist? That came from me.

And where did that humble and holy man come from?

That also came from me, my boy. I suffered much from poor grandfather, no use complaining. You must have patience, well, and you get reconciled.

And what about that other grandmother, that pious and saintly one?

She, poor dear, was an evil woman. Full of anger, envy, and avarice, and that's why she made a saint of herself. You've got that from her, don't you know.

What?

Why, that you envied everybody and wanted to be the best of them all, my poor duckie.

And what have I got from the other grandfather?

Perhaps that you served. That one, my lad, was still a bondsman, and he had to do menial labour for his squire, like his father and grandfather.

And where did the poet come from?

A poet? That wasn't in our family.

And that hero?

No hero. We were, my boy, all ordinary people. Why, weren't we and aren't we as numerous as people at a village wake?

You're right, grandmother, you're right, like people at a village wake. And then a man shouldn't be born as an average of so many people! From everybody he gets something, and together it's so ordinary and average—thank God!

Thank God!

Thank God, that I was that ordinary man. Indeed, it's just that that is tremendous—in it you, all of you, so many of you, resting with the Lord!

Amen.

And how many there are of us—like people at a village wake. So many people together—why, it's like a big festival! You wouldn't say, good Lord, you wouldn't even think that life is—such a glory!

. . . . .

And what about us, your possible brothers?

Where are you? I can't see you——

No, you can't see us, we can only be imagined. For instance——

What, for instance?

For instance, I should be a joiner, and take over the workshop from father. Don't you think that it would be a big workshop by now, twenty workers—and what a lot of machines! We should have to buy that potter's yard to spread into, in any case there's no potter's workshop any longer.

Daddy thought of that.

Of course he did, but when he had no son a joiner! It was a pity. After all, it wouldn't be bad.

It wouldn't.

But not me, I should be something different. Man, I should have shown that painter's chap! Frank would have taught me how to fight, and that would be that. He would get something, that blighted painter's chap!

And what would you like to be then?

It's all the same. To smash rocks with a pickaxe, for all I know, stripped to the waist, spit in my hands, and dig. Those muscles, my boy, you would see.

Go away, to smash rocks! I should go to America or somewhere. And not only dream about adventures, that's nothing. To have a go, damn it, to try your luck and set out into the world. At least you enjoy something and learn.

Enjoy something—you can only do that with women. I should let them have it, chaps? Whether it was a slut or a princess in a tweed suit——

And that canteen woman?

And that canteen woman with her breasts on her belly.

And that whore on the bridge?

That one, too, man. She must have been—gee whiz!

And that . . . little girl with frightened eyes?

That one specially, that one specially. I shouldn't let her go! And altogether. By Jove, I should have some fun.

And what about you?

I, nothing.

What should you be?

Well, nothing, nobody. Only just so, don't you know.

Should you beg?

Perhaps even beg.

And you?

I? . . . I should die in twenty-three years. For certain.

And you wouldn't have enjoyed anything?

Nothing. But because of that everybody would pity me.

Hm, to think that I should have been killed in the War. Crikey, it's silly, but at any rate you're with pals. And when you're kicking the bucket at least you're all worked up, so dreadfully and beautifully worked up as if you're spitting in somebody's face. You swine, what have you done?

And none of you would be a poet?

Ugh! When once you've begun, then something decent. What you, you were almost the weakest of us, you couldn't do what we—well, it's good that you remembered us, brother. After all, we're all of one blood. You beggar, adventurer, joiner, ruffian, and rake, the one who fell in the War and the one who died early——

We're all of the same blood.

All. Have you already seen, brother, someone who couldn't be YOUR BROTHER?

CHAPTER XXXIII

STILL to be a poet, he has it nice; a poet sees what's in him and he can give it a name and a form. There's no phantasy, nobody can think out what wouldn't be in him. To perceive and to hear, in that is the whole miracle and the whole revelation. And to think out to the end what is only suggested in us. And he finds a whole man, and a whole life in what for others is only a tremor or a moment. He is so overcrowded that he must send it into the world. Go, Romeo, and love with the savagery of love, murder, jealous Othello; and you, Hamlet, hesitate as I did. All these are possible lives who lay claim to be lived. And the poet can let them have it with a miraculous and omnipotent fullness.

If like the poets I could give free rein to those lives which were in me then they would look different. Christ, I should make something else out of them! That ordinary man wouldn't be a station-master; he would be a farmer, an owner who farms his own land; he would curry his horses and plait their manes, two heavy brown geldings with their tails to the ground; he would grab his oxen by the horns and he would lift that cart with one hand, such a whopper. And the whitewashed homestead with red roofs and a wife on the doorstep; she wipes her hands on the apron, and Come, eat, master. We should have children, wife, for our field would yield. Why work if it isn't for ourselves?—It would be an obstinate and testy farmer, like a slave-driver with his people, but, on the other hand, a nice farm, and what a lot of animals and life swarming there! That, sir, isn't any longer an enclosure of chips, it's a real chunk of the world, and real work. Everyone can see what work I've done for myself here.—This, then, would be the real story and the complete, full, not partial truth about an ordinary man. That farmer apparently would risk his neck for his homestead: not because it would be tragic; on the contrary, because it's obvious; isn't that fine holding worth a man's life? Maybe he's working in the fields, and in the village someone rings the alarm bell, there's a fire somewhere. And then the old farmer runs, his heart isn't good enough, but he runs; it's dreadful what a heart like that can do. As if it would burst, as if it were contracting terribly, and couldn't expand again, but the farmer still runs. Just a few steps, but it's no longer a heart, it's already just an overwhelming pain. And here we are, here is the gate and the yard, whitewashed walls and red roofs; why is it turning upside down? No, these aren't whitewashed walls after all, it's the sky. But there always used to be a farm here, the farmer wonders; but then people are already running out from the building and are trying to lift the heavy body of a man.

Or the one with the elbows: that would also be quite a different story. First he would get on better, an official table wouldn't be enough for him; I don't even know what he'd have to be to satisfy his ambition. And he would be more reckless, he would have a dreadful will to power; he would trample over corpses to achieve his aim; he would sacrifice everything for his career—happiness, love, men, and himself. At first small and humble, he would scramble up at all costs; a model pupil who always crams and helps the teachers on with their coats; a zealous little official who devours work, flatters his superiors, and denounces his colleagues; then he himself can order others about, discovers what it tastes like. Masterful and callous, he pesters people, like a slave-driver cracking his whip; of course, now he's becoming an important and useful personality, and he develops faster and faster, always more and more lonely and more and more powerful and always more and more hated. And still he hasn't got enough, never can he be enough of a master to blot out the humbleness of his beginnings; he still must bow to a few, it's a wonder that he doesn't snap in two with eagerness and respect; so that there is still that feeling in him of being small and servile which he hasn't overcome yet. Well, farther yet, still a bit higher, exert himself to the utmost—and then the one with the elbows stumbles over something, and at once he's down, he's in disgrace, degradation, and the end. That's the reward for wanting to be great, it's a just retribution. A tragic figure, look at it; he was such a severe gentleman, and now he sits and holds his hand to his heart. Did he ever have a heart? Well, at one time he hadn't, and suddenly there's something that aches deeply and horribly. This, then, is his heart, this pain and anxiety; who would have believed that a man may have so much heart!

Or that hypochondriac; just to get him finished properly and he would be a real monster. His story, that would be a prodigious tyranny of weakness and fear, for a weakling is the most terrible tyrant. Everything must turn round him, awestruck and on tiptoes. Nobody must laugh, nobody enjoy life, for there is a sick man here. How can, how is anybody allowed to be healthy and cheerful! Put an end to it, you rascals, may your faces twitch, with pain, may you dry up with fear and depression! At least for you, my kinsmen, I shall poison days and nights with thousands of pettifogging demands, at least you I shall compel to wait upon my illness and weakness—am I not ill, and isn't it my right, pray? So look at them, they will die sooner! It serves them right, that comes from being healthy! And in the end he alone remains, the hypochondriac; he outlived them all, and now he has no one to pester; now he's really ill and he's alone with it; there's no one with whom he might be annoyed, whom he might blame for being worse again to-day. How selfish of those people to have died! And the hypochondriac who tormented the living begins silently and bitterly to hate the dead who have forsaken him.

And what could be made of that hero—he wouldn't escape with a whole skin; sometime in the night the soldiers would arrest him—how he would look at them with haughty, burning, derisive eyes, like that painter's son; he would be shot on the spot, apparently with a bullet in his heart; only one painful twitch, and he would lie between the rails on his back. The mad captain with a revolver: Take that dog away into the lamp room! Four railwaymen drag the body—God Almighty, how heavy such a dead man is! By this time the poet would have been dead long ago, he would have drunk himself to death; he would die in hospital, swollen and dreadful; what's all this rustling, is it the cocos palms or wings? The sister of mercy prays over him, she holds his hands so that they don't wander much in his delirium. Sister, sister, how does it go on: Gentle Jesus, meek——? And the romantic, what about him? something would have happened, some great and unusual misfortune; and he would be dying, without a doubt, for that beautiful stranger; his head would be in her lap, and he would whisper: Ne pleurez pas, Madame. Yes, that would be the proper end, these are the right and complete lives as they ought to have been.

And are these all, and are they all dead? No, there's still that little beggar of God left yet; he isn't dead yet, then? No, he's not, perhaps he's eternal. He always was there where everything came to an end; and perhaps he'll be at the end of everything, and he'll be looking on.

CHAPTER XXXIV

Everyone of us is plural, everyone is a host that fades away into the invisible distance. Just look at yourself, man, you are nearly the whole of mankind! That is what is so dreadful about it: when you sin the blame falls on them all, and that huge host bears all your pain and pettiness. You mustn't, you mustn't lead so many people along the path of humiliation and vanity. You are myself, you are leading, you are responsible for them; all these you were supposed to bring somewhere.

Yes, but what is one to do when there are so many lives, when there are so many possibilities? Can I lead them all by the hand? Shall I look eternally into myself, and turn my life inside out and outside in—isn't there anything still left? haven't I perhaps overlooked some little crouching figure which, God knows why, is hiding behind the others? Shall I perchance drag out of me some addled embryo of a possible life? But at least there were nearly half a dozen of them that one could pretty well make out, and call by name, and even that's more than enough; each would be sufficient for a WHOLE life—why seek farther! If you did you wouldn't even live, but just rummage about in yourself.

And so let that rummaging be, it wouldn't lead anywhere. Don't you see that all the other people, whatever they are, are like you, that they also are hosts? But you don't even know what you all have in common with them; only just look—indeed, their life ALSO is one of those countless possible ones that are in you! Even you could be what the other is, you could be a gentleman, or a beggar, or a day-labourer stripped to the waist; you could be that potter, or that baker, or that father of nine children smeared with jam from ear to ear. You are ALL THAT because in you there are those various possibilities. You can look at all people, and in them discern all that is man in you. Everyone lives something of yours, even that ragamuffin whom the gendarmes led away in handcuffs, and that wise and silent lamp attendant, and that drunken captain who drowned his grief—everyone. Look, look carefully so as to see at last all that you might have been; if you search you will see in everyone a fragment of yourself, and then you will recognize with amazement in him your real neighbour.

Yes, it is like that, thank God, it is like that; and no longer am I so much alone with myself. My friends, I can't go among you any longer, I can't look at you from a near distance, I can only look out from the window—maybe someone will pass by: a postman, or a child to school, or roadman, or a beggar. Or that youngster may go this way with his girl, they will press their heads together and they won't even look up at my door. And I can't even stand any longer by the window, I have such swollen and lifeless legs, as if they were growing cold; but I can still think about people, whether I know them or not—they are as numerous as people at a village wake, such an immense host! God, so many people! Whoever you are, I recognize you; for indeed we are most on a level in that each of us lives some other possibility. Whoever you are, you are my innumerable self; even if I hated you, I shall never forget how terribly near you are to me. I shall love my neighbour as myself; and I shall fear him as if it were myself, and I shall resist him like myself; I shall feel his burden, I shall be vexed with his pain, and I shall groan under the iniquity that is done to him. The nearer I shall be, the more I shall find myself. I shall set limits to the egoists for I myself am an egoist, and I shall serve the sick, for I myself am sick; I shall not pass by a beggar at the church door because I am poor like him, and I shall make friends with all who labour for I am one of them. I am what I can understand. The more people I learn to know in their lives the more my own will be fulfilled. And I shall be all that I might have been, and what was only possible will be reality. The more I grow the less there will be of that self that limits me. But, indeed that self was like a thief's little lamp—there was nothing but what was within its own compass. But now you, and you, and you, you are so many, we are as numerous as people at a village wake; God, how much bigger does this world grow with other people! one wouldn't admit that it is such a space, such a glory!

And that is the real, ordinary life, the most ordinary life, not that which is mine, but that which is ours, the immense life of us all. We are all ordinary when there are so many of us; and yet—such a festival! Perhaps even God is quite an ordinary life, only to perceive him and know. I might find him perhaps in the others, since I have not found him and known him in me; he might be met perhaps among the people, he might perhaps have quite an ordinary face like us all. He might reveal himself . . . perhaps in the joiner's yard; not that he would appear, but suddenly one would know that he was there, and everywhere, and it wouldn't matter that the planks bang and the plane sings; father wouldn't even raise his head, Frank wouldn't even stop whistling, and Mr. Martinek would look with beautiful eyes, but he wouldn't see anything particular; it would be quite an ordinary life, and at the same time such an immense, amazing glory. Or it would be in the wooden hut, shut with a hasp and smelling like a beast; such a darkness with light only coming in through a chink, and then everything would begin to stand out in a radiance strange and dazzling, all that muck and that misery. Or the last station in the world, the rusty line grown over with shepherd's-purse and hair-grass, nothing beyond, and the end of everything; and that end of everything would just be God. Or the lines running into space, and meeting at infinity, lines which hypnotize; and no longer should I set out along them after who knows what adventure, but straight, straight, quite straight into infinity. It might be that it was there, that EVEN THAT was in my life, but I missed it. Perhaps it's night, a night with little red and green lights, and in the station the last train is standing; no international express, but quite an ordinary little train, a parliamentary train that stops at every station; why shouldn't an ordinary train like that go into infinity? Bim, bim, the workman taps the wheels with his hammer, the porter's lantern flickers on the platform, and the station-master looks at his watch, it would already be time. The doors of the compartments bang, they all salute, ready, and the little train gathers speed over the points into the darkness along that infinite line. Wait, but there are plenty of people, Mr. Martinek sits there, the drunken captain sleeps in the corner like a log, the little dark girl presses her nose to the window and sticks out her tongue, and from the van of the last carriage the guard greets with his flag. Wait, I'm coming with you!

. . . . .

The doctor was in his garden when Mr. Popel came to return the manuscript, again so carefully tied round as if it were a fascicle of completed deeds.

"Have you read it?" the doctor asked.

"I have," murmured the old gentleman, unable to think of anything else to say. "Listen," he blurted out after a while, "but it couldn't have done him any good, to write things like that! It's clear from his handwriting how unsteady he was towards the end, as if his hand was shaky." He looked at his own hand; no, thank God, it's not so shaky yet. "I think that it must have upset him, don't you? In his state of health——"

The doctor shrugged his shoulders. "Of course it was bad for him. It was still lying on the table when they asked me to see him. He must have just finished it—if it really is finished at all—down to the last dot. Of course, it would have been better for him if he had played patience or something like that."

"Perhaps he might have been still alive, eh?" surmised Mr. Popel hopefully.

"Oh, yes," mumbled the doctor. "A couple of weeks, or a month or two——"

"Poor man," said Mr. Popel with emotion.

The garden was silent, except that somewhere on the other side of the fence a child was shouting. The old gentleman thoughtfully stroked the turned-up corners of the manuscript. "Tell me," he said suddenly, "what ought I to say of my own life! It wasn't just simple and . . . ordinary like his, my friend. You are still young, you don't know yet what kind of things a man can fall into. . . . Where should I get to if I tried to explain it all somehow? Well, it was, and what's the use of talking. And you, you, of course, as well——"

"I haven't time for such-like things," said the doctor. "To potter about inside oneself, or that sort of thing. Thanks very much, I find enough muck in other people."

"So you say," Mr. Popel began hesitatingly, "better to play patience——"

The doctor glanced at him quickly; don't you worry, I shall not examine you here! "It depends," he said curtly, "on what one does best."

The old gentleman blinked thoughtfully. "He was such a good, orderly man——" The doctor turned and made as if he were pinching off a withered flower. "Perhaps you'd like to know," he murmured, "I've changed those aquilegais in his garden there. So that now he's gone everything is left in order."

AFTERWORD by Karel Čapek

The end of the trilogy. It's as if the guests have gone — the house was full of them and now, suddenly, it's silent; there's a slight feeling of relief and a slight feeling of desolation. It is in this moment that we remember one thing or another that we wanted to say to those who have gone, and didn't, what we had meant to ask them, and didn't; or we remember what sort of person each of them was, and recall what he said and how he looked at us. Fold your arms and, for a few moments more, think about those who are no longer here.

For instance, Hordubal the farmer. A cattle man who falls foul of a horse man, a conflict between a man who, out of solitude, turned completely inward, and the simple, or brutal, facts that surround him. But that isn't it, that isn't the real tragedy of Hordubal. His real and most bitter lot comes only with what happens to him after his death. With how his story becomes coarse in the hands of men; how the events, which he lived in his way and according to his inner law, become obscure and oblique when policemen reconstruct them by means of objective detection; how it all becomes corrupted and entangled and contorted into another, hopelessly ugly picture of life. And how Hordubal himself appears crooked and almost grotesque when the public prosecutor, the mouthpiece of moral judgment, calls his shadow to witness against Polana Hordubal. What remains now of Juraj Hordubal? Only a helpless, feeble-minded old man— Yes, among those human proceedings Juraj's heart was lost; that is the real, tragic story of Hordubal the farmer—and, more or less, of us all. Fortunately, we do not usually know how our motives and acts appear to other people; perhaps we would shrink in terror from that crooked and obscure picture which even those who think kindly of us have. One must become conscious of what is hidden of the real man and of his inner life in order to try to learn to know him more justly—or at least to respect more fully what we do not know of him. Hordubal's story will have been written in vain if it is not clear what a dreadful and common injustice was done to a man.

Our knowledge of people is generally restricted to allotting them a definite place in *our* life systems. How differently the same people and the same facts appear in Hordubal's version, in the eyes of the policemen, and in the moral preoccupations of the court! Is Polana beautiful and girlish, as Hordubal sees her, or is she old and bony, as the others say she is? This question seems simple and rather irrelevant; and yet it is on this point that the question turns: whether Stepan Manya (who in the real story was called Vasil Manak, just as Hordubal was called Juraj Hardubej) committed murder for love or for profit; the whole story will look different according to the answer given to that question. And there are heaps of such uncertainties. After all, what was Hordubal like, or Polana? Was Stepan a sullen brute or a charming uncle whom the child, Hafia, adored? And what about that question of the fields and the stallion? A story at first simple breaks up into a series of insoluble and debatable uncertainties as soon as it is fitted into various systems and subjected to various explanations. The same events are related three times: once as Hordubal lived them, then as the policemen ascertain them, and finally as the court decides them; the farther we go the more it creaks with all the discrepancies and inconsistencies—it is in spite of this, or just for this reason, that truth has to be ascertained. By this it is not meant that there is no truth; but it is deeper and weightier, and reality, too, is more commodious and more complicated than we usually accept. The story of Hordubal ends with a wrong unreconciled and with a question that has no answer; it sinks into uncertainties just when the reader expects to be dismissed in peace. What, then, is the actual truth about Hordubal and Polana, what is the truth about Manya? What if that truth is something still broader, which encompasses all the accounts, and even surpasses them? What if the real Hordubal was both weak and wise, if Polana was beautiful as a lady and worn as an old washerwoman, what if Manya was a man who kills for love as well as a man who murders for money? At first glance it is a chaos before which we are helpless and which is not at all to our taste; and it is for the author somehow to put in order, as much as possible, what he has allowed.

And then we have *Meteor,* the second phase of the trilogy. Here, too, the life of a man is portrayed in a triple or quadruple way, but the situation is inverted: in every possible way people try to find the lost heart of a man; they have only his body, and they try to fit to it a corresponding life. But this time the point is not how far they diverge in their explanations, which, after all, they had to conjure out of their own wits (we may call it intuition, daydream, imagination, or whatever); what is so striking is that here and there, in some things, they coincide with or hint at the probable reality—but even this isn't so much the point. Each one places the given fact—the unconscious body of a man—into a different life-story; each time the story is different, depending on who is telling it; each one includes himself, his experiences, his trade, his methods, and his inclinations. First is the doctors' objective diagnosis; second—a story of love and guilt—the feminine sympathy of a sister of mercy; third, the abstract, intellectual construction of a clairvoyant; and finally, the creative work of a poet; it would be possible still to think up innumerable other stories, but the author had to have sense enough to stop in time. All these stories have this in common: that in them is mirrored more or less fantastically the one who is telling them. The man who fell from the sky gradually becomes a doctor's case, a nun's, a clairvoyant's, and a poet's; it is always him and, at the same time, the other one, the one who is preoccupied with him. Whatever we look at is that thing and, at the same time, something of us, something of ours, something personal; our knowledge of the world and of men is like a confession. We see things differently according to who and what we are; things are good and evil, beautiful and dreadful—it depends upon the eyes with which we look at them. How terribly big and complex, how spacious is reality when there is room enough for so many different interpretations! But it is no longer a chaos, it is a distinct plurality; it is no longer an uncertainty, but a polyphony. What threatened us like a blind conflict tells us that we are listening not only to different and inconsistent testimonies, but also to different people.

But if what we apprehend is always encompassed by our I, how can we apprehend this plurality, how can we approach it? No matter what, we must look into the I that we impose on our interpretation of reality; that is why *An Ordinary Life* had to come with its probing around in the interior of a man. And here it is, here again we find this plurality, and even its reasons, too; a man is a host of real and possible persons—and at first glance it look like a worse confusion, like the disintegration of a man who has torn himself to bits and has thrown his I to the winds. Only at this point did it become clear to the author: it *is* in order; the reason we can apprehend and understand this plurality is that we ourselves *are* such a plurality! *Similia similibus:* we apprehend the world through what we are ourselves, and in apprehending the world we discover ourselves. Thank God, now we are home again; we are of the same stuff as that plurality of the world; we are at home in that spaciousness and infinity, and we can respond to those numerous voices. It is no longer only I, but we people; we can come to an understanding through the many tongues that are in us. Now we can respect a man because he is different from us and understand him because we are his equals. Fraternity and diversity! Even that most ordinary life is still infinite, immense is the value of every soul. Polana is beautiful, had she been ever so bony; the life of a man is too big to have only one face, to be sized up at a glance. No longer will Hordubal's heart be lost, and the man who fell from the sky will live through more and more stories. Nothing ends, not even a trilogy; instead of ending, it opens wide, as wide as man is able.